FOREST OF
FOES

FOREST OF FOES

THE BERNICIA CHRONICLES: IX

MATTHEW HARFFY

An Aries Book

First published in the UK in 2022 by Head of Zeus
This paperback edition first published in 2023 by Head of Zeus,
part of Bloomsbury Publishing Plc

9 7 5 3 1 2 4 6 8

A catalogue record for this book is available from the British Library.

ISBN (PB): 9781801102346
ISBN (E): 9781801102353

Cover design: Ben Prior
Map design: Jeff Edwards

Printed and bound in Great Britain by
CPI Group (UK) Ltd, Croydon CR0 4YY

MIX
Paper | Supporting
responsible forestry
FSC® C171272

Head of Zeus
5–8 Hardwick Street
London EC1R 4RG

WWW.HEADOFZEUS.COM

Forest of Foes
is for my wife, Maite.
The strongest woman I know.

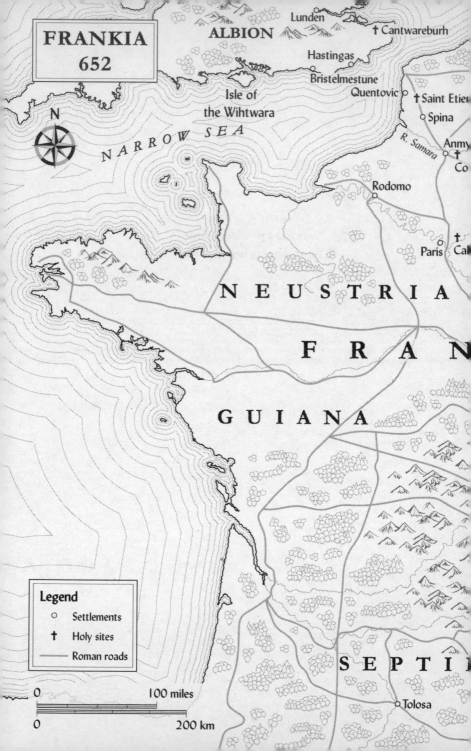

FRANKIA
652

ALBION

Lunden

† Cantwareburh

Hastingas

Bristelmestune

Quentovic

Isle of
the Wihtwara

† Saint Etien

Spina

R. Samara

Anmy

Co

NARROW SEA

Rodomo

Paris

† Cal

N E U S T R I A

F R A N

G U I A N A

S E P T I

Legend

○   Settlements

†   Holy sites

—— Roman roads

Tolosa

0 ——————————— 100 miles

0 ——————————— 200 km

Place Names

Place names in Dark Ages Britain vary according to time, language, dialect and the scribe who was writing. I have not followed a strict convention when choosing what spelling to use for a given place. In most cases, I have chosen the name I believe to be the closest to that used in the early seventh century, but like the scribes of all those centuries ago, I have taken artistic licence at times, and merely selected the one I liked most.

Ægypte	Egypt
Ad Buisi	La Boisse, Ain, France
Albion	Great Britain
Anmyin	Amiens
Baetica	Southern region of the Iberian Peninsula, loosely corresponding to modern-day Andalusia
Bebbanburg	Bamburgh
Bernicia	Northern kingdom of Northumbria, running approximately from the Tyne to the Firth of Forth
Burgundia	Burgundy, one of the three main polities that formed the Frankish realm, together with Austrasia and Neustria

Cala	Chelles
Cantware	Kent
Cantwareburh	Canterbury
Cerdun	Cerdon, Ain
Deira	Southern kingdom of Northumbria, running approximately from the Humber to the Tyne
Eoferwic	York
Frankia	France
Guiana	Frankish province roughly corresponding to the Roman province of Aquitania Secunda
Gwynedd	Gwynedd, North Wales
Hereteu	Hartlepool
Hithe	Hythe, Kent
Lindisfarena	Lindisfarne
Liyon	Lyon
Mercia	Kingdom centred on the valley of the River Trent and its tributaries, in the modern-day English Midlands
Muile	Mull
Neustria	Frankish kingdom in the north of present-day France, encompassing the land approximately between the Loire and the Silva Carbonaria
Northumbria	Modern-day Yorkshire, Northumberland and south-east Scotland
Quentovic	Frankish trading settlement. The town no longer exists, but is thought to have been situated near the mouth of the Canche River
Rheged	Kingdom approximately encompassing modern-day Cumbria in England, and Dumfries and Galloway in Scotland. Annexed by Bernicia in the early seventh century
Rodomo	Rouen, France

Rôno	Rhône, France
Saint Etienn	Fictional minster near Quentovic
Samara	River Somme
Secoana	River Seine
Septimania	Visigothic kingdom in modern-day southern France that roughly corresponds to the former administrative region of Languedoc-Roussillon (now part of Occitanie)
Sona	Saône, France
Spina	Lepine (Pas-de-Calais)
Suriyah	Syria
Tolosa	Toulouse
Ubbanford	Norham, Northumberland

Anno Domini Nostri Iesu Christi
In the Year of Our Lord Jesus Christ
652

PART ONE

STRANGERS IN A STRANGE LAND

Chapter 1

"Did you hear that?" Beobrand asked, stifling the hacking cough that had settled on his chest during the long months overwintering in the crowded settlement of Quentovic. He wasn't sure what he had heard in the distance. The horses and the blustery day muffled all but the loudest sounds. Beobrand shivered. The wind that soughed around the bones of the winter-bare oak and beech trees held the bite of snow and frost. He pulled his sodden cloak about his shoulders and once again cursed this trip. He glanced over at Cynan. The Waelisc warrior was wrapped up against the cold, but the younger man was straining to listen, sitting in the saddle straighter than he had been since the rain had begun to sheet down bitterly from the granite-dark sky.

Unable to hold back the cough any longer, Beobrand hawked and spat phlegm into the churned mud of the road they were following south. Gods, how he wished they had never come to this accursed land. And they had scarcely begun their pilgrimage, only now heading inland from the coast of Frankia, despite having left Albion months ago.

He looked up, ready to snap at Cynan impatiently. It was a simple enough question. Could the man never merely do what he was asked? But before Beobrand could say anything, Cynan raised a gloved hand for silence. The other riders reined in.

"Listen," Cynan hissed.

"What is it?" asked Wilfrid, his breath steaming. The young man's straight nose was red, but there was no other sign that he felt the cold. He was enveloped in thick furs of fox and beaver, gifts from one of the ladies he had befriended while they had tarried in Quentovic.

"Hush," snarled Beobrand, feeling the scratching at his throat that presaged another bout of coughing. He suppressed it with an effort. Wilfrid raised an eyebrow. Beobrand growled deep in the back of his throat. Damn the young man's insufferable calm. Nothing seemed to upset him.

The line of riders was spread some way down the path. Narrow now where it wound between the looming trees, it was not wide enough for all sixteen of their number to amass. At the rear, Attor, who, if he had been healthy, would have been riding ahead as a scout, was racked by a violent coughing fit. The sickness that ailed Beobrand had also sunk its fangs into the slim warrior's chest. Beobrand shook his head. They should not have left the warmth of the trading settlement, but they had all been desperate to be on the move and it had appeared that the incessant rain had finally abated. He hoped they would find the warm shelter they were heading for soon. After all the battles they had fought in together, he could barely countenance the idea that Attor might be struck down by a fever. And yet, Attor was not a young man, and the gods knew this damned cough had often enough made Beobrand feel like he might die. He had not imagined such a straw death for Attor. He had always thought the warrior would be taken by a stab under the shieldwall, or a foe-man's blade in a bloodfeud. But all men must die, and few can choose the manner of their passing. Woden would take Attor when it was his time. There was nothing Beobrand, or anyone else, could do to alter his wyrd.

The men, pale-faced and hunched in their saddles against the wind and rain, listened, striving to hear what had caused Cynan to halt the column. The day was filled with the wind-whisper of the forest, the groan of boughs, the sigh and drip of the rain, the stamp and snort of the mounts, and the jangle and creak of bridles and harness. No other sound came to them on the breeze.

A stocky, broad-shouldered man nudged his horse forward. The fingers that gripped the reins were thick and stubby; the hands of a farmer.

"What did you hear?" he asked.

Cynan frowned, but Beobrand was not angered by Baducing's failure to remain silent. He was so unlike his fellow novice monk. Both Baducing and Wilfrid came from noble families, but where Wilfrid was often haughty and carried himself as one destined to rule others, Baducing, still young, but a few years Wilfrid's senior, was a quiet, sober presence, thoughtful and humble. There could be no denying though that both men were quick-witted and knowledgeable, and Beobrand could not believe how long they each spent reading.

"Perhaps it was nothing," Beobrand said, shrugging. "A trick of the wind maybe."

Cynan did not look convinced.

"We have so long been surrounded by men and women in Quentovic, we have forgotten what silence is," said Baducing.

Beobrand sniffed. His nose was not clear, but he could smell well enough to note the scent of the wet loam, the lichen on the tree trunks, fungus on a rotting branch. The heavy aroma of the life and death of the forest.

"And I'd forgotten what clean air smells like," Beobrand said. "How's your leg?"

Baducing reached down and rubbed below his left knee.

"It aches," he said, offering Beobrand a thin smile. "And yet it pains me less than your chest, I fear. Or Attor's." He flicked a glance over his shoulder. The scout had stopped coughing, but looked small and pallid astride the dappled mare he rode.

The first mishap they had suffered on this journey occurred only three days after leaving Cantwareburh and before they had even reached Frankia. Rough seas had not dissuaded Ferenbald, master of the *Saeslaga*, from taking them across the Narrow Sea, but a badly secured barrel of mead had fallen, breaking Baducing's leg. He had been lucky not to lose the limb. They had found an old woman in Quentovic who the locals said was an expert in leechcraft, and for a price she had agreed to tend to the injured novice. Even so, it had taken several weeks for Baducing's leg to heal. By the time he could walk again, albeit with a pronounced limp, winter storms were battering the coast. First blizzards had kept them in the town, then, when the snow had begun to thaw, torrential rain had made travel impossible.

Annoyed at their talking, Cynan trotted his horse forward a few paces further along the path where he sheltered from the worst of the rain beneath a beech tree.

"I do not miss the stench of the city," Beobrand said. "But we should not have ridden today. We would have done well to wait for spring."

"We had waited long enough," said Baducing. "I yearn to see the wonders of Roma. Much as some seemed happy to linger a while longer enjoying the pleasures of Quentovic, I for one felt the time had come to ride."

Wilfrid shook his head at Baducing's veiled jibe at him.

"I too think it was time to leave," he said. "There are many more wonders to witness on our journey."

"Wonders," said Baducing, shaking his head. "Yes."

Wilfrid had made no attempt to hide his dalliances with the women of the town. His behaviour had upset Baducing, who believed it contrary to the teachings of the Christ. Beobrand had cared nought for which furrow young Wilfrid chose to plough. However, the husbands of the ladies were not so understanding.

That very morning, an angry man, made a cuckold by Wilfrid, had come looking for the young novice, murder on his mind. Beobrand, Cynan and the rest of the warriors, armed and imposing as they were, had sent the aggrieved husband on his way. But the man would return with friends and family, perhaps warriors of his own, and Beobrand would not be able to protect the novice forever. He had been tasked to watch over Wilfrid and see him safely to Roma, and he meant to do his duty. Only then could he return to his beloved Northumbria. To Ubbanford. To his kith and kin.

And to Eanflæd.

"Halinard," he called over his shoulder, feeling another cough building up within him. "Do you think we'll reach that hall before nightfall?"

"I know not this land well, lord," said the Frank, walking his squat grey stallion forward. His Anglisc words were heavily accented, but their meaning was clear enough. "If what the wine merchant told us be true," Halinard went on, "we will arrive at Spina by dark. Or soon after. But we must push on now. There is not much light left in the day and this rain is cold."

Unable to hold in his cough any longer, Beobrand hacked, cursing inwardly at the sign of weakness. He knew the men, both his gesithas and the warriors from Baducing's father's warband, looked to him for his strength.

By Woden, he was Beobrand of Ubbanford! The half-handed lord of the fearsome Black Shields. His name was famed throughout the kingdoms of Albion. But by the gods, this cough had left him tired. A warm bed and some hot food were what he needed. The sooner they were out of this rain, the better. This sickness would not do. Men do not wish to be led by the infirm.

"Come then," he said, spitting into the leaf mould at the edge of the road, "let us ride."

"Wait," said Cynan, turning in his saddle. His tone was sharp, like a blade drawn from a sheath. "Hear that?"

For a heartbeat Beobrand heard nothing out of the ordinary, and then, as the wind gusted towards him, he knew with a terrible certainty that they would not be riding straight to the warmth of a local hall just yet. For on the breeze came a sound he should have recognised the instant he first heard it wafting through the drizzled woodland. It was a noise he had heard many times before, and though it never brought happiness, he could not prevent a thrill of excitement rippling through him.

Echoing through the woods came the sudden, unmistakable clash of sword blades.

Chapter 2

"Attor," Beobrand shouted, his voice carrying easily over the wind, rain and distant clangour of fighting, "stay back and watch Wilfrid."

Without prompting, his black-shielded warriors unslung their shields and readied their weapons. At a nervous nod from Baducing, the novice's men did the same. Beobrand's voice was strong, all trace of weakness fled now. This was the man who had slain the mighty Hengist, captured Cadwallon of Gwynedd, and retrieved the head and limbs of the saintly king Oswald after the battle of Maserfelth. This was the warlord who had broken countless shieldwalls, whose sword had sent so many men to the afterlife that they could not be numbered.

This was the Beobrand warriors gladly followed into battle.

Beobrand's gelding, picking up on the change in its rider's mood, wheeled about, skittish and shaking. Beobrand tugged at the reins, pulling the young horse's head back towards the sound of battle. Another noise reached them then. One that all too often accompanied the sword-song music of war. Carried on the sigh of the chill wind, they heard the terrified screams of women.

Without waiting, Beobrand kicked his heels into his horse's flanks. He wished it was his black stallion, Sceadugenga, but this gelding was a solid enough mount, and it sprang forward. Forgotten now were his tiredness and the barking cough. Those things could wait. For somewhere nearby in the bruised shadows of the rain-spattered forest, womenfolk were in danger.

The rain lashed at Beobrand's face as the gelding reached a gallop. On his left, Cynan, a far superior rider, spurred his own mount on, quickly catching up with Beobrand. For a time they rode side by side, their mounts' hooves throwing up great clods of earth and muck behind them. They careened down a slope, following the path through the trees as it veered to the right. Beobrand cast a glance over his shoulder and was satisfied to see his men were all close behind. When he was a younger man, he might have laughed at the thrill of speed and the headlong rush towards danger. He could not deny that the prospect of taking out his frustrations on a foe lifted his spirits, but he was not the impetuous fool he had once been. Men followed him into the fray now. Oath-sworn men who trusted him, and it was his duty that they not be led into unnecessary peril.

As they rounded the bend in the track, the sounds of fighting grew louder and Beobrand was able to take stock of the situation they had ridden into. The path before them was choked with men and horses. As he watched, a mount reared, screaming as a man drove a spear deep into its guts. Its rider toppled from the saddle and was instantly set upon by several figures, hacking and chopping with axes and wicked-looking knives.

Beobrand slowed his horse to a canter. They would be upon the fighting in a few heartbeats and he needed time to understand what was happening. All was chaos, with at least a dozen horses and perhaps twice as many warriors on foot attacking the riders. The ground rose up on either side of the path here, creating a perfect place for an ambush, and as he thought this, Beobrand saw how the attack had taken place.

Beyond the fighting closest to them, a large oak had been felled, blocking the path. A few horsemen, who all wore cloaks of deep blue, had dismounted and encircled a sumptuously caparisoned covered waggon that was pulled by four mules. The men had their backs to the waggon, defending it from the numerous attackers who surrounded them. From between the waggon's curtains, Beobrand caught a glimpse of golden hair and a young woman's pale face. A second cart, presumably bearing supplies and covered with a simple sheet of leather, had been halted behind the first. The oxen yoked to the vehicle lowed, rolling their eyes in fear.

Beobrand could imagine the waggon and cart, accompanied by the troop of blue-cloaked warriors, halting before the fallen tree. The leader of the escort would have barked out orders to his men, sensing a trap. And then, the men who had been hidden in the forest, had attacked, sweeping down from both sides of the road.

Beobrand scanned the fighting at the rear of the column. In a moment he would be upon the warriors. There was no time to think, but he must make a decision. He could rein in and try to ascertain who the two sides of this combat were, or he could take advantage of the element of surprise. The path was too clogged for them to ride far into the melee, but as he contemplated pulling his gelding to a halt, he saw another of the blue-cloaked horsemen toppled from his mount. At the sight, a woman's scream emanated from the waggon.

Surrounded by the dark-garbed, grimy men who must have created this ambush, the unseated blue-cloaked warrior, a tall man with long dark hair and a jutting beard, pushed himself to his feet and swung his sword about him in an effort to keep his attackers at bay. There was something noble in the futility of the gesture, for he was surrounded by iron-tipped spears and he could not hope to prevail, alone and separated from his men as he was.

But he was not alone.

Beobrand made up his mind in that instant and heeled his

gelding forward. The men around the lone swordsman were intent on jabbing at him with their spears and avoiding his flashing blade, so had not noticed Beobrand and his gesithas bearing down on them from the rain-riven afternoon. Beobrand might no longer be the young fool he had once been, but he yet carried within him that streak of rash battle-madness that made him so formidable. Without pause, he urged his steed onwards, hoping to clatter it into the dirt-streaked men he had decided must be brigands of the forest, wolf-heads intent on plundering the wealthy occupant of the waggon.

But the gelding was not bred for war, nor did it have the stout heart of Sceadugenga. Before the animal collided with the men fighting in the mud, the horse locked its legs, skidding to a halt and lowering its head. For the merest of moments Beobrand thought he might cling onto the saddle, but in an eye-blink he knew he would be thrown and so, with a bellow of fury, he leapt from the horse's back, launching himself at the throng of warriors.

He crashed into the mass of fighting men with the force of a boulder striking saplings. The wind was driven from his lungs as he sent two of the ruffians tumbling into the mud. Struggling to draw breath, he staggered to his feet, pulling Nægling from its scabbard and moving towards the blue-cloaked horseman. The bearded man spun to face him, confusion on his features, sword raised, ready to attack.

"Friend!" gasped Beobrand in Frankish. He had no skill with languages, but they had been in Quentovic long enough for him to have picked up a few words.

To accentuate his meaning, Beobrand buried Nægling's sharp blade into the skull of one of the men he had toppled who was now attempting to climb to his feet. Blood and brains splattered the earth and the man collapsed lifeless in the mire.

"Friend!" Beobrand repeated, his voice stronger now.

The rest of the men were recovering from the fair-haired

thegn's sudden appearance. They levelled their spears at him. Beobrand wished he had his shield, but he had lost it in the fall.

"Friend," he said for a third time and trusted that the man understood his intentions. The first spear lunged at him, and Beobrand parried the blow, catching the haft in his left half-hand. Stepping quickly inside the reach of the weapon, he hacked down savagely into the spear-man's neck. More blood spurted, bright and hot in the cold day. The brigand fell back and Beobrand leapt to the blue-cloaked warrior's side. There was no time for talk, but even if the man had not understood his poor Frankish, it seemed his actions spoke loudly enough. The man nodded to him, saying something he could not make out. But his meaning was clear, they should stand back-to-back. Beobrand fell into position, coughing now as the chill, damp air filled his lungs.

They were surrounded by spear-men and neither he nor the Frankish horseman had a shield. Beobrand looked around them and wondered how long they could hope to last against so many.

Every battle was like a living thing, pulsating and shifting with its own balance of power. Beobrand had been in enough fights to be able to sense the way a battle was going, much as a skilled skipper could follow the tides and currents of the sea merely by the thrum of the tiller and the way a ship handled and flexed in the water. But Beobrand did not yet have his bearings in this fight. He could not make out the ebb and flow of it. It was all he could do to draw breath and prepare to fight for his life.

His fight would not last long if the spear-men attacked at once. Not without help. All about them, the fighting raged. The familiar forge sound of metal on metal, the shouts of enraged men, the grunts and screams of the dying, echoed in the wet air, reflected and amplified back to them from the tree-lined slopes to fill the killing ground with a chaotic cacophony.

The spear-men had been unnerved by Beobrand's sudden arrival and the death of two of their number in as many heartbeats. But that initial fear and confusion had soon turned to renewed anger. One of them, a balding man with a broad nose and straggly beard, screamed orders, bringing them back together, reminding them that they outnumbered the two men before them. They closed ranks and prepared to surge forward. Beobrand growled and spat, ready for them.

That was the moment Cynan attacked.

The Waelisc warrior had slid from his saddle, effortlessly hitting the ground at a run. Hefting his black-daubed shield and drawing his sword, he had perhaps thought to wait for the arrival of the rest of Beobrand's gesithas, but seeing his lord's predicament, he threw himself into the momentarily stunned brigands. Cynan scythed through them like a reaper harvesting barley.

The instant before the spear-men rushed Beobrand and his Frank companion, Cynan's sword flashed and blood sprayed. The bald man, who had been exhorting his men to greater efforts, half-turned, only to have his shouts cut short by Cynan's deadly sword. The man's words turned into a gurgled, bubbling scream and he fell back, clutching at the ruin of his face. Two more men fell before they even knew what was happening. Cynan reached Beobrand, and turned to face the remaining attackers.

"Sorry I didn't come immediately, lord," he said, grinning. "But I prefer to dismount in a more leisurely fashion."

"I thought you had stopped to admire the view," replied Beobrand, the joy of bloodletting lending his tone a levity that had been missing of late. "Good of you to join us in the end."

The remaining spear-men were wary now. They shuffled backwards, fearful. A couple of them turned, looking for a means of escape, or easier foe to face. They found neither. The thrumming of horses' hooves rolled over them as Beobrand's gesithas galloped down the slope. Eadgard with his huge axe jumped down, joined by his shorter, though no less deadly brother, Grindan. Gram, his greying hair slicked by the rain, climbed more slowly from his saddle, but as he deliberately dragged his sword from its scabbard and joined the others with his own black shield, the many rings on his arms glimmered and there could be no mistaking the movements of a skilled warrior. Halinard reined in beside him and hurried to join the others in the shieldwall that was quickly forming. Cynan's men, Ingwald, and the erstwhile thrall, Bleddyn, dismounted and moved to join their Bernician companions. The shieldwall was already six men strong and, behind the milling horses, Baducing and his father's five warriors were readying themselves too.

The spear-men, seeing their chance of escape blocked, turned back to Beobrand, Cynan and the blue-cloaked Frank. There were still perhaps a dozen men around them, but Beobrand sensed the tide had turned, at least here, to the rear of the waggons. Further away, where the felled oak blocked the path, he could hear that the fighting was furious and he could not tell which side had the upper hand.

"Death!" he screamed. Hesitation would only serve to give the spear-men a chance to regain their composure. "Death!" he cried again, glancing at Cynan, who took up the battle cry with a nod. "Death," they shouted together and leapt forward. The blue-cloaked warrior came with them and together they routed the spear-men.

The brigands, in disarray now, tripped and fell in their haste to be away from the warriors' swords. Beobrand's hand throbbed as Nægling cut savagely, almost severing an arm before embedding deep in the thick bone. Wrenching the blade free, he parried a feeble slash at his face. Without slowing, he stamped forward, chopping down with his sword into his attacker's shoulder. The man howled and fell. Beobrand finished him with a stab to the throat.

To either side of him, more men were slain. Cynan, as deadly as Beobrand, dispatched one, while the Frank, clearly a skilled swordsman and filled with burning fury, took another with a deep gash to the groin that saw the man's lifeblood pump steaming into the mud.

In moments it was over, Gram led the Black Shields, along with Baducing's men, forward, and with Beobrand and the others attacking from the other side, the brigands' force was shattered. Soon, the mud was strewn with bodies of the dead and dying. The air was redolent with the acrid stench of spilt bowels.

Beobrand was seized by a bout of coughing and he cursed as he shivered. The trembling was partly from the cold, he knew, but mostly it was the usual tremor that always gripped him after combat. But the fighting was not over yet. Men were still locked in battle near the fallen tree and the waggons. Clenching his mutilated left hand into a fist against the shaking, he strode over to retrieve his shield. It was smeared with mud, having been trampled during the fighting.

Three other blue-cloaked warriors joined them. One had a terrible gash on his face and his skin was pale beneath the blood and mud, but they seemed like doughty men. They addressed the Frank whom Beobrand had fought beside as if he were their leader. The bearded swordsman snapped commands at them, then shouted something at him, but Beobrand shook his head.

"What is he saying?" he asked Halinard.

"He says his name is Brocard and he thanks you, but he says we must get to the waggons. His mistress is there."

"Who is his mistress?" asked Beobrand, recalling the golden hair and pale skin behind the curtains.

Halinard spoke quickly to Brocard, who was retrieving a shield from the muck. Before he could respond, a sudden movement from the ground made Beobrand start. One of the men he had believed to be dead had snatched up a seax from the earth and attempted to slash his ankle as he passed. Only Beobrand's heightened battle-senses and cat-like reflexes saved him from the cut. Stepping quickly aside, the seax missed him by a finger's breadth. Beobrand swatted the blade away with Nægling, then, without pause, he drove the blade through the man's hand, pinning it to the earth. He knew better than to leave injured foe-men on the field of battle. He had lost his lord, Scand, to one such cruel death blow from beneath the shieldwall. Cursing, he pulled his sword free and was preparing to take the man's head from his shoulders when Cynan shouted a warning and something heavy struck him, knocking Beobrand from his feet.

Rising quickly, ready to defend against this sudden, unexpected threat, Beobrand saw that it was no new foe-man, it was one of the Blue Cloaks' horses, wounded in the action. It was now fleeing, blood-streaked and eyes white-rimmed with terror. Desperate to be away from the death-stench of the battle, the beast had sent Beobrand tumbling into the mud. Galloping some way up the path, it slowed, seeming to find some comfort in the company of the horses from Beobrand's party.

Remembering the man who had tried to cut him, Beobrand looked down, ready to finish what he had started, only to see the man sprawled on his back and gazing vacantly at the grey sky. For a heartbeat Beobrand was confused, and then he saw the curved shape of the wound on the man's forehead. Blood oozed from the crescent moon cut where the crazed horse's hoof had struck him.

A piercing scream cut through the cold air. Brocard shouted something, the dismay clear in his tone. He beckoned for Beobrand to follow and sprinted towards the waggons where his mistress was still under threat. Beobrand turned away from the trampled man.

"Men of Albion," he shouted in his strident battle-voice, "let us help our Frankish friends finish off the last of these accursed wolf-heads. I am cold and tired and they stand between us and a warm hall."

Chapter 3

Beobrand slid and slipped through the churned mud of the road. Riderless horses whinnied and shied away from the clash of fighting and the smell of blood. The animals crashed through the undergrowth beneath the winter-bare trees, snapping twigs and branches as they fled the battle.

Beside the fallen oak the fighting had not gone well for the Blue Cloaks. Five lay dead or dying in the quagmire, leaving only three still valiantly standing against the ambush. They had their backs to the waggon and had acquitted themselves bravely. There were more wolf-head corpses in the muck than blue-cloaked warriors, but they had been sorely outnumbered. A dozen or more brigands still confronted them, vicious-looking men with scarred faces and deadly, blood-slick weapons. If Beobrand's band had not stumbled upon this ambush, the outlaws would have slaughtered the escort and taken what they wished from the cart and the waggon's passenger.

But such is the way of wyrd, he thought. No matter the plans of men, none can alter the path that fate has chosen for them. And it was the wyrd of these brigands of the forest, no doubt starving and desperate for food after the harsh winter, to have their attack thwarted by a group of some of the most accomplished and formidable warriors of Albion.

Seeing how close Brocard's men were to being overwhelmed, Beobrand sprinted forward, roaring in his battle-voice in an effort to distract their assailants.

"Death!"

Cynan and the others came with him, taking up his cry. Brocard, flanked by his three companions did not hesitate. Screaming their own indecipherable challenge, they rushed headlong at the enemy that had slain so many of their comrades and now threatened their mistress.

It was not an ordered attack, but it was savage. One moment the brigands had outnumbered their foe, and their victory had seemed assured. An eye-blink later, they were being assailed from the rear by more warriors than there had been when they first ran down the slopes to ambush the column. At first, they tried to stand their ground, but they were no match for Beobrand's Black Shields and Brocard's men's fury, fanned anew to flames by the arrival of these unknown allies.

Eadgard bellowed like an ox as his axe smashed through a man's skull, carrying on with his great strength, before burying its blade deep into the outlaw's ribcage. Gram took a strike on his shield and seemingly without effort sliced his sword into his opponent's throat. Blood spurted. Bleddyn, despite not having lifted a sword before the previous year, now looked every bit the warrior in his polished byrnie and black-painted shield. Screaming, he drove a snaggle-toothed, squat man backward with a shove of his shield boss, before burying his sword deep in the man's guts.

All along the ragged line of their attack the men were fighting viciously, showing no mercy. One of Brocard's men fell, impaled on a low-lunged spear. The man with the gash to his face avenged his comrade, hacking his sword into the spear-man's wrist, severing the hand, and then reversing the blade to smash his jaw.

A dark-haired youth, with a straggly fuzz of hair on his upper lip, blocked Beobrand's path. His eyes were terrified and blood poured from his nose. The boy must have been younger than Beobrand's son, Octa. Just a child. Beobrand hesitated. He did not wish to kill a mere boy. And yet the youth had chosen to pick up a weapon today. His own decisions had brought him to this place and to this fate. Beobrand lifted his sword and the boy flinched. With a snarl, Beobrand pushed him away with his shield. The boy tripped over one of his dead companions. Wide-eyed and panting, he scurried away, first on all fours and then, rising from the mud, he sprinted up the slope to the south-east. Beobrand let him go.

The boy's escape seemed to turn the tide of the battle. As if they were following some secret signal, the remaining brigands pulled back from the fighting and, where they could, they turned and ran into the woods. A couple were slain as they retreated, but at least half a dozen made it away to the shelter of the trees. Some of the blue-cloaked warriors made to follow them, but Brocard called them back.

Eadgard roared and started after the fleeing men.

"Hold him," shouted Beobrand, and Grindan hurried after him, pulling his brother back and whispering to calm him. The axeman often lost his wits to the battle-rage. Grindan was the best at bringing him back to his senses.

Beobrand took in the destruction in the dell. He noted that Baducing had blood on his sword. He was pale-faced, but his eyes gleamed. Beobrand nodded at the young noble. He was pleased to see Baducing was good for more than reading and praying to the Christ god.

"See that none of those bastards try to steal our horses," Beobrand said. "And fetch Attor and Wilfrid." Without comment, Baducing nodded and called to his father's men.

Looking back at the tangled bodies of the fallen, Beobrand felt his hands begin to shake once again. At his feet lay a corpse that had died trying to hold in his gut-rope. The man's entrails had spilt from his belly where they steamed in the cold drizzle. Beobrand's gorge rose and he quickly wiped the worst of the blood from Nægling's blade on the man's kirtle. Stepping away from the body, it took Beobrand two attempts to scabbard the sword, such was his trembling.

One of Brocard's men rose from where he had slit the throat of a wounded man. Brocard, who had been moving towards the waggon, said something, his tone hard. The man nodded, grumbling quietly to himself.

When Brocard was yet several paces from the waggon, the curtain was thrown back and it was as if the sun had broken through the clouds to shine into the gloomy clearing of that chill forest. The golden-haired beauty Beobrand had glimpsed earlier climbed down from the vehicle. She somehow made the descent seem elegant, even though she had to clamber over the edge and jump down into the mud. She wore a long robe of red silk, embroidered with swirls of golden thread that matched the shimmer of her elaborately braided hair. To further accentuate the lustre of her tresses, the plaits were bound with ribbons of red, yellow and green. The woman's limbs were slender and long, and despite her obvious wealth, there was a muscular, athletic nature to her movements that spoke of one not unaccustomed to hard, physical work. An ornate, heavy gold and garnet necklace hung at her neck, accentuating the rise of her breasts. She swept her gaze across the men surrounding her. Her eyes met Beobrand's, and he swallowed against the sudden dryness of his mouth. It was as if he saw beyond the veil of death. This woman was a stranger to him, but her beauty, golden locks, and the hard focus of her stare, were so similar to Sunniva, his long-dead wife, that his breath caught in his throat.

And just as he remembered Sunniva when last he saw her with life, this stranger's belly swelled with new life. It was as if he was witnessing his love brought back from the dead.

The young woman contemplated him for a few heartbeats, as

if she too saw in him someone she had once known. Beobrand was opening his mouth to speak when a sudden movement behind her halted him. A mud-smeared man surged up from where he had been hidden beneath the waggon. Beobrand tensed, ready to rush the brigand. But before he could close the distance, the man wrapped a dirty arm around the lady's throat, holding her tightly to him. Brocard and Beobrand both stepped quickly forward. They hesitated when the man shouted something, fear making his voice quiver. A glint of metal reflected from the knife he pressed against the woman's throat.

Brocard spoke in his native tongue. His tone was calming, such as one would employ with a frightened animal. Beobrand dropped his hand to Nægling's pommel. The woman grew very still. She stared at Beobrand and then looked to Brocard. Beobrand saw no fear on her delicate features.

A high-pitched scream pierced the stillness that had descended on them. Beobrand recognised the cry from the shrieks that had summoned them to this place of death and mud. And yet the woman being held by the outlaw had uttered no sound. Beobrand saw then that there was another woman in the waggon; the noble woman's servant, presumably. She was a beauty like her mistress, but her clothes less extravagant and her body was not adorned with jewels and gold. Her hair was black, her dark eyes wide with fear. She did not have her mistress's poise. She continued to scream until the captive woman calmly told her to be quiet. The maid in the waggon placed a hand over her mouth, as if that was the only way she would not cry out. Her eyes brimmed with tears and she shook like a leaf in a storm.

Ignoring her, the muddy man spoke quickly, much too fast for Beobrand to comprehend. But he could easily hear the terror in the man's words. The wolf-head looked about him at the grim-faced warriors. His eyes were never still as he searched for a way out of his predicament. He was alone, surrounded by warriors who had slain a score or more of his comrades and, whatever else he might be, he was no fool. He understood that they would not allow him to leave this place alive. So he clung to the woman, pressing his knife to her pale, perfect skin, and shouted at Brocard.

"What is he saying?" Beobrand asked Halinard in a quiet voice. The woman's eyes flicked to him as he spoke, her expression questioning, no doubt surprised by his use of the Anglisc tongue. Beobrand marvelled at her apparent lack of fear.

"He says he will kill her, if let him go we do not," said Halinard, his words clumsy, yet clear.

"I hardly needed you to tell me that," replied Beobrand.

"I tell you what he says," said Halinard, shaking his head. "He says nothing interesting."

Brocard spoke to the man in the same calming tone he had used before. The brigand shouted more loudly, his voice cracking with his anger and fear. Behind him the maidservant looked ready to swoon.

Beobrand stepped closer to Brocard, beckoning for Halinard to follow him.

"Ask him his name," he said in a low voice. Halinard translated. Brocard looked askance at Beobrand, then, with a shrug, he spoke to the brigand.

"Omer," replied the brigand, narrowing his eyes as though he expected a trick.

Beobrand nodded.

"Offer him a horse," Beobrand said. Halinard whispered his words in Frankish.

Brocard hesitated. One of his men, the one with the great bleeding wound on his face, growled something. Brocard held up his hand for patience and offered Omer a steed.

Omer replied and Beobrand understood enough to know he wanted two mounts, one for him and one for his hostage.

"No," Beobrand said in Frankish. He held up a single finger. "One horse."

Omer shook his head and began to shout. Beobrand could not make out all the words, but it was clear Omer was not happy with the answer. Beobrand watched the knife blade waver at the woman's lovely throat. Omer must know that if he killed her, he would surely follow the woman to the afterlife in moments. And yet men under such pressure do not always act reasonably and Beobrand became increasingly worried that the brigand might yet cut her throat by accident.

"Tell him he can have two horses," he said. Halinard translated for him. Omer again looked as though he suspected he was being lured into a trap. He spoke quickly, urgently, but Beobrand could barely make sense of any of it. He was pleased though, to see that some of the tension had left Omer's shoulders. The knife had lowered slightly from the lady's neck. Brocard spoke up in anger at Beobrand's offer. But before Beobrand could respond, the lady being held hostage moved with the speed of a striking serpent and Omer's speech came to a sudden, choked halt. For a couple of heartbeats he stood there, unmoving and silent, mouth opening and closing without sound. Then his hand fell, the knife tumbling from lifeless fingers.

The man's right eye seemed to wink. A garnet glimmered there, as red as blood, set in the golden hilt of a small, straight-bladed knife. The lady had pulled the hidden weapon from her gaudy necklace and had buried the sharp spike up to the hilt.

She stepped away as Omer collapsed, dead, into the mud. Looking down at her hand, she wiped at a spot of Omer's blood. Behind her in the waggon, her maidservant began screaming again.

"It seems the lady did not need our help," Beobrand said, his voice quiet.

"Still, your aid is most welcome," she replied, looking up and meeting his surprised gaze. Her voice held no tremor of fear. Only a slight breathless excitement gave away any emotion. "No need to look so shocked. Of all the surprising things that have occurred this day, my ability to speak your tongue is surely not at the forefront."

Her voice was as youthful and elegant as her form, and her Anglisc came to her naturally, as one born and bred on the island of Albion. Beobrand shook his head at her calm demeanour. She was staring at him, but he did not know what to say. When the silence grew uncomfortable, he cleared his throat.

"At your service, my lady," he said, his words gruff.

"And to whom do I owe my gratitude?" she asked.

"Beobrand of Ubbanford," Beobrand replied, feeling strangely self-conscious under the young woman's stare.

"Lord Beobrand of Ubbanford, master of the famed Black Shields and champion of King Oswiu of Northumbria," said a new voice. Turning, Beobrand saw Wilfrid striding through the mud and stepping over the dead. The young novice bowed low, then flashed the lady a broad grin. "It is unlike you to be modest, Lord Beobrand," he said with a smile. His tone was infuriating.

"And who might you be?" asked the lady.

"I am but a humble student of Christ's teaching, my lady," he said in a tone that sounded anything but humble. "My name is Wilfrid. Lord Beobrand is the leader of my protectors. I did not know the roads were so dangerous." He lowered his head and looked up at her through his lashes, in what Beobrand assumed was a pretence at shyness. "Nor that such fair roses grew along these dark forest paths."

The woman smiled at his flattery.

"Well, we are safe enough now, it seems. Thanks to your Beobrand," she said, "and my Brocard. Now, we must see to the fallen and be away from this place. I fear I am one rose who would wilt if I were to spend the night in this cold forest."

Her attitude changed suddenly then. She turned to Brocard and they spoke quickly in Frankish. Brocard and the blue-cloaked warriors hurried to do her bidding.

The maid was quietening now and Beobrand noticed that

Bleddyn had lifted her down from the waggon. The Waelisc man now embraced the poor girl who sobbed on his shoulder.

"Now, Lord Beobrand," the noble lady said, turning back to him. "Would you please have your men help mine clear the path?"

"Of course." Beobrand was quietly pleased that she seemed to understand who had the power here, despite young Wilfrid's confident air. "Halinard, see to it that the men do what is needed so that we can all move on." He glanced up at the dark sky through the branches of beech and oak, trying to gauge how much daylight there was left.

"If we hurry, we should reach Spina by nightfall," the woman said, interpreting his thoughts. A sudden bout of coughing gripped him. When it abated he was loath to spit the phlegm out in front of this lovely lady. He swallowed it with a grimace and cursed.

"You are not well," she said, concern in her voice.

"I am hale enough to kill the likes of the bastards that attacked you." His tone was rough as he tried to hide the embarrassment of his weakness. "Do you know who they were?" he asked, trying to change the course of the conversation away from his poor health. "Why they would attack you?"

She looked about the clearing. Brocard already had men tying ropes to the oak. The oxen from the cart would easily drag it aside. Other men were carrying the corpses of the brigands to the edge of the track. As he watched, Eadgard and Ingwald unceremoniously dropped one of the men Beobrand had killed onto the pile. The dead man's eyes seemed to stare at him accusingly. The dead rarely seemed to accept their wyrd without reproach to the one who had slain them. Here was another face to haunt his nightmares. Beobrand looked away.

"The winter has been cruel," she said. "Many of the folk are hungry. They will do anything for food."

Beobrand scanned the bodies. Despite their poor clothes and

dirt-smeared faces, none of them seemed to have wanted for food. Stooping, he picked up a fallen seax from where a wolf-head had dropped it. He ran his thumb on its edge. It was sharp. Good steel. The handle was carved horn. It was not a rich man's weapon, but nor was it a beggar's. He slid the blade into his belt.

"We can speak later of who these men may or may not have been," said the lady. Beobrand wondered if she might not be thinking the same as him. "But first, we must get you into the warm. That cough sounds bad. And if I am to be truthful, I am weary. Carrying this child does tire me so." She stroked her belly with a long-fingered hand. "So, you will ride with us to Lord Marcoul's hall, where we are due to spend the night, and then, if you are well on the morrow, you will ride with us to meet my husband."

Much as Beobrand looked forward to the warmth of a hall and the company of this beautiful woman, the thought of meeting her husband did not interest him. Besides, they were already several weeks behind where they should be, and he longed to return home. He missed his friends and family. This lady's swollen belly made him think of his daughter, Ardith. She would have given birth by now. He realised with a pang that he must be a grandfather, if the child lived. He dared not think of the danger to Ardith. The thought that childbirth might snatch her away, as it had his beloved Sunniva, filled him with dismay, so he pushed the fear away. His daughter and new grandchild would be well, he told himself. To think otherwise was a pointless torture. He desired to go back to Ubbanford and see once more his kith and kin, but almost more than that, he could not bear not knowing how the shift in power had affected the north. He could almost feel the great tafl game of kings playing out in Northumbria in his absence. He had set some of the pieces in motion when he had taken Oswine's life, and it had felt like a betrayal to have ridden away, leaving Northumbria to its fate. Not that he had been given a choice.

"We are heading south," he said. "I thank you for your hospitality this night, but we have already wasted much time since crossing from Albion. We will escort you on this road for as far as our paths run together. Then we must be on our way."

"I insist you join me at my husband's hall in Paris."

"Insist, do you?" He raised an eyebrow, struggling to hold in the cough that scratched his throat.

"I do." She met his gaze without blinking.

"I am sorry, but I must insist that we cannot tarry."

"Lord Beobrand," said Wilfrid, placing a hand on his arm. "Paris is on our way, and even if it were not, we could surely spare some days from our journey to accompany the lovely lady to her home. After all, we are guests in this foreign land and it would do us well to make friends wherever we are able."

"It is as your young friend says," replied the lady, smiling at Beobrand's scowl. "And it would not do to ignore my wishes. And my husband is one whose friendship I think you will value."

Her self-possessed tone and certainty rankled. Beobrand wished to blurt out that he would be damned if he would do her bidding. They had saved her life by intervening, that was enough. And yet, something in her words warned him not to speak rashly. He choked back his retort and his building need to cough.

"What is your name, my lady, and who is your husband?" Wilfrid asked, cutting directly to the heart of the matter.

She turned her radiant smile on the young novice.

"My name is Balthild," she said. "And my husband is Clovis, second of his name, son of Dagobert, King of Neustria and Burgundia, ruler of the Frankish people."

Chapter 4

Beobrand picked up the goblet of wine and sipped the rich liquid, enjoying the feeling of warmth as it trickled down his throat. He could feel the cough still threatening, rasping, but the wine soothed him and after an initial violent bout of coughing when they had first come inside out of the incessant rain, he had managed to suppress it for the most part. He was glad of that. He had been tired before the fight, but once the trembling he always suffered after combat had passed, the exhaustion of his illness, coupled with the aches and bruises from the battle, made him feel old. He smiled grimly. He was old, he supposed. Closer to forty summers than thirty now. A grandfather.

He carefully placed the expensive glass beaker back on the linen-covered board and looked over to Balthild. The queen sat beside their host, Lord Marcoul. Sensing Beobrand's gaze, she glanced in his direction and offered him a smile. She was not much more than ten years his junior, but her smooth skin and the unborn babe in her swollen belly reminded him of Ardith and made him feel much older.

A thrall stepped up to refill his glass. Muttering his thanks, Beobrand looked about the sumptuously decorated hall, marvelling at the wealth on display. Gaudy drapes embroidered with golden thread hung against the walls, and the food was served on embossed silver plates, such as Beobrand had only seen in the halls of kings. As far as Beobrand could ascertain, this Marcoul was only a minor noble, but clearly his lands provided him with plenty of treasure.

They had reached the hall after dark, but for a time after leaving the gloom of the forest, they had ridden through an open land of low hills and tilled, richly fertile fields. Beobrand sipped his wine again and thought back to that long, bedraggled afternoon. He had been pleased to leave the woods behind. Under the trees he had sensed hidden eyes on them, peering out from the shadows. Stragglers from the band of brigands who had attacked Balthild's column, no doubt. It seemed unlikely they would risk another attack, but he did not like the sensation of being watched.

Out in the open, he had felt the tension easing from him. But with the removal of the threat of another ambush, so they lost the shelter from the trees that had helped to protect them from the worst of the weather. The wind picked up and the rain lashed at their faces as they rode. Balthild and her servant had vanished behind the curtains of the waggon that was now driven by one of Brocard's men. They had found the waggoner, lying in a pool of his blood, his throat opened. Brocard and Beobrand had set scouts ahead of the column and organised the rest of the men to ride protectively about the vehicles. Once they were on their way along the road, none of the men seemed inclined to speak.

Beobrand had ridden with his head down and cloak drawn up around his shoulders. Lost to his thoughts, he had dozed for a time, before being woken by coughing. Attor had lolled in his saddle, held steady by Gram, who rode close by. Beobrand exchanged a look with the older warrior. They were both worried about Attor. He had been excited to travel to the holy city of Roma, to the seat of power of the Christ followers. Attor worshipped the Christ passionately and, despite admitting he didn't always understand the finer points of the teachings the monks and priests preached in the small chapel at Ubbanford, he delighted in the idea that he would get to see where Saint Peter himself had been martyred.

"They hung Saint Peter upside down from a tree," he had said, excitedly, one day in Quentovic when they had talked of the journey ahead and their final destination. "He said he was not worthy to die like Jesu Himself."

"He will not still be hanging there, you know?" replied Beobrand.

"Of course not," Baducing said, making the sign of the cross at Beobrand's blasphemy. "But it is the most holy of places."

"The most holy of places," echoed Attor, nodding. Beobrand thought he detected a slight air of disappointment though, now that Attor knew he would not see Peter's crucified corpse.

Attor's cough had worsened as they had trudged through the rain-dark afternoon. When they had arrived at Marcoul's hall, the injured had been taken to a smaller guest building, where they were to be tended by a healer woman summoned from the nearest village. Two of Baducing's men had taken bad cuts, as had Eadgard, who fought with such abandon he seldom thought of defending himself. Fulbert, the man with the slash to his face, along with two others of Brocard's men, also needed treatment. They all protested that their wounds could be seen to after they had feasted, but Brocard, Baducing and Beobrand had insisted they all receive treatment before they could return to the hall. Attor was the only man amongst them who did not ask to be allowed to eat first. He had slid from his mount, almost stumbling, and followed a thrall without complaint or comment.

Beobrand sighed. He hoped that the cunning woman would have some ointment or potion that could help Attor. Stifling a cough behind his fist, Beobrand reached for a spoonful of salt pork`stew. Perhaps he too should have joined Attor. But surely he was not as unwell as the scout. He would rest soon, and mayhap the woman from the village would be able to give him a healing draught. He drained his glass, once again relishing the flavour. Besides, this wine was working wonders and it would not do to miss a feast with the queen of Neustria and Burgundia.

"My lord Beobrand," Balthild said suddenly, "Lord Marcoul has asked me to remind you that this wine is heady stuff."

Expensive too, thought Beobrand. He had seen the way the man's eyes had narrowed when they had ridden into his courtyard. The lord might well be rich, as his lavish hall with its cut stone walls and gold-threaded hangings attested, but he was certainly not overly pleased to have to feed the queen's entourage along with this group of travellers from Albion who had somehow gained her favour.

"Please thank Marcoul for his kindness and his hospitality. I am finding that his wine is proving a balm for my throat. I already feel much improved."

She relayed his words and Marcoul muttered a reply. She smiled in response.

"Then he bids you to drink as much as you wish, but he asks that you do not hold him to account in the morning when you feel your head is being split by a woodsman's axe."

A few of Beobrand's men laughed. Eadgard, who had returned from the healer with a white strip of cloth binding his forearm, lifted his own cup and emptied it in one gulp.

"Here's to splitting heads!" he roared.

The men laughed more loudly. Marcoul scowled, before forcing himself to grin and to raise his glass in salute to the men who had helped rescue his queen.

Beobrand cleared his throat and held out his glass to the nearby thrall.

"The mention of woodsmen makes me wonder. Does Marcoul know anything about the men who attacked you in the forest?"

Balthild hesitated, meeting Beobrand's gaze without speaking for a moment, before turning to their host and repeating the question. Marcoul spoke lightly, spreading his hands and gesticulating as he talked.

Halinard, who sat to Beobrand's left, translated for him in a quiet voice.

"He says he knows nothing of the men of the forest. There are – how do you say? – heads of wolf, in all woods."

"Wolf-heads," Beobrand mumbled. The name was used for men outside the law, who could be slain as if they were nothing more than beasts.

Halinard nodded distractedly. Lord Marcoul was still speaking animatedly and Halinard was listening.

"He asks why the queen travels with so few warriors."

Balthild replied to the lord of the hall, her tone frosty now. Halinard continued to interpret their words.

"The land is in peace. There has never been tell of so many outlaws attacking together."

Marcoul shrugged.

"It has been a hard winter. People are hungry. Desperate."

"Then you must be thankful," said Beobrand loudly, once he had heard Halinard's translation, "that your queen, along with the unborn child of the king, were not slain. Had it not been for our chance arrival, I fear the outlaws would have slain everyone in that column."

Marcoul's face clouded.

"Of course we offer praise to the Lord Almighty for our good queen's deliverance. And I will send out men to scour the woodland for any of the perpetrators who survived. But," he went on with a nod towards the leader of the queen's guard, "I have no doubt that brave Brocard and his men would have prevailed against a handful of ruffians."

"These were no mere ruffians," said Brocard. His words came to Beobrand through Halinard, but the warrior's anger was clear. His voice was as sharp and cold as a blade. "There were close to two score men, armed and organised. We rode with sixteen guardsmen, all strong, valiant men, and though it pains me to say it, Lord Beobrand is correct. Without the intervention of his men, we would surely have all been killed and..." he hesitated, biting his lip. "And the queen lost." He lowered his gaze in shame, but his words were still clear as he went on. "Of course, when we are safely back in Paris, I will relinquish my command. I have failed you, my lady. And I have failed my king."

"Nonsense, Brocard," Balthild said, waving away his concerns. "You are my most trusted servant. I would not dream of having you replaced. As to Beobrand's arrival, I do not believe in chance. I have been speaking to Wilfrid and Baducing, both learned men and good Christians. And they are certain that the Lord's hand was in this. Could it be chance that Christ-loving pilgrims, travelling to Roma, the holiest of cities, should be the ones to come to my rescue? Surely none can believe there is not divine will in such a thing."

"We had planned to travel many days earlier, after Plough Day," said Wilfrid, clearly pleased to have been mentioned, "but the weather kept us at Quentovic until this morning." He paused, giving Balthild time to translate his words. Without bidding, she did so. Marcoul frowned. Beobrand did not like the man, but he understood the lord's discomfort. He felt it too. Wilfrid so easily commanded the hall and every flame-lit face was turned towards him. It was clear that the young novice basked in such attention. "And who controls the wind and rain," Wilfrid continued, gesturing with his hands at the sky above the hall, "if not our Lord God?"

Outside the rain still fell, hissing against the tiled roof. Beobrand chose not to mention that it was Thunor's hammer that smote the skies with lightning. Something else had been troubling him.

"How is it that you were travelling so close to your confinement, your highness?" he asked.

"Why, that is simple. I was visiting the minster of Saint Etienn.

I have been working with the abbess there. Like you, I was held longer than I intended by this terrible rain."

"Working with the abbess?" Wilfrid enquired. "I must say I am most intrigued by this. Please tell us what holy endeavours are being carried out by the mother of a priory and the mother of the Franks."

Balthild smoothed the cloth on the board before her, brushing away crumbs. For the first time since they had met, Beobrand thought the young woman seemed lost for words.

"There are several women at Saint Etienn," she said at last, "who once were thralls. They are now free, and I wished to speak to them."

"Speak to them?" asked Wilfrid. "What for?"

"To learn from them. To understand what they require now they have been freed."

Wilfrid frowned and rubbed a hand over the short hair that had grown to replace his shaved tonsure. The golden ring he wore gleamed in the firelight.

"This sounds like the work of the abbess and her sisters in Christ, no doubt," he mused. "But why is the queen of the land concerned with such matters?"

"Once again, that is simple," she said, with a quick, almost embarrassed smile. "I freed them."

"That is laudable," he said uncertainly.

"I would free all slaves, if I could," she went on, her voice growing in strength. "To keep children of God in chains against their will is barbaric." Her words took on a hard edge and colour flushed her cheeks.

Beobrand glanced at the thrall who had refilled his glass. He had paid no heed to the young woman before. Now he saw how she was staring at the queen, her eyes glimmering fervently. The queen looked at the girl and nodded.

"No man or woman should be enslaved," Balthild said. Her voice shook. "None."

Silence had descended on the hall. The fire crackled in the hearth. Outside, the rain thrummed against the roof. A sudden coughing seized Beobrand and all eyes turned to him. He held up a hand in apology as he caught his breath. Cynan was staring at him. He had once been a thrall. Beobrand had freed him and made him a warrior in his warband. Beobrand could not interpret his expression. The previous year, Cynan had disobeyed him to travel into the west to help a woman who had once been Beobrand's thrall. The woman, Sulis. The slave who had killed Beobrand's woman, Reaghan, who too had been a thrall in her time, before Beobrand had given her her freedom.

Beside Cynan sat Bleddyn, another erstwhile thrall. Cynan had slain Bleddyn's master to protect Sulis. Freed from his bonds of thralldom, Bleddyn had joined Cynan's growing comitatus.

Beobrand had never felt easy with the idea of slavery. He treated his thralls well, saw them fed and clothed and seldom beaten, but could the queen be right? Was it wrong to enslave humans as one might saddle a horse, or yoke an ox to a plough?

He sensed there was more to this than he understood. Balthild had barely flinched when a man had held a knife to her throat and she had killed the brigand as quickly, and with as little remorse, as a trained warrior. But now, at the mention of thralls, she was shaking with passion.

"This seems like a subject close to your heart," said Wilfrid, clearly thinking the same thing.

"Oh, it is, Wilfrid," she replied, her voice controlled, her grip tight on her emotions once more. "Forgive me, I forget that you are not from Frankia. My story is well known here."

"Your story, your highness?"

"Yes," she replied, smiling a sad smile. "Before I became the bride of King Clovis, I was a thrall."

Chapter 5

They set out early the next day. The rain had stopped, and a watery sun tried to shine through the clouds. It did little to warm the land or to dry the puddles, and the mud was still thick in the courtyard and the road heading south towards Anmyin. It might have been more prudent to stay at Marcoul's hall another day, allowing the road to improve and also to give the injured and sick men time to recover, but Balthild was adamant that they should leave. Beobrand and Brocard did not disagree.

"I will feel safer when we are far from Marcoul's lands," Brocard whispered, his words translated in hushed tones by Halinard.

Beobrand coughed loudly, hawking up phlegm and spitting into the mud of the yard where the men were saddling the horses and preparing the waggon and cart for travel. He had slept poorly, but the wine and warmth, and a potion of sage, horehound and betony that the cunning woman had given him seemed to have done him good. The brew was foul-tasting, but he had forced himself to swallow a couple of spoonfuls and awoke feeling as if perhaps he had seen the worst of this accursed cough.

"Do you believe Marcoul had something to do with the attack?" Beobrand asked.

Brocard shrugged.

Beobrand sensed that Brocard did not like him, perhaps resenting that Beobrand and his Black Shields had needed to rescue the queen whom he had been tasked with protecting. On top of that, Beobrand and his fellow pilgrims had the advantage that they shared Balthild's land of birth and her mother tongue. The leader of the queen's guard did not hide his dislike, but the man seemed honest, and he clearly respected Beobrand enough to trust him with his concerns.

"I know not," said Brocard, scratching at his neck where his byrnie chafed, "but I am not blind, and any fool can see that the lord of the hall does not love our queen. I have my eyes wide open. I know that many nobles resent her rise to power, but in the palaces of Paris and Liyon, people are more subtle about their loathing."

"Balthild is so widely hated?"

"Oh no," replied Brocard. "The people, the normal people, those who work the fields and whose toil brings silver and gold into the coffers of the nobility and the church, they all love her. The farmers, peasants, craftsmen and even the thralls, adore her. They see her as one of their own." He smiled to himself. "This enrages the nobles even more. That she is beautiful, intelligent and just, serves to fan the flames of their anger."

Beobrand could barely believe that one as lovely as the queen could be hated by anyone, but he had witnessed the souring of the mood in the hall as Balthild had spoken of her past and her rise to become the most powerful woman in the kingdom. Marcoul's disapproval had been clear. The lord had glowered, exchanging dark glances with his frowning wife, who sat silently throughout the feast. Their children, a chubby boy and a sharp-faced girl, also sat in silence. The boy devoured everything that the thralls placed before him, while the girl seemed to only pick at her food. But neither of them uttered a sound, instead watching with wide eyes as their queen recounted her tale.

"My family hails from East Angeln, in Albion," Balthild had

said in Anglisc. "I was but a child when my father sold me to a trader from Frankia."

"Your father sold you?" asked Beobrand, his voice jagged. His own daughter, Ardith, had been sold into slavery by the man she had believed to be her father. That man was now dead, as were many others who had stood in the way of Beobrand and the men who had gone in search of Ardith.

"He did." The queen met Beobrand's sombre gaze. "He is long dead now, but I bear his memory no ill will."

Beobrand snorted. Halinard looked sidelong at him. He had met Beobrand when he had first come to Frankia. He had seen what he was capable of to rescue his kin.

"Think what you will, Lord Beobrand," Balthild said. "I can no more change your mind than I can alter the weather. But I tell you there was no malice in my father and he did what he needed to do for his family. If he had not sold me all those years ago, we might all have died, for we were poor and food was scarce." As if to accentuate her words, she picked up a sliver of venison from her trencher, inspected it briefly and then popped it into her mouth.

"I found my way into the household of Erchinoald, the *major domus*."

"*Major domus*?" asked Beobrand. The words meant nothing to him.

"A most powerful man at court," explained Balthild. "Erchinoald is second only to the king himself. The kingdom is administered under his wise counsel." She raised her ornate goblet, turning it so that the candlelight flickered in the green glass. Taking a sip, she replaced it on the table. "It was whilst I was serving in the palace that Clovis spied me."

Marcoul's lady, perhaps understanding Balthild's words or merely at the mention of the king, let out a small cough. It sounded almost like a scoffing laugh. Brocard tensed. The queen ignored her.

"It does not do to question the wishes of a king," she said in a flat tone, "and so, shortly after we met, we were wed."

Beobrand was incredulous. Balthild was no doubt beautiful, with a quick wit and keen mind, but surely there must be more to this tale than she had told. Kings could bed whichever thrall took their fancy. They certainly didn't need to marry them. He had wanted to ask more, but despite the flow of ale and wine, which the men were enjoying, the atmosphere in the hall had become cool and, as if suddenly feeling a cold draught, Balthild shivered, then stood. There was a scraping of benches and seats as everyone rose. Beobrand noted that they had to wait for several heartbeats for Marcoul and his lady to push themselves reluctantly to their feet.

Brocard had set a guard outside the queen's quarters. Beobrand offered his men to share the duty and Brocard grudgingly agreed, pairing his men with Beobrand's, thus ensuring that none of the men from Albion were left alone outside the queen's door. The man was clearly prudent and trusted nobody. Such distrust seemed sensible to Beobrand.

"How's the arm?" Beobrand called out to Eadgard. The giant axeman was helping an hostler attach the cart's yoke to the oxen. His face was pale, but he seemed hale enough and Beobrand suspected that his pallid complexion had more to do with the amount of ale he had consumed than his injury.

Eadgard grunted with the effort of lifting the yoke into place. The oxen's breath clouded the air around him.

"It will be as good as new in a few days, lord." He wiped sweat from his brow, despite the cold of the morning.

"And Attor?" asked Beobrand. "How does he fare?"

"I will do well enough, lord," said a voice close behind him.

Attor stood there, his features pinched, his eyes dark-rimmed. He had a blanket wrapped about his shoulders. He looked haggard and old, but he seemed more alert than the previous night. And he was on his feet, which was something.

"I give thanks to see you are on the mend," said Beobrand.

"I feel much better, lord. That muck the old woman fed us last night has done wonders." He grimaced. "It tastes like dog shit though."

"I wouldn't know," replied Beobrand with a grin. "I haven't got your taste for such things."

Attor started to laugh, but his laughter quickly turned into a cough. The strength of it bent him double. His hacking breath steamed in the chill air. As if in answer to Attor, Beobrand could feel his own cough building, but he held it in.

"You may be better than yesterday, my friend," he said, "but you still need rest."

"You'll not be leaving me here, lord?" Attor looked aghast at the prospect.

"No," said Beobrand, "you'll not shirk your duties that easily. But I think you would be better riding in the cart today. You need to build your strength."

"I will not travel like a woman or a child," Attor grumbled.

"No, no," said Beobrand, glad he had thought to discuss Attor's situation with Brocard beforehand. There was no need to further hurt Attor's pride. "The cart needs a driver," he nodded to where Eadgard and the hostler had finished attaching the oxen. "And you would do well not to ride for a day or two."

Attor was not pleased, but Beobrand insisted. So, complaining that he was a gesith not a ceorl, Attor clambered onto the cart that held the provisions and baggage for the royal party.

All around them, the horses were ready and the men were pulling themselves into saddles. There were several empty horses that would be led by the riders. The corpses of the men who had fallen would be buried in the way of the Christ followers by the local priest, a short, fastidious man. He had nodded obsequiously as the queen had given him instructions for the men's burial, but his eyes had been hard and his lips pressed tightly together at the thought of so much work.

When Brocard handed him a small pouch of silver, the priest's demeanour brightened noticeably.

"Your highness," said Beobrand, bowing to Balthild who had stepped out of the hall. "Let me help you." He held out his hand.

"Thank you," she replied, and without hesitation she took his outstretched hand gently in hers, allowing him to guide her to her waggon. The waggon was waiting as close as possible to the doors of the building, but the ground was slippery and treacherous.

Brocard frowned, perhaps thinking that this role should have fallen to him. He said nothing, instead turning to adjust his horse's bridle. Beobrand smiled as Bleddyn hurried forward and offered his arm to the queen's pretty maidservant.

Once both women were safely in the covered waggon, Brocard jumped up onto his horse and trotted to the front of the party. He shouted something and rode out of the courtyard. Attor lashed the oxen with a hazel switch and the man driving the waggon flicked the mules' reins. The wooden vehicles rattled and creaked, then groaned as they squelched through the mud. Men touched heels to their mounts' flanks and, with a clatter, the column moved out.

Beobrand swung himself up onto his gelding. Bleddyn was close by. They kicked their horses into a canter to catch up with the other Black Shields. Cynan turned in the saddle at their approach.

"I'm surprised to see you here, Bleddyn," he said, smirking.

"Where else would I be, lord?"

"Well, the day is cold and I thought you might have decided to ride on the waggon to keep a certain maid warm."

Bleddyn blushed and the men who heard the exchange laughed. Bleddyn had disappeared for a long spell in the evening, and it had not gone unnoticed that the queen's attractive servant had also been missing from the feast for a time.

"I really don't understand it," said Ingwald with a grin, his teeth bright in his dark, leathery face. "Bleddyn can speak but a few words of Frankish and I do not think the girl can speak our tongue. So I know not what they could find to do together."

"I have no idea," said Cynan with a wink. The men laughed again. Beobrand felt suddenly lonely. He was pleased for Bleddyn, but it had been a long time since he had been with a woman. Queen Balthild reminded him of Sunniva, lost all those years ago. He sighed. The women he had loved were all dead, apart from one.

And she could never be his.

Noticing Cynan rubbing at his shoulder, Beobrand changed the subject.

"No better?" he asked.

Cynan sighed.

"A little," he said. "But it still hurts."

"I still can't believe it was a horse that got you in the end."

Cynan had followed Beobrand headlong into the fight and even though he was in the thick of the action, he had escaped unscathed. It was only afterwards, when he had helped to round up the scattered horses, that he had been injured.

"Tell me again," Beobrand said, "how the best rider in Northumbria found himself scratched and battered by a mare."

"It was a stallion," murmured Cynan.

"Easy mistake, lord," said Ingwald, biting his lip to stifle a guffaw. "You picked the wrong Waelisc warrior. It is Bleddyn here who tumbles with a Frankish mare."

Bleddyn's cheeks flushed. Cynan and Beobrand chuckled.

"My lord," spluttered Bleddyn, "I assure you—"

Beobrand held up his left hand. The scars on the stumps of his mutilated fingers were stark in the pale morning light.

"No need to explain yourself, Bleddyn. It is perfectly natural. We don't wish to hear all the dirty details of your rutting."

"But, lord, I—"

Beobrand cut Bleddyn off again.

"Well, if you insist, then later you can tell all, but first I would have Cynan tell us of his adventure in the forest. He rode into the woods unhurt and returned as if he had tried to bed a wildcat."

Cynan glowered. As well as the shoulder that clearly pained him, his cheeks were scratched and his left eye was swollen and bruised.

"I have already told my tale," he snapped, "and I will not tell it again for your amusement." He kicked his heels into his horse's ribs and galloped away towards the front of the line.

"But your lord wishes to be amused!" shouted Beobrand at his departing back. The men laughed, but Beobrand quickly regretted shouting in the cold, damp air. A fit of coughs seized him and his gelding shied and sidestepped, startled by his rider's sudden movement and barking cough. The men's laughter subsided and they looked at him sidelong. He spat into the long grass and nettles that grew beside the road. Shaking his head, he rode on in silence for a time, thinking about the story Cynan had told them the previous afternoon when he had ridden out of the forest leading a pair of horses.

He had gone deep into the woodland in search of the stray animals, wary of any stragglers from the band of brigands who had attacked Balthild's column. But the men had vanished, swallowed into the damp dark beneath the dripping branches of the trees.

The first two horses had been easy enough to capture. The third he had found was hurt and Cynan had cursed when he had recounted how he had been impatient to catch it and return. It was never easy to control an injured animal, and it had been foolish to attempt to bring it back to the waiting warriors and waggons along with the other two mounts. No sooner had Cynan pulled on the stallion's reins, than the beast had refused to budge, digging its hooves into the rotting leaves and staring at him balefully. He should have let it remain there then. He knew horses well enough to understand this animal would be trouble, and he could see the blood wet and slick on its flank. But he had been in a hurry, so, stupidly, he had wrapped the reins in his fist and tugged hard. The next thing he knew he had been pulled from the saddle, losing his hold on the first two beasts, while the third, injured and in pain, had dragged him through mud, nettles, bracken and brambles before he'd managed to free himself from the reins.

He'd let the wounded horse run after that.

When Beobrand had first seen Cynan and Ingwald returning, he worried they had encountered some of the fleeing brigands. Many had disappeared into the protection of the forest, some with terrible wounds that would surely see them perish. They would be desperate, dangerous, and he had cursed himself for allowing his men to split up in search of the scattered horses.

Beobrand thought of the assault on the queen and wondered how likely another attack might be. If the men who had ambushed Balthild's party were indeed wolf-heads, desperate men who had organised themselves in an attempt to rob a wealthy traveller, they would see no more of them. The brigands had lost many, and whilst the survivors might well prey on other travellers in the forest, they would not dare leave the sanctuary of the trees. Besides, to pursue them would be folly. They were armed and clearly able to defend themselves. But none of this made sense. Why would a band of ruffians risk attacking a waggon and cart with a mounted, well-armed escort of hardened warriors? No matter how many times he thought of this, he could not fathom it.

His mood darkened and they rode on without speaking for some distance. Either side of the road, the land rolled away flat and sparsely wooded. Beobrand began to relax, before reminding himself that a sizable force of men could hide in a small copse of trees, or lurk, crouched in a ditch or hollow.

"How bad is his shoulder?" he asked Ingwald without warning.

The older man turned sharply, startled out of a doze.

"It pains him," he said. "But he'll recover soon enough. There is none tougher. His pride took the worst blow."

Beobrand nodded. The bald, tanned warrior was steadfast and loyal to Cynan. Beobrand liked him.

"Perhaps it is a good thing that this happened."

"Lord?"

"It can do us good sometimes to find we are just as likely to fall as the next man. It helps us to keep focused."

They rested at midday in a small hamlet. The houses were ramshackle and dilapidated. The daub had fallen off in great patches from the walls of the buildings, exposing the wattle beneath. The thatch on the roofs was mossy and mildewed. Despite the obvious poverty of the place, the lady of the largest house invited Balthild inside her home. Brocard, stern-faced and on edge, pushed past the woman and went into the hovel first. Moments later, he returned and ushered the queen into the gloom.

The goodwife, a hard-bitten, raw-boned woman, scowled at him and Beobrand thought he was lucky that she was not armed.

"This is still Marcoul's land," Brocard muttered, and Beobrand was surprised to find his Frankish must have been improving for he understood him.

Beobrand looked about the tumbled fences and mean houses, the skinny sheep in a nearby field and a hollow-chested nag that stood, head down, cropping at the weeds near the gate. From inside the smoky gloom he could hear their hostess chattering away at the queen. Balthild's replies were light and friendly, and as the old woman bustled about her hearth, preparing food and drink for her unexpected guest, Beobrand pondered how the warmth of a welcome could not be measured by wealth.

Chapter 6

Balthild smiled to the old woman as they left, handing her a small brooch as a token of her thanks. The goodwife dropped to her knees and kissed the hem of the queen's dress. Brocard needed to pull the woman to her feet so that Balthild could climb up into her covered waggon. The queen smiled and nodded at the woman, but Beobrand saw that Balthild's eyes were dull and she appeared to collapse onto the pillows as her maid, Alpaida, lowered the curtains.

When they had left the hamlet behind, Beobrand rode alongside Brocard. He signalled to Halinard to join them.

"How far to Paris?" he asked.

Brocard shrugged.

"Ten days. More if the weather is bad."

Beobrand shook his head.

"The queen is tired. I do not know if she can travel so far."

"She is stronger than you think."

Beobrand thought of how she had killed the man who held a knife to her throat.

"I do not doubt her strength," he said. "But no matter how strong, she cannot stop a baby coming when it will. I am no expert in these matters, but it seems to me she should be in her confinement already."

Brocard frowned.

"The abbess at Saint Etienn said as much, and I know Alpaida worries too. But the queen assures me there is still time. We should have left Quentovic long since, but Balthild has vowed to have this, her first child, delivered at Cala. And it is not for me to gainsay the queen."

"No, it is for you to protect her," said Beobrand. "Perhaps some decisions cannot be taken by the queen. Mayhap this journey is too dangerous."

Brocard's face darkened.

"When we reach Anmyin, we will rest a day and I will speak with her highness again. Perhaps she will change her mind and enter her confinement there." He rubbed a hand over his face and sighed. "But I doubt it. She has set her heart on Cala and you have seen that it is not a simple matter to dissuade the queen from a course of action."

"Did you say Cala?" asked Wilfrid, who had trotted his horse past the royal waggon to join Beobrand and Brocard at the head of the column. "I thought the queen was heading to Paris." Beobrand felt a stab of envy at the young man's facility for the language of the Franks. It was all Beobrand could do to follow the simplest of conversations, but he understood enough to hear that Wilfrid spoke the tongue well.

"Indeed we are travelling to Paris," Brocard replied, "but the queen's final destination is Cala, a minster close to the city."

"I know of Cala," said Wilfrid, "though of course, I have never visited. In fact, it seems that this journey is not out of our way at all. We bear messages and gifts from Hild, a most holy sister at the Abbey of Hereteu. Hild's kinswoman, Hereswitha, resides at Cala."

Brocard nodded.

"Abbess Bertila is a good friend, and the queen refuses to allow anyone else to tend to her in her lying-in."

Beobrand glanced back at the waggon.

"She may not have a choice," he said under his breath.

They had just ridden up a small rise. It was barely perceptible to the horses, but the heavy waggon was wallowing in the thick mud at the foot of the slope. The blue-cloaked warrior who now drove the vehicle was shouting at the mules and lashing them with the reins, but strain as they might, the waggon did not budge.

Behind the waggon, Attor had halted the ox-drawn cart. There was nowhere to go until the waggon was over the low hill.

With a sigh, Beobrand wheeled his gelding around.

"Come on," he said. "Looks like we are going to get muddy. And if these roads don't improve, we won't be reaching Cala, or even Anmyin, before Balthild's child is born."

Men were already dismounting to help push the waggon out of the mire, but before he rode down to them, Beobrand looked around. There was a stand of aspen a few hundred paces to the east and a sudden prickle of unease scratched down his spine.

"Brocard," he called.

The leader of the queen's guard reined in and followed his gaze.

"Good place for an ambush," he said.

"Aye."

"I will stay here with a guard, while the rest of you help with the waggon."

Beobrand looked down at the men who were already up to their knees in dark, clinging mud. As he watched, the waggon shifted and Grindan stumbled, falling forwards into the muck. The men laughed as he rose. He was caked in the stuff and looked more beast than man.

Beobrand coughed and spat.

"I didn't like being clean and dry anyway," he said with a twisted smile to Halinard. The Frank grunted, and together they rode down the hill.

It took them a long time to free the waggon from the quagmire.

By the time they had rocked and shoved and heaved it to the top of the rise, most of the men were smeared with great dollops of cold, cloying mud. It stank too, the smell acrid and thick in their throats. The men joked about how much of the mud was actually manure from horses, mules and cattle that had passed that way. Beobrand, wiping a gobbet of the noisome stuff from his cheek, found little enough to laugh about.

Still, they had learnt from the experience with the waggon and they managed to get the cart up the hill much more quickly by skirting the road and trampling over the long grasses and nettles that grew beside it. The oxen lowed angrily, and the cart slipped and slid over the wet foliage, but it was much easier going than trying to force the vehicle through the deep, rutted mud.

When they were all on the brow of the hill, the only men not covered in ordure and mud were Brocard and Fulbert, who had stood watch. They grinned at the mud-smeared men who cursed their cleanliness, but despite being dirty and wet, the humour of the men was buoyant. There had been no fresh ambush, as some had feared, and there was a sense of achievement at having worked together to get the vehicles up the incline.

They all cheered when Balthild pulled back the curtains and thanked them for their efforts. The sun, that had been so elusive, now shone down on them from between the grey clouds. The light was warm on their faces, a promise of the spring that would soon awaken the earth from its winter slumber. They rode on in good spirits.

They spent that night in a small hall. It was much less grand than Marcoul's, but again, just as at the small cottage, they were made to feel welcome. The lady of the hall, a homely, plump woman with warm eyes and pink cheeks, took one look at the queen's swollen belly, pale skin and pinched expression, and, tutting and complaining at how badly she had been looked after, she whisked Balthild off to her sleeping quarters. There, the lady fussed over the queen, frequently sending out Alpaida to bring hot water, warm, watered-down wine, toasted bread and honey, and a bowlful of broth. When it became clear to the lord of the hall, a solid, cheerful man called Theodulf, that neither the queen, nor his wife, would be returning to the main hall, he clapped his hands and called for more ale. A large fire blazed on the hearth and the travellers' clothes steamed in the warmth. Theodulf's table was of simple fare, mutton, pottage and coarse bread, and there was no expensive wine, but he was generous, and the sound of laughter and jesting soon echoed in the hall.

The ale flowed and the men became rowdy. When several of them broke into a song led by the drunken lord of the hall, Theodulf's wife burst out from the sleeping quarters, shouting furiously at them. The queen needed her rest and if they could not be quiet, they could all go and sleep in the barn. Several of the men laughed, but one glare from the hitherto jovial-looking lady silenced them.

She vanished back behind the partition, and the men, chastened now, grew hushed. Conversations were murmured in the shadows as the fire died down. Theodulf and some of the men were soon snoring. Attor, wrapped in a blanket near the fire, was already asleep. He had seemed much better when they had arrived. Though his shoulders were slumped from fatigue and he was still coughing terribly, he ate and drank before stretching out to sleep. And both Beobrand and Attor had taken another sip of the foul-tasting potion the cunning woman had given them.

Seeing Brocard's cup empty, Beobrand picked up a large earthenware pitcher and poured ale till it frothed over the side and onto the linen cloth.

"My thanks," said Brocard, drinking with obvious relish.

Beobrand smiled.

"It's good," he said, refilling his own cup.

He had slept poorly these last nights and after the day's riding, he was tired. But he wished to find out more about the kingdom they were travelling through, and what perils might await them. Until now he had only seen Brocard fighting, or wary that enemies might be lurking nearby. Seemingly at ease now, the man looked several years younger than Beobrand had first thought.

"You think there will be more attacks on the road?" Beobrand said, nudging Halinard to translate for him. The Frank, who had been almost dozing, sat up straight and mumbled something to Brocard.

The captain of the guard scratched at his beard and took another swig of ale.

"I don't know," he said at last. Some of the worry lines began to furrow his brow once more and Beobrand felt sorry that he was not able to leave the man alone for tonight. He needed rest too, and Beobrand knew well enough the pressures that came with responsibility. And yet he also had a duty to his people, and he needed to know what they might face on the road.

"But you think there might be," he said. It was not a question. "Who would attack the queen?"

Brocard sighed.

"No king nor queen is without enemies."

Beobrand thought of the seax he had retrieved in the forest, of the numbers of dead.

"Enemies from within the kingdom, or from without?"

Brocard shrugged.

"Who can say?"

A thought came to Beobrand.

"Does the king have any blood-kin?"

"His brother, Sigebert, rules over Austrasia." Brocard shook his head. "But this is not the act of a king and there is only love between the sons of Dagobert."

Beobrand recalled Oswine, the king of Deira's, bloody death in a darkened hall. Oswiu had ordered his kin's killing. And for what? Land and power.

"I hope it is as you say. But if those who attacked you were sent by enemies of the queen, there will be more."

Brocard emptied his cup and held it out for more ale.

"I fear it is true," he said. "But if they were not outlaws, one thing is clear."

"What?"

"Those enemies who move against the queen, whoever they may be, are not so brave as to strike openly. They hid behind the rags and mud of brigands, even if they carried the blades of warriors. If they plan another attack, it will take time to bring together another force strong enough to guarantee success. Perhaps if you did not ride with us, they might try again." Brocard sniffed, clearly unhappy with the acknowledgement that his men were not enough to assure the queen's safety. "But at Anmyin I will be able to call on more men to bolster our number from Lord Riquier's warband."

"You will be able to trust this Riquier's men?"

Brocard bit his lip, but did not answer the question directly.

"I think if we can ride through to Paris without delay, we should reach Cala safely."

"And once the queen reaches Paris?" asked Beobrand. "Will she be safe then?"

"Who can say they are ever truly safe? The queen has many friends and allies, more than enemies, I think. Theodulf here, for example. The men and women of the land. But it is not the number of enemies she has that worries me."

"No?"

"Her enemies may be few, but they are powerful."

"Who is she?" asked Beobrand, saying the words in his poorly accented Frankish.

"She is my queen," replied Brocard, raising his chin and meeting Beobrand's ice blue gaze.

"She spoke of being a thrall," Beobrand said. "Of being sold by a father who could not afford to feed his family. Can this be true? Why would a king marry such a woman? I have seen how she speaks to nobles and ceorls. She is at home with both. And how would a thrall from such a lowly family command such loyalty and respect from her subjects? And why would she have such powerful foes?"

"These are many questions, Lord Beobrand," Brocard replied after listening to Halinard's translation. "You have heard from the queen's lips how she came to be a thrall, and how it was that Clovis took her for his wife. If there is more to her tale, then it is not for me to say." He fell silent, staring into the dying flames of the fire. Taking a mouthful of ale, he set the cup aside, as if he had made up his mind about something. "I know not the truth of these things, and I have no reason to doubt my queen's word. And yet, there are those who say that she is kin to Anglisc royalty."

Chapter 7

They reached the city of Anmyin without further setbacks. It rained at times, but only a light drizzle fell, rather than the teeming, seemingly never-ending downpour that had kept them in Quentovic for weeks. Whilst the roads were still clogged with mud in places, they were passable, and neither the waggon nor the cart became bogged down again. The men became adept at driving the vehicles up hills, and the queen's guards and the travellers from Albion bonded over the shared effort. The warriors also grew accustomed to sharing guard duties. Brocard, whilst not becoming warm towards Beobrand and the rest of the pilgrims from Northumbria, at least trusted them to stand watch.

Anmyin was a sprawling place and a pall of smoke hung over it like low cloud. They had spent so long in Quentovic with its huddle of thatched buildings, barns, warehouses, stables and bustling timber wharfs, that the sheer size and history of Anmyin shocked Beobrand. They rode south through the outskirts along mud-thick streets between thatched buildings with timber frames and daubed walls not unlike those in Quentovic, but every now and then, they would spy to the south, over the dark waters of the wide Samara river, the red tiles of a Roman roof. Close to the water, a crumbling colonnade of stone jutted from a weed-tangled patch of ground where dogs fought over scraps of offal. A thickset man glanced at their passing from where he was butchering a cow's carcass atop a blood-soaked stump. In the distance, looming over the city south of the river, rose the remains of a great circular building, like the one in Cantwareburh he had visited as a boy. Beobrand recalled the resignation and fear on the faces of the thralls awaiting their fate on the old stained sands. He wondered if the Franks held slave markets here too, and if they did, what the queen thought about the practice of selling people like animals.

They crossed over a stone bridge, another reminder of the grandeur left by the men of Roma, to an island in the Samara. The smoke and stink of the city oozed over the water, but the air was relatively clear here and the buildings sparser and further apart. This was where Lord Riquier and his wife, Fastrada, welcomed them. The lord's hall and its outbuildings had been constructed on the site of a noble Roman villa. Riquier was a slender man with strong, angular features. His dark eyes held a sadness about them, but both he and his wife seemed genuinely pleased to see Balthild. And yet, no matter their host's sincerity, the riders were still nervous. They had not forgotten the battle in the forest which had seen so many of their number killed or injured. There were guards at the gate and as the party clattered into the courtyard behind the high wall, Beobrand could not shake the feeling they were being trapped. He glanced at Halinard and he knew that he too was remembering a similar courtyard, not so far away in Rodomo.

Beobrand wanted to ask Balthild about her past, but she was exhausted from travelling, so after the brief welcome, she retired quickly and asked for food to be brought to her quarters.

The decision not to travel on the subsequent day clearly did her good. The day was dry and Beobrand saw Balthild sitting in deep conversation with Lady Fastrada in the walled garden where herbs and flowers grew sheltered from the wind. It was warm and still there, and in the afternoon sunshine it was easy to forget the dangers of the road. And yet, was Balthild truly safe here? Was Riquier friend or foe to the young queen? Brocard stood in the shade of a wall. He was never far from the queen's side. Beobrand nodded to him, assured by his prudence.

That evening, her hair brushed so that it shone like spun gold in the light of candles and oil lamps, Balthild joined them for a feast. Beobrand, as a guest of honour, had been seated alongside the queen, Riquier and Fastrada. Wilfrid and Baducing too were given places at the high table either side of a plump Christ priest, Bertofredus, the bishop of Anmyin. When the holy men became engrossed in a debate about some matter of their religion in that impenetrable old Roman tongue they spoke, Beobrand decided to ask the queen directly about her heritage.

She smiled and he was glad to see the gleam had returned to her eye and that the day's repose had brought back the colour to her cheeks.

"If my father were a king or atheling, do you imagine he would have sold his daughter to be the possession of another?"

Beobrand thought of all the daughters of kings who were given to men to weave peace between two kingdoms. Was that not also a form of thralldom? He was wondering how he could say such a thing without causing offence when Balthild drew in a sharp breath and placed a hand on her belly.

"My lady," said Beobrand, anxiety sharpening his tone, "is it time?"

Balthild chuckled.

"It is time for more food and wine," she said. "And then we must rest, for tomorrow we ride on." At his concerned expression, Balthild's smile broadened. "Do not fear, Lord Beobrand, The babe is merely kicking me from within. Reminding me that I must hurry to reach Cala before I am forced to lie-in." She sipped her wine. "I cannot imagine a worse thing than being forced to remain a-bed for weeks." Beobrand could think of many worse things, but he said nothing. He could quite imagine that for one such as Balthild, so vivacious and full of energy, being cooped up for weeks on end would indeed feel like a torture. He recalled how Sunniva had hated to be locked inside, and how they had both longed for open spaces and freedom after long weeks in the crowded fortress of Bebbanburg.

"I too prefer to be outside, where the air is clear." He smiled. "Resting can be so tiring."

Balthild laughed, a joyful, infectious sound.

"Finally," she said, "a man who understands me."

"I don't believe any man can truly understand a woman's mind."

She laughed again.

"Perhaps you are right at that. But I think you know me well enough not to attempt changing my decision."

Beobrand knew that Brocard had already urged the queen to remain at Anmyin. Fastrada was a mother and grandmother, and said there was a fine midwife she could call upon. There was plenty of space. Riquier's buildings were comfortable, and he would be honoured to house Balthild during her confinement. The queen was resolute. She would not hear of it. They would leave after morning prayers.

"I know it is not my place to argue with a queen," Beobrand said with a raised eyebrow, "whether she is the daughter of royalty, or not."

"You speak from experience, I'd say. I wager that your wife's word is heard loudly in your hall, queen or no queen." She offered him a radiant smile.

Beobrand's features tightened at the mention of his wife. Misunderstanding his reaction, the queen leant forward and placed a hand on his arm.

"I meant no insult, Lord Beobrand. Please accept my apologies. I am sure you command your hall without dissent from your womenfolk."

Despite himself, he chuckled at that.

"No, you have the right of it, and no mistake. My wife's every wish was as a command to me and all of my men. Nobody could deny Sunniva. Everybody loved her."

He fell silent and reached for his wine. Balthild's hand slid from his arm. He wished he had not moved. He could sense her eyes upon him.

"I am sorry, Lord Beobrand," she said, her voice tender, softened by concern. "I mean to speak lightly and all I do is upset you."

Beobrand shook his head.

"It is no matter. Many years have passed."

"Some losses never leave you."

"No," he said, taking a sip of the wine. "And I will never forgive myself for Sunniva's passing."

He glanced at Balthild. She was leaning forward, her hand resting on the linen tablecloth. For a moment, Beobrand wondered whether she would reach out again and touch his hand. Her eyes shone. He sensed she was holding herself back, curbing her curiosity, though she longed to ask him more about Sunniva.

"You remind me of her," he said, taking control of the conversation, steering it away from questions he did not wish to answer.

"Indeed?"

"You both have the same strength. Like steel wrapped in the softness of silk." He thought briefly of Eanflæd. She too had the same quality of beauty enfolded around a core of iron. "Sunniva's father was a smith. He taught her to forge metal." He smiled at the memory of her standing at the forge, hammer in hand, sweat plastering her hair to her scalp.

"She sounds stronger than me then," Balthild said.

He recalled the queen standing proudly in the mud of the forest while Omer held her captive.

"I am not sure of that," he said, with a thin smile that quickly turned into a frown. "But it matters not. Neither her strength nor mine could protect her."

Balthild placed her hand over his. Her skin was cool and soft.

"Well, Lord Beobrand, you protected me, and for that I thank you."

"I do not think you needed my protection at all," he said, remembering how she had dispatched Omer as ruthlessly as any warrior.

"That is where you are wrong, Lord Beobrand," she replied, removing her hand from his, as if she had suddenly noticed they were touching. "I am in need of as many friends as I can find. And if they have swords, so much the better." Her eyes twinkled. "I trust that we are friends."

"Of course," he said, feeling his face grow warm, "I am honoured. My sword and those of my men are at your service. I promise I will do all in my power to keep you free from harm."

As he uttered the words, he regretted them. Who was he to vow such a thing? He knew better. It was impossible to keep anyone safe. But the memory of Balthild's touch lingered on the back of his hand and he could not take back the words now they had been spoken. Looking away from the face that so reminded him of Sunniva, Beobrand drank deeply of his wine. He hoped there would be no further incident on their journey south that would put to test the rash promise he had made.

The next morning, Balthild said she wished to travel some way west along the river to view a plot of land at a place called Corbie. It seemed she had ordered a minster to be built there and wished to see how the work was progressing. At this, Brocard drew the line and refused her request. Beobrand felt sorry for the man, but could not completely hide his smirk as the leader of the guard's face reddened with barely suppressed fury. Beobrand was not envious of the man's position, and he nodded in agreement when Brocard firmly told the queen that they would not be diverting from their course.

For a long moment Balthild held Brocard's gaze. The men, already mounted and ready to ride, waited in awkward silence, unsure who would win this battle of wills. Beobrand cleared his throat.

"Your highness," he said, "Brocard has the truth of it. There is no time to waste. We must ride south directly." For a few heartbeats more, Balthild stared at Brocard. In that moment Beobrand saw again the hardness he had witnessed in her when she had stood in the mud beside her waggon and slain the man who threatened her. At last, she turned away from Brocard and nodded at Beobrand.

"Very well," she said. "Perhaps you are right." Without another word, she allowed Alpaida to help her into the waggon.

Brocard let out a sigh.

"My thanks," he said to Beobrand in a voice so low he barely heard it. Swinging up into his saddle, Brocard signalled for the men to ride out.

And so they left Anmyin, crossing the river from the island over another bridge, though this one was timber and could not have been more than a few years old. The brown waters of the Samara surged white around the wooden piles and the crumbling, weed-entwined columns of an older bridge that had long ago fallen into the river. They did not tarry in the busy streets of the city and were soon heading south on the Roman road towards Paris, refreshed after their brief respite from the rigours of travelling, but glad to be free of the stench and noise of Anmyin.

Brocard had chosen not to bring on any more guards at the city, despite Riquier offering some of his own men.

"You were right," he said to Beobrand as they rode through the flat land. "I would have to watch any new men. We cannot be sure that Riquier is a friend of the queen."

"Let us hope that the men in the forest were merely hungry wolf-heads."

Brocard nodded sombrely. Neither of them said any more on the subject, but despite the days of peaceful travel and the sun that now more frequently warmed the land and lifted the riders' spirits, a dark certainty settled on Beobrand that the queen was not safe.

"You worry too much," said Cynan to him on the second day south of Anmyin.

"Do I?" Beobrand coughed briefly. The cold air of the morning still brought on his cough and after sundown he would often be racked by bouts of debilitating coughing, but whatever was in the brew he and Attor had been drinking each day, it was seeing them both improve.

"She is not our queen," Cynan replied. "Not your queen."

Beobrand shot him a sharp glance. He gripped his reins tightly and set his jaw. Surely this was a jibe about Eanflæd.

"No," he said, "she is not our queen." His words were bitten off and sharp. "But still I would not see harm come to her. All I have witnessed tells me she is a good woman."

"She does seem to be that," Cynan said, nodding. "And nobody would like to see such a beautiful woman come to harm."

Cynan looked at him sidelong, perhaps wary that he had pushed his lord too far. Beobrand sighed. Cynan knew how to anger him and seemed to relish doing so. But there was no denying that in his barbed comments there often nestled the seeds of truth. Would he have cared so much for the queen of the Franks had she been old and ugly? Did it truly matter?

"She is a comely woman," he replied, "of that there is no debate. And she is also one who bears the heir to the king of the Franks. And for that alone, I would say we should keep her safe."

Wilfrid had dropped back to ride near them and had overheard the last part of the conversation.

"It is clear that the Almighty guided us to this place that we might aid the queen and travel with her," he said, "thus forging an alliance that might benefit us as we journey through the lands of her husband. An alliance that might also profit our lord king, Oswiu."

"I believe it is our wyrd to be here," said Beobrand, uneasy at this talk of the Christ god exacting power over them.

"Wyrd, or Christ's hand," replied Wilfrid with a shrug, "what is the difference?"

Beobrand frowned. Wilfrid annoyed him even more than Cynan. He found infuriating the young man's softly spoken words and his uncanny ability to cut to the heart of any matter.

"I suppose it matters not the reason we are travelling with the queen," Beobrand agreed, grudgingly, "just that we are doing so."

"No," said Wilfrid, "what is important is how our situation can help us, God, and our king."

Beobrand thought on this often over the following days, as they rode south without further incident.

"Wilfrid's not wrong, you know?" Cynan said to Beobrand one evening as they made their way outside the hall they were staying in that night. They walked away from the building, the sounds of conversation and merriment muffled by the walls and the distance, but still loud in the hushed darkness.

"About what?" asked Beobrand.

Cynan chuckled.

"About most things, it seems to me. And he is right about the queen. It is good for us to have her as an ally. And it will stand you in good stead with Oswiu, if you take back news of this alliance when we return home."

They followed their noses and soon found the ditch that had been dug near the midden. Loosening their breeches, they both let out a stream of hot piss into the sodden hole in the earth. The cold air steamed and the stink of the place hit the back of Beobrand's throat. In the quiet night an owl hooted.

"You dislike him because you don't understand him," Cynan said.

"I dislike you, and I understand you well enough," growled Beobrand, wishing he had come to the midden alone. "And who said I dislike him?"

Cynan chuckled and belted his breeches.

"Wilfrid is clever. Much cleverer than you or me," said Cynan. "His mind is cool, where ours are hot. How many times have we allowed our hearts to govern us? Our anger?" He hesitated. "Our love."

Beobrand frowned in the dark. He did not like to be confronted with such thoughts.

"What about those women in Quentovic?" he asked. "Wilfrid seemed to follow his heart then."

"Did he?" replied Cynan. A sudden peal of laughter from within the hall reached them like distant waves on a shingle shore. Cynan halted and Beobrand stood near him, listening. "It seems to me," Cynan went on, "that Wilfrid measures everything by how much profit he can gain. As I recall, he did not leave empty-handed from ploughing any warm furrow in Quentovic. And there are few situations I have seen him walk away from with less treasure, power or influence than when he started."

"I care nought if helping Balthild will bring me fortune, and I certainly don't care if it will help me with Oswiu." Beobrand spat, as if the name of his king had left a bad taste in his mouth. For a time they stood in silence, listening to the murmurs of the throng in the hall. "I just feel it is right," Beobrand said at last.

"I know, lord," whispered Cynan, his voice almost lost beneath the sounds of merriment inside. "And that is why we follow you."

Chapter 8

Cynan stretched his right arm as he rode, rolling the shoulder and wincing. The joint still ached from where the injured horse had dragged him along the forest floor, but the pain no longer woke him at night and the scabs on his face had begun to peel off, leaving smooth, pink scars that would pale in time. Another reminder on his body of a foolish decision. One of many. His leg throbbed some mornings, or after a long day's riding, the pain not allowing him to forget his fight with Brunwine the previous year. And yet, that was a wound he was glad to have sustained. If he had not thrown himself into the path of that great bear of a champion, the man might have slain Beobrand. And Cynan did not think he would have been able to forgive himself if that had happened. To lose his lord would have been terrible, but for Beobrand to have died while still furious with Cynan for his disobedience, and what he saw as his betrayal, would have been unbearable.

But they had both survived. By dint of skill, luck or, if you asked Wilfrid or Coenred, divine providence. Beobrand would call it their wyrd. Whatever the reason, Cynan was glad for the chance to regain the lord of Ubbanford's trust.

Beobrand had remained sullen and angry with him for months, and Cynan had begun to wonder if things would ever return to the way they had once been. But as the snows melted, and the rains had begun to fall from the leaden sky over Quentovic, there had been small signs that Beobrand's frostiness towards Cynan was also thawing.

Both men had been grumpy over the long winter, each wanting to be back in Northumbria for their own reasons, but each accepting this quest to escort Wilfrid and Baducing to far-off Roma as suitable punishment for their sins. Beobrand had maintained a surly distance from Cynan as they had finally begun their ride south, but after the clash with the brigands in the forest, the lord's mood shifted and Cynan found himself more often talking to Beobrand with something like the warm camaraderie they once had. He was not sure if the change in his lord's demeanour came from having a purpose in protecting Balthild, or from the company of the young queen herself. He suspected it was a bit of both. Whatever the reason, he was glad of the change. And Cynan couldn't deny that he too felt pleased whenever the queen smiled at him or offered a word of greeting. There was something about Balthild, he mused, that made all the men anxious to see her safe.

Sometimes, he would catch himself watching the queen over his cup in one of the halls they visited, and he would berate himself for a fool. Eadgyth was waiting for him at Stagga and he knew he should never have ridden away when she raised the question of marriage. By the gods, how he missed her.

The day before, as they rode from the steading where they had slept, the farmer's children, two girls and a boy, none above ten summers of age, ran after them, whooping and hollering, the farm dogs yapping at their heels. The sight of them brought a grin unbidden to his lips and, with a start, he realised he not only missed Eadgyth, he missed Athulf and Aelfwyn too. They might not be his children, but he had been like a father to them all these years. He had not seen them now for months. A lump came to his throat when he thought of how they must have grown.

"Do you think we'll see the queen again," asked Bleddyn, shattering Cynan's maudlin daydreaming.

He glanced over at the dark-haired warrior. He knew the real question Bleddyn wanted to ask. At another time Cynan might have teased him about it. But now, missing Eadgyth and her children as he did, he could not bring himself to make fun of the man's affections for the queen's handmaiden.

Cynan looked west where the sun glinted on the broad waters of the Secoana. The light hazed in the smoke that hung over Paris there. Then he cast his gaze along the road they followed that led south-east. From between the trees ahead, he could just make out a cluster of buildings. Fulbert had galloped by just moments before, excitedly declaring they had reached their destination. For the buildings belonged to the small minster of Cala, and Balthild and Alpaida would remain there for the queen's lying-in.

"I do not know, Bleddyn," Cynan said, keeping his tone flat. "I fear the queen, and her maidservant, will stay at the minster for some time."

The confinement would probably last for several weeks after the royal birth, and he could see no way that they would remain for so long in Paris.

Bleddyn said nothing, but his lips pressed tightly together as he stared fixedly ahead, as if he could will the minster gates to remain at a distance. Ever since Bleddyn had comforted Alpaida in the aftermath of the forest attack, the two of them had found every opportunity to be together. The men laughed to see Bleddyn, a man who was usually quiet and in control of himself, become like a young boy whenever Alpaida was near. In truth there was jealousy in their jests. The queen's servant was lovely, and the two of them, the handmaiden who served the thrall-turned-queen and the warrior who had been a thrall, had formed an instant and close bond. Cynan too was envious. He had shared a hall with Eadgyth for years and had been too foolish to understand his feelings for her. And now she was at the other end of middle earth while he was lonely riding on a quest through distant realms.

"I know you'll miss the girl," said Ingwald, addressing Bleddyn, though the younger Waelisc man did not turn in his saddle, "but it will be good to make better progress."

"That it will," said Attor, from where he sat behind the oxen who pulled the cart stolidly along the road. "I for one cannot wait to be in the saddle again. I have seen enough of these oxen's backsides to last me a lifetime."

Bleddyn didn't respond and soon his sour mood settled over them all like a drizzle. They plodded on towards the minster, but even at this slow pace, it was not long before Cynan could see the details of the timber gate and the tall elms that grew either side of it. Beyond that, the newly built stone chapel, thatched cells and long refectory caught the light of the early afternoon sun.

A large congregation of women, all wearing habits of the plainest wool and white wimples that covered their hair, greeted them when the waggon and cart trundled through the open gates and into the area before the buildings. A few lay folk also waited in the yard. Men fidgeted and gripped their hats. Women clutched their children tightly to their skirts in an effort to keep them still. All of them watched excitedly for a glimpse of their queen.

Brocard dismounted and hurried to the waggon where he held out his hand to assist Balthild. For the first time that Cynan could remember, the Frankish warrior was smiling. Cynan thought he had earned the right to be pleased with himself. He had delivered the queen to her destination safely, which in her state and with the attack they had suffered and the possibility of more enemies lurking along their route, had not been a certainty.

Balthild said something quietly to Brocard. His smile widened. Bowing, he ushered her towards the waiting abbess, a slight woman with a thin mouth and large eyes. The queen and abbess embraced as old friends.

At the sound of someone approaching at a run, Brocard turned, suddenly alert, his hand falling to the hilt of his sword. For a moment, the leader of the guard tensed, but then he laughed to see it was Bleddyn. The Waelisc man had cantered forward, leaping from his horse and sprinting up to offer his hand to Alpaida, clearly not wishing to miss this last opportunity to be close to her.

He helped her down and, unable to contain his emotion, he encircled her in his arms and planted a kiss on her cheek. Alpaida let out a small cry of shock. Cynan and the rest of the men could not keep themselves from laughing. This only served to make the handmaiden angrier, and Alpaida slapped her delicate hands against Bleddyn's chest, pushing him away. With a furious glare, she moved away from the warrior, hurrying to join her mistress and the waiting nuns.

Bleddyn stared after the servant forlornly.

The women fussed about the queen and seemed ready to whisk her away into the nearest building when Balthild held up a hand to halt them. She turned to face them, her beauty undiminished despite her obvious weariness from the long journey.

First she spoke in Frankish, and Brocard and his men nodded and smiled, then she addressed the men from Albion in their own tongue.

"You came to my aid when all seemed lost," she said, "and I thank each and every one of you for your assistance against my enemies and for helping to escort me here. You will be given the finest food and wine in my husband's palace in Paris, for you have more than earned it." Eadgard gave a loud cheer at this. "Masters Wilfrid and Baducing, this is Sister Hereswitha, for whom you bear missives from her kin, I believe." She indicated a tall, somewhat haughty-looking woman. The nun did not smile, but her eyes glimmered at the mention of messages.

"Lord Beobrand, Wilfrid, Baducing," she went on, looking at each man in turn, "I thank you for your generosity of spirit. I know that riding with my waggon has slowed you, but I hope you have not found the journey too hard. I have enjoyed the chance to converse with fellow countrymen in my mother's tongue." She smiled, and it was as if the sun shone warmer. "May the Almighty guide you on your journey. And if you should return this way, it would bring me joy to see you once more." She looked at them all one last time. Cynan felt his heart tremble when her eyes met his. She made to follow the abbess, then halted without warning and turned. "And Bleddyn," she said, "I believe I do not speak out of turn when I say, should you come back this way, a warmer welcome might await you than the farewell you received. Parting from a loved one can make a lady sorrowful and peevish."

Bleddyn blushed crimson. He could find no words for the queen, so merely bowed low. Cynan and the others laughed again and their laughter accompanied the queen and the other womenfolk into the buildings.

"Did you hear that?" asked Bleddyn. "She said Alpaida loves me."

Cynan clapped him on the back. Ingwald began to speak. He had the gleam of mischief in his eye and Cynan shook his head, silencing him. They had had enough fun at Bleddyn's expense.

Wilfrid and Baducing disappeared to deliver their messages to Hereswitha.

Brocard's men helped unload the cart and waggon, carrying the chests and trunks into the minster buildings and placing them wherever a stern-faced nun ordered. Eadgard, Halinard and Bleddyn helped, while the rest of the men stood in the yard, feeling awkward and out of place.

A short while later, ale, bread and cheese were brought out and three pretty young women, cheeks red and eyes glimmering at the looks and compliments they received, served the warriors who slouched in the afternoon sun. When they had finished eating and were wondering where they would spend the night, Wilfrid and Baducing returned with the answer.

"We are to sleep in the palace," said Wilfrid.

"We cannot sleep here?" asked Beobrand, impatience in his voice.

"It is a nunnery, lord," replied Baducing. "The abbess will not countenance so many men remaining under the roof of the minster."

"Surely the queen cannot be left unguarded."

"No. Brocard and his guards will stay. Fulbert has been given the order to show us the way to the palace."

Cynan could see the tension in Beobrand's stance and thought he might seek to argue with the abbess. He understood his lord's displeasure. They had travelled far and risked their lives for Balthild. It was not right to be turned away thus. But as he watched, Beobrand let out a long breath. His decision made, he turned to Fulbert. The Frank offered Beobrand a conciliatory shrug and a lopsided smile. Fulbert's long scar was healing well, but if he had ever been a handsome man, those days were behind him now. He was well-liked by the men; quick to laugh and slow to anger. He spoke rapidly now to Halinard, who relayed his comments to the waiting men of Albion.

"Fulbert says that without the waggon and cart, we will make good time. The horses have been rested and watered, so we will make Paris shortly after nightfall." Fulbert said a few more words and vaulted into his saddle. "He says he knows you are sorry to be leaving so many nuns behind, but he assures you the women of Paris are more friendly, and the table at the palace will be richer and better than that kept by the abbess."

"Well, men," said Beobrand, walking to his gelding and climbing into the saddle, "what more do we need to know?"

The promise of good food and drink, and perhaps willing women to accompany it, gave the men renewed purpose. Quickly they were all mounted and following Fulbert at a fast trot. The only one of them who did not seem overly pleased to be leaving Cala was Bleddyn, who gazed over his shoulder morosely as they rode away.

Chapter 9

Beobrand interlaced his fingers behind his head and pulled until he heard a satisfying click. His body was stiff from riding and he could feel his eyelids drooping as the warmth and sound of the hall washed over him. For a time he had tried to keep up with the conversation, but as the night wore on and the wine flowed, he found it increasingly difficult to pick out words from the river of sound. He felt like a bear leaning over a waterfall and snatching at leaping salmon. Every now and then he would grasp a word, but his understanding of Frankish was poor, so even then, the meanings were often lost as soon as he thought he had caught hold of enough to understand the flow of the talk.

For a while after they had arrived, Wilfrid and Baducing, both of whom had managed to gain a more solid grip on the language of the Franks, had acted as interpreters in Halinard's stead. But ever since they had begun to talk in earnest with the bishop of Liyon, they had turned away from Beobrand. At first, he had listened intently to what they said, trying to glean the meaning, but soon he realised they were no longer speaking the tongue of the Franks, but the old Roman language used by the Christ priests. He shook his head at his own stupidity and wasted effort, putting it down to the noise in the hall and his tiredness that he had laboured trying to comprehend a language that had no meaning for him.

Wilfrid raised his voice, and Beobrand glanced over, but it seemed to him that the discussion, whilst becoming heated, was well meaning. The bishop was still smiling, and Wilfrid and Baducing would do nothing to jeopardise their welcome at the palace.

Raising the blue glass beaker to his lips, Beobrand drank. The wine was dark and rich, carrying the memory of long warm summers and the flinty tang of frosty mornings. It was every bit as good as the wine Marcoul had served them. If they stayed in Frankia for long, Beobrand thought he could get a taste for the stuff. Absently, he wondered how easily he would be able to have wine shipped to his hall back in Ubbanford.

Looking around him, he pondered how similar the surroundings were to his own great hall in Bernicia, and yet also how different. The sounds of merriment, the heat from the hearth, blazing against the chill of the night, the flicker of candles, the rushes on the floor, the sensation of rich food filling his belly. All these things were familiar to him. And yet he felt out of place and as far from his home as he had ever been. Of course it was true, he was in a foreign land, but there was more than the difference in the language. From the glass goblets, rare in Albion, yet seemingly commonplace here, to the straight-cut stone walls of this hall, to the lingering taste and scent of unusual herbs and spices, and the tartness of the wine on his tongue. All these things made him feel awkward and alone.

Baducing and Wilfrid, both much younger men of noble birth, who had studied the scratchings of learned scholars on parchments and in books, seemed at ease and relaxed surrounded by these aristocratic Franks.

A brief conversation with Halinard shortly before they arrived at the palace had further unsettled Beobrand. As they had ridden through the darkening streets of the city, Halinard had moved his horse close.

"Be careful here, lord," he'd said.

Beobrand had looked at him sharply. The man's tone held a brittle edge.

"I am always careful," he'd said, forcing a smile.

"I have been to Paris before." Halinard had hesitated. "With the man I served then."

Halinard's words unnerved Beobrand. They seldom spoke of Vulmar.

"I see."

"It is a nest of vipers," said Halinard. "Take care not to get bitten."

Now, surrounded by Frankish nobles who peered at him and whispered behind their cups, Beobrand wished he had gone with Halinard, Cynan and the rest of the gesithas to dine with the palace guards. He was sure he would have felt more at home there, away from the serpents surrounding the throne that Halinard had warned him of. He knew where he was amongst warriors.

But he was the lord of Ubbanford, and as such he was an honoured guest here. And when Erchinoald, the *major domus* of the palace, had heard from Fulbert how Beobrand had been instrumental in saving the queen's life, the man had seemed genuinely thankful. He had grasped Beobrand's hand, muttering his gratitude. It was clear then that there would be no escaping this feast with the nobility of Paris. Beobrand wondered at the position of the *major domus* within the court. He sat at the centre of the high table, the host in the king's absence, and bishops and nobles treated him with deference. Beobrand had thought him to be a kind of steward or reeve, but watching how men of obvious wealth and import hung on Erchinoald's words, it was clear he was much more than an administrator, though it seemed there was some of that within the title. Beobrand barely understood, but when he had enquired as to the man's role, Erchinoald, a tall man with an aquiline nose and receding, greying hair, had smiled.

"I am blessed to govern matters of the realm for the king in his name." The idea made little sense to Beobrand. Surely the king ruled the kingdom and the lords of each estate enforced his laws. And yet, watching the self-assurance with which Erchinoald carried himself and how others fawned over him, it seemed that the *major domus* acted almost as a king in his own right. Beobrand would have liked more answers, but before he could ask further questions, Erchinoald was introducing a short woman.

"This is my wife, Leutsinde," said Erchinoald.

She curtsied.

Beobrand looked down at the woman. Most men were shorter than him and he had never met a woman who matched his height, but Leutsinde was diminutive and her head barely reached his chest. She wore a silk dress that clung to her buxom breasts, her tiny stature accentuating their size. Gold and jewels glimmered at her throat and wrists. Golden thread was plaited into her elaborately styled hair, and her fingers were heavy with rings. She offered Beobrand a coy smile, looking up through her lashes.

He bowed to cover his discomfort at Erchinoald's wife's obvious flirtation.

"My lady."

"Fulbert here says that you stopped the queen from being slain," Erchinoald said, seemingly oblivious of Leutsinde's behaviour. Halinard whispered the translation of his words. They had not long since arrived, clattering over the bridge to the island in the wide river, where, like at Anmyin, the walled palace lay. The warriors had not yet gone to their meal.

"I am pleased to say that we helped stop an attack," Beobrand said, pointedly ignoring Leutsinde, though he could sense her intense stare upon him. "When we learnt that it was the queen who was in danger, we could not refuse to accompany her south."

"And now she is safe at Cala," said the *major domus*. It was not a question and Beobrand wondered how he knew the queen's whereabouts. Had Fulbert told him as much? Or did Erchinoald have spies on the road?

"She is," he said, "but if I were you, I would send men to reinforce Brocard there. He has few men and it seems to me that the queen has many enemies." Erchinoald nodded sombrely and snapped some commands at a nearby courtier, who vanished into the shadows at the edge of the courtyard. Beobrand immediately regretted giving away information. He had no idea of the identity of Balthild's foes. Surely she would have told him if she did not trust Erchinoald. But had the man not been her master once? Perhaps he did not take kindly to having a former thrall become his queen. Beobrand watched Erchinoald's face closely. His concern seemed real, but Beobrand knew well enough that a man could hide his true feelings behind a sincere-seeming mien.

"Has the babe come?" asked Leutsinde, her voice strangely loud and strident for one so small.

"No, my lady," he replied. "Abbess Bertila said there are still several days until the baby is due."

"The queen should not have travelled so close to her time," she replied, shaking her head. Her voice trembled and rose in pitch and she glowered at Beobrand. She was a comely woman, but there was a hardness in those eyes, he thought. "Thank God she arrived safely."

"Thanks to Beobrand and his companions," said Erchinoald, placing a hand on his wife's arm to calm her rising fury at the risks they had taken with the queen's health.

"Yes," she said, forcing herself with an effort to quieten her anger. "For that we must give thanks. The king will be pleased she is safe and, with God's grace, he will return in time for the birth. Do you think that is possible, husband?"

"Clovis will be here soon enough," he said.

Beobrand had understood some of this exchange, but Wilfrid had picked up on much more.

"The king is not here?" Wilfrid asked, speaking to the *major domus* for the first time. Beobrand wondered if the others could hear the note of disappointment in Wilfrid's tone. He had been excitedly anticipating meeting the king of the Franks.

Erchinoald raised an eyebrow to hear the novice's clear words in the Frankish tongue.

"Unfortunately, he is not," he said. "He was needed far to the south, at Septimania to settle a dispute there. But do not fear. As his representative, I will see that you are all well recompensed for your care of his queen. Clovis will be most pleased to hear of your exploits and most grateful for your part in Balthild's rescue. I too am overjoyed to learn of Balthild's safe delivery to Cala. We had worried so for her, hadn't we, dearest?"

Leutsinde nodded absently, but was still visibly shaken.

True to his word, Erchinoald had proceeded to treat Beobrand and the others as if they were visiting royalty. They had been taken to a small timber building where there was water to wash off the dirt of the road. Thralls brought them clean clothes of linen and wool. Beobrand was glad to change out of his travelling clothes and was impressed that the servants had found a red tunic and tan-coloured breeches to fit his large frame. Wilfrid, though annoyed at losing the opportunity to meet the king, was pleased to be given a deep blue kirtle edged with red and gold woven hems.

"Perhaps we can remain here at the palace until the king returns," he said, after he had changed. He stroked the smooth fabric of the pale blue linen breeches that had been laid out for him, appreciating the fine weave of the cloth.

"We will do no such thing," snapped Beobrand. He was already tired and they hadn't even started the meal yet. "Erchinoald said it would be weeks until Clovis comes back, and I will not waste any further time. My task is to escort the two of you to Roma, not to join the court of the Frankish king."

Baducing smiled his thanks at Beobrand. He too was impatient to be on their way. He had eschewed the finery the thralls had brought for him, instead asking them to shake out and brush his habit. He pulled the newly scrubbed robe back over his head and cinched his plain belt at his waist.

"Beobrand is quite right. Let us enjoy the food tonight, and perhaps rest our mounts tomorrow, but more than that we should not delay. I long to see the catacombs of Roma. The crypt of Calixtus. The sepulchres of Milix and Pumenius. Too long have we dallied in Neustria."

Wilfrid was not pleased at their response and he had been withdrawn as they were led to the hall. But when they had seen the crowd of nobles and clergy who awaited them, he'd seemed to forget about the disagreement, throwing himself into the task of meeting everyone and making a good impression on each of them.

Beobrand felt uncomfortable in his borrowed clothes. On several occasions, he found his hand reaching for Nægling at his side only to remember he had left the sword with the palace door wards. And yet surely he had no call for a weapon here. They must be safe within the walls of the palace. Safe from attack perhaps, he mused, but not, it seemed, free from barbed looks and snide comments. As he met the different people within the hall, Beobrand felt awkward under their gaze. He did not believe himself to be a vain man, but here, surrounded by Frankish nobles, all of whom seemed born to wear silks and gold, he was painfully aware of his scarred face, his bulk and his mutilated left hand. He was the son of a farmer, but in Albion, his name was spoken with awe. He had reputation. Here, he was looked upon as an oddity, a hulking northern brute whose lack of ability to communicate made him appear more like an animal than a man to be reckoned with. He could see the fear in the eyes of the men who conversed with him. They were wary of him the way they would be scared of a wolf. They did not respect him as a lord of men, a warrior who had altered the very future of kingdoms with his actions.

The only men who had responded differently to him were Dalfinus and Annemund. They introduced themselves as brothers, but there was little to mark them as kin except for a certain vitality and force of will that burnt in the eyes of both men.

Dalfinus was of slender build, with narrow hips and long, expressive fingers, while Annemund was broad-shouldered and taller than his brother. Annemund had hands that looked as though they could crush rocks and, despite his greying hair, Beobrand could easily imagine the man standing resolute in a shieldwall where his bulk and strength would serve him well.

Dalfinus was careful, almost diffident in his movements, and where his brother was solid, so he appeared delicate. He would not have been out of place bearing the tonsure and sitting with the scribes in a minster. Both men smiled when introduced to Beobrand and seemed interested to listen to him. The brothers were important men in the southern city of Liyon. One was the *comes*, the lord of the city, while the other was the bishop. It was only after they had been talking for some time, with Wilfrid and Baducing serving as interpreters, that Beobrand realised the error of his assumptions about the two men. He had believed that the slender Dalfinus was the priest, while the stocky, well-built Annemund was the lord who would stand in battle if called to defend the kingdom. In fact, Annemund was the bishop, and Dalfinus the lord.

They smiled tiredly when Beobrand's mistake became clear.

"You are not the first to think this, Lord Beobrand," said Annemund, "and there are no doubt men of the cloth who would say I would be better suited to fighting than praying. But I fight with my faith, with the word of God as my sword and the

Holy Ghost as my shield. My brother may not look like much, but I assure you, he is deadly in a fight."

"Though I try to avoid fights, if possible." Dalfinus raised his glass in a gesture of salute. "At least those I cannot easily win." Beobrand noticed the knotted muscles of Dalfinus' forearm, and the thin, pale scars there.

"I would wager you are a skilled swordsman," he said.

"When I was young, perhaps." Dalfinus must have been at least a decade older than Beobrand, but he was still hale and strong if the sinewy cords of muscle on his arms were any indication. "Now I have others do my fighting for me." Dalfinus shrugged. "Such is the way of things. We are all getting older by the day." Stroking his white-streaked beard, he narrowed his eyes and stared at Beobrand. "I believe I might have heard tales of your sword-skill, though I cannot place where or when. Perhaps there are songs of your exploits when you were young."

Beobrand was needled with annoyance at being thought of as old, but he felt a swelling of pride to think men sang of his battle-fame here, across the Narrow Sea.

"Perhaps," he said.

In a room filled with stuffy nobles, flatterers and sycophants, it was good to speak with a fellow warrior who did not see the need to coat his words in honey. Beobrand liked Dalfinus, and by extension Annemund, with whom he felt an affinity due to his height, bulk and strength, not to mention the trait he shared with his brother of speaking straight, without subterfuge and veiled meanings. He felt sufficiently at ease with the brothers to inquire as to the whereabouts of the king.

They listened as Wilfrid relayed Beobrand's question.

"The king is far to the south on the frontier with Septimania," said Dalfinus. "A sorry business with the Iudaea there." He sneered. "It seems they do not know their place and are not content to remain in Narbona."

"Iudaea?" Beobrand struggled with the unfamiliar word. He wondered if it was a Frankish tribe.

"The Iudeisc," explained Baducing. "The people who nailed the Christ to a tree."

Beobrand frowned. After all these years and many conversations with his old friend, the monk Coenred, he still did not understand the Christ followers.

"But wasn't Jesu slain hundreds of years ago?"

"Yes," said Wilfrid, shaking his head at Beobrand's ignorance, "but the Iudeisc forever carry the sin of what they did."

Beobrand rubbed a hand over his eyes. They were gritty with exhaustion.

"The sins of the father pass to the son?" Unbidden he saw the face of the man he had believed to be his own father. The spectre of fear that he would become such a man as Grimgundi, a bully of children and abuser of women, had plagued him all his life.

"It is not so simple as that," said Wilfrid. He softened his tone, perhaps noticing the tension in Beobrand.

"Oh, but it is simple," said Annemund, when Baducing had interpreted Wilfrid's Anglisc words. "For did not all the people say unto Pontius Pilatus, 'Let him be crucified'? And when Pilatus washed his hands of Jesu Christ's blood, did the mob not shout, 'His blood be on us, and on our children'?"

"Yes," replied Wilfrid, "so it is written in the Scriptures, but it is also written," and now, for the quote from the holy book, Wilfrid switched to the Latin in which he had learnt it, "*anima quae peccaverit ipsa morietur filius non portabit iniquitatem patris et pater non portabit iniquitatem filii iustitia iusti super eum erit et impietas impii erit super eum.*"

Baducing struggled to keep up his translation of the two men.

"The son shall not bear the iniquity of the father, neither shall the father bear the iniquity of the son: the righteousness of the righteous shall be upon him, and the wickedness of the wicked shall be upon him."

Annemund smiled, glad to be sparring with such a bright student. Wilfrid for his part was serious, but his eyes gleamed. Beobrand recognised the glint, he had seen it in men in battle. He had felt it himself often enough. It was the joy of the conflict, of crossing blades with a worthy adversary.

"You have clearly read widely for one so young," said Annemund, "and I am glad your teachers had you memorise the Lord's words, thus they are always with you."

Wilfrid received this praise with a gracious smile. Beobrand watched the exchange and imagined a duel. Wilfrid believed he had struck the winning blow. But then, just as a more experienced warrior might feint, only to send a cut higher or lower than expected, so now did Annemund return Wilfrid's grin.

"And, as an able student, you surely have not forgotten that it is also written in the book of Numbers, chapter fourteen, I believe: 'The Lord is long-suffering, and of great mercy, forgiving iniquity and transgression, and by no means clearing the guilty, visiting the iniquity of the fathers upon the children unto the third and fourth generation.' For the iniquity of the murder of his son, surely there can never be forgiveness."

The conversation was making Beobrand's head spin. He was not sure he wanted to understand the intricacies of the Christ followers' religion, but even if he did, to listen to arguments in more than one tongue made it nigh on impossible for him to keep up with the men's points.

Dalfinus clearly felt something similar, for he held up his hand as Baducing stumbled over the translation of this last tirade.

"Enough, brother," he said. "All you need to know about the Iudaea, Beobrand, is that Clovis' father, Dagobert, forbade them to remain in his kingdom unless they converted to the one true faith. Many did, and those who did not were put to the sword."

"So why has Clovis needed to go south, to..." He had forgotten the name of the place, but Wilfrid reminded him.

"Septimania," he said.

"Yes, Septimania," Beobrand said, with a sidelong glance at the novice that made Dalfinus chuckle.

"The Iudaea on the border are not behaving themselves. There has been talk that they have stopped worshipping the Christ and have reverted to their old ways. But enough of this," Dalfinus said, snatching a jug of wine from a nearby slave and filling first Beobrand's glass and then his own, "let the priests talk of religion, while we drink."

Beobrand drank deeply, again thinking how he liked the man who seemed so unlike the other nobles in the hall.

"Though, if I know my brother, there will not be enough time in one evening for all the talking they will do."

Annemund laughed.

"I fear Dalfinus knows me too well. It is not often I meet such learned young men, and from far-off Albion no less. And you say you knew the great Aidan?"

"I did," said Wilfrid, making the sign of the rood in memory of the abbot of Lindisfarena.

"Ah, you must tell me all about him, may the Lord keep his soul. And I would show you my scriptorium. And the relics I have accumulated over the years. I have bones of saints Sacerdos and Nicetus and even thorns from the very crown worn by our Lord Jesu the Christ."

"I think I speak for both Baducing and myself," said Wilfrid, his eyes shining, "when I say we would be honoured."

"Then it is settled," said Annemund with an expansive grin. "You will come with us to Liyon, as our guests."

Baducing began to protest, but after a few words from Annemund, he too smiled.

"I thought you did not wish to waste more time," said Beobrand, his frustration with these young men building.

"Ah, but Lord Beobrand, this will not be wasted time."

Beobrand scowled. His head was beginning to ache.

"Not for you, perhaps," he said, "but I wish to reach Roma and then return to my home, as soon as I am able."

"But, you see, the city of Liyon is on the road we must follow as we travel through the kingdom of the Franks. Travelling with Lord Dalfinus and His Excellency will make our journey safer."

"And you will have the best lodgings possible in the great city," interjected Annemund.

Baducing nodded, interpreting the bishop's words.

"You see?" he went on. "It will be no bad thing to spend a few days there recuperating. Wilfrid and I would study the marvels in the bishop's library. It would be madness to miss such a chance. Perhaps you might even find something to interest you there."

"I doubt it," Beobrand replied. But he could not deny that Baducing's words made sense.

"I can take you hunting," said Dalfinus, pouring more wine into Beobrand's glass. "I do so love a hunt, don't I, brother?"

"Oh, he does," replied Annemund, his eyes twinkling. "My brother's hunts are quite something. There are all manner of interesting animals to stalk in the south."

"Men come from all over Frankia to attend," Dalfinus went on, suddenly serious. "You simply must attend as my guest, Lord Beobrand."

Beobrand was not keen on hunting, but he could see that the decision had already been made and it would do him no good to object further.

"Very well," he said, finally allowing the warmth of the wine and the food to relax him. "We thank you for your invitation."

Beobrand had sat back, leaving Wilfrid, Annemund and Baducing to whatever obscure passages of the holy scriptures they discussed in the old language of the men of Roma. For a time, Beobrand spoke in his halting Frankish to Dalfinus, but soon it became apparent that the *comes* of Liyon was content to drink in companionable silence. Beobrand could grow fond of such a man.

He lost count of how many glasses of wine he imbibed, but Dalfinus saw to it that his goblet was not empty for long, and the slim lord had matched him glass for glass. Both men were drunkenly slouched and Beobrand was struggling to keep his bleary eyes open, when a sudden commotion at the doors of the hall dragged him away from the approaching embrace of sleep.

The hall was suddenly silent. A figure was hurrying towards him. Absently, Beobrand wondered if this was an attack. He pushed himself unsteadily to his feet, ready to meet his would-be attacker, even unarmed as he was. A man stood before him, but he did not strike. It took Beobrand a moment to see it was Halinard, panting and beaded with sweat. The sight of the man was like a sobering slap. Beobrand shook his head as if stepping from a stream and clearing his face of water.

"What is it?" he snapped. He was pleased that his words were not slurred.

"It is Cynan," replied Halinard, his voice breathless. "You must come quickly."

Chapter 10

Cynan followed Fulbert to a large timber structure that backed on to the wall of the royal enclosure. From inside came the sounds of many men. Fire-glow and the scent of smoke and food oozed beneath the door into the darkness of the courtyard. Fulbert was clearly at home in the palace, for he did not hesitate as he nodded to the men on guard and pushed the door open.

Heat and noise rolled out. Fulbert stepped inside without a backward glance.

"Behave yourselves," Cynan growled to the men behind him. They had all left their weapons with the door wards of the palace. But even unarmed men could cause trouble, and, counting Baducing's gesithas and the Black Shields, the warriors from Albion numbered more than a dozen men. Cynan wished Beobrand was with them. The men would do as he said. He was not so certain that he would be able to control the warriors once the ale began to flow.

He ushered them into the hall and out of the night. Waiting for them to file in, he rubbed at his shoulder. The reminder of his foolishness annoyed him.

Attor was the last man. He halted at the threshold to cough; a wet, hacking sound. When the coughing passed, he spat into the darkness beside the door, before ducking inside.

"How are you feeling?" Cynan asked.

"I believe I will live to see Roma." Attor snorted, as if he had heard a jest. "A fortnight ago, I was not so sure of that."

Attor had been a part of Cynan's life ever since Beobrand had brought him north from Mercia. Cynan had soon outgrown him in stature and strength, but Attor had always been filled with seemingly boundless energy. Cynan admired him, and the Northumbrian scout had taught him much about riding and fighting. In battle, Attor was fearless and deadly, wielding his two seaxes with frenzied skill. To see Attor brought so low by this sickness, and for Beobrand to come down with it too, had been a shock to Cynan, and he had noticed the worried glances from the other men too.

"I am glad to hear that," Cynan said.

"As am I," replied Attor, with a grin that stretched the skin over the sharp ridges of his cheeks. He had never been a stout man, but he had lost weight these last weeks. "God is great." Attor made the sign of the cross and touched the crucifix that hung at his throat.

Cynan was unsure what to say to that. Transferring his attention away from Attor, he saw that a large fire crackled in the hearth and the room was lit by several oil lamps. The interior was hot and heavy with the fug of food, smoke, sweat and spilt ale. The gathered men fell silent at the new arrivals. Hard faces turned towards them, but Cynan saw more inquiry than confrontation in those gazes.

Fulbert said something in a loud voice, presumably announcing who the newcomers were. One of the men sitting near the fire asked a question. Fulbert replied and some of the men laughed. Cynan stiffened. He saw Gram's hand drop to his hip, where his sword would normally hang. A warrior's pride was easy to prick. Cynan touched Gram's arm.

"Easy now," he said.

Gram looked at him for a heartbeat before nodding. Cynan understood how the older man felt. He too was tired and irritable. Nothing about this journey had been easy and they still had a long way to go.

The laughter died away and the conversations picked up where men had left off, but many of them still stared at Cynan and his companions with interest.

"Perhaps a table for our men, apart from the others?" Cynan whispered, nudging Halinard.

Halinard spoke briefly to Fulbert, who in turn conversed with the men at the board farthest from the door. Only four men sat at the table. A dozen or more men could easily fit on the two long benches at either side. Looking about the hall there was plenty of room at the other tables to accommodate the four men, but they did not seem inclined to move. Cynan sighed. He had hoped that by keeping the Northumbrians separate from the Franks, he might avoid confrontation.

A tall man with a long, thick beard and hair that draped in two pendulous plaits over his shoulders, slammed his fist into the board, rattling the cups and platters. He rose menacingly, turning to face Fulbert and Halinard, who had been attempting to convince the four men at the table to give up their seats.

Cynan swallowed back his anger as he watched his hopes of a peaceful night rapidly dissipating. Halinard said something in a placatory tone. In response, the bearded man snarled and shoved him backwards. The atmosphere in the hall was as taut as a bowstring now. Nobody spoke. The tall warrior surged away from his bench and moved toward Halinard with a growl.

Without hesitation, Cynan stepped between them, placing his hands on the angry warrior's chest. The man was massive; taller than Cynan. Their eyes met. The man's breath was strong with garlic and sour ale. Cynan did not want a fight, but if one was needed, better to end it quickly. Perhaps then they could still eat and drink in peace. Cynan readied himself. He would not throw the first punch, but the moment the bearded man attacked, he would put him down as fast as possible.

If he were able.

The man was broad and strong, and the scars on his face and the twisted cant of his nose told the tales of many past brawls. And there was a madness in his eyes that spoke of a lust for combat.

It would not be a simple matter to defeat this foe.

Cynan waited for any sign of movement, his focus never wavering from the warrior's bloodshot stare. It would be the man's eyes that first gave away his intention to attack. And so it was. With the slightest twitch of his eyes, the warrior prepared to fling himself forward. Cynan, sober and prepared, began to drift to the right.

"Gunthar!" snapped a cold voice. It was not a shout, but the voice sliced through the tension in the hall like a sharp seax through lard.

Cynan tensed, ready to receive the bearded warrior's attack. He was certain it would come now. The moment had passed when the man might pull back from this course. The fury of battle was in his eyes and his muscles were already bunched and uncoiling.

But the attack never came. The voice halted him, and Cynan marvelled at the power of the man who had spoken, and the discipline of the bearded warrior to be able to arrest himself.

"Gunthar," said the voice again, softer now. The bearded warrior took a step back towards his bench and looked at the speaker. Cynan followed his gaze.

The man who spoke had close-cropped hair that was so pale it might have been white. His cheeks and jawline were angular and hard, as if he had been chiselled from a slab of granite. He glowered at Gunthar, but there was no glimmer of madness in this man's eyes. Cynan thought there was no emotion there at all. His eyes could have been those of a fish, or a serpent. He spoke again, his words barely above a whisper now, but carrying easily over the hush. Gunthar lowered his gaze, and, turning, he gathered up his cup, bowl and spoon, and silently made his way to one of the other benches. The men shuffled along to make room for him.

The three remaining men who had been seated at the far board rose without a word and followed their comrade.

Cynan let out a long breath and nodded his thanks to the man who had averted the fight. He smiled at Cynan briefly, but no humour reached his eyes.

The men from Albion were sitting themselves down now. Cynan noticed the glowers and scowls that flashed between them and the Frankish warriors who filled the rest of the room.

Fulbert said something to Halinard, who nodded.

"The blond one is named Thagmar," Halinard said. "It is best to avoid a fight with him."

Cynan did a quick count of the men in the hall. The men from Albion were outnumbered at least three to one.

"We would do best to avoid a fight with any of these men," he said, as much for the benefit of the men around the table, as in reply to Halinard. "We are all tired and have ridden for many days expecting attack at any moment, but we are warm and dry here, and the queen is safe in her minster." A thrall placed a large pot on the board, while another handed out wooden bowls, cups and spoons. "There is food and ale, so let us eat and drink our fill, and then sleep soundly tonight. We are guests here and it would not do to disturb the peace by fighting."

"Not to mention that we would lose," said Ingwald, loud enough for them all to hear.

"Yes," said Gram, with a lopsided grin, "much as I hate to say it, there comes a point when it is more foolhardy than brave to seek a fight."

Grindan took up the ladle that jutted from the pot and dished out the thick, spicy pottage of tripe and onions to the hungry men. The thralls brought over a couple of large, crusty loaves, which the men tore up and used to mop their bowls. Clay jugs were placed before them, and soon the cups were filled with good ale.

The hubbub in the hall reverted to what it had been when they arrived. No doubt many of the conversations were now about the newcomers, but as long as there were no other incidents, Cynan would be happy enough. He massaged his aching shoulder again, then stretched, knuckling the small of his back. Like his arm, it had been stiff ever since the fall in the forest. Picking up his cup, he drank a deep draught of the ale.

"How much further to Roma?" asked Ingwald.

Cynan shrugged.

"Wilfrid and Baducing say it will be weeks of travel yet."

Ingwald shook his head to think of such a distance.

"Then it must be further than the length of the whole of Albion."

"Let us just hope we do not get delayed any further," Cynan said, some of his frustration colouring his tone. "I had not imagined we would be away for so long. But if we have weeks of travel ahead, and then the same to return, the gods alone know when we will be able to return to Stagga."

Cynan frowned at the thought and drank more ale. He did not like to think of what lay ahead for it only made him miss Eadgyth more. He wondered what she was doing now. How he longed for her calming company, sitting in the warm glow of his own hearth fire. For many years he had thought of her as his friend's widow, but now she was something more in his mind and he would sometimes find himself dreaming of her body next to his, hot skin against his beneath his bed's furs. He wondered what it would be like to lie with her, after all these years as friends.

"What are you smiling about?" asked Ingwald.

Cynan blushed.

"Nothing."

Ingwald looked at him askance and snorted. His gesith was an astute man and he often surprised Cynan by seeming to know the thoughts that ran through his head. Ingwald pointed at Bleddyn with his chin.

"I never imagined Bleddyn to be one to grow lovesick."

Cynan glanced over at the young man, glad that Ingwald had not chosen to pry further into his own musings.

"No man is immune to a woman's charms," he said.

"That depends on the woman, I'd say." Ingwald drank. "And the man."

Cynan thought on that for a spell.

"Aye, but there is no denying Alpaida is a beauty few men would be able to resist."

Ingwald smirked.

"I'm only jealous, really," he said. Cynan nodded, hearing the truth behind the words. Ingwald was not the only one to be envious of Bleddyn.

All along the board, the tense anxiety that had twisted the men's nerves these last days of travel began to unwind. They had needed to be on guard, expecting another attack on Balthild at any moment. Now that they had delivered the queen to her destination, they could finally allow themselves to relax and, as the food filled their bellies and more jugs of ale were brought to the table, so their talk grew louder and increasingly jocund. Gram, eyes gleaming and red-cheeked in the fire's warmth, began recounting riddles. Most were known to them all by now, having spent long weeks together in Quentovic, but the old warrior seemed to have a never-ending supply of riddles with which to regale them.

"A young lad came up to where she rested in the corner," Gram declaimed in the serious, sonorous voice he employed when riddling. "He stepped up to her, this strapping ceorl, heaving up his robes with his hands. He thrust under her girdle something stiff—" Eadgard hooted with mirth and the others laughed. Gram paused, waiting for the men's laughter to abate. He held up a hand for quiet and then continued. "The boy worked his pleasure, and they both shook." Eadgard could barely breathe now. Tears streamed down his cheeks while the others shouted at him to hush. Gram, sensing he might lose his audience, raised his voice and bellowed: "The fellow quickened, forceful by turns, a most excellent servant, yet he was exhausted, vigorous at first, he sooner than her wearied himself with the work."

"Have you been watching Bleddyn with the queen's maid?" shouted Grindan. The others laughed uproariously. Bleddyn's face reddened. He stared into his cup and did not laugh.

"Please, friends," said Gram, "I have not finished the riddle."

"The boy in the riddle has finished already," wheezed Eadgard, wiping his eyes.

"There," went on Gram, gesturing as if rummaging beneath a woman's skirts, "under her girdle began to grow what good men often heartily desire and will purchase with silver."

"I know I would pay good silver for a chance to get beneath that servant girl's dress," roared Eadgard.

Some of the men drew in a sharp breath. The big man was drunk, but some things should not be said. Such talk about a man's woman could even lead to bloodfeud and murder. Cynan flicked a glance at Bleddyn. The Waelisc man sat still, looking down at the cup before him. Bleddyn, like Cynan himself, had been a thrall for many years, but unlike Cynan, Bleddyn, whilst brave and able with shield and spear when called upon to use them, had spent many more years a thrall and he had buried the hot streak of his fury deeply within himself. He was able to ignore insults and jibes, and Cynan did not believe he had ever seen Bleddyn lose his temper. Perhaps that made him a better man, but just as even the stoutest oak could snap in a storm, every man had a breaking point. Bleddyn's face was thunderous.

"You are a fool, Eadgard," said Cynan, "everyone knows the answer is not a woman, but a butter churn."

Eadgard looked confused for a moment. Then, slowly, the sense of the riddle with this meaning dawned on him. He mimicked plunging a wooden paddle into the milk and churning. He beamed at the riddle's devious wording and shook a finger at Gram.

"I thought—"

"We all know what you thought," said Cynan. A smattering of laughter. Bleddyn looked up, anger still burning in his eyes. "Now, Eadgard," Cynan went on, "beg forgiveness for your words."

"I meant nothing by it," the huge man whined.

"Then you will have no problem saying so to Bleddyn."

Eadgard hesitated for a heartbeat, before lowering his eyes in embarrassment.

"Sorry," he mumbled. "I wasn't thinking."

"You never think," said Grindan, slapping his brother on the shoulder. "That's your trouble."

"I know, I know." Eadgard's face was scarlet now, and he blinked at Bleddyn imploringly.

Bleddyn's expression softened and he offered Eadgard a thin smile.

"I know you are just jealous," he said at last. He looked around the table. "All of you, eh, Ingwald?"

Cynan laughed with the others, glad that the moment had passed. He sipped his ale and met Ingwald's quick, wide-eyed look. Bleddyn's ears must be keen indeed.

The mood lifted once more. And Gram soon launched into another riddle, this one without lewd overtones.

On the other tables, games of dice and knucklebones had started up. Fulbert, clearly bored with the riddling he could not comprehend, drifted off to join one of the games of chance. Cynan watched him go, momentarily worried at the reception he might receive. But Fulbert appeared to know some of the men, for they welcomed him warmly.

Gram was telling another riddle now, this time about a one-eyed onion seller of all things. It was a silly old rhyme, but the men, glad of its familiarity so far from their homes, laughed uproariously. Eadgard had recovered from his humiliation it seemed, and he now shook with mirth. He had moved to sit beside Bleddyn, and the Waelisc man appeared more at ease than he had been earlier too.

Cynan was pleased. He closed his eyes, enjoying the sensation of the good-natured laughter washing over him. He could almost imagine he was back in his own hall at Stagga. It felt good to be surrounded by these men, many of whom were like family to him.

A raised voice, more strident and jagged than jovial, made him open his eyes. Cynan's heart sank. It was Gunthar. The bearded warrior was shouting something over the din, directing his words at the table of men from Albion. His comrades waited with expectant smiles on their flushed faces.

"What does he say?" Cynan asked Halinard.

Halinard sucked his breath through his teeth and Cynan knew it was going to be bad before the Frank translated the words.

"He asks what it was like to bed the queen's maidservant."

Fulbert was signalling with his hands for Gunthar to be quiet. Cynan understood what had happened in an instant. Fulbert, tongue loosened with drink, had no doubt been asked about the recent disagreement on Cynan's table. In explaining the cause of the clash, Fulbert must have mentioned Bleddyn's trysts with Alpaida. Gunthar, clearly not over the confrontation earlier and now with several more cups of ale inside him, had decided to use the information to goad the men of Albion into the fight he had earlier been denied.

On hearing the words Gunthar had spoken, Bleddyn's face

clouded and he pushed himself up from the bench. It seemed the wind had finally blown strong enough to splinter even Bleddyn's self-control.

Across the hall, Gunthar rose up, rolling his neck, flexing his huge arms and clenching his fists. The man was a brute. Cynan recalled the mad glint of violence in his eyes, and the slabs of muscle beneath his kirtle. He had been unsure if he could best the man in a fist fight. Bleddyn had been a thrall all his life until the previous summer. He was brave and tough, and had picked up the use of weapons quickly, but he was a full head shorter than Gunthar, and had never proven himself to be much of a brawler. If he stood up to Gunthar, Cynan was in no doubt they would have another seriously injured man to contend with. Or worse.

Cynan stood, holding a hand out to halt Bleddyn.

"Tell that bastard, Gunthar," he snapped at Halinard, his voice loud and clear, "that for him to understand what it felt like, he would need to have swived at least one woman himself."

"This is madness," said Halinard.

Cynan waved his concern away.

"Speak my words, Halinard."

Halinard swallowed, then spoke.

Some of the Frankish men chuckled at the retort. Gunthar paled. He yelled something and stepped forward. Cynan wondered if Thagmar would intervene again, but a glance told him that the pale-haired man had decided to let this new situation play out.

"What does he say?" Cynan asked.

"He says he has had plenty of women," replied Halinard.

Cynan had worried there would be violence ever since they'd arrived in the hall. He had done what he could to avoid it, but sometimes the only course of action that remained was to fight, or to lose face. He sensed that moment had arrived. If he could dispatch Gunthar quickly, perhaps he could avert further fighting. But one thing was certain, Gunthar would not back down now.

"Tell him," said Cynan, stepping away from the board, "that his mother and sisters do not count."

Halinard hesitated.

"Tell him," growled Cynan.

Halinard uttered the words, and Gunthar rushed at Cynan. He was a massively strong man and if he had come at Cynan warily, his strength might have served him up a victory. But as Cynan had hoped, his derision had prodded Gunthar into a rage. The tall Frank came in swinging wildly. Most men would have retreated before such brutish brawn and fury. But Cynan had anticipated this mad onslaught, taunting Gunthar into rushing him. He stepped inside Gunthar's great hooking blows, taking the right swing on his left forearm and driving a straight right fist into the Frank's nose. Such was the man's forward momentum that the punch lifted him off his feet and he clattered onto his back on the reed-strewn floor.

Cynan was aware of other movement in the hall now. Voices shouting. Tables and benches tumbling. But he did not look away from his prey. Gunthar was a fighter, of that there was no doubt. He rolled over, shaking his head to clear it, sending droplets of blood flying from his broken nose. Cynan could have stepped back then, allowing the man to rise to his feet so that they might exchange blows toe to toe. But Cynan did not want a fair fight. He wanted to end this and to stamp out the prospect of further fighting as quickly as possible.

As Gunthar got his hands on the floor, preparing to launch himself once more at the Waelisc warrior, Cynan stepped in and kicked him hard in the face. Gunthar crumpled over. For an eye-blink, Cynan thought he had knocked him senseless. Then Gunthar moaned and, spitting blood, he started pushing himself up once more. Cynan knew that he could not let him up onto his feet. The man was a beast. Most men would already be out cold, yet Gunthar still seemed full of fire. Without giving him a chance to rise, Cynan threw himself down onto the Frank, using his weight to send him crashing onto his back. Then, without pause, he began pummelling Gunthar's face, first with his right fist, and then his left.

He had only hit him twice when strong hands grabbed him from behind, dragging him off. Cynan spun around, lifting his blood-smeared fists, ready to defend himself. Thagmar stood there, a strange expression on his face. He shook his head.

"Enough," he said, and Cynan understood his meaning.

The blond man flashed his teeth in a wolfish grin as if he had enjoyed the spectacle of the fight. Cynan gradually became aware of the fact that, somehow, the hall had not descended into a chaos of brawling men. One of the boards had been overturned, spilling plates, cups and jugs onto the rushes. Several of the benches were also upturned, and all of the men were on their feet. And yet, despite the storm-crackle tension in the room, the two sides had not charged; instead, as Cynan had hoped, they had watched to see the outcome of the fight between him and Gunthar.

Cynan offered a small smile to Thagmar at the same instant that the pale-haired warrior's eyes opened wide in shock. With a growling roar, Eadgard, perhaps believing that Thagmar meant to strike Cynan, leapt forward and, taking hold of the Frankish leader by his collar and belt, heaved him bodily into the air.

"No!" shouted Cynan, but it was too late. Eadgard was blinded by the battle-rage that made him a formidable opponent. The only one who had any chance of penetrating the fog that clouded his judgement was his brother. Grindan was already moving towards Eadgard, but he had no hope of reaching him in time and deterring him from his path.

For a moment, Thagmar was held above Eadgard's head, as if he were little more than a child, and then, with a savage shout of triumph, Eadgard spun and flung him across the room. Thagmar clattered heavily into one of the fallen benches. As he fell, his flailing legs tripped another man who tumbled over with a curse.

Thagmar was on his feet again as fast as a cat. Snatching up a cloak from the floor, he wrapped it around his left forearm in quick fluid movements. In his right hand suddenly glinted the blade of a wicked-looking knife that he had pulled from his leg bindings. Any sign of a smile had vanished now. His eyes blazed with a cold fire as he dropped into the warrior stance, crouched, knees bent, left, cloak-wrapped arm extended like a shield, knife held back, ready to strike.

Despite the heat of the fire in the hall, Cynan felt a chill run through the gathered men. There had been violence brewing in the fug of that room for a long time, but that had changed now. Where before there had been the threat of a brawl with its bruises and the risk of a broken bone or two, now naked steel gleamed in the firelight. In moments, there would be blood spilt here, and Cynan could see no way to prevent it.

Thagmar scowled and stalked forward, leading with his left foot and following with his right. He moved with the confident ease of a skilled killer, his eyes never leaving Eadgard's, his knife held still and unwavering.

Eadgard stood panting, as broad and tall as a bear. Grindan was hurrying forward. Ingwald and Bleddyn were also moving to stand before the large axeman. But even as he watched, Cynan could see it would do no good. Thagmar would not halt, and even if he was not able to stab the object of his anger, one of the others, unarmed as they were, would be gravely injured, or worse.

All he could think to do was to rush Thagmar and attempt to wrestle the knife from him. Perhaps if he could reach him while he was distracted by Eadgard and the others, he might yet avert a murder.

Cynan's muscles were bunching, ready to leap, when two voices shouted at the same instant. One he did not recognise, but the other Cynan knew as well as if it belonged to his own kin. That voice was now raised in the tone his lord used in the shieldwall, and even men who did not know it paid that battle-voice heed. That voice brought Cynan and the Black Shields up short.

"Stop this!" bellowed Beobrand.

The other voice barked an order. With a deep breath, Thagmar straightened. Without turning away from Eadgard, Thagmar reached up and wiped a spot of blood from his cheek.

For several heartbeats, nobody moved. Cynan risked a look at the doorway. There were Beobrand and Wilfrid in fine clothes that Cynan had not seen before. Baducing and Halinard stood in the shadows behind them. Beside Beobrand was a man with greying hair, trimmed beard and stern eyes.

This man said something to Thagmar, who now stepped back from Eadgard. Cynan let out a ragged breath. He was suddenly acutely aware of how tired he was. And gods, his shoulder and back ached terribly. His right hand throbbed and he wondered if he might have broken a finger when punching Gunthar.

The man in the doorway spoke quietly to Wilfrid. The novice's face was pallid as he took in the upheaval in the hall, but he forced a smile, nodded and interpreted the words in a clear voice, addressing Beobrand.

"Dalfinus says that it seems your men have met his warriors already. The man with the knife there is Thagmar, master of his guard."

PART TWO

THE BISHOP'S BARGAIN

Chapter 11

Beobrand reined in his gelding and took in the great expanse of the city that sprawled out below his vantage point. The day was sharp and bright, and so clear that he could make out the snow-clad peaks of huge mountains in the distance beyond the city. The range loomed massive like a bank of far-off clouds. Not knowing how far away they were, it was impossible to judge their true size, but Beobrand was sure they dwarfed the mountains he had encountered in Rheged and Pictland. He wondered if the path to Roma would lead them across those purple peaks. He pushed the thought away. That was an obstacle for another time. For now, the sight of the city was all he could contend with. Like the mountains, this city was the largest settlement he had ever seen.

Beobrand had ridden out of a forest of oak, beech and holly that covered the hills to the north-west of the city. He now sat on his horse, blinking at the sudden brightness of the midday sun. Beneath him, spread over the convergence of two great rivers, was Liyon, the home of Lord Dalfinus and his brother, Bishop Annemund.

"By Tiw's cock," Beobrand whispered, as much to himself as to anyone, "now it begins to make sense."

"Lord?" asked Cynan from where he sat astride his own

mount beside Beobrand. Cynan's eyes were narrowed against the glare of sunlight that flashed from the wide rivers.

"Imagine the riches the lords of such a city must possess," said Beobrand, shaking his head in wonder. "Finally seeing Liyon answers many questions I have had about Dalfinus and Annemund."

Cynan patted his mare's neck and reached up to rub his right shoulder with his left hand. He had been doing this less of late, but it was clear his arm still pained him. Beobrand knew how he felt. The weather was bright and dry now, but when the days were dank and filled with rain, Beobrand's body reminded him of many of his past injuries. Those battle memories didn't improve with age.

Cynan whistled quietly, perhaps picturing the vast wyrm's hoard of treasure the brothers must have.

"It explains how they are able to travel in more luxury than the queen," he said. "And with more men to guard them."

Beobrand nodded, scanning the sweep of buildings that were hazed here and there by smoke rising languidly from cooking fires. He watched as the column of riders wound its way down the road that sloped towards the stone wall encircling the west of the city. The number of warriors accompanying Dalfinus and Annemund had surprised them all. They were the combined escorts of the two brothers, of course, both important men, but they travelled with a total of some sixty warriors, all of whom answered to Dalfinus' man, Thagmar. Considering Balthild had been escorted by sixteen men, the size of the brothers' force seemed excessive. Unless, of course, they feared an attack. When Beobrand had asked about the size of the warband, Dalfinus shrugged.

"We brought with us the tributes of the Burgundian people. Such treasure would be a tempting prize indeed, and the time of our journey is well known. So it is prudent to travel with enough men to dissuade even the most determined thieves. The lands are never truly peaceful." Dalfinus had hesitated then, as if weighing up whether to say more. After a moment, mind made up, he raised his eyebrows quizzically and continued. "The question you should really ask yourself is why the queen was allowed to travel with so few protectors."

Beobrand had pondered that as they had travelled southeast through Neustria towards Burgundia. Could it be that the queen's guard had deliberately been made small to aid the attack in the forest?

He reached up and touched the Thunor's hammer amulet that hung from a leather thong around his neck. Beside the hammer was a new object and its touch brought back to him the morning they had left Paris. Erchinoald had handed him a golden ring bearing an engraved sigil.

"You have my eternal thanks for what you did for my queen," he said, his tone earnest, his long fingers pressing the gold band into Beobrand's hand.

Beobrand had been embarrassed.

"I do not need your gold."

"No, no," replied Erchinoald, waving away the words that Halinard had translated. "Of course not. This is my token I give you. If ever you find yourself in need, this ring will grant you safe passage and an audience." He had gripped Beobrand's hand firmly. "I will not forget what you have done. And as thanks I give you my friendship, which is a thing of some value in this land."

Beobrand thought often about Balthild and Erchinoald. He was sure there was more to the attack than was apparent at first glance, but the further they travelled from Paris, the less pressing the matter seemed to him and the less likely he would see either the queen or the *major domus* again. This was not his land, he told himself, and Balthild, lovely as she was, was not his queen. Her safety was Brocard's concern, not his.

One thing he did not need to worry about on their southward

journey was the threat from marauding brigands and wolf-heads. Travelling in such numbers, only a warhost could have attacked them with any chance of victory. And yet, that did not mean there was no peril on the road. But any danger there was came from their travelling companions.

The massive brute Gunthar's face was mottled and swollen after the beating he had received from Cynan. His bruises served as a constant reminder of the clash in the palace hall, and, whilst many of the men were on friendly terms after a few days' travelling together, there were many more who still glowered darkly at the men of Albion.

Dalfinus had not failed to notice his men's aggression, and he had been keen to prevent further conflict.

"Keep your men in check, Lord Beobrand," he'd said on the first night after leaving Paris, "and I assure you there will be no more incidents. Thagmar has my orders on the matter and I can trust him to follow my commands as obediently as a hound."

Beobrand stared down the hillside where Thagmar rode close beside Dalfinus at the head of the column. As he watched, the lord of Liyon wheeled his horse around, and kicked it into a loping canter up the hill towards his position on the hilltop. Dalfinus raised a hand in greeting. Beobrand returned the gesture with a smile, but found his memory pulling him back to a storm-dark night a fortnight earlier, when Dalfinus' hound had been called upon to follow his master's orders, no matter how bloody they might prove to be.

It was the second night out of Paris when Dalfinus' command over his men had been tested. The party of travellers had been put up in the hall of a local landowner. The man's hall was not large enough to house all of the men, only the nobles and a few of their hearth-warriors. Most of the warriors found space in the barns and stables. In an effort to keep the peace between his men and the Franks, Beobrand bade his Black Shields and Baducing's warriors camp beneath a lean-to propped against the enclosure wall. The men grumbled about the cold. It was raining heavily and the lean-to provided poor shelter, but keeping the men apart from the Franks seemed prudent and more important than their comfort.

The food and wine in the hall had been hearty and warming, and the farmer had seemed almost desperate to please, bowing and scraping whenever he addressed Dalfinus and Annemund. He stumbled over his words like a nervous boy, rather than a man who had seen well over forty summers. Beobrand had already been on edge, unable to relax, and the farmer's attitude only served to make him more uneasy.

Such was the disquiet in the hall, it had almost been a relief when the door had been flung open and Ingwald had shouted inside for help.

It had been dark and confused in the rain-drenched night, but it didn't take long to find out what had occurred. One of Baducing's warriors, a quiet man called Aculf, had gone to the midden to relieve himself. A couple of Dalfinus' men had been waiting there. They had set upon Aculf, coming at him unawares in the darkness and beating him badly.

When Dalfinus had taken in what had happened, he apologised to Beobrand and barked an order to Thagmar. Grim-faced, the leader of the warriors had the two attackers dragged before the *comes* of Liyon. The men had clearly been drinking, but the thunderous expression on the face of their lord was enough to sober them like a slap. One of the two threw himself into the mud at Dalfinus' feet. The man gibbered and moaned, begging and pleading pathetically.

Beobrand enquired after Aculf to Baducing.

"He'll be eating soup and porridge for a time, lord," replied the stocky novice. "But he'll live."

"Good. Tell Dalfinus as much." Beobrand had been angry about the assault on their comrade, but he knew it was impossible to have so many warriors in close proximity without altercations like this. It was in the nature of men of war to fight. "And let him know that I will see to it that our men stay out of trouble from now on."

Gram had pushed his way through the mass of men.

"Lord," he said, fury twisting his features in the flickering light from the camp fires that hissed and crackled in the rain. "This was none of Aculf's doing. His only crime was that he needed to piss."

Beobrand bit back his own anger and placed a hand on Gram's shoulder.

"I hear you, and I know the truth of it. But we have not started this journey on a good footing with our hosts' men, and we still have many days of travel to go. It would do us best if we kept away from them at night."

Dalfinus waited patiently for Beobrand to finish speaking to his man, and then said a few words to Halinard, who translated.

"Dalfinus says he gave his word no fighting there would be. His men broke the peace, now they will be punished as he had ordered."

The man crouching before Dalfinus let out a howl on hearing this. The other man paled and swayed on his feet. Beobrand felt a sudden chill.

"What is to be their punishment?" he asked.

Dalfinus, either understanding the question in Anglisc, or guessing what Beobrand had asked, replied directly. Halinard's face hardened as he listened. His words were clipped as he interpreted for Beobrand.

"He told the men that any who harm his guests be killed."

"Killed?" Beobrand's mouth was dry. "They are drunk. Men fight. Could they not be flogged?"

Dalfinus snapped something.

"He says his word is like iron," translated Halinard. Beobrand scowled. He too had once prided himself on his unbreakable word.

"I understand," Beobrand said. "A man's word is important." He looked imploringly at Dalfinus. "But they were merely brawling." He did not wish to see these men slain for a drunken mistake; besides, the Frankish warriors would ultimately blame their friends' deaths on the foreigners from across the Narrow Sea.

Dalfinus shook his head. He would not back down. Beobrand protested, but it soon became apparent that Dalfinus would not relent. However, after listening to Beobrand, Dalfinus did agree on a single concession. Instead of Thagmar having both men slain, only one would be killed as an example to the others.

Beobrand had clenched his fists at his side, impotent and angry. His head had ached and the damp night made his ribs throb with the memory of old war wounds.

"They are his men to lead as he wishes," Cynan had whispered.

Beobrand said nothing, but a glance at Cynan told him they both had the same thought, that perhaps if Cynan had not fought with Gunthar in Paris, none of this would have happened. Not wishing to see a man killed, Beobrand had returned to the hall. There he had sat for a time, with no company but for a grizzled dog that lay stretched by the hearth. Beobrand reached down and stroked the animal's wiry fur. The dog stretched its limbs, but otherwise ignored the tall, fair-haired man who watched the flames dance, and listened to the sounds of the rain and the men outside. There was a brief spell of shouting, and then what sounded like a collective sigh. The dog's ear twitched.

After a while, the men returned, solemn-faced and soaked from standing in the rain. The hound lazily lifted its head to watch them enter the hall, then, seeing nothing of interest, it let it flop back.

"It is done," said Cynan, as he slid onto the bench beside Beobrand and filled a glass with wine.

"Which one?" asked Beobrand.

"The one who begged."

Beobrand nodded.

"If I'd had to choose, it would have been him." For an instant, he had a memory of a corpse swinging from a yew tree, many years ago and far away.

"Oh, Dalfinus didn't choose him."

Beobrand frowned.

"No?"

"No," Cynan said, his tone flat, "he gave them each a sword and had them fight."

That was the only time Beobrand had seen Dalfinus angry. On every other occasion he was easy-going, good company. But he had been scowling when he came in out of the rain that night.

Beobrand offered him a glass of wine.

"I am sorry one of your men had to die," he said, through Halinard, who was pale and clearly shaken by what he had witnessed.

"I have plenty of men," replied Dalfinus, taking the glass and sipping its contents. Beobrand poured another glass for Halinard. He took it with a trembling hand. He drank while Dalfinus continued speaking, then translated his words. "I am not angry that one had to die. I am angry that they do not all obey me."

In the morning, Dalfinus had risen in a mood as jovial and ebullient as before, and for the remainder of the journey he had often sat with Beobrand and Halinard, late into the night, drinking and talking of their pasts, foes they had vanquished and marvels they had witnessed. Beobrand once again grew to remember why he had liked the older man when they had first met. And there could be no denying that the harsh punishment Dalfinus had meted out had the desired effect. There was no further clash between the two groups of warriors, though Beobrand was not blind to the dark glances, and he sometimes heard the hissed insults when the men from Albion passed close by.

Dalfinus and Thagmar were feared and respected by their warriors, but looking down the hill now at the city of Liyon, Beobrand wondered how safe it would be for him and his men in that warren of alleys and jumbled streets. They would have to be careful, for any manner of accident could befall a stranger in this strange land and even Dalfinus' iron word would not protect against a knife in the dark.

Chapter 12

"It is quite some sight, is it not?" said Dalfinus with a grin, pulling his horse to a halt. Beobrand's gelding nickered in welcome.

"It is that," said Beobrand in his faltering Frankish. Though he never thought he would become fluent in the language, he found increasingly that he did not need to wait for Halinard to interpret for him to understand simple phrases and statements. Still, there was no way he could endure any lengthy exchange, and he cast about, wondering where Halinard had got to. Lately he had noticed that the Frankish gesith often seemed to find a reason to be absent when Beobrand required his services as interpreter. Perhaps the man grew tired of the task, or mayhap he did not enjoy the company of the Burgundian lord with whom Beobrand was spending so much of his time. He would have to speak to Halinard about it.

Dalfinus pulled his horse's head round to face the city once more.

"Come," he said, touching his heels to the animal's flanks and beckoning for Beobrand to follow him.

Beobrand glanced at Cynan, who shrugged, and they both started off down the hill alongside Dalfinus.

Dalfinus called something over his shoulder, as they cantered past the other riders. Beobrand heard him mention the city, but didn't understand more than that. He was just about to ask Dalfinus to repeat himself, something he knew infuriated the man, when Wilfrid, riding easily on a fine-looking black horse, peeled away from the main group and joined them. Baducing spent much of his time conversing with Annemund about whatever it was that concerned Christ priests, but Wilfrid, determining that the real power of the brothers lay with the *comes* and not the bishop, had taken to acting as interpreter for Beobrand whenever Halinard was unavailable. Come to think of it, Beobrand would not put it past the ambitious young man to have somehow coerced or cajoled Halinard into stepping aside and allowing him the chance to rub shoulders with the powerful lord of Liyon. The novice monk was as crafty as he was ambitious.

As his horse fell into stride beside Beobrand and Cynan, Wilfrid translated Dalfinus' last comment.

"He said that Liyon was once the capital of the Roman province of Gaul." That Wilfrid had assumed Beobrand had not understood Dalfinus irked him. What annoyed him even more was that Wilfrid was right. He bit back his irritation. There were still many weeks of travel ahead of them, and he could not afford to let his dislike of Wilfrid show. Besides, the man had his uses.

"I have never seen a city as grand," Beobrand said, knowing that Wilfrid would interpret without prompting.

Dalfinus beamed as if he himself had built the city with his bare hands.

"There are many things that I would show you. The *thermae*, the *forum*, the *amphitheatrum*. All of these things you will have seen in great cities before, but none so well-cared for, or so large as in Liyon." Beobrand wasn't sure what these things were, but he said nothing, not wishing to give Wilfrid the pleasure of explaining. In any case, there wasn't the chance, as Dalfinus continued speaking enthusiastically without cease. "Where others have allowed the buildings of the men of old to decay and crumble, my masons are the best in the world. They repair what they can, and what they cannot repair they build anew. You will see the palace they have built for me. Grander than any of the king's residences. And Annemund's church is a gem in Liyon's crown."

They were at the head of the column now. Shortly before, Beobrand had seen Thagmar lead a detachment of some twenty guards ahead at a gallop, presumably to announce the arrival of the *comes* and the bishop. Beobrand looked along the tree-lined stretch of road they were on. It reached all the way to the city wall. The stone wall rose taller than the height of two men and there was evidence of what Dalfinus had talked about with such obvious pride. There were sections that had been patched with rocks that differed from those of the original structure, their lighter hue stark against the aged stones of the Roman wall. Beobrand thought of the great Wall that divided Albion from east to west. It was a huge, almost unbelievable feat to have constructed such a thing. Many believed the Wall and other stone edifices had been built by giants, not men. And yet, no matter how impressive, in Albion, the memories of the men of Roma were, for the most part, heaps of weed-tangled boulders, like the bones of long-dead behemoths jutting from the earth.

When they reached the gates, the path had been cleared for them. Wall wards, all carrying red and blue shields bearing Dalfinus' white lion emblem, stood to either side, holding back the men and women who were gathered there. Carts, waggons and mules laden with produce thronged the muddy verges.

Dalfinus nodded to the wardens, who bowed, only chancing a glance at the riders once they had trotted past. After they clattered through the gatehouse, ten of the men who had been sent ahead rejoined the front of the column to protect their lord and to clear the way.

"The wall looks strong," said Beobrand.

"It had collapsed in places," replied Dalfinus, "but it does not pay to grow soft. The city is protected from the east by the great rivers Sona and Rôno, but to the west, the wall is the only defence."

Beobrand glanced up at the ramparts and the armoured spearmen who stared down at the passing riders.

"Are you planning for a war?" he asked.

Dalfinus slowed his horse, so that Beobrand could catch up and he did not need to shout.

"I pray for peace, but plan for war," he said. "You can never know who your enemies might be, or when they might attack."

Beobrand nodded.

"Wise words."

Dalfinus grinned and rode on down the shadowed street. The forward riders had gone before them, announcing the approach of the lords' cavalcade and clearing the path as best they could, but even so, the city was bustling. They frequently needed to halt while some of Dalfinus' men pushed people and animals aside.

After two weeks travelling through open country, the sounds and smells of the city made Beobrand's head spin. The crack of their horses' hooves and the jingle of the harness echoed back from the buildings that loomed to either side. Hawkers and traders shouted to passers-by. A mangy-looking dog rushed out of an alley, snarling and barking at the horses. Dalfinus' horse shied and the lord was almost unseated. Catching hold of his mount's mane, he righted himself. A man scurried out after the dog, shouting. On seeing whose horse his hound had frightened, he paled and bowed low. Dalfinus' eyes narrowed, but then he smiled, and said something to the dog's owner. Beobrand could not make out the meaning, but the man smiled and bobbed his head in thanks. With a pat on his horse's neck, Dalfinus pulled the animal back in the direction they had been going.

"I love the city," he said, over his shoulder, "but its pleasures can wear thin. I think you will approve of my palace. It is over the river on a great hill." He waved his hand airily ahead, but Beobrand could see no further than the next bend in the thoroughfare. They rode past a group of women who laughed and leered at the warriors. One pulled down her dress to expose huge, wobbling breasts. Wilfrid had been doing a good job of translating Lord Dalfinus' words, but Beobrand couldn't help smiling as the young novice's voice trailed off at the sight of the woman's pale flesh, shaking and jiggling. His open-mouthed shock made the whores howl and cackle with laughter.

"The air is cleaner over the river," said Dalfinus, Wilfrid stammering to regain his composure. "When we become tired of the excitements Liyon has to offer," Dalfinus winked, "I will take you hunting. Perhaps we will find a stag, such as the one your friend slew and placed on his hall, eh? And there are more exotic animals we can hunt too." His eyes glimmered. "For my truest friends, nothing but the best."

Beobrand wondered what manner of unusual animals lived near to the city, but before he could ask, Dalfinus had spurred his mount ahead. Beobrand rode after him.

The smell of roasting meat and baking bread wafted to them over the stench of the ordure-thick streets.

"I hope you are hungry," Dalfinus said. "I will have my cooks prepare you all of our local delicacies. We will have fish, and tripe, and snails." Wilfrid wrinkled his nose. Beobrand shrugged. Attor had acquired a taste for snails ever since trying them in Rodomo, years before. He had eaten them a few times in Quentovic, but he said none tasted as good as those he had tried down by the wharfs on the Secoana. "But perhaps first," Wilfrid went on, interpreting Dalfinus' next thought, "we can have some sweet ice. It has been unseasonably warm."

It was true that it had been mild these last few days, and when not in the shadow of the buildings, the sun warmed their faces. And yet Beobrand was uncertain Wilfrid had understood

Dalfinus, for surely it had not been cold enough for there to be ice or snow for several weeks now.

"Did he say ice?"

"I think so," replied Wilfrid. "Sweet ice." He asked Dalfinus a question, and the *comes* turned in his saddle, smiling.

"Oh, we have ice here all the year round, even in the height of summer. It is so cooling on a hot day. My cook sweetens it with fruit and honey. I have it brought down from the mountains. There is a great expanse of ice there and men chisel out blocks of the stuff and bring it here on waggons. When the weather warms a bit more, I shall take you up the mountains and show you the sea of ice."

Dalfinus continued to speak as they rode, pointing out other things of interest. They passed through a more sparsely built part of the city, where trees grew and there were even some ploughed fields. When they finally reached the river, Beobrand's head was aching and he longed for quiet. Dalfinus liked to talk at times, especially when he had drunk too much wine, but Beobrand had never known the man to speak so incessantly.

A long timber bridge crossed the river. Beyond it, on a high hill, lofted one of the strange circular buildings so favoured by the men of Roma.

"My palace is there," Dalfinus pointed up the steep slope. "My brother resides closer to his flock." He nodded south along the river. Steep cliffs dropped down from the city to the west bank of the Sona. "The church of Saint John is yonder. Behind those trees. The bishop's palace is not far from there."

They waited beside the bridge for Annemund and the other riders to catch up. Beobrand looked up at the tall stone circular building on the hill. Turning, he stared back through the trees and fields at the sprawl of the city. On the river, a broad-bellied barge drifted downstream. The weather-beaten steersman gaped unblinking at the gathered horsemen. Beobrand's eyes met his and the sailor spat into the mud-dark waters. Further south, where the two rivers combined in a wide waterway, he could make out wharfs and jetties, teeming with many more ships and boats of all shapes and sizes. It reminded him of Rodomo. He had thought that city huge, but Liyon was larger by far.

Dalfinus followed Beobrand's gaze.

"There the Sona joins the mighty Rôno," he said, "and then it flows all the way south into the Great Sea. Here you can find anything in the world. Salt, gold and ivory from the lands of the Berbers. Cinnamon, pepper, nutmeg and clove from the east. Everything is carried by ship on the Great Sea. It is the heart of commerce." Dalfinus took in a deep breath of the warm afternoon air as if he could smell the far-off brine. "And the Rôno is one of its arteries, carrying wealth and prosperity to the Burgundians."

And to its lords and bishops, thought Beobrand, looking at the golden torc around Dalfinus' throat, and the rings that glimmered on his fingers. Annemund, his retainers and armed escort were arriving now, and the small esplanade before the bridge was suddenly crammed with jostling horsemen. The afternoon sun glinted on polished helms and spear points. The bishop himself had changed out of his drab riding clothes and had entered the city wearing shimmering silks. Around his neck hung a thick chain of gold. Yes, thought Beobrand, these brothers certainly knew how to squeeze wealth from the lifeblood of this region.

Baducing rode his horse with difficulty through the press of men and animals.

"The bishop has invited us both to stay with him at his palace," he said to Wilfrid. "There is not enough space for us all, I am afraid." He gave Beobrand an apologetic look, but quickly turned back to Wilfrid, his excitement making his face glow. "I cannot wait to begin reading from Annemund's copy of Origen's Hexapla."

"I too am excited to look through the bishop's library,"

said Wilfrid, picking his words with care, "but I have decided to accept the hospitality of Lord Dalfinus and stay with him instead."

"Oh, I had assumed..." Baducing said, clearly disappointed. Wilfrid's decision did not surprise Beobrand. The young man had obviously already made up his mind that Dalfinus was the brother with whom it would best serve him to curry favour.

"It will only be for a few days," said Wilfrid breezily. "It will do us no harm to stay in separate residences." He smiled broadly.

"No, of course," replied Baducing.

"I for one will miss you," Beobrand said, and it was true. His primary duty was to protect Wilfrid, the man under Eanflæd's patronage, but he much preferred Baducing's company.

"Thank you, Lord Beobrand," said Baducing, cheering up as quickly as he had become downcast. "As Wilfrid said, it will only be for a few days, and I am sure we will see each other frequently. The bishop has been promising all manner of feasts." He leaned in closer and lowered his voice. "I am sure that our abbots and teachers back in Cantware and Bernicia would never have approved."

"Well," said Beobrand, with a chuckle, "they are far away."

"Yes, but God is everywhere." Baducing seemed genuinely worried by the prospect that he might be judged for feasting too much. Beobrand rubbed his callused left hand over his face. He thought he would never understand these followers of the Christ. His own mind was troubled enough by his actions without the need to worry about what the gods thought of him.

"I am sure the good bishop Annemund knows what is right and proper in the eyes of the Lord," said Wilfrid.

"Of course." Baducing did not look convinced, but it seemed the thought of the books in the bishop's library was enough to assuage any concerns he might have, for he turned his horse and rode back to Annemund with a smile on his face.

Beobrand watched him go, accompanied as always by his

father's gesithas. On seeing Aculf's face, still mottled like a storm cloud from the beating he had taken, Beobrand called after Baducing.

"Be careful," he shouted.

Baducing raised a hand and nodded.

"He'll be fine," said Cynan. "Baducing's no fool, and nor are his men. Besides, that blond bastard, Thagmar, and that brute, Gunthar, are coming with us."

The bishop's party, which included a score of the Frankish guards, rode south and were soon lost to sight. As Beobrand kicked his gelding forward to follow Dalfinus across the timber bridge, he felt a prickle of worry. He would have rather all the pilgrims from Albion remained together, but Wilfrid was right. It would only be a few days. He just hoped Cynan was also right about Baducing.

Chapter 13

Cynan stretched his shoulders, grasping his hands and straightening his arms over his head. The muscles and tendons he had strained when being pulled from the saddle by the wounded horse no longer pained him. Panting from his run around the perimeter of the amphitheatre, Cynan picked up the clean linen cloth Dalfinus' slaves left for him every morning and wiped the sweat from his face.

Across the sand of the arena, Beobrand was sparring with Attor. Like Cynan, the two older men were both stripped to the waist. He watched them lunge, parry and counter, the crack of the wooden practice swords reaching him a moment after the contact, such was the size of the training ground. He could tell that their hearts weren't really in the bout, but neither man had anything to prove. The main reason they came here several times a week was to prevent themselves growing fat, slow and soft.

He watched them a moment longer. Despite them not fully committing to the fight, they were both still fast, their balance good as they glided across the raked sand. It brought joy to his heart to see the two men hale again. The rest had done them good and neither Attor nor Beobrand coughed any longer.

"Do you wish to cross blades with me?" said a voice. "I could use a lesson in sword craft." Cynan turned to see Ingwald walking towards him from where he had been seated in the sunshine, watching the men train. The bald warrior had always tanned easily, but here, after weeks in the southern sun, he was as brown as a chestnut. The sun just made Cynan's skin burn red, leading to painful, sleepless nights. Eventually his burnt skin would slough off in dusty flakes, leaving fresh smooth skin beneath, ready to be burnt anew. He had learnt not to stay in the sun for too long and, despite the taunting of his comrades, he had taken to wearing a straw hat on hot, sunny days. And those days were more frequent now they had passed Eostremonath. Spring had come without warning, but after the deluges and storms of winter, little rain had fallen. The long dry days made ceorls in the fields shake their heads and bemoan the state of their crops that longed for moisture, but Cynan was glad to see the end of that long, freezing and wet winter.

He shook his head, draping the cloth over his shoulder and making his way back to retrieve his kirtle from one of the stone steps that served as benches for spectators who came to witness events. Dalfinus had told them that the Romans once staged combats to the death here. Wilfrid had even said that the men of Roma would bring lions and other exotic animals from far-off lands to fight in this very place, but Cynan did not truly believe such tales. Now, on holy days and feasts, people would gather in this place of spectacle that Dalfinus had repaired, to watch running races, fist fights and games of chance. Cynan thought back to the day of Eostremonath, that the people here called Pascha, the day they celebrated the rebirth of the Christ. The place had been so crowded it seemed that everyone in Liyon had made their way into the arena. The sound of the throng had been as loud as a gale as men wrestled, raced and fought for their entertainment.

Pulling on his kirtle, Cynan drank water from the earthenware pot that was always kept full at the edge of the arena floor.

"It's too hot to stay out here." He squinted over to the far side of the circular sandy area where some of Dalfinus' men were training. Thagmar, hair almost white in the brilliant sunshine, danced and spun gracefully, while two warriors circled him warily. They would do well to be cautious. Thagmar was as naturally gifted a fighter as Cynan had ever seen. The man unnerved him. Thagmar seldom addressed the men from Albion, and when he did, he was always civil. But there was an empty coldness behind Thagmar's eyes. Cynan had known many killers. He was feared as a slayer of men himself. And yet he did not believe he had ever before met a man like Thagmar who seemed to feel no fear and no remorse. As he watched, Thagmar leapt forward, parrying a clumsy attack and driving his wooden practice blade hard into his assailant's sternum. Then, anticipating his second opponent's move, Thagmar twisted, caught the scything cut on his sword and, without pause, kicked his adversary hard between the legs.

The man collapsed in a heap, retching and spitting. The first warrior was on his knees, gripping his chest and struggling for breath.

Thagmar did not revel in his victory. He seemed indifferent as he handed his practice sword to one of the onlookers, a man called Hincmar. The tanned warrior glanced over at Cynan and raised the sword in salute. Cynan offered a smile in response. Hincmar was friendlier than most of Dalfinus' men. He had an easy way about him, and they had shared several jugs of ale and wine these past weeks, often sitting in the shade after weapon practice and watching the others in the arena. In the Pascha festivities they had wagered against each other on many of the games, enjoying a good-humoured rivalry that saw Hincmar take several gold coins from Cynan's pouch.

"It was the right decision," said Ingwald, continuing a conversation they had started several days before.

"Yes," said Cynan, "I wouldn't have wanted to shame our host's man. It would have been rude."

Ingwald smiled sidelong at Cynan.

"Yes, lord. Very rude."

This was a game of words they had played together ever since the Pascha celebrations. Dalfinus had issued an open challenge to any swordsman in Liyon. Anyone who could best Thagmar in the arena would be awarded with a purse of gold coins minted with the face of the *comes* of Liyon himself. It was a handsome prize, but nobody won it. Beobrand forbade any of his men from accepting the challenge. Grindan had said that the lord of Ubbanford would surely be able to best the man himself. Beobrand had shrugged and said he was not yet fully recovered from his winter sickness. Cynan was not sure that was the only reason. He had watched Thagmar training, as had they all, and he was uncertain whether Beobrand, or indeed any of them, himself included, would have been able to beat him.

Certainly not a single one of the warriors who entered the ring that warm spring day was able to touch Thagmar with their wooden blades. Half a dozen brave or foolish men dared to face him; three left the arena with broken arms or wrists, two hobbled away, thankful they bore nothing worse than bruises, and one unfortunate was carried out with blood oozing from his ears where Thagmar had cracked his skull. They heard later that the poor man never awoke, succumbing to his injuries three days afterwards.

"I'm thirsty and hungry," said Cynan, looking up at the clear sky and the bright sun. "Besides, it must be after noon and we said we would meet with Baducing."

Looking back, he saw that Beobrand and Attor had finished their practice and were making their way towards them.

"We're going to be late," Cynan called, waving for them to hurry. Neither Beobrand nor Attor made any sign of speeding up. Grindan and Eadgard rose from where they had been basking in the sun on one of the tiered seats and sauntered over to join them. The taller of the two grinned. A tooth was missing and his left eye was still bruised, but Eadgard had not once complained about the injuries he had sustained in the Pascha games. Cynan should not have been surprised. He had stood beside Eadgard often enough in the shieldwall to know the man was a towering strength in battle, but he did not believe he had ever seen a man take such a pummelling and remain on his feet.

For the games, Dalfinus had also put forward the giant warrior, Gunthar, as his champion fist fighter. At first, Beobrand had told his gesithas that it would not do to stand against their host's man, but Gunthar was as loud as he was big.

Their initial concerns about the possibility of attacks from the Frankish warriors had proven unfounded and, apart from a couple of scuffles late at night after too much ale, there had been no serious incidents. But ever since he had been beaten in Paris, Gunthar had accused Cynan of cowardice. He had said that he would not be able to stand against him in a fair fight.

"Any fight is fair if you win," Ingwald had said.

Cynan had smiled. And yet the truth was that to stand toe to toe with Gunthar would be madness. The man was taller and stronger, and Cynan remembered how hitting him had felt like punching the trunk of an oak.

But Gunthar's continuous insults and jibes eventually led Beobrand to relent, and the night before the festivities, he had announced to Dalfinus that his man would have his chance at revenge.

"Do you hear that, Gunthar?" Dalfinus had called out to the big man. In honour of the part he was to play in the upcoming games, he had been seated at the high table in the great feasting hall of the palace. "You will get your wish."

Cynan had picked up most of this exchange from his growing understanding of Frankish, but Gunthar's snarled response was unintelligible to him. He had glanced at Wilfrid for a translation.

"He says he will knock your teeth out and ugly that pretty

face of yours," Wilfrid said, smiling and taking more pleasure than he should, it seemed to Cynan, from relaying the man's threats.

"Oh no," said Beobrand, holding up a hand, "your man misunderstands. Cynan is my closest gesith and it would not do to have him brawling with the likes of Gunthar." He paused, glancing at Cynan. "At least, not again. No, it is my man Eadgard who will stand against Gunthar. That is, if the challenge still stands. Of course, if Gunthar does not wish to face my man, I understand."

Gunthar had blustered then, saying that he could beat any fighter Beobrand chose. But Cynan had noticed how he had glanced at Eadgard as the night drew on, growing ever more subdued and sullen.

For his part, Eadgard was overjoyed.

"Don't you worry," he had said to Cynan the following morning, "I'll finish what you started."

The only thing that had truly concerned Cynan was that he might lose face by not fighting Gunthar himself. But apart from him, nobody else seemed to care. In the eyes of the Black Shields, Cynan had bested the man with guile and skill, and now it was Eadgard's turn to defeat him with brute strength and tenacity.

The two giants had slogged it out, watched by thousands, until they each ran with blood from cuts to their cheeks and eyebrows, and the cloths that wrapped their knuckles were stained crimson. The crowd had bellowed and roared, and Cynan had imagined the people of Roma baying for blood and death centuries before.

The sound had been deafening when eventually, exhausted and wheezing like an injured bull, Gunthar had crumpled first to his knees and then, slowly, onto his side, where he lay, his only movement his heaving chest.

"About time we left," said Eadgard now, slapping a meaty

hand on his belly. "It takes a lot of food to keep my strength up, you know?" He grinned his gap-toothed smile and nodded a welcome to Beobrand and Attor.

"Is the big man complaining about his belly again?" asked Attor.

"To be fair," said Cynan, clapping Eadgard on the shoulder, "he is not the only one who is hungry. We should have left long since. If we don't hurry, there won't be any food left."

"There is little chance of that," Beobrand said. "Genofeva could feed the whole garrison and have food to spare."

"Enough of this talk about food," grumbled Eadgard. "Let's go and eat."

He strode off through the shadowed archway that led out of the arena. Beobrand caught Cynan's eye and they both chuckled.

"I should never have let your brother fight that brute," muttered Beobrand to Grindan, with a shake of his head. "He was bad enough before, but ever since, he's walked about the city as if he owns it."

"He thinks his battle-fame is as large as his stature, it's true," said Attor.

Grindan smirked, hurrying to keep up with the pace set by Eadgard.

"It is perhaps almost as large as his fat head," quipped Grindan.

"I may have a fat head and thick ears from Gunthar's punches," shouted Eadgard over his shoulder, "but I am not yet deaf."

Laughing, they followed the giant warrior through the twisting streets that had become so familiar over the last weeks. It didn't take them long to reach the timber bridge across the Sona. They crossed quickly, ignoring the street vendors who offered them all manner of trinkets and food. These warriors from afar were known to be wealthy and could be relied upon when drunk to part with their silver easily. But they were sober now, and swept past the hawkers, oblivious to their shouts. Cynan marvelled at how quickly they had come to accept this way of life. When they had first arrived some six weeks earlier, they had blinked and gawped about them like blind men seeing for the first time. Now, they hurried along the ancient, cobbled streets as if they had been born in the city. With a pang, he thought of how different life was here from what he had known in Bernicia. He still missed Eadgyth and the children, but did he truly miss the quiet life of Stagga? There were times when the bustle of Liyon became overpowering, but there was no denying it had its benefits.

As soon as they had crossed the river, Eadgard led them down some steps to the left. A couple more turns through the cool shade between mouldering warehouses, and they had arrived. Cynan thought they would never have found this place without Hincmar's recommendation. Now, the men from Albion met here several times a week. On days of rain, the interior was smoky and cramped, but on a sunny day like today, there were tables and stools set up outside the small timber-framed building. The sound of conversation and laughter reached them as they rounded the last corner.

Baducing and his gesithas, along with Gram, Halinard and Bleddyn, were slouched around a couple of tables they had pushed together. As they had suspected, the men had already begun eating and the board was cluttered with bowls, jugs, cups and plates.

"Nice of you to join us," said Gram, holding aloft his clay cup in mock salute.

"I hope you have saved us some food," gnarred Eadgard, lifting a jug from the table and draining its contents in a couple of massive gulps. "I have a hunger to match my thirst!"

"Never fear," said Gram, kicking a stool towards Eadgard. "We told Genofeva you were coming, so she probably has half a mutton roasting just for you."

"Excellent." Eadgard settled his massive frame onto the small stool and reached for half a loaf on the table.

Pulling up stools and a long bench, the newcomers sat. The thought of mutton made Cynan's stomach grumble. The men chattered and joked around him. Halinard beckoned to one of the widow Genofeva's young daughters, a plain, plump girl with wide, perpetually frightened eyes, and ordered more food and drink. Soon they all had a cup of wine in their hands with the promise of more of the widow's tasty food.

Genofeva was a serious woman. Her husband had been a sailor who had never returned from a voyage some years previously. Now, with the help of her five children, she served wholesome vittles, mainly to the men who worked the wharfs and the fields. Genofeva's had become a popular establishment with Dalfinus' and Annemund's guardsmen too. The widow was always generous to the warriors, with an extra pitcher of ale or wine, on the understanding that they would assist her with any patrons who might prove unruly. If any drunken ceorl or sailor was stupid enough to make a nuisance of himself, there were always several willing warriors at Genofeva's tables ready to beat some sense into him. As a result, there was seldom trouble.

Cynan sipped the watered wine and watched the men talk. The sun was hot in this secluded patio and he wished he had thought to bring his hat. Gram was still teasing Eadgard, while Halinard was telling anyone who would listen about the wonderful fish pie. The Frank was at ease and happy here in Liyon, surrounded by folk he could understand and who understood him. He missed his family back in Ubbanford, but where this crowded city was a novelty to Cynan, to Halinard, who had lived much of his life in the city of Rodomo, it was like returning home.

The rest of the men laughed and talked, relaxed and happy in the sunshine of another fine day. The only ones who did not appear content were Baducing and Beobrand. Cynan wasn't concerned about Beobrand. The thegn of Ubbanford was prone to dark moods and they all knew it was best to avoid him when he was in such a humour. Cynan seldom tried to speak to Beobrand at such times. He knew from bitter experience he would receive only curt words in return for his interest. Beobrand would no doubt drink more than usual that evening, before falling into a troubled sleep. With any luck, whatever dark thoughts assailed him would have passed like a storm in the night, and he would awaken, bleary-eyed and with a throbbing head, but in a brighter mood.

Baducing was another matter. The stocky novice monk had seemed happy these last weeks. He had been overjoyed to read Annemund's books, and he had bored everyone with his excitement each time he discovered another tome his masters in Albion had spoken of. Most times when they all got together, Baducing would end up sitting apart with Wilfrid, deep in conversation about the things they had found in Annemund's library. But now, Baducing seemed ill at ease. Where he was usually quick to smile, now his mouth was twisted in a scowl. And where he would normally regale anyone who would listen, and even those who did not wish to, about his latest revelation, now he sat in glum silence, staring into his cup of wine.

Cynan wondered what was troubling him. It was Baducing who had sent a messenger to Dalfinus' palace that morning asking for them all to meet here at noon. Cynan was about to ask him why he had summoned them, when Genofeva came out of the house carrying a large pie.

"Ah, magnificent," said Halinard, smacking his lips and grinning at Eadgard. "Now you will know the taste of heaven, my friend."

The men cleared a space and Genofeva placed the steaming pie on the table, then bustled about them, first serving the men, and then collecting empty bowls and plates.

Eadgard lifted a slice of the pie to his face and sniffed it.

Genofeva stood by, balancing the teetering piles of plates, watching expectantly.

"Go on," urged Halinard. "I promise you, you will not be disappointed."

Eadgard cut a piece with his eating knife, blew on it to cool it, then tentatively placed it in his mouth. As he chewed, he began to nod and then to smile. "Delicious," he said in Frankish to Genofeva, before shovelling more of the food into his mouth.

The normally sombre widow beamed with pleasure, then made her way back inside. Cynan was not overly fond of fish. He preferred meat and had been looking forward to the mutton Gram had mentioned, but Eadgard's response to the pie, and Halinard's praise, filled him with anticipation.

Taking a bite, Cynan savoured the rich flavours and textures. The pastry crumbled, the hot filling was creamy, with chunks of firm fish, steeped in a thick herb-rich sauce.

"Hmm," said Eadgard, wiping his bearded face with the back of his hand. "Tastes like a kelpie's cunny."

Laughter erupted around the table and it was all Cynan could do not to spit pieces of fish and pastry. As the laughter subsided, Cynan noticed that Baducing had not joined in with the mirth. Unlike some Christ followers, he was not usually one to frown on bawdy jesting, and again Cynan wondered what vexed the man.

Baducing met Cynan's quizzical stare.

"Where is Wilfrid?" he asked without warning.

Cynan shrugged.

"I thought he would have met us here. We came directly from the arena."

"Weren't you supposed to be looking at a relic together today?" asked Bleddyn.

The men around the table had quietened now, listening intently.

"Yes, we were," Baducing said with a sigh. "A sliver of the

shin of Saint Orientius; a thing of great wonder. Annemund also has a copy of Orientius' *Commonitorium*. But it seems Wilfrid's interest in books and relics has waned of late."

So that was it. Baducing was angry with his friend.

"It seems to me," said Ingwald, "that as fascinated as Wilfrid is with the Scriptures and saints' bones, he finds what lies beneath a lady's skirts vastly more interesting."

"Don't we all?" said Gram.

Ingwald smiled. Eadgard guffawed.

"Few things capture my attention more," he said around a mouthful of pie.

Several of the men chuckled, but Beobrand's face was stony.

"Are we going to have an angry husband come looking for him then? Like in Quentovic?" he said. "Or worse," and a frown furrowed his forehead, "has one perhaps already found him?"

"If any man is angered by Wilfrid's dalliances," said Attor with a twinkle in his eye, "it will be more likely a father, not a husband, who comes looking for the lad."

"A father?" asked Beobrand. "Who?"

"You must be the only one who doesn't know," said Baducing.

"Know what?" asked Beobrand, his tone hardening.

Attor shook his head at Beobrand's confusion.

"That Wilfrid has been drinking from the waters of a forbidden pond."

When Beobrand still seemed uncertain, Baducing sighed.

"I thought it was common knowledge that Wilfrid has become... close to Dalfinus' daughter."

"He would not dare," said Beobrand, aghast. "Surely he is not such a fool."

"He is young," said Cynan, as if that was enough explanation for foolish actions. "And what he has been up to is obvious to any with eyes. But you have perhaps not been looking far afield of late."

Beobrand glared at him and Cynan immediately regretted his words. Beobrand was in no mood for taunting.

"I meant nothing by it," Cynan said. "Just that you have seemed..." He hesitated. "Distracted."

"And well I might," growled Beobrand. "We should have left Liyon long before now. We still have far to travel and I swore an oath to Oswiu and Eanflæd that I would see Wilfrid safely to the holy city. I will fulfil my duty. My word still has some meaning." He rubbed his half-hand against his forehead as if his head hurt. "But we all heard the rumours of war once again coming to Northumbria." A few days earlier, they had met a merchant who told tales of disquiet to the north of Bernicia, in the lands of the Picts. "My place is there, defending our land. Protecting our people. It is not my task to dally in this city while young Wilfrid..." He cast about for a suitable turn of phrase. "Dips his quill."

The men grinned at that. They had grown comfortable in Liyon. And Wilfrid was not the only one to have found a woman to keep him warm at night. And yet Cynan noted that several of those gathered around the table were nodding in agreement with their lord's sentiment. It seemed Beobrand was not the only one to have grown restless.

"I am glad to hear you say as much," said Baducing. "I had hoped that Wilfrid would be here. I thought that perhaps we could all agree, for my mind is made up."

"Indeed, Baducing," said Beobrand, "and what is it that you have decided?"

"I have enjoyed Bishop Annemund's hospitality for long enough. I could spend many more weeks reading his books, but Liyon was never my goal. A group of merchants are setting out southward in two days' time. They are heading for Roma. That has ever been my destination, so my father's men and I will be leaving with them."

Chapter 14

Wilfrid drew the warm spring air into his lungs. The sunlight dappled through the canopy of trees above him. The afternoon was alive with the drone of insects in the undergrowth. The scent of clover and sage was heady after the stench of dung and the refuse from the thousands of inhabitants of Liyon. The smell of cities was something he wasn't sure he would ever grow accustomed to. Even far up on the hill where Dalfinus' palace was built, the stink of the place was ever present.

Sighing, he wandered down the slope, following the well-worn path that threaded between the trees, down from the small settlement, where he had left Thagmar and the others, towards the waterfall that the old man in the village had told him was there. Far off, back up the incline where the riders were, distant shouting reached Wilfrid's ears. Evidently someone did not like having to pay their taxes. He smiled at that thought. Who liked parting with their property? He paused for a moment to listen, but could not make out what was being said, or by whom. With a shrug, he pressed on. He had more important worries of his own and was already imagining the sensation of dipping his feet in the cool water of the stream that flowed in the valley.

The shouting faded as he strode further down the slope. Pleased to be alone for once and far from the arguing and noise, he smiled as the tranquillity of the forest enveloped him. Now he could collect his thoughts. In the city there was never a moment of true peace. Even when walking in Dalfinus' walled garden, there would be the muffled rumble of the city streets. Shouts from hawkers, the calls of boatmen on the river far below. And whilst the thralls in the palace often stood in demure silence, their presence was unnerving.

The only time the streets were quiet was after dark, but then they were more dangerous than the densest forest. But instead of wolves that might prey on a lonely traveller, in Liyon, cutpurses and thieves could spring from any shadow to relieve an unsuspecting man of his coin, or even his life. Despite often finding Beobrand's boorish company stifling, Wilfrid could not deny he had been glad of the man's presence and that of his Black Shields when needing to traverse the city at night. They had all heard tell of the men who had gone missing after staggering into the darkness, sodden with wine, never to be seen again. Perhaps they had fallen into one of the rivers, people mused. More likely, it seemed to Wilfrid, they had been robbed, murdered and then thrown unceremoniously into the deep, cold waters of the Sona or Rôno, hiding any evidence of the crime.

He thought back to the years he had spent on Lindisfarena amongst the brethren. Speaking had been frowned upon there. Wilfrid had lost count of the times he had been scolded and even beaten for raising his voice, or speaking during silent meal times. He had thought then that he yearned for the noise of a great hall, like his father's home – the hall that should have been his – filled with the laughter and riddling of gesithas, men loyal to him alone.

But now that he had spent months in the company of warriors, residing in the halls and palaces of rich men, his desires had begun to change. And now his future had taken a sudden turn he could never have anticipated.

Ahead he could make out the sound of cascading water, and

he hurried down to a place where the land loomed, rocky and sheer above the narrow valley floor. On the far side of a large, shallow pool, water rushed white in a torrent down the slick face of the rock, to fragment and shatter into rivulets on a huge boulder. The myriad small waterfalls formed there, tumbled into the tranquil pond below. The ground was muddy here, and Wilfrid could imagine where the womenfolk would wash their clothes, slapping and scrubbing them on the flat rocks.

The old man had been right to speak in awed tones of the cascade. It was majestic and soothing. To look at it, he would have imagined it would have filled the vale with noise, but its constant, distant whisper was calming.

He listened to the afternoon. Doves cooed somewhere far off, their voice still clear over the sigh of the water. A lone woodlark sang its piercing, fluty trill. There were no other sounds but the hissing of the cataract. Unlacing and tugging off his shoes, he made his way cautiously through the shallows to a dry expanse of rock that was lit in a lancing beam of afternoon sunshine. He sat there, dangling his bare feet in the cold water, revelling in the sensation of warmth on his face and coolness on his feet, and of being alone and without the commotion that had been such a constant part of life these last weeks. He needed to think. His course had been set out for him and yet, was there a way he could still alter his path? Did he even want to?

One of the only truly quiet places he had found in Liyon was Annemund's library, with its high windows and dusty, familiar smell of vellum and ink that brought back memories of the scriptorium on Lindisfarena. Wilfrid enjoyed reading in companionable silence, sitting across from Baducing. The two of them could remain like that, with their heads lowered, poring over passages of the Hexapla and the other fine manuscripts as the day grew old and it became impossible to continue reading by the dimming light that pooled around the windows.

Within the library it was always cool and quiet, and Wilfrid would often break off from his reading to marvel at the thickness of the stone walls and how straightly the slabs were cut. He had begun to question his own ambition of having a hall like his father's, with a high thatched roof and great oaken beams swirled with carvings of animals. He had known nothing larger than the mead halls of lords and kings in Albion, so that is what his mind had conjured whenever he'd looked to the future. But recently, he'd started dreaming of stone buildings, with columns and statues so realistic they looked as if they could begin to move at any moment. The further south the pilgrims had travelled, the more lavish the buildings, and the more the Frankish nobles attempted to emulate the men of Roma with their own constructions.

The future that in Wilfrid's mind's eye had always been filled with the flicker of great hearth fires and the roaring sound of gathered warriors, now changed to quiet, towering buildings of stone, rising up from the windswept hills of his homeland of Bernicia. For what better way to display power than by constructing buildings grander than any that remained on the island of Albion? This was one of the reasons he had been so keen to build a rapport with the noble brothers of Liyon. Beyond possessing the wealth and power that he coveted, they also had access to the craftsmen and artisans who could help him create his dream. Had that dream been shattered now? Or had it been transformed into something equally impressive, or perhaps even more so?

One evening, Baducing and Wilfrid had sat at a table in a corner of Genofeva's warm house, drinking wine and eating marinated herrings. It was raining hard and the place had been crowded. After the day of silent reading and reflection in the library, the harsh sound of so many men battered Wilfrid's nerves as he told Baducing of his ambitions.

"One day," he said, raising his voice to be heard over the din, "I will build a great stone edifice. It will be the largest and most important place of worship in all of Albion." At Baducing's perplexed expression, he added, "All this I will do to honour the name of our Heavenly Father, of course."

"Of course," replied Baducing, and Wilfrid thought he detected a hint of sarcasm in his friend's tone. "Such a place sounds wonderful, as long as there is a scriptorium. Somewhere I can read the word of the Lord in peace, that I might grow closer to Him."

"Oh, there will be books and calm." Wilfrid had sipped on his wine, letting his imagination flow like the stream in which his feet now soothed. "And there will be richly decorated sleeping quarters for you and other visiting dignitaries."

Baducing shook his head.

"You know me," he said. "I do not need comfort. Just the Scriptures and somewhere to worship. And I think that is how it should be, don't you? Is that not what we have been taught? That it is through hard work, poverty and prayer that we will attain glory?"

Wilfrid had said nothing in response to that. Too often he had felt the rebukes from the pious Baducing. He liked the man well enough. He was a stalwart companion and despite the look of the ceorl about him, he had the keenest mind of anyone Wilfrid had met. And yet, in spite of his numerous virtues, Baducing did have a blind spot that led him to appear hypocritical in Wilfrid's eyes. Baducing's father had provided him with his own warrior escort, and he seemed content enough to accept Annemund's hospitality, but still he preached to Wilfrid about poverty.

The following day, after Baducing had headed to Annemund's library following mass, Wilfrid had approached the bishop. At first, Annemund's guards barred his way, but the grey-haired prelate saw him from the gilded litter he rode in, carried on the broad shoulders of four burly slaves. Annemund smiled and waved Wilfrid forward. The guards opened ranks and Wilfrid fell into step beside the bishop's covered chair. It was a warm, humid day after the rain. Rivulets of sweat trickled down the slaves' faces and necks. Their linen robes were soaked and plastered to their skin. The smell of their bodies mingled with that rising from the churned mud and manure underfoot and the countless other odours that wafted along the streets near the west bank of the Sona.

Each day for mass, more frequently on holy days, Annemund made this journey from his palace to the church of Saint John. A score of scarlet-cloaked warriors marched in serried ranks around the bishop and the slaves, keeping the faithful safely away from Annemund. Two servants handed out small slivers of silver to the beggars that thronged the street awaiting the passing of the bishop and his almoners.

"It does them good to receive more than just spiritual sustenance from me," said Annemund. "Reminds them that God is great."

Wilfrid's gaze flicked to the golden thread in Annemund's robes. The silken cap upon the bishop's head was adorned with coloured crystals and pearls. The golden pastoral staff he held in his left hand was studded with garnets.

Annemund, seeing where Wilfrid was looking, smiled.

"You disapprove of my wealth?"

Wilfrid felt his face grow hot. He did not wish to anger the bishop, but, despite his own ambitions, he could not deny that he felt a certain unease at Annemund's display of riches before the paupers. He could not bring himself to openly criticise the bishop, but he knew how his teachers on Lindisfarena would have felt about such pomp.

"Baducing says that by prayer and poverty we learn to be nearer Christ."

Annemund grinned. Wilfrid could not be certain if he was smiling at what Baducing had said, or at Wilfrid's clumsy attempt at veiling his own criticism behind Baducing's words.

"Does he indeed?" replied Annemund, waving absently to the passers-by who peered at him as he swayed above the heads of the burly thralls and warriors. "That is perhaps sufficient for men like Baducing. But he lacks your ambition, Wilfrid. Do not look surprised. My brother and I have both seen it in you. We are not young and we have seen men rise to power and then, all too often, lose everything. You are no ordinary man. You are destined for more than the life of a lowly monk, I would say. I am certain you will rise to a prominent position, and I would not be surprised if you hung onto your power once you are there." He appraised him with a sidelong look. "You have that way about you."

Wilfrid blushed, gladdened by the man's praise.

"And what way is that, Your Excellency?"

Annemund chuckled.

"You know how to set your sails with the prevailing wind so that it always carries you towards your goal. That will serve you well, even in stormy weather."

Ever since he had been forced to leave his father's hall shortly after he had remarried, Wilfrid had dreamt of acquiring enough power to own more land than any of his kin. At first he had been dejected to have been sent to Lindisfarena, surrounded by praying, poor monks. But over time, he came to believe that within the church, he had found the path that would lead him to that power. He recalled the first time he had read the story of Yosef in the book of Genesis. Wilfrid had instantly identified with the young man destined for glory who was turned upon by his own family, only to have them return to him years later begging for food, when he had risen to be a mighty lord in Ægypte. Wilfrid wondered whether he would be as forgiving as Yosef in the same situation. He longed for the day in which his father, his second wife – Wilfrid could never bring himself to refer to her as his mother – and his three brothers would all look up to him and comprehend that the young man they had underestimated now held authority over both their earthly forms, and their immortal souls.

He wondered if Annemund's words were mere flattery. But to what end? What reason could such an influential man have to flatter him, a young novice from the north? Besides, had not Queen Eanflæd also believed in him enough to provide him with funds and guards for him to achieve his goal of visiting Roma? He had been amazed how quickly his plans had fallen into place after that. He would soon reach the holy city, and there he would cultivate relationships with bishops, cardinals and even the *Pontifex maximus*, the bishop of Roma himself. With Eanflæd's gold, he planned to acquire relics and books that would elevate his status and help him to further his ends in Albion.

"What value is there in learning," the bishop continued, cutting into Wilfrid's thoughts, "if you are defenceless?" Annemund waved a hand to encompass the guards around them. "Poverty is for peasants, not for bishops. A bishop must show the people that God has power. That is his duty, as much as it is to guide them and provide the poor with alms."

Wilfrid's heart soared to hear Annemund speak words that echoed his own thoughts. Wilfrid had felt like an outsider on Lindisfarena, but here was one of the most powerful men of the church in Frankia, giving him permission to pursue his dreams of wealth and influence within the structures of the church.

"How do things go with Rotrudis?" Annemund asked, turning the conversation in a direction Wilfrid had not anticipated. They had reached the bishop's palace and Wilfrid stepped back as the litter was lowered slowly to the ground. The mention of Dalfinus' daughter had shaken him, and he offered his hand to assist Annemund, taking the moment to gather his thoughts.

Rotrudis had at first been an unexpected pleasure in the palace household. She was young, pretty and plump, and when he had noticed that she was drawn to him, without thinking, he had focused his attention on her, as he had learnt to do over this last year. Ever since his stay in Cantwareburh, where his handsome angular features and quick mind had found him sharing the bed of a wealthy widow, he had realised this was something he could use to his advantage, both in obtaining physical pleasure, but also riches and influence. Putting his newfound skills to good use, he had found it easy enough to secure a rich lover in Quentovic. She had diverted him through those long, cold days. Such was the ease with which he'd seduced these women, it had even crossed his mind that perhaps the queen of Northumbria might have been more interested in his charm and his youthful body, than in helping him to enrich his immortal soul. Eanflæd was a beautiful woman and on more than one occasion he had lain awake at night regretting not having pursued the matter. When he returned to Albion, he vowed to see whether he could persuade the queen to part her legs for him. The idea of bedding a queen always sent a shiver down his spine.

And so it was that when Rotrudis had approached him, he'd seen a chance of advancement he would not squander. He had laughed at the girl's jokes and listened to her inane chatter about her maids and the latest gossip. Soon they had been sharing secretive kisses in shadowed corners, and she had become increasingly passionate in their embraces.

He had known it was foolish, but the flesh is weak, he told himself when first he had lain with Rotrudis. To his horror, she had cried out when he had thrust into her, and there had been blood on her thighs and sheets after their coupling. His first thought had been that Dalfinus would kill him if he found out that his guest had deflowered his daughter. Then, immediately after that thought, he wondered if it were possible for a woman to bear a child from her first time with a man. The woman in Cantwareburh had taught him enough to spill his seed outside of her body to avoid an unwanted pregnancy, but she had warned that the method was not always effective.

"Especially with such a young, virile stallion as you," she had said, her cheeks flushed and her forehead beaded with sweat from their exertions. "But the risk is worth it."

He had thought the risk a small one to him then. He cared nothing for what might happen after he had gone. In Cantwareburh his lover was a widow with no close kin. In Quentovic the biggest threat to him was that the woman's husband would find out. But here, in Liyon, Rotrudis was the daughter of the *comes*, the niece of the bishop, both men whom he hoped would help him on his climb through the echelons of the church. He could not allow the soft flesh of the girl to distract him from his path.

In truth, he would rather bed Rotrudis' mother, Gudula. He had seen the hunger in the eyes of the lady of the palace when she looked at him. She was a handsome woman, and he remembered fondly how willing and grateful his older lovers in Quentovic and Cantwareburh had been. But if he had been concerned that a dalliance with Dalfinus' daughter might lead to trouble, the thought of being caught with the *comes'* wife was beyond imagining.

So he had taken to avoiding them both. When the desire came upon him, he had found one of the thralls, a lithe, dark-haired thing from Baetica, did not complain at his advances. When he caught her alone, lifting up her skirts and satisfying himself, it seemed to him that she even enjoyed the experience.

Keeping out of Rotrudis' path became increasingly difficult. The more he avoided her, the more besotted with him she became. She would have the servants and thralls inform her of his whereabouts, and soon there was nowhere within the palace walls where he was safe from her simpering, clinging presence. He cursed his own weakness and vanity that had helped to nurture the young girl's love for him. He did not know how to push her away without having her moping about the palace weeping pitifully, which would not do. He lived in fear that she might tell her father about their trysts.

He supposed in some ways he should thank her, for her obsessive nature had driven him away from her father's palace, which meant he had spent much longer than he might have done in Annemund's library. In the bishop he saw an ally he must cultivate. He had believed at first that Dalfinus was the more powerful of the two brothers, but he had quickly come to understand that if he was to advance his position within the church, Annemund would prove the more valuable of the two. Besides, it seemed to Wilfrid that, despite the usual bickering between siblings, Dalfinus never denied his younger brother anything, meaning that to be close to one, brought the favour of the other.

That day when he had approached Annemund on the way back from mass, Wilfrid had believed he was finally done with the worry of Rotrudis. A week or more had gone by since he had last seen her, apart from afar at a feast where she had mercifully spent most of the time ignoring him and speaking with a minor noble from a nearby province. Wilfrid had thought she had forgotten about him, that maybe she had redirected her affections to this lordling from Tolosa. But at the mention of her name by Annemund, Wilfrid's breath had caught in his chest.

"You look as if you have spied a ghost," chuckled the bishop, stepping down from the sedan chair. "I thought you liked the girl."

"I do. Of course I do," Wilfrid replied quickly, forcing a smile.

Without a word, the slaves hefted the empty chair and carried it away, leaving Wilfrid alone with Annemund. Or at least out of earshot of any servants, thralls or guards. The gate to the city was closed and the clamour of the beggars was reduced to a muted murmur.

"I know the girl thinks much of you, young man. Many men have approached my brother for her hand, but Dalfinus dotes on the girl and no suitor has lived up to his expectations."

Wilfrid had listened, nodding, his mind racing. He did not

like the way this conversation was going, but he could see no way to avoid what was coming. Annemund placed a hand on his shoulder.

"Lords have come from as far afield as Guiana, seeking to take Rotrudis as their prize. They have offered lands and gold, but Dalfinus has turned them all away. But in you, I believe he sees a young man worthy of his daughter. Do not look so scared, Wilfrid." The bishop squeezed his shoulder. "I have no son and I have long thought of who would be my heir. In you I believe I have found one who could govern in my stead." Annemund spoke the words with conviction, as if he had long rehearsed them. Wilfrid could scarcely believe what he was hearing. He had grown close to the bishop over these last weeks, but this was unexpected and sudden.

"I would have you stay here, with me," the bishop went on, holding Wilfrid tightly and fixing him with an earnest stare. "You would become the spiritual ruler of some of my lands to the south. The tithe from those parishes would go to you. I have already spoken to my brother, and I am sure I can convince him to allow you to wed Rotrudis. Thus, you would gain an uncle, a father and a wife."

Wilfrid swallowed against the dryness in his throat.

"Your Excellency," he said at last, his tone giving away his surprise, despite his attempt at appearing calm, "this is a most generous offer, and one I had not expected." A question scratched at his thoughts. "But what do you get from such a bargain?"

Annemund laughed out loud. Some of the guards at the gate glanced at the two of them quizzically.

"That is one of the things both Dalfinus and I admire about you. You are as direct as you are ambitious. I need a man by my side whom I can trust. Someone who is clever enough to understand that the church cannot be separate from the games played at court. Who can see several moves ahead of the king, queen, the lords and the *major domus*. A man who understands languages easily, who can speak to peasants and princes alike, and someone who can broker agreements with the royal houses of Albion. You are all of those things, Wilfrid, and I predict a great future for you."

A kingfisher flashed in the sunlight over the water, catching Wilfrid's eye with the streak of its brilliant red and blue plumage against the white of the waterfall. He sighed, noting how the sun had lowered perceptibly. He would have to return to the riders soon.

His head still reeled when he remembered the conversation with Annemund. He had thought he would need to work for years to build up his reputation and power, and then, in a moment of humid sunshine in the courtyard before the bishop's palace, everything he had yearned for had been offered to him.

He had stammered for a time, unsure what to say about any of it, especially the proposed marriage with Rotrudis. The thought of spending his life with the vacuous girl had darkened his mood, but when he had expressed his concern that Dalfinus might not agree with the match, Annemund's face had grown hard.

"Perhaps you would care to tell him how you sullied his daughter, taking her maidenhead before she was wed?"

Wilfrid had blanched, but had not sought to deny the accusation. To do so would only weaken his position.

"My niece is not as discreet as she could be," Annemund went on, his face stern. "And the woman who washes her sheets is a good Christian. She confesses all to her priest."

The bishop's steward, a tall, austere man, began to approach, but Annemund held up his hand to halt him.

"And her priest confides in his spiritual father. By my reckoning, it will yet be some months before her gravid state begins to show."

"She is with child?" asked Wilfrid. He could not entirely keep the whining tone from his voice.

"Truly only God and time will tell the truth of that, but she has said as much to her maidservant, and there is no reason to doubt the girl. She is young and foolish, it is true, but she is no idiot." He applied more pressure on his grip of Wilfrid's shoulder, making him wince. "And I note that you do not deny that she could be, or that you are the father. If you are married before her belly swells, my brother need never know what occurred between Rotrudis and you. I need not remind you that he is not a forgiving man."

Wilfrid felt his strength leaving him. He wished he could be seated, but the bishop held him firmly. This had been his worst fear. That all his plans and ambitions might be destroyed because of a moment of weakness and lust. And yet, at the same moment as he was hearing the news of Rotrudis' pregnancy, so too was Annemund providing him with a solution, a way of escaping Dalfinus' wrath and also advancing his own fortunes drastically.

The idea of Dalfinus as his father-in-law filled Wilfrid with dread, but even as the threads of his thoughts tangled and unravelled, he could see that if accepting the marriage to Rotrudis would gain him everything else Annemund had spoken of, it was a price worth paying. He could do much worse than her, he reasoned. At least the girl would prove a willing and energetic mate. She had made that very clear. And there would always be thralls when he tired of her.

"The offer you have made me is generous," he said, pleased that his voice was steady now. "More generous than anything I could have hoped for, and yet I am still unclear as to why you would want to offer such things to me."

"The fact that you are asking this question, answers it in part. You have a cold mind, Wilfrid. Perhaps you are yet too young to know how rare such a thing is, but the likes of you are not common."

"Baducing is clever."

"He is. Pious too, and perhaps more learned than you will

ever be. But the man I seek needs many more traits. Besides, Baducing would never be content to stay here. His mind is set on reaching Roma."

"I could not carry on to Roma?"

"Perhaps, after the wedding and the babe is born. But even if Baducing were interested in staying here, he does not have your many gifts. Such as your ability to befriend men." He hesitated and raised an eyebrow. "As well as women. Dalfinus has not warmed to him as he has to you. And it would serve me well to have another pair of eyes and ears close to my brother."

These last words had made Wilfrid ponder everything he thought he had known about the two siblings. He had believed them to be so close that they shared everything, including their secrets, but this conversation made him wonder. Did Annemund not trust his brother? He spoke of obtaining information from servants in Dalfinus' palace. What other spies did he have there? Were some of the warriors who seemed to serve both masters truly reporting to the bishop? Was their loyalty to one brother or the other, or both? And what of the blond-haired killer, Thagmar?

Thinking of the leader of the guards brought Wilfrid back to the present. His feet were numb from the cold stream water. He pulled them out of the current and shuffled further up the rock so that they could dry in the rays of the sun that still filtered through the trees. Pulling his cloak from around his shoulders, he dabbed at his feet to dry them. Rising, he sprang over the shallow water to the bank where he had left his shoes. His movement startled the kingfisher that had been sitting on a twig, watching the water for prey. In a fluttered flash of brilliant feathers the bird vanished into the tree-shade further downstream.

Lacing his shoes, Wilfrid gave one last lingering look at the cascade. It was peaceful here and he longed to tarry, but he knew that was not possible. Turning away from the water with a sigh, he headed back towards the small cluster of houses where he had left Thagmar and the other riders. Thagmar had said they would not take long and he did not wish to anger the man. Wilfrid had enough to contend with, without provoking the fair-haired warrior with the cold, killer's eyes.

He had wondered for a time how Annemund permitted himself to be aligned with such a man as Thagmar, who seemed to enjoy violence. But he thought he was beginning to understand the bishop now. To Annemund, Thagmar was a tool, just like any other. A knife he could wield, through his brother's commands perhaps, to perform acts that would be frowned upon by the more sanctimonious members of the flock.

"The man's methods may be distasteful to me," Annemund had said to him, "but he does what he is commanded and he gets tasks done."

Wilfrid supposed Annemund looked upon him in the same way. How had he underestimated the man so? When Dalfinus had asked him to accompany Thagmar on this trip, Wilfrid had at first taken it at face value: that Thagmar was travelling to some small settlements that had not yet paid their annual tithes to the church or the *comes*, and one of those settlements, a small village called Cerdun, was near the site of the cave in which Saint Lienard had dwelt. Wilfrid had never heard of this Lienard, but Dalfinus had assured him that he was a most holy hermit, and that the place of his isolation would without a doubt be of interest to Wilfrid, himself a holy pilgrim.

However, Wilfrid soon learnt that it was Annemund who had suggested he go, and if it were merely for the chance to visit the grotto where this Saint Lienard had lived, then surely Baducing would have been invited too. Perhaps Annemund wanted Wilfrid far from Liyon while he spoke to his brother about Wilfrid's future with his daughter. Wilfrid wondered what reception he would receive on his return.

Or maybe this trip was some sort of trial Annemund had set for Wilfrid. Was it a test of his loyalty to him? He was certain that any number of the warriors that rode with him would report back to the bishop. He would have to be on his guard at all times.

In any case, he had been pleased to leave the city, with its stench and noise, and at first he had been happy to be away from Beobrand and his dour judgemental presence. But as they grew more distant from Liyon, and the mountains loomed ever higher on the horizon, Wilfrid wondered whether it would have been more sensible to have brought Beobrand and his warriors with them. The man was oath-sworn to protect him. And yet, surely Thagmar and his score of warriors would be protection enough from any foes. Unless – and with the thought came the prickle of fear under his scalp – Thagmar had been given some other instructions to which Wilfrid was not privy. Beobrand, and perhaps his Waelisc man, Cynan, were the only warriors Wilfrid knew who might stand a chance against the Frank.

He hurried up the slope through the cool puddles of shade beneath the trees. A forest creature shrieked further up the hill. He shivered. He should have told Beobrand where he was going. He was a fool not to have brought him. Thagmar was Annemund's instrument, a killer who would do his master's bidding without question. What Wilfrid had not thought about until this moment was that he had his own implacable warrior in his service. Beobrand might not obey his every command, but whatever he thought of the man, Wilfrid knew he could be trusted. And like a fool, he had left Beobrand, arguably the deadliest warrior in all of Albion, back in Liyon.

The animal cried out again, a piercing, high-pitched scream.

Wilfrid's skin prickled. The scratching finger of fear ran down his back, making him shudder. That was not the sound of a woodland beast, he realised with a jolt of panic. It was the howling scream of a man. A man in agony, and in fear for his life.

Chapter 15

Beobrand kicked his gelding's ribs hard to urge the beast to canter up the steep rise. The horse snorted and shook its head in annoyance. Beobrand reined in and patted the animal's neck.

"Sorry, boy," he whispered, ashamed of his actions. None of this was the dumb beast's fault. There could be nobody to blame apart from that fool Wilfrid, and perhaps Beobrand himself for not seeing what had apparently been known by all his men.

Attor caught up with him, slowing his own mount to stand beside the gelding as the others lumbered up the slope to join them. Cynan and Ingwald had ridden some way ahead to scout, and Beobrand saw their shapes through the trees in the valley below from time to time.

"We won't catch them any quicker if you push the horses too hard," Attor said.

Beobrand glanced at the older man and sighed. His pleasure at seeing Attor strong and healthy again was diluted by the fury that he was unable to completely control.

"I know you speak the truth," Beobrand said, as Halinard, Eadgard, Gram, Grindan and Bleddyn trotted up to the knap of the hill in a clatter of hooves and jingle of harness. "But I cannot throw off the feeling that Wilfrid is in danger."

"You think Dalfinus knows?" asked Attor.

Beobrand frowned, running the fingers of his half-hand through the gelding's long mane.

"He gave nothing away if he does, but the man is no fool, and I would wager he has had his eyes open wider than mine have been of late."

Following Baducing's declaration that he was leaving, Beobrand had gone in search of Wilfrid at the *comes'* palace. There had been no sign of the novice and eventually, after enquiring of the steward, servants and thralls to no avail, Beobrand had been ushered into a cool room where he was told Dalfinus would meet him. A servant had filled a glass goblet with watered wine, but Beobrand had barely sipped at it. His stomach churned as he thought of what might have befallen Wilfrid. His only task was to protect the young man. If he failed to do that, Eanflæd would never forgive him. That thought stabbed at him like a seax blade.

After a long wait, Dalfinus had swept into the room. Pouring himself a glass of wine, he turned to Beobrand.

"I hear you are looking for young Wilfrid," he said, just as Beobrand was about to speak.

Halinard began to interpret, but Beobrand understood enough Frankish by now to gather the gist of Dalfinus' words.

"Yes," he said, forcing a relaxed tone, "that is true."

Dalfinus took a deep draught of wine, holding Beobrand's gaze over the rim of the blue glass. Dalfinus did not blink and his cold glare felt like a challenge. There was something about that look that spoke of shadowy depths and hidden secrets. Not for the first time, Beobrand wondered what Dalfinus had done to Wilfrid. He recalled the men who had broken the peace on the journey from Paris. Dalfinus would have no qualms about slaying a man who sullied his daughter's honour.

Dalfinus lowered his glass and smiled, showing his teeth.

"If only all questions I am asked had such easy answers," he said. "Wilfrid is with Thagmar."

At the mention of the blond captain of the guard, Beobrand tensed, but he did not let his anxiety show.

"Oh, and where are they? I have looked all over the palace."

Dalfinus chuckled.

"You will not find them here." He paused again to take another mouthful of wine. It seemed to Beobrand that the man knew exactly what he was doing and was enjoying dragging this out. Beobrand could feel his anger building inside him, so he clenched his fists at his side and fought to remain calm.

"Indeed?" he said. "Where should I look then?"

"They are heading to Cerdun. It is a few days ride from here. They should return in a sennight, or perhaps a few days more."

"Why are they riding so far from Liyon?"

"Thagmar had his orders to travel there. There are taxes and tithes to be collected." Halinard was struggling to keep up with some of the words in Anglisc now and Beobrand gestured impatiently for him to continue. "I told Wilfrid he could see the grotto where it is said Saint Lienard dwelt for many years. The cave is near Thagmar's destination. He seemed all too pleased to accept. Truth be told, I think he was becoming tired of the city."

On hearing this, Beobrand had hurried back to Annemund's palace, where he asked Baducing to delay his departure. He had an uneasy feeling that Dalfinus was hiding something, but if he could reach Wilfrid and return to Liyon, they could all then continue on their way to Roma. It was becoming ever clearer that their welcome in the city would soon turn sour. If Dalfinus did not already know of the encounters between his daughter and Wilfrid, it was only a matter of time before he found out.

But Baducing was adamant. He had tarried long enough and apparently he had asked Wilfrid repeatedly these past weeks if they could travel on. Now he saw an opportunity to travel safely onwards and he would wait no longer.

"If you can return here before we leave," he said, "I would of course be more than happy to have you as my travelling companions. If not, I hope we meet again on the road, or in Roma itself."

Beobrand could not blame the man for wanting to move on. He felt the same way, but was tethered to Wilfrid like a ship tied to an anchor rock. He bade Baducing a safe journey and gripped his forearm in the warrior grip, for the man had proven himself a valued addition to the warband during the fight in the forest.

Thinking of the ambush on the queen put Beobrand further on edge. He recalled the strangeness of the attack. The number of brigands with their well-honed weapons. He wondered if Brocard had unearthed any further information about the ambush and who might have been behind it. He guessed he would never know, unless they happened to cross paths again when he travelled back from Roma. But for that, he must first find Wilfrid and escort him there.

"You think we will reach the place by nightfall?" he asked Attor.

"Dalfinus said we would get there before dark and you have been pushing the horses. From what he told us, I think it will be just over that hill. The other side of those trees."

Beobrand looked up. The sun was not far past its zenith and the sky was clear apart from some white wisps of cloud far off to the east over the mountains that rose in the haze.

"I hope you are right," he said, heeling his gelding into a trot and fighting the urge to gallop. "With luck, they might have stayed there and we can press on back to Liyon and join Baducing." Even as he said it, he thought it unlikely. Dalfinus had told them the names of several places Thagmar needed to visit and the captain did not seem like the kind of man who would seek rest when there was work to be done.

It was cool under the trees. Puddles of sunshine lit the earthen path. In many places, where the shade remained for most of the day, the track was churned, dark mud, and there were stagnant puddles of scum-covered water left from the spring rains. Despite the warmth of the days, some of those puddles would remain wet for most of the year, he thought. Perhaps only drying in the height of summer.

They rode close together, the sounds of their mounts echoing back from the densely packed trees, giving them the impression there were more riders out there in the wood-shade, beyond their sight. They passed a narrow, overgrown track that led into the darkness beneath the thick tree canopy. At the entrance, from the boughs of an ash dangled tattered ribbons and crudely fashioned straw dolls, most weathered and tattered by time. Beobrand slowed and peered into the gloom, but saw nothing save trees and bracken. A crow cackled high above them. Attor crossed himself and Eadgard cursed, spitting into the mud and reaching to touch the iron head of his axe.

"It's only a bird," said Beobrand. Without thinking, his fingers caressed the Thunor's hammer amulet he wore. The unfamiliar shape of Erchinoald's ring dangling beside the amulet made him aware of what he was doing. He lowered his hand. "Come on."

Cynan and Ingwald were waiting for them where the forest thinned. Beobrand's gelding whinnied a greeting to the other horses, who nickered in response.

"Down there," said Cynan, pointing with his chin, not bothering with greetings of his own. "I thought we'd wait for you. I'm not sure that the inhabitants will offer us a warm welcome."

Beobrand stared down the path. His eyesight had never been keen, but it was sharp enough that he could make out a cluster of small, thatched hovels. There were a few fenced-off animal pens and a slightly larger building that might be a barn, or a small hall. To the north, an arm of the forest encircled the settlement. To the south, there were some ploughed fields, and beyond them, a straggled hedge of blackthorn and then a stand of alder.

This must be Ad Buisi, the first place Thagmar had been due to halt. On the edge of the settlement a sizable group of people were gathered. Beobrand squinted, but could not discern any details.

"Thagmar's men?" he asked, though he had not noticed any of the tell-tale glinting he would have expected from weapons and armour.

"No," replied Cynan, shaking his head slowly. "But I wouldn't be surprised if we are witnessing Thagmar's work."

"How so?"

"Those people are burying one of their own. What you see down there is a funeral."

Chapter 16

In an attempt not to frighten the inhabitants, they rode slowly down the hill towards the hamlet. The sun gleamed from their byrnies, helms and warrior rings. The afternoon sunlight glimmered on the gold and garnet pommels of Beobrand's and Cynan's swords. The silver and gold decorations on the warriors' belts and scabbards flashed brightly. These were clearly men to be feared, no matter the speed with which they approached. Their very mounts, sleek and bred for riding, rather than pulling a wain or a plough, marked them as warriors and men of worth just as plainly as their finery, armour and weapons.

The faces of the villagers turned towards them, fear etched into their features. There was the certainty on those faces that, if they so wished, these warriors could easily butcher with impunity all the men, women and children that were huddled about the freshly dug grave. Even if they were later brought to trial for the offence, it was evident these riders were rich and would easily be able to afford the weregild that would be demanded for the life of such peasants.

At a stern command from one of the men, the womenfolk snatched up their children and hurried away into the scant protection of the houses. The score or so men remained where they were, defiantly glowering at the riders. Beobrand respected them for that. There was no point in trying to flee, but it took bravery to admit that and to hold one's ground. None of the villagers was armed. There were a couple of wooden shovels leaning against a fence, but even if they had been carrying spears and shields, they would have proven no match for Beobrand and his Black Shields.

Halting his gelding, Beobrand swung his leg over the saddle's cantle and slid to the ground. His shield and helm were both tied to his saddle and he made no move to reach for his sword or the seax that hung from his belt. Without prompting, Halinard also dismounted and joined his lord.

"Ask them who they are burying," said Beobrand, keeping his tone low.

Halinard spoke and an angry-looking man of perhaps forty years took a pace forward and snarled an answer. He was balding, with a full, long beard. He wore on his head a small cap, as did all the men. The cap seemed vaguely comical to Beobrand. It softened the man's features somehow, and Beobrand had already dismissed him as no threat. But the bearded man's eyes did not flinch when they met Beobrand's, and he began to re-evaluate the situation. Perhaps this man was not so defenceless as he had thought. Maybe he had once borne weapons. There was an icy hardness to his gaze, and despite his muscled shoulders and broad back, he moved with the lithe grace of a fighter.

"He says they are burying his father. And they would like to be left in peace to grieve and pray for him as is their custom."

Beobrand nodded. He noticed that the man's dark kirtle was torn just above his right breast, revealing pale skin beneath. A glance about the rest of the men who stared at him with open animosity showed they all bore similar tears or cuts to their clothes.

"Tell him I am sorry for his loss. To lose a father is a terrible thing." He grimaced at the thought of Grimgundi, the man whom he had believed to be his own father. For an instant he could almost hear the bastard's final pleading wails as their house burnt around him. "We do not wish to interrupt their rituals. All we want is information, and we will ride on."

"You have already interrupted the *Levaya*," said the man, with Halinard speaking his words in Anglisc. When Beobrand enquired about the strange word, the Frank shook his head.

"The funeral," snapped the man, by way of explanation. "If you allow us to finish the *Kvura*," he frowned, "the burial, I will answer your questions."

Beobrand felt his impatience building within him like a stream rising behind a dam, but he drew in a calming breath and stepped back. He glanced down. A swaddled corpse lay at the bottom of the hole. These people had lost a loved one. He knew the pain of loss. These simple folk were not his enemies. Nodding, he went back to his horse.

"Tell him we will wait," he said quietly to Halinard, who relayed the message.

The bearded man stared after Beobrand, as if he expected a trick of some kind. He watched without speaking as Beobrand led his gelding away from the funeral, followed by the rest of the warriors. When they dismounted, tethered their mounts to a fence, and lounged or sat leaning against the fence, the man seemed to finally believe there was no artifice in Beobrand's actions.

He called out to the women and children, who slowly, nervously returned. The womenfolk were all dressed in dark clothes and their heads were covered in shawls. They watched Beobrand and his warriors warily as they led their children out from the shelter of the buildings to stand once more beside the grave.

One of the men began to chant in a language none of the Black Shields could understand. The song was haunting, its music strangely guttural, yet beautiful.

"Who are these people?" asked Beobrand in a quiet voice.

"Iudaea," replied Halinard. "Their rituals are not those of the Christ followers."

Beobrand shook his head. Just how many gods were there in middle earth?

"The Iudeisc killed Jesu, the son of God," said Attor, making the sign of the rood over himself to ward off evil.

"Hush," said Beobrand. "Whatever their forebears may have done, these people do not look hundreds of years old to me. I do not think they are any danger to us."

Attor looked unconvinced.

"I thought they were not permitted to worship their false god in Frankia," he said.

Beobrand recalled the conversation with Dalfinus and Annemund in Paris and nodded.

"That is the law here, or so I was told."

"Well," said Cynan, raising an eyebrow, "it would seem that these Iudeisc have decided to ignore that particular law."

They waited in silence for the rest of the chants and prayers that were said at the graveside. There was a sombre austere beauty to the ritual and as they watched, Beobrand's admiration grew for the man he had spoken to, and for these quiet, dignified people.

When at last they had finished, first the son of the deceased, and then each of the others, took turns in shovelling three heaps of earth into the grave from the pile of soil beside it.

"Remain here," Beobrand said to his men. "And keep quiet." He fixed Attor with a stare. Beckoning to Halinard to follow him, he walked across the open area between the buildings.

As they approached the mourners, Beobrand pulled his cloak over his head, making a hood. He urged Halinard to do the same. The covering of the head seemed to be a mark of respect for these people, and he did not wish to cause them offence.

The people stared at him sombrely as he drew close. Nobody

spoke until he held out his hand to take the shovel from a young man who had finished dropping clods of damp earth into the now half-full grave. A glance showed Beobrand that no sign of the deceased in his shroud remained. All that could be seen now was moist, dark earth.

The young man hesitated and took a step back, placing the shovel on the ground, out of his reach.

"Tell him I wish to pay my respects to the dead," Beobrand said, biting back his anger at the youth's rudeness. Halinard spoke and the bearded man, whose father lay entombed beneath them, replied.

"He says it is bad to hand the shovel from one person to another. It might pass the sadness to you."

With a nod of understanding at the young man, Beobrand stooped and lifted the spade. The smell of the loam was rich and heavy and it brought with it a distant memory from his childhood of walking behind the plough while gulls shrieked and flocked to eat the worms lifted to the surface by the blade. Cutting into the depleted heap of turned earth, he quickly shovelled three loads of dirt into the grave. When he had finished, he placed the implement on the ground.

Another mourner retrieved it without comment and deposited his own three shovelfuls of soil into the hole. Soon, the grave was filled and covered in a domed mound of earth.

The son of the buried man stepped forward.

"My name is Binyamin," he said. He said more, but Beobrand had to turn to Halinard for a translation.

"He says it is an honour you do," said the Frank. "That his father cannot repay you for your kindness, but you are welcome to eat with his family as they begin to sit *Shiva*. Which I think means the time after someone has died."

"Mourning?"

"Yes, mourning."

Beobrand inclined his head to Binyamin. The sun had dipped

in the sky and the shadows were lengthening in the fields, but he pushed aside his impatience.

"It would be my honour," he said.

A willowy woman moved close to Binyamin and, together with their three children, a boy on the edge of manhood, and two younger girls, they led the way across the hamlet to a small hut. Beobrand signalled to Cynan that all was well, and ducked inside the shadowed interior. No fire burnt on the hearth and the only light came from the open door and the small opening in the thatch that would allow smoke out.

Binyamin's wife offered Beobrand and Halinard a seat each. Her husband sat on a stool, and their son, haughty and serious, pulled up another. The girls, eyes wide and gleaming as they stared at Beobrand, sat on a bed at the rear of their home.

Nobody spoke. Beobrand looked from one of them to the next, and was met with unblinking, dark eyes at each turn. This had not been a good idea. He should have demanded the man tell him what he knew. He was wasting his time here. What did he care about Binyamin's father. Surely it would be better if he left these people to their grief and continued after Thagmar and Wilfrid.

Just as he was about to voice these thoughts, several people entered the small building. They greeted Binyamin and his family in their throaty, musical tongue, speaking with soft solemnity. One of the women opened an earthenware pot she carried and offered it to each of them. Beobrand peered in, wondering what strange food these Iudeisc might eat. Inside were a dozen eggs. Taking one, he watched to see what Binyamin did. He tapped it on the edge of his chair, peeled off the flaking shell, and bit into the hard white egg within. They were boiled and had been left to cool. Beobrand cracked his egg's shell on the side of the bowl and pulled off the brittle covering, careful not to drop the slippery egg when he held it in his half-hand.

Binyamin had already finished his egg. Beobrand ate his in

two mouthfuls. He was glad of it and thought of the hungry men outside. One of the newly arrived women poured him a cup of ale, and he drank. It was light and flavoured with a gruit of bog myrtle and rosemary.

Binyamin said something in Frankish and, after washing down his mouthful of egg with some ale, Halinard interpreted.

"He says it is tradition to eat eggs, a symbol of life, at the..." He hesitated, unsure of the words.

"*Seudat Havraah*," said Binyamin.

"What is that?" asked Beobrand.

"The meal of consolation," translated Halinard. "The first meal after a burial. He says you are gracious with them, but he thinks you do not wish to hear more about the ways of his people."

Beobrand nodded in response to this.

"He asks your name," continued Halinard, "and from where you come?"

"My name is Beobrand," he said in his halting Frankish. "I come from a land far to the north," he gestured with his half-hand to indicate a great distance. "On the island of Albion."

Binyamin nodded, as if he met men from Albion every day.

"What information do you seek, Beobrand from Albion?"

"We are looking for a friend. He is travelling with a man named Thagmar."

At the mention of the fair-haired captain's name, Binyamin spat into the cold ashes on the hearth stone. One of the women hissed.

"Any friend of Thagmar's is no friend of ours," Binyamin said. Such was the change in him and so potent his fury that Beobrand thought the Iudeisc might launch himself at him.

Beobrand held up his hands.

"Thagmar is no friend," he said quickly in Frankish. He pointed outside. "Thagmar? He did that?"

Scowling, Binyamin nodded.

"What happened?" asked Beobrand.

Binyamin let out a ragged breath, then took a drink from his cup. His hands shook and Beobrand looked away so as not to shame the man by seeing his weakness.

Binyamin began to speak in a bitter monotone. Halinard translated his words.

"Thagmar came for more taxes. We have given all we can afford. We told him so. The spring storms destroyed the crops. If we pay more, we will not have enough food to feed our children."

"Can you not petition the *comes*?" asked Beobrand. "Ask for clemency?"

Binyamin laughed, a harsh, jagged sound, devoid of humour.

"We have tried. Neither Dalfinus nor his brother the bishop care for the plight of the likes of us."

"But if you die, there will be no taxes. No tithes for the church."

Binyamin shook his head at Beobrand's naivete.

"If we die, there will be other farmers. Lovers of Christ, no doubt, who will pay their taxes. Perhaps if they have a bad harvest," he said bitterly, "Annemund would be more lenient with them. But I doubt it."

"Why did Thagmar kill your father?" asked Beobrand.

"My father told that devil we had nothing to give. Thagmar would not listen." Binyamin's face clouded at the memory, and Beobrand noticed that his son had grown pale. "Thagmar knocked him down and beat him." He shook his head. "It was a coward's thing, but he would not stop, even when my father lay still. In the end, to make him halt, I brought out the small amount of silver we had hidden. Thagmar took it all." Binyamin bit his lip and stared into his cup as if searching for something he had lost. "If I had given him the silver earlier, my father would still live."

Several men had entered the hut now, and they grumbled

and growled at the retelling of the old man's killing. They were angry, but also ashamed, and more than one of them wiped tears from his cheeks. It is no easy thing to witness such brutality and stand by, and yet Beobrand knew it would have been madness for them to have stood against Thagmar and his warriors. If they had, there would be many more fresh graves outside.

Binyamin had fallen silent, and for the first time, his wife spoke up. Halinard, adept at his role of interpreter now, translated her words without being asked.

"Avram was alive when they left. We brought him inside, near the fire and cleaned his wounds. For a time he seemed calm as he slept, but then, as night fell, his spirit became angry. His body shook and his limbs thrashed. He never awoke. His spirit left him some time in the night."

Binyamin snapped something in their Iudeisc language. His wife replied with a burst of invective. Beobrand had no idea of the meaning, but the tone was clear enough. Binyamin was not the only one who had suffered, and his wife had as much right as he did to speak of what had occurred.

"Was there a young man with them?" Beobrand asked. "One who was not a warrior, but wore the robes of a monk?"

"Yes, he was with them," said Binyamin, his tone chastened now, following his wife's rebuke.

The thought of Wilfrid riding with Thagmar filled Beobrand with dread. Why had the young man left Liyon without telling him? And with Thagmar no less. If Dalfinus knew of Wilfrid's actions with his daughter, had he given his captain instructions to deal with the novice when they were far from the city? A murder could easily be disguised as an accident. And yet, no matter his worries for Wilfrid, and whatever the young man's faults, Beobrand was disappointed to think that Wilfrid had done nothing but watch as Thagmar's brutes abused these poor peasants. He had thought better of the lad.

"I am sorry that our friend could not stop Thagmar,"

Beobrand said, setting his empty cup down carefully beside the cold hearth.

When Halinard had interpreted his words, Binyamin shook his head.

"He was not here."

Beobrand stiffened. Had Thagmar dealt with Wilfrid before beating the old man?

"Where was he?" he asked.

"He had gone down to the river, to see the cataract." Binyamin's face darkened. "When he asked the way, it was my father who had told him. The old man always loved that waterfall and was happy to tell people where it was. He was proud of it, as if he somehow had a hand in its beauty. The old fool." His voice caught in his throat and he fell silent.

"Avram was always a kindly man," said Binyamin's wife. "When your friend returned and saw what Thagmar had done, he shouted at him. I thought Thagmar might kill him too, but he did not raise his hand against the monk, even though his hatred for him was clear."

Binyamin looked up at Beobrand. His eyes were dark.

"I do not envy your friend," he said. "For he travels with a serpent."

Beobrand flicked a look at Halinard and saw reflected in the Frank's face his own fears for Wilfrid. How long would Thagmar stay his hand? He wondered whether Woden stalked these lands, as he did in the north. Even now, was the all-father watching with glee at Beobrand's predicament? Woden, god of frenzy and death, loved blood and mayhem above all else. If Woden and his kindred gods held any sway over these southern lands, Beobrand could imagine them grinning at the prospect of more death. If Wilfrid were slain, Beobrand did not know how he would be able to return to Bernicia. Certainly Eanflæd would never forgive him.

Beobrand rose and thanked Binyamin and his wife for their

hospitality. They nodded solemnly, but made no move to follow him outside. Blinking in the brightness of the afternoon sun, Beobrand strode across the open ground to the waiting warriors.

"I hope you have rested," he said, untying his gelding from the fence and pulling himself into the saddle. "For we will ride through the night. With any luck, we will reach Thagmar and Wilfrid on the morrow."

He ignored the protests from the men, kicking his horse into a trot and leaving them to catch up. He was done with talking. His face was grim, and his shadow was long and dark on the path before him as he rode towards the forest and the distant mountains.

Chapter 17

Wilfrid glanced at Thagmar as they rode. The captain had not spoken to him since the beating of the old Iudeisc man. Wilfrid bit his lip and recited the paternoster silently. He had caught himself praying more frequently of late, and it had surprised him. He did not often resort to the consoling effects of the Lord's words, preferring instead to rely on his own quick wits. And yet some problems could not be solved with cunning and intelligence, and he had found recently that the prayers he had learnt on Lindisfarena brought him some solace from the swirling fears and thoughts that threatened to overwhelm him.

He wondered why he felt such outrage at the treatment of the old man at the hands of the captain of the guard. Wilfrid had seen violence before, and he cared nothing for the poor Iudeisc farmers and their families. But there had been an unhealthy gleam in Thagmar's eyes as he had punched and kicked the old man. It was as if he was punishing him for some unspeakable crime, being Iudeisc perhaps, but it made no sense to Wilfrid.

"They must be taught to obey their lord," Thagmar had panted, out of breath from the exertion of knocking the old man senseless.

"You will kill the man!" Wilfrid had shouted. He recalled the old Iudeisc's toothy grin when he had told him where to find the waterfall. He had seemed proud of the natural spectacle of the falls near his home. Now the man was sprawled on the ground, unmoving, his face bruised and bloody.

All about them, the women and children wept and wailed. The bearded men glowered and clutched their spades, hoes and axes, but none of them dared attack the armed warriors.

"One less Iudaea mouth to feed," spat Thagmar, kicking the insensate form of the old man once more. Swinging about to face the gathered villagers, he spoke in a clipped voice, as cold and deadly as steel. "Now, will you pay what you owe the lords of Liyon, or," he glared at a solid-looking, balding man with a thick beard, "shall I start on him next?" He pointed at a boy, gangly and awkward, just on the verge of manhood. Two of Thagmar's men moved forward to grab the boy. The bearded man cried out.

"Wait!" He stared down at the broken form of the battered man on the ground. "Wait." His voice was small now, defeated and shattered like the body of the old man. "We have some silver."

"Of course you do," Thagmar sneered.

When the man brought out a small purse containing a handful of clipped gold coins and shards of hacksilver, Thagmar had weighed it in his hand. He nodded to his men and they shoved the youth they had been holding into his mother's arms. The boy's face had been as white as curds and for an instant his eyes had met Wilfrid's. The Iudeisc boy must only have been a few years younger than him.

Thagmar tossed the purse to Gunthar, then wheeled on Wilfrid.

"Never question me again, boy," he hissed, standing so close that his breath was hot on Wilfrid's cheek. "Tread with care, or you'll share your protector's fate."

Thagmar growled in the back of his throat and pushed past Wilfrid.

Wilfrid's Frankish was not perfect so he was not sure he had understood Thagmar's words, uttered as they were in a rush of anger and contempt. He went over them again and again in his mind that afternoon as they rode, and later as he lay, ignored by the warriors, sleeping beside a large fire in a clearing of the forest. Who was the protector Thagmar had referred to? What could the captain of the guard mean? Could he be speaking of Annemund? Or Dalfinus? Perhaps he was alluding to Beobrand. But what fate did he speak of? A sudden black thought gripped Wilfrid in the darkness. Was it possible that Thagmar knew something of the queen of Bernicia? Could it be that he had heard that Eanflæd, his patron, was dead?

Lying there in the gloom he listened to the night and repeated the Frankish words in his mind. A breeze whispered through the beech trees. The dying fire glowed more brightly, crackling and popping as a fresh log ignited. A man coughed. Another rolled over and farted. Wilfrid closed his eyes and turned Thagmar's words over the way a mason will rotate a piece of stone searching for just the right place to strike with his chisel. But no matter how long he thought, and how hard he focused, no further meaning came to him.

When he finally slept, his dreams had been filled with the sound of the brethren of Lindisfarena chanting psalms during the nocturns. All the while, he had seen the staring, terrified eyes of the young Iudeisc boy. Eyes that had been so similar to those of the old man who had lain senseless, bloodied and unmoving on the earth.

He had awoken in the dawn chill, and, just as the previous afternoon, none of the warriors spoke to him. Thagmar ignored him completely and the only man to pay him any attention was the huge warrior, Gunthar, who passed him an oatcake that one of the men had made on a hot stone in the embers of the fire. The gesture unnerved Wilfrid almost as much as Thagmar's cold indifference, and he wondered whether he wasn't being offered the last meal of a condemned man.

The day was warm and bright again and they made good time. Wilfrid surveyed the land they passed; the dense stands of alders, the fertile, dark soil of the wide valley floors, the occasional marsh, dotted with puddles and pools, where midges and flies swarmed in the sunlight. He wondered what the land that Annemund had offered him would be like. Was this perhaps why the bishop had sent him on this journey? So that he would see what was needed to bring in the tithes and taxes from an unwilling peasantry?

They trotted into a farmstead beside a stream, perhaps a loop of the same river that made the waterfall he had visited the previous day. Men and women stood in doorways and on the edge of their fields, weather-beaten faces set against whatever misfortune these mounted warriors brought with them.

Wilfrid's guts churned as they approached the steading. He wondered what he would do if Thagmar once again proceeded to beat one of the ceorls. He did not know if he would be brave enough to stand up to him again after the man's hissed threat the day before, but he vowed that when he became the master of land, and people paid their dues to him, he would not allow such savagery. It was right that men paid a tribute to their lord, and a tithe of their goods to the church, but they should not be treated like disobedient animals for failure to do so. There were laws. And those laws must be followed.

Thagmar reined in and called for food and drink for the men. Farm boys led the horses down to drink at the stream, and women brought out bread and ale for the warriors. When they had all eaten, they remounted and rode away. Wilfrid had barely been able to swallow any of the bread he had been offered. His stomach was in turmoil, and it was only when they were riding away that he realised again that he was repeating the words of the paternoster over and over in his head.

His unease must have been clear on his face, for Thagmar turned in his saddle and laughed at him.

"Those were good Christ-following folk," he said. "And they paid their taxes on time. No need to look so scared. I am no monster."

Wilfrid said nothing. He looked away, unable to meet Thagmar's chill glare for long. He was terrified of the man. Not for the first time, he wished he had brought Beobrand and his Black Shields with him. Even as he thought this, he hated his own weakness.

He wondered if, in his absence, Annemund had convinced Dalfinus to allow him to marry Rotrudis. He had made his peace with the idea, for surely it would be a small price to pay for the power the bishop had promised him. When he was the husband of the *comes*' daughter, he would not need to fear Thagmar. With the influence he would have, he would see to it that the man was sent away from the palace. Perhaps, Wilfrid fantasised, he could even have Beobrand kill the man. Though in truth he was certain the thegn of Ubbanford would never do his bidding. In fact, the Bernician warrior would probably leave Liyon as soon as he found out what he had agreed with Annemund.

But none of that would matter if Dalfinus had other plans for Wilfrid.

He rode on as the sun rose high in the pale sky, feeling the weight of the furtive glances from the warriors around him. Were they waiting for the moment the trap would be sprung and something dreadful would befall him? Murmuring the paternoster under his breath, Wilfrid gripped the reins so tightly that his fingers ached, and followed behind Thagmar's rigid back as they rode further into the hills and ever further from Liyon.

It was early afternoon when they spotted the haze of smoke on the horizon. They had turned from the road shortly after midday and followed a winding track into the hills. Cresting a low rise, Wilfrid saw another steading, not dissimilar to the others they had passed. A collection of thatched huts, a couple of larger buildings, some animal pens. On the hill they rode down were dotted a dozen or so sheep. A dog barked at the riders, but was quickly silenced by the shepherdess. She was a young, slender girl, and wore the now familiar dark garb, with the shawl over her head, that marked her as Iudeisc.

Thagmar barked an order to a couple of his men and they peeled away from the column and cantered across the field towards the girl, scattering sheep as they went.

"What are they doing?" asked Wilfrid.

"You'll see soon enough," snarled Thagmar and one of the men laughed.

That was what Wilfrid was worried about. He had no desire to see this young woman hurt or tortured.

"In the name of the Lord our God, Christ our saviour," he said, slowing his horse and forcing his voice to be firm, "you will do no harm to that girl."

"We won't do too much harm to her," Thagmar said, "if she doesn't struggle too much." He shrugged and, again, some of the warriors chuckled. "But these Iudaea don't always know their place and often insist on fighting back."

The two riders had reached the shepherdess now. The dog was barking angrily and one of the men raised his spear. The girl shouted an order and the dog turned and ran after the sheep, circling about them to bring them together. As the other warrior made to drag the girl up onto his mount, she bit his hand and then toppled him from the saddle.

All the riders had reined in now to watch the fun and they laughed uproariously to see their comrade's ungainly display, shouting encouragement to the girl and hurling insults to the man.

"She's a fiery one," Thagmar laughed. "Collecting taxes can be tedious, but it does bring moments of pleasure."

"This is not the way to treat one of the Lord's flock," Wilfrid said, disgusted.

"These are Iudaea," spat Thagmar, "not Christ followers. Their kind cared nought for our Lord. Why should we care for them?"

"The bishop will hear of this."

"And he will thank you for the tale." Thagmar grinned. "Be sure not to spare any details. His Excellence does like to have a picture painted for him."

The other warrior had dismounted now, and after a brief chase across the field that had the watching men whistling and screaming with laughter, the two guards caught up with the shepherdess. The one she had bitten punched her in the face, and she went limp. Wilfrid's gorge rose, burning his throat. There was a casual brutality about these men that horrified him. As far as he knew, the girl was a free person, Iudeisc or not. Wilfrid treated thralls with more respect than this.

The dog returned, barking and snapping at the men as they carried the girl back to their horses. But she regained her senses enough to mutter a command and the beast obediently lay down in the grass, staring hatefully at the men who had captured its mistress. They slung her over the back of one of the horses and made their way back to the path and the waiting warriors.

People had come out of the houses in the farm at the sounds of horses and the commotion on the hill. They thronged at the entrance of the steading, where the track passed through a small gate, pale faces staring out from a mass of dark clothing, shawls, hats and thick beards. Wilfrid reckoned there to be about a dozen people, mainly women, children and older men. From the far side of the buildings, he could make out a handful of men sprinting down a hill. They were shouting, but still some way off. It seemed unlikely they would reach the steading in time to halt whatever horror Thagmar had planned. Not that those few men would be able to stand against the armed killers from Liyon in any event.

Thagmar rode straight at the group of ceorls without slowing, forcing them to part and allow him through. Wilfrid wanted to ride away, but his horse followed Thagmar's, and the other warriors' mounts were close behind him, crowding him forward. The women cried out, some screaming in their Iudeisc tongue. A stout woman with a round, flat face shouted in Frankish to let the girl go.

Thagmar's horse whinnied at the noise. He yanked hard on its reins, making it sidestep and wheel about. The men and women backed away.

"You know why I am here," he said. He did not need to shout; his voice cut through the noise like a sword blade. "I have come to collect what is owed to my masters. Pay what is due and we will leave."

A wizen-faced man with a long white beard took a step towards Thagmar. His eyes were rheumy and sad, but there was a defiant strength there too.

"We cannot pay what we do not have," he said.

Thagmar clicked his fingers at the man who held the girl over his saddle. This must not have been the first time they had performed this routine, for without a spoken command, the warrior slid from his horse and pulled the shepherdess down. A couple of the other men dismounted. One uncoiled a rope. The girl struggled at first, shouting and fighting, then, when she realised she could not escape, she began moaning and pleading. Wilfrid wanted to turn away, but found himself transfixed as the men dragged her to the nearest fence and began to tie her there, her hands outstretched along the cross-beams, her back towards the onlookers.

The rest of the guards leapt from their saddles, formed a line and advanced on the farmers, holding them back with the threat of their spears.

Thagmar slid from his saddle with languid slowness.

"We have travelled a long way to return empty-handed," he said. "If you cannot pay, I will have to take another form of payment." The girl cried out as the men tightened her bonds.

"We have the sheep," said the old man, his defiance gone now, replaced by the terror of what would happen to the shepherdess. "You can have some of them. They will fetch good coin in Liyon."

"Alas, I am not a farmer," said Thagmar, shaking his head in mock sadness. "And I do not satisfy myself with beasts. I draw the line at Iudaea."

Clicking his fingers again, one of his men, grinning widely at the prospect of what he was about to witness, pulled the shepherdess' skirts up to reveal her pale legs.

The girl screamed and fought, kicking and struggling until one of the men drew a seax and placed it at her throat. She grew still, but her back rose and fell with her sobbing. The women babbled and yelled, begging with Thagmar and praying to their god.

"No," said Thagmar, taking in the sight of the pale, quivering flesh of the girl's legs, and then surveying the gathered farmers, "I think this payment might well suffice for now."

Licking his lips, he reached out and stroked the girl's white thigh. She trembled and cried out. Sliding his hand up, he reached her undergarments and suddenly, savagely, tugged the garment away with a ripping of linen. The man who held the knife at her throat swallowed and leaned forward, to get a better glimpse of the girl's half-naked body.

The girl shuddered and moaned in pain and fear at Thagmar's probing touch. Some of the warriors guarding the ceorls looked over their shoulders to see what their leader was doing. Wilfrid noticed that Gunthar was not watching. Their eyes met and Wilfrid thought he saw a tortured pain in the huge man's eyes.

If Gunthar had any qualms about what his captain was doing,

Thagmar had none. Clearly enjoying himself, the blond leader worked his hand between the girl's thighs. She whimpered, but no longer moved. The old men looked away and the women prayed, covering their children's eyes.

"Perhaps," said Thagmar, lifting his hand to his face and sniffing his finger, "she would like to feel a whole cock inside her, and not one of those pathetic cut things you Iudaea have between your legs."

He looked down at the girl's naked buttocks, dropping his hand to his breeches. Then, without warning, he spun on his heel and drew his sword in a flash of steel. The youngest of the men from the field had reached the steading, hurdling a fence and rushing at Thagmar, axe raised ready to slay the shepherdess' pale-haired tormentor. He had come from behind the houses, and none of the distracted guards had seen him in time to intercept him. But Thagmar must have been aware of his approach all along, for quick as a serpent, he stepped close to the young man, catching the axe haft in his left hand and forcing it harmlessly away from his body. In the same instant, he plunged his sword into the man's guts.

The onlookers cried out with fresh anguish, while the poor girl, straining to see what was happening behind her, let out a howling wail of such pain that Wilfrid felt tears prick his eyes. Whether the man was her husband, her brother, or another kinsman, she was more distraught now than ever and she fought with renewed fury at her bonds and the men who restrained her.

Thagmar pulled his sword blade from the young farmer's belly. The man collapsed to the ground, where he lay, blinking and gasping in agony.

"Hold them back," snarled Thagmar, tugging at his belt and loosening his breeches. "You'll be dead soon," he hissed at the man who lay in an expanding pool of blood at his feet, "but you'll live long enough to see me take my payment."

Turning towards the girl, trusting now to his men to protect him from the angry villagers, Thagmar pulled his engorged member from his breeches. The girl, knowing what was coming, tensed, but before he could thrust into her, a bellowing shout came from the path and the sound of thrumming hooves reached them.

Wilfrid followed Thagmar's startled gaze. Perhaps God had answered his prayers, for galloping down the path, followed by the barking dog, came nine riders. Their cloaks billowed behind them and the afternoon sun gleamed from polished byrnies and helms. At the head of the column rode two massive warriors, both strong and grim-faced. The older of the two shouted out "Stop this!" in a booming voice. He spoke in Anglisc, but no translation was needed for the Franks to understand his meaning.

Thagmar's men scurried to form a protective line, and Thagmar hurriedly pulled up his breeches.

Wilfrid sighed in relief, offering up a silent prayer to the Almighty. Beobrand had come and whatever Wilfrid thought him, he knew the lord of Ubbanford would not allow the girl's torment to continue.

Chapter 18

Cynan had seen what was happening before Beobrand was able to make out the details.

"Thagmar is violating some poor woman," he'd snapped after staring down the slope for a few heartbeats.

"Bastard," spat Beobrand. "You are sure?" He peered towards the steading, but his eyes were older and he was unsure what was transpiring down in the valley.

"He has her tied like an animal while her folk watch." Cynan's outrage had flooded through him as sudden as a spring tide washing over the sands of Lindisfarena. Beobrand looked about at the other riders, perhaps thinking of how best to approach the situation. They were visitors in this land, guests of the bishop and his brother, the *comes*. A wise man would not rush headlong into a fight with the captain of Liyon's guard and his men.

But Cynan did not consider himself a wise man. He did not pause to prepare himself for combat. He already wore his byrnie, but rather than his helm, on his head was the wide-brimmed straw hat that protected him from the sun.

Kicking his heels into his mount's ribs, Cynan set off at a gallop down the slope. As he rode he tugged his sword free of its scabbard. The straw hat caught the wind and flew from his head. Glancing over his shoulder he saw his hat flutter onto the stone-strewn packed earth of the path. Beobrand and Ingwald's horses narrowly avoided trampling it. Cynan was pleased to see them both so close behind. Neither were great horsemen, but despite his impetuous charge, they would not allow him to ride alone to face the Franks.

"To me!" bellowed Beobrand, and as one, the rest of the Black Shields spurred their horses forward.

As they drew closer, Cynan saw in more detail what was happening. He watched as Thagmar turned from the half-naked woman and cut down the man who had run at him to protect her. The woman screamed, her tear-streaked face contorted in terror and pain. With a start he realised she was just a girl, scarcely old enough to be called a woman. She looked young, perhaps younger even than Aelfwyn back at Stagga, and the idea of someone abusing Eadgyth's daughter in this way sent a jolt of fury through him like a spear thrust.

Beobrand, presumably close enough now to see what was taking place, screamed in his battle-voice for Thagmar to halt what he was doing. Cynan did not know if the Franks understood him, but they had certainly noticed the riders' approach.

The warriors at the steading were hurrying to form a protective line just behind the gateway into the open area before the buildings. A few of the men were with Thagmar, and those, along with the captain of the guard, were rushing forward too, leaving the girl tied to the fence, the dying man at her feet.

Beobrand was shouting for his gesithas to make a shieldwall. That made sense. They would dismount and form up, and then face off against the Franks. Beobrand probably hoped in this way to avoid bloodshed. His Black Shields were formidable opponents, and though outnumbered, the difference in numbers was not enough to make a fight a sure thing. In a heartbeat, Cynan weighed up what would happen. The two leaders would talk as the warriors glared at each other, perhaps hurling insults. Eventually, they might well reach a compromise. Perhaps that was what a leader should aim for. And maybe that was the best course of action.

But Cynan chose to ignore Beobrand's yelling. The girl at the fence was pale and frightened, and these men had been enjoying her anguish. The same men who had beaten the old man at Ad Buisi to death. No, he would not halt his headlong charge. A stand-off between the two shieldwalls would be a precarious thing in any event. If Cynan could bloody their opponents first, that might give the Black Shields an advantage. A small voice whispered inside him that it might also make peace impossible, leading to slaughter, but his rage at the sight of the terrified girl, and the young man bleeding to death on the earth behind her, drowned it out.

He pressed on, telling himself that once, when he was younger, Beobrand would not have halted either.

As Cynan reached the gate, half a dozen of the Frankish warriors had already formed a ragged wall. For an instant, he considered kicking his horse on, but even though his mind was filled with the flames of anger at what these people had been forced to endure, he had not lost all sense. He still recalled the pain and ignominy of the horse pulling him from the saddle in the forest. If he was to drive his steed at the shieldwall now, no matter how unprepared the warriors were, the animal would as like as not throw its rider. The thought of being helpless, sprawled on the earth at their feet, was enough to make him pull hard on the reins, bringing his horse to a scraping halt. As the horse skidded in a spray of pebbles and dust, Cynan jumped down, pulling his shield from his back.

"Shieldwall!" bellowed Beobrand behind him. He could hear the horses slowing, the men yelling as they dropped to the ground. "Cynan! To me!"

He hesitated then, his lord's voice tugging at him. Obedience was not his strongest quality, and Beobrand had not yet forgiven him for disobeying his command to remain in Ubbanford the previous year. Cynan was all set to pull his horse away and hurry back to Beobrand and the rest of the Black Shields when one of the Franks, a mean, weasel-faced man called Letard, joined the line and shouted something directly at Cynan, his lip curled in a taunting grin. Cynan did not understand the man's words, but it was clearly an insult of some kind. Or a challenge. If it had just been the tone and sneer in the man's voice, Cynan might have been able to suppress his rage for long enough to turn and join Beobrand and the others, but Letard had been one of those holding the girl while Thagmar violated her. The man said something else, spitting at Cynan, then laughing. The man was clearly a fool as well as a bully and violator of young girls, for only an idiot would goad the tall Waelisc warrior who stood alone and unafraid before the Frankish shieldwall.

Perhaps sensing the shift in Cynan, Beobrand hollered again, his voice cracking with the effort.

"Cynan! Come back!"

Cynan did not take his eyes from Letard's. He hefted his black-painted shield and sent his horse away, slapping its rump with the flat of his sword.

"You're mine," he hissed, and for the first time he saw fear dawning in Letard's eyes.

The other Franks were tightening up their line and Cynan knew that once they were set, he would stand little chance on his own. Thagmar was shouting at them, and in the moment of disarray as he arrived at the shieldwall and they shuffled along to allow their captain access, Cynan struck.

Bounding forward, he raised his sword high, throwing his shield wide to cover his left flank and also to entice attacks high on his right. A spear-tip glimmered in the sun as it flicked towards his face. He caught the attack on his sword, pushing the spear out of line and sliding his blade down the ash haft. The wielder was experienced enough to realise he would lose his fingers if he did not move and so, as Cynan had anticipated, the spear withdrew. He deflected another blow on the rim of his shield and a third spear bit into the hide-covered linden board.

This was the most dangerous of the blows, and Cynan fought against the weight dragging his shield away and down. With a growl, he twisted his wrist, fighting not to be slowed in his attack, wrenching the spear from the splintering boards. At the same instant, with Letard crouched behind his shield to receive him, Cynan dropped to the earth and skidded to close the distance. He held the shield above his head to ward off the attacks he knew would come, but relied on his speed, audacity, and the unexpectedness of what he had done to protect him as much as his leather-bound board. Swinging out with his sword, he felt it bite into Letard's shins. The man squealed and collapsed. Cynan surged back to his feet and danced backwards, away from the shieldwall.

Again, he was forced to parry a spear thrust with his now blood-smeared sword. He caught another darting strike on his shield, but without breaking their ranks to follow him, he was out of range from the Franks within an eye-blink.

"Come on, you whoresons," he screamed at them, urging them to attack him. If their discipline was bad and they came at him in a rush, he was sure that Beobrand and his gesithas would take advantage of the confusion and join him in the fray. They would break them then, of that he was certain. A man beside the giant, Gunthar, shouted and took a pace forward. With a pang of regret Cynan saw it was Hincmar, but a barked command from Thagmar and Gunthar's huge hand on the man's shoulder pulled him back.

The warriors glowered at him over their shields. Letard whimpered and cried, lending his wails to those of the women and children who looked on in abject terror.

Turning his back on the Franks in a show of bravado, Cynan walked slowly back to Beobrand and the Black Shields who awaited him in silence. Without a word, they parted for him and he took his place at Beobrand's right.

"I told you to come back," muttered Beobrand under his breath.

"Did you, lord?" Cynan replied. "I'm sorry, my hearing is not what it once was. But I am back now."

"Damned fool," Beobrand said. "Now you have killed one of Thagmar's men. Woden knows how we are going to get out of this without more fighting."

"We're ready for more fighting, aren't we, lads?" said Cynan, raising his voice so they could all hear him. The Bernician gesithas replied with a shout. "Besides," Cynan went on more quietly, "I haven't killed anyone. Just cut him down to size a bit."

"He could well die yet."

"True," said Cynan, without sympathy, "and if he lives, he'll have a nasty limp to remember me by."

They fell silent as Thagmar stepped through his ranks to stand in the gateway to the steading. He called over his shoulder and a moment later, Wilfrid joined him. The novice was pallid and nervous. He made the sign of the cross over himself and spoke.

"Lord Beobrand," he said, "Thagmar asks why you attack his men? You would do well to remember that you are guests in Burgundia."

"Tell him I cannot easily forget that. But I cannot stand by and watch women abused and old men beaten." He hawked and spat into the long grass that grew beside the path. "Or worse."

Thagmar shook his head. He spoke in a quiet tone, while Wilfrid continued to interpret.

"He says his methods for punishing those who do not pay their dues are no concern of yours. He does not come to Bernicia and tell you how to govern your people."

"No," replied Beobrand, "he does not." Cynan could sense Beobrand growing angrier with each word. He readied himself, in case his lord's infamous rage got the better of him and he called for them to attack. "But," Beobrand went on, "if Thagmar did come to my land, he would not find me raping girls and killing old men. What next? Does he plan to torture some babes in arms? I had thought him more of a man than that. But these are not the ways of men, these are the actions of cravens. Nithings."

Wilfrid hesitated.

"Speak my words, Wilfrid," said Beobrand, his voice hard and cold. "Or I will have Halinard do it."

Wilfrid swallowed and then translated. The colour drained from Thagmar's face. He spoke and his words hissed like a sword being dragged over a whetstone.

"He says it is not wise to insult him."

"Tell him I am not known for my wisdom."

Cynan blinked, the similarity to his own thoughts surprising him. Hincmar stared at him from where he stood in the Frankish shieldwall. Cynan hoped he would not have to kill the man. He liked him.

"Tell him," Beobrand went on, "I am known for the sharpness of my blade, my quickness to anger and slowness to forgive. And that I do not allow my men to harm women, children or the old."

"He says he is not one of your men."

"No, he is not. I would not have one such as he in my warband. I do not have cowards in my shieldwall."

There was a moment of tension and Cynan wondered if Beobrand had pushed too hard. Then Thagmar smiled, showing his teeth like a wolf scenting prey.

"Your words are hollow," he said. "You are a fool to cross me and my master."

Chapter 19

"By Tiw's cock," snarled Beobrand. "We should have left the boy to his wyrd with his new friends. We could have travelled half the way back to Bernicia by now."

Cynan shook his head. Beobrand knew what he was going to say and the truth of it infuriated him.

"You know I wish to return home as much as you," said Cynan, "but what of the promise you made to Eanflæd?"

Beobrand grabbed his cup of ale, spilling some of its contents. He was careless in his anger. By Woden, he was furious. He drank, then dried his half-hand on the wool of his breeches. Beobrand felt as though he had been constantly filled with rage ever since they had ridden down into that farm where Thagmar was abusing the poor Iudeisc girl. That had been ten days ago, and they had been back in Liyon for two stultifying days.

Beobrand refilled his cup and drank yet more of Genofeva's fine ale. He had already drunk too much, but he welcomed the dulling of his senses. How he wished he had ridden away from Liyon weeks ago. He looked about the small yard where they sat. It was thronged with boatmen from the river. On the far side of the brazier that glowed with embers were a group of a dozen warriors, drinking and talking in raucous voices. They were Dalfinus' men and Beobrand recognised a couple of them from their recent journey. One of them returned his gaze with a dark look. Beobrand placed his cup on the board before him. He would have to slow down the drinking. It was already dark and he had an early start the next morning. He looked up at the sky. It was a dark blue and the first stars were showing, but to the west it still held the memory-glow of sunset. It had been a warm day with a cloudless sky, and Beobrand had spent much of it drinking and eating here with Cynan, Halinard, Ingwald and Gram. They had reminisced over the last couple of weeks and the more they had talked and drunk, the more Beobrand's discontent had grown, as if the conversation and ale fuelled his anger.

Despite saving the girl from further torment, Beobrand's plans of taking the fool, Wilfrid, away from Thagmar and riding with all haste back to the city had been dashed the moment he mentioned the idea.

"I thank the Lord you came when you did," Wilfrid had said to Beobrand, once the two bands of warriors had separated, and the imminent threat of further bloodshed had dissipated. "I have been praying you would come."

"You would have had no need of prayer, if you had not left Liyon without telling me. What madness possessed you?"

Wilfrid had looked sheepish.

"I wanted some peace away from the city, and Annemund and Dalfinus invited me to accompany Thagmar. They said I would like to see Saint Lienard's grotto..." His voice trailed off as he heard the inadequacy of his explanation.

"Did you find the peace you craved?" snapped Beobrand.

Wilfrid had the good sense not to reply.

"Well, while you were out here watching your new friends murder and rape peasants, your friend Baducing has almost certainly left Liyon by now."

"So soon?" Wilfrid at least had the decency to look upset. "I had thought he might wait for a few more weeks."

"Well, he has grown tired of waiting, as have I. If we hurry back, we might yet join Baducing and the merchants he is due to travel with to Roma."

"We cannot leave yet," said Wilfrid in a small voice.

"Do not tell me what we cannot do," roared Beobrand, his anger bubbling over.

Wilfrid bit his lip and flicked a glance at where the girl had been tied. There was a dark stain on the ground from the blood of the young man Thagmar had killed. It transpired the man was her brother. The sight of his lifeless form further angered Beobrand. There is such certainty in youth. The boy, for he could barely be called a man, had not faltered in his sister's defence. He had run at Thagmar without a thought for his own safety, propelled onward by righteous anger and certain in the knowledge that what he did was right. It was his duty to protect his kin. The boy was younger than Octa and Beobrand thought of his own children, and the grandchild he had not yet met. How many loved ones had he tried to save in his lifetime? So many were gone now; ashes and bones. And yet he remained. He wondered if this was part of the curse that had been placed on him all those years ago in a cave on Muile. That he was doomed to outlive all his loved ones and die alone. He had watched in silence as the young man's body was carried inside. There the womenfolk now tended to him, preparing him for burial.

"I have seen one Iudeisc funeral already," said Beobrand. "I do not wish to witness another."

"The lad speaks the truth," Cynan said.

"How so?" Beobrand asked, glaring at the Waelisc man for a moment. But despite his initial anger with Cynan for not obeying his order instantly, that particular fire had burnt out quickly. Of all the things that enraged him, seeing Cynan shatter the shins of that whoreson, Letard, was not one of them.

"Unless you wish to hear of many more funerals, we will have to ride on with Thagmar as he collects taxes for his masters."

"The Almighty brought you here," said Wilfrid, "for which I offer Him thanks. But yes, now I fear we must continue with Thagmar until he returns to Liyon. We have seen how he treats these people. Can you imagine how badly he would abuse them now that you have crossed him?"

Beobrand groaned, seeing that they spoke true.

"Your god did not bring me here," he replied. "Unless he is a gelding." Beobrand had stalked away then, trembling with exasperation, fists clenched at his sides. He knew Wilfrid was right. He could not now ride away and leave these people to their wyrd. But even after he had made the decision, he did not make peace with it, and the ire that had been building for weeks grew stronger each day, as if a furnace were being stoked within him.

On the first night that they had camped near Thagmar's warriors, Beobrand had stared into the fire, trying to see sense in the dancing flames.

"If we plan to leave for Roma soon," Gram had said, breaking into his reverie, "what is the point of travelling with that whoreson now? As soon as we are far from here, he will return and do whatever he wishes to these people."

Beobrand spat into the fire.

"I know as much," he said. "I learnt long ago that I cannot keep everyone safe." He searched for the faces of loved ones in the coals and flickering flames, but saw none. A fox shrieked in the night and Beobrand pulled his cloak around his shoulders. The cloudless nights were chill. "But nor can I stand by and allow innocents to be harmed. While I am yet here in Burgundia, Thagmar will do no more harm to these people. And if he tests me, I will gut him like the pig he is."

"Not if I get to him first," interjected Cynan from the shadows. The rest of the men laughed at that. They had all loved to see Cynan's bravery, as he faced the line of warriors alone.

And so it was that they had ridden with Thagmar under an

uneasy truce. They had stopped at four other farms and hamlets, and at each one the people had paid what they could. Thagmar had told them that he would return at harvest time and demand their rightful share. The threat was clear, as was the fear in the faces of the farmers and their families. They knew Thagmar and what he was capable of. Beobrand understood he could not prevent time from passing, and had consoled himself with the knowledge that at least he had given the wretched peasants a few months' respite.

Now they were back in Liyon and Wilfrid had once again refused to travel on towards Roma. Beobrand stretched his spine, leaning back until it clicked. He always ached after a lot of riding, but he would put up with the discomfort to be far from this place and that bastard, Thagmar.

When they had returned to the city, Beobrand had told Wilfrid they would be riding on within the week. The novice had nodded and Beobrand had believed that finally, they would be on their way. And now Wilfrid came to him with this foolishness.

"Can the boy truly believe Dalfinus will give him his daughter's hand?" Beobrand snapped suddenly, his anger bubbling up from where it had simmered.

"Hush, lord," said Cynan, flicking a glance at Dalfinus' warriors.

It was unlikely the men would understand him, but Cynan was probably right to be cautious. Who knew what spies Dalfinus had in Liyon?

Beobrand was still reeling from what Wilfrid had said to him about the sudden change to his prospects. He rubbed a hand over his face. Reaching for his cup, he found it empty. Fighting the temptation to refill it, he slammed it down on the board and growled. A few of the warriors glanced in the direction of the noise. A couple of leather-faced boatmen scowled at him before looking away quickly.

"It does seem passing strange," said Cynan, "but sometimes powerful people lift up young men in whom they sense potential." He raised an eyebrow. Beobrand shook his head, but smiled thinly at the Waelisc man's words.

"This is hardly the same as that. You were a thrall who had done me a service. Wilfrid says Annemund means to elevate him to be his heir, to give him land and riches."

"You gave me land, and wealth," replied Cynan.

Beobrand frowned. Cynan was as infuriating as a pebble in a shoe.

"After I had heard your oath," Beobrand said. "And you had been in my service for years. And you had proven yourself to me many times over."

Gram poured himself some more ale and offered the jug to Beobrand, who, after a brief hesitation relented and held out his cup.

"Perhaps Wilfrid has done Annemund and Dalfinus a service," Gram said, pouring the ale.

Beobrand sipped the drink, forcing himself to calm down. To think.

What could the boy have done to warrant such reward? Wilfrid was clever, no doubt, but Beobrand could barely believe that would be enough for Annemund and Dalfinus.

"Surely there must be more to this than we can see," he said at last, his tone low and measured.

"Perhaps," said Halinard, "but what? If there is intrigue here, I cannot believe Wilfrid knows of it."

"No." Beobrand sighed. "He certainly seemed to believe it when he told us."

"Annemund and Dalfinus could be playing him for a fool," mused Cynan.

"Wilfrid is many things. He is young and ambitious. But a fool? And even if they were able to have him act in some scheme without his knowledge, to what end? And would Dalfinus allow the boy to sully his daughter to further some plot? No, I cannot see the truth in that."

Gram emptied his cup and signalled to one of Genofeva's daughters to bring a new jug. He winked at the pretty girl, whispering in her ear as she bent to retrieve the pitcher. She blushed and hurried away.

"We will know the truth of it all tomorrow, one way or another," he said, watching the sway of the girl's hips as she vanished inside the tavern. "I cannot imagine Dalfinus has invited you just to hunt boar. Surely he will speak to you of this and other things too."

"That is what I am worried about," replied Beobrand, running his hands through his long hair.

Before the church bell had rung for midday mass, Wilfrid had brought the message that they were to attend one of Dalfinus' fabled hunts the following day. Nobles from across the land had been invited. Wilfrid was excited. It seemed it was a great honour, coveted by all. Beobrand was not interested, but Dalfinus had been a gracious host, and they would be leaving soon. And perhaps it was as Gram said and he would be able to receive the answers he needed from the *comes* during the hunt.

"You think it could be a trap?" asked Cynan. He had not been invited, and he was clearly not happy about that. It was his duty to protect Beobrand, but Wilfrid had relayed Dalfinus' steward's explicit instructions that only Beobrand, Halinard, who would act as his interpreter, and one other could go. Places at the event were limited and exclusive. Cynan had expected Beobrand to offer him the third place, but Gram had pleaded to be allowed to attend. He loved hunting, and he could not bear the thought of missing such an opportunity after hearing so many hushed comments about Dalfinus' famous hunts. Beobrand had acquiesced quickly.

"The thought did cross my mind," Beobrand said, "but the idea is madness. If Dalfinus wanted to cause me harm, he could have killed me many times over. We travelled together for a fortnight and then we have been his guests for weeks. Why wait till his precious hunt to seek to hurt me? It makes no sense. The man has shown me nothing but friendship."

"Well," said Cynan, scratching behind his ear, "you hadn't crossed Thagmar before." He shrugged. "And I hadn't cut short Letard's fighting career."

"More reason for you not to accompany me. It was you, not I, who wounded Thagmar's man."

Letard yet lived and it seemed he would survive Cynan's blow to his legs. But his wounds were healing badly. He could barely hobble with the support of a stick and he was in constant pain. He was often insensate, choosing to dull the agony with milk of the poppy mixed with wine. It seemed unlikely Letard would ever walk unaided again. His fighting days were over.

"Perhaps Dalfinus means you no harm, but Thagmar might have other plans," said Cynan.

Beobrand shook his head.

"In these last weeks there have been better places to settle a score with us than at his master's hunt. Thagmar would gladly cut both of our throats, I am sure, but not like this, not before his lord's guests. No, I will be safe enough. I will press Dalfinus for the truth of Wilfrid's future. And whatever it may be, we will leave the day after tomorrow."

"Your mind is made up then?" Cynan sounded relieved. They were all getting restless, despite the comforts of Liyon.

"Yes," replied Beobrand, and at the realisation, he felt his own relief flood through him like a cooling stream washing over parched earth. "Whatever I learn about Wilfrid's future tomorrow, we will leave the next day. As you are not invited to the hunt," he said, smiling despite himself, "gather the men from the brothels and ale-houses and see they are not too drunk by sundown. And buy provisions for the journey. On the morning after the hunt, we ride."

"To Roma?" asked Halinard.

Beobrand shrugged.

"If Wilfrid is to come with us, then yes, I will complete my mission. But if he decides to stay here, I will wash my hands of him. We will turn about and ride north, for the Narrow Sea and Albion."

Beobrand lifted his cup to his lips and drained the last of the ale. He knew not what tidings tomorrow would bring, but if what Wilfrid had said to them was true, the day after tomorrow they might be riding for home.

Chapter 20

The sun was already hot in the unclouded sky as they rode up the slope towards the looming shape of the stone-built edifice of the arena. Beobrand squinted and held up his hand against the glare. He wished he had thought to obtain a hat like Cynan's. If they were to ride on a hunt all day in this sun, he would regret leaving his face and neck unprotected. His skin was not as pale and prone to burning as the Waelisc warrior's, but he had suffered enough times from working in the fields as a boy to know that the sun could be a fickle mistress. Still, there was no time to return to the palace now. He would have to make do. They were already late, and Wilfrid was almost shaking with his pent-up nervous energy as he rode beside him.

They had been delayed waiting for Gram to join them. He had eventually been roused, but he was bleary-eyed and tousle-haired. He had clearly continued drinking long after Beobrand had left the tavern down by the river. Beobrand wondered fleetingly, with a needling of envy, whether the older man's flirtations with Genofeva's daughter had borne him fruit. Judging by the warrior's rueful smile, he thought perhaps it had and Beobrand's jealousy grew. But there was no time to dwell on such matters now.

When Wilfrid had come to accompany them to the agreed meeting place for the hunt, the young novice had again made his plans clear.

"Dalfinus will today announce my betrothal to Rotrudis," he'd said, as they had mounted their horses in the palace stable.

Beobrand still thought this unlikely. He was tempted to deride the boy, but he bit his tongue. If Wilfrid was mistaken, they would learn of it soon enough. And no matter what Beobrand said, the truth of it would not change. Either the *comes* of Liyon and his brother, the bishop, had great things in store for the youth, or Wilfrid was deluded.

"Well," Beobrand had said, pulling himself up onto his gelding, "if you are to marry Dalfinus' daughter, I take it you will be staying here."

"That is most likely," replied Wilfrid stiffly. The fact that he did not apologise for having kept them here all these weeks, rankled Beobrand. Again, he wanted to say something of the matter, to voice his anger at the young man. Instead, he gritted his teeth and pondered the selfishness of youth. If all played out as Wilfrid believed, tomorrow Beobrand and his gesithas would be riding homeward. He could not hold onto his anger in the face of such a possibility.

The path up to the huge Roman building was familiar to them. They walked this way several times most weeks, but this was the first time they had ridden. As they reached the wide expanse of shade before the soaring stone walls, Beobrand saw a large number of horses penned in a temporary corral. There were a dozen crimson-cloaked guards standing near the animals.

Beobrand's gelding stepped in a pile of fresh dung, its hoof slipping against the cobbles. Reining in, Beobrand slid down from his saddle. It was cool in the shade and he welcomed the moment's relief from the sun. Throwing his reins to the nearest guard, he turned and waited for Wilfrid, Halinard and Gram to dismount.

From within the walls came the muffled murmur of raised voices and the occasional echo of laughter.

"Sounds more like a feast than a hunt," he said. "I am surprised we are not riding out by now."

"Dalfinus said there would be refreshments before the hunt," said Wilfrid. "He seems most proud of the arena and the work his masons have done to repair the structure. He wants to show it off to the men who have travelled from far afield to participate in this year's hunt. And what better place to welcome everyone? And," he raised an eyebrow, "where better to make any announcements before we ride? Of course, for that, everyone must be present."

Beobrand took the hint about their tardiness and strode towards the main entrance. The huge oak doors were closed. Before them stood another four city guardsmen. Beobrand did not recognise any of them and none of the men made any effort to allow them to pass or to open the doors.

"Tell them we are here at the invitation of their master."

Halinard spoke quickly to the spear-men. The tallest of them, a red-faced man with a dark beard and dull, slate-grey eyes, replied and nodded curtly at the large, iron-bound chest that stood to one side.

"He says we must leave our swords before we enter. They will guard them until we depart."

Beobrand scowled. Unbidden, his left half-hand had fallen to rest on Nægling's pommel. He did not wish to be without his blade. The guard stared at him, unblinking and expressionless. Beobrand felt a prickle of misgiving.

"Lord?" said Gram, his voice croaky.

Through the timber of the doors came the clatter of plates and a titter of laughter. Beobrand shrugged.

"It is normal not to wear a sword in a lord's hall," he said in response to Gram's inquisitive look. "This is no different." Unbuckling his sword belt, he handed the scabbarded weapon to the guard. He turned to Halinard. "Tell him that if anything happens to Nægling, I'll be making an ale cup from his skull."

Halinard said something, but Beobrand doubted he had translated his words faithfully for the guard's expression did not change. After the briefest hesitation, Gram and Halinard deposited their own swords with the guards. Still they made no move to open the doors.

The grey-eyed guard said something, looking down. Beobrand followed his gaze and understood.

"We will keep our seaxes," he said. "There is food in there. Would he have us eat like animals?"

Halinard translated his words. The guard glowered at them each in turn. Beobrand stared at him with his unwavering icy glare. He pulled himself up to his full height, hoping the man would decide it was not worth the trouble to argue with them about this. He readied himself for further confrontation, expecting the man to say that the small eating knives they wore would suffice.

After a drawn out, awkward moment, the guard made up his mind. He nodded and stepped aside, giving the command to his comrades to pull the doors open. The sound of revelry that had been muted before, now rolled over them like a wave, echoing down the shaded tunnel. The bright light of the sun on the sand shone at the end of the passage.

Beobrand moved past the guards without another glance, pleased at his petty victory over them. He chuckled to himself at that. What had become of him? The thegn who had defeated the mighty Hengist, the warrior who had brought victory to his adopted kingdom of Northumbria in countless battles, revelling in giving up only his sword and not relinquishing his seax as well. He shook his head as they walked into the gloom. He had been city-bound for too long, enjoying the life of a foppish Frank noble. It had softened him.

Beside him, Gram stumbled on an unseen crack in the

flagstones. Beobrand caught his arm, preventing him from falling. Gram grinned sheepishly. His breath was foul from his over indulgence the night before. Beobrand turned his face away.

"Get some food inside you," he growled, "and no more drinking. You can barely walk and you are not the best of riders even when sober."

"I am hurt, lord," said Gram. "Everyone knows I ride better when I'm drunk. What are we hunting, anyway?"

"Dalfinus would not say," said Wilfrid. "As far as I can recall, on all the occasions he has talked of his special hunts, he has never mentioned the huntsmen's prey. When I pressed him on it yesterday, he said he liked it to be a surprise for first-time hunters."

"I don't like surprises," grumbled Beobrand.

"He also said that nobody has ever been disappointed with one of his hunts."

"Perhaps," said Gram, his tone more animated now as they drew close to the much-anticipated hunt, "he has captured exotic animals, like the men of Roma used to do. Some of the men were speaking of such things when we first trained here. How savage beasts had once been brought here and released within the walls of the arena for men to fight them while the people watched." A sudden thought struck Gram. "Do you think they might have lions? Do they have lions in Frankia? I have heard tell of them, but I'm not really sure what they are. Perhaps their meat is good."

"I'm sure it will be nothing more exotic than a boar, or a deer, and we have those in Bernicia."

"Perhaps Frankish boars are bigger and more dangerous."

"Perhaps."

They stepped out onto the circular arena floor, blinking in the bright daylight after the dark of the tunnel. They had trained here many times, but much had changed since last they had visited. Near the doors where they had entered, several tables had been set up. They were covered in fine white linen and laden with exquisite arrangements of all manner of food. One board was dotted with cups and silver pitchers that winked brightly in the sun. A couple of servants bustled over to the newly arrived guests, offering them titbits of seared chicken livers and slices of blood sausage from polished platters. Another carried one of the ornately decorated silver jugs, and several small silver goblets on a tray.

"Wine?" he asked.

Gram was quick to accept.

"I'll ride better," he said with a grin in response to Beobrand's disapproving expression.

Beobrand accepted a goblet of wine and looked about him, trying to take in everything at once. This was like no hunt he had ever attended. As had happened so often since arriving in Frankia, he felt out of place. The sand was thronged with dozens of men. Most wore gaudy linens and silks. Gold jewellery flashed in the sunlight and seemed to adorn every throat and wrist. Many of the men wore extravagant hats, several with feathers protruding from them. They conversed in small groups. A few, sensing the new arrivals, stared openly at the men from Albion. Beobrand could feel them judging him, questioning his worth. Well, he may be a barbarian from the north, but he was no pauper. He reached his right hand up and touched the golden arm ring he wore on his left arm. There was more precious metal there than on many of these nobles. He wondered if they knew the ring signified he had slain his foe-men in battle. He glowered at them, knowing that his face would tell the tale well enough, the scar beneath his left eye, his piercing glare, his bulk and lithe movements marking him as a warrior.

To Beobrand's surprise, Wilfrid hurried away, threading his way between the people, until he reached Dalfinus on the far side of the arena. Beyond the *comes* of Liyon were what appeared to be several crates of differing sizes. Beobrand could not be certain what they contained, for they were covered in great sheets, so large that perhaps they were sails from ships that travelled the rivers.

"Do you think there are lions under there?" asked Gram, his mouth full of chicken liver.

"More likely the hounds for the hunt," Beobrand replied, though in truth, he had never known a pack of dogs to be so quiet. The gathering before a hunt was usually a cacophony of snarling and barking as the hounds sensed the excitement to come. It seemed unlikely that the crates were filled with dogs. But what then?

Beobrand knew nothing about lions, but he had an uneasy feeling that he would not like what was beneath those sheets. He thought of the tales they had heard of the contests against beasts here in the days of old, and the gleam of excitement in Dalfinus' eyes whenever he spoke of his special hunts. Until a moment ago, Beobrand had believed they would be riding out of the city in search of some local animals, but now, seeing the numbers of men within the arena, and thinking back to the numbers of horses outside, he thought he might have been wrong all along. But surely if there were wild animals within crates hidden beneath the sailcloth, releasing them within the arena would not be a hunt. It might be a sport of some kind, he supposed. But not a hunt. Perhaps the word meant something else to the Franks.

He was about to put some of these thoughts to Gram, but before he uttered a sound, a voice cut through the general hubbub of the throng.

"Lord Beobrand of Albion," said the voice in Frankish. "It is a pleasure to see you here."

Turning, Beobrand looked down at a man who stood more than a head shorter than him. He recognised the man's face, but for a moment he was unable to recall where he had met him before. And then, in an instant, memories of the dark and rain-filled days of winter came to him. He pictured the man surrounded by wealth and gaudy decorations. Upon his head he wore a cap of shimmering silk, and in his hand he held out a silver cup that glimmered in the morning sun.

"Lord Marcoul," Beobrand said, raising his own goblet in greeting. "We are far from your hall."

"Indeed we are," said the lord from the north, "but not as far as we are from yours. And I never miss one of Dalfinus' hunts." He wagged a finger at Beobrand conspiratorially. "I see your grasp of our tongue has improved since last we met."

Marcoul was speaking too fast for Beobrand now, and with the background noise of conversations, he struggled to comprehend the exact meaning of Marcoul's words. He looked to Halinard, who interpreted.

"Please tell him he is too kind, but," Beobrand gave a thin smile, "as he can see, my language skills are still sorely lacking."

Marcoul returned the smile with obvious insincerity and Beobrand was reminded of how he had disliked this man when he had stayed at his hall. Brocard had been sure he'd had something to do with the attack on the queen and they had hurried away from Marcoul's lands as quickly as they were able. To see him now, in this strange setting, was unnerving.

"It is wonderful to meet you again," Marcoul said, looking Beobrand up and down. He smiled, strangely nervous now, and seemed to be almost embarrassed, though by what, Beobrand could not tell. Halinard translated his words and then continued. "He says this is the first time he has known one of Dalfinus'…" Halinard faltered, searching for the correct words. "Guests of honour," he concluded.

"You mean Wilfrid?" Beobrand surmised. "He is excited to hear what Dalfinus will say today of his future."

Marcoul listened to Halinard as he interpreted Beobrand's words. The strange smile on his face broadened.

"No, Lord Beobrand," he said. "I meant you."

Beobrand thought he understood the man, but he was

confused as to his meaning. Before he could ask for clarification, the doors from which they had entered the arena were slammed shut. The crashing noise startled Beobrand and he turned quickly. Just as outside the building, four guards stood before the doors. Scanning the rest of the arena, Beobrand counted several more guards dotted about the edge of the sand. There were perhaps a score of them in total and they each stood to attention, helms polished and shining, spears planted firmly on the ground next to them.

"I've got a bad feeling about this," muttered Gram.

Without thinking, Beobrand reached for the pommel of his sword for reassurance. His fingers met only air and he cursed silently. He agreed with Gram. He sensed a shift in the gathered men. There was an energy about them now, a crackling power such as is felt before lightning strikes.

Forcing himself to breathe slowly, he sipped his wine and swept his gaze over the arena. A few of the people were looking in his direction, but none had moved or shown any aggression towards him or his companions. Surely he was worrying unduly. There were so many men gathered here, his presence must only be as one guest more. But what of Marcoul's words? Had he misunderstood him?

Looking over at where Wilfrid stood close to Dalfinus, Beobrand noticed a stocky man with long hair, pulled back from his face and secured in a ponytail. There was something vaguely familiar about the man, though Beobrand could not place him. Something in the way he moved perhaps. The man reached out to snatch a pastry from a passing servant. His hand was scarred, red skin puckered from some past wound. He moved like a warrior, wary and stepping lightly, as if ready to fight at any moment.

"Who is Dalfinus talking to?" Beobrand asked.

Halinard interpreted.

"That is Agobard," said Marcoul.

Beobrand peered at the man.

"Who is he?"

Marcoul thought for a moment, as if weighing his words before speaking. Then, with a shrug, he replied.

"He is one of Dalfinus' men. A trusted messenger. He accompanied me all the way from my hall."

Frowning, Beobrand tried to think where he had seen Agobard before, but the man's face was turned away and partly in shadow. Perhaps he had been at Marcoul's hall the night that Beobrand had been there. That would explain his familiarity. He was about to ask Marcoul if that were the case, when Agobard turned towards Beobrand, as if he had sensed the thegn of Ubbanford staring across the sand at him.

Their eyes met and in a flashing memory of chaotic shouts, clangour of weapons against shields, splattered mud, driving rain and the thrumming of hooves, Beobrand knew exactly where he had seen Agobard before.

Above the man's eyes, which were widening as he realised that Beobrand had recognised him, there was a crescent moon-shaped scar. Beobrand remembered the thud of the horse's hoof hitting the man's forehead. The raw scar on Agobard's hand came from Beobrand's blade. He had thought the man dead, but here he was, standing beside Dalfinus, having arrived with Marcoul, on whose land the ambush had taken place.

In a rush, the tangled threads of Beobrand's thoughts began to weave together, revealing a tapestry of deceit and perfidy. This Agobard had been one of those who attacked Balthild in the forest near Quentovic. If he was Dalfinus' man, then the *comes* of Liyon's hand must surely be one of those directing the plot against the queen. But how many others were involved? Brocard had been suspicious of Marcoul. The fact that he was here, and had even travelled with Agobard, could not be a coincidence.

Beobrand's mind reeled. The anticipation in the air was thick with treachery. Faces were turning towards him, picking up on the shocked realisation on Agobard's features. Beobrand could still not make sense of everything that was happening. He was yet unsure how some of the threads fit into the traitorous weft and warp of plots and plans. His invitation to this place could be no mere accident of chance. But what reason could Dalfinus have for bringing him to his hunt? If he had suspected that Beobrand knew of his part in the attack on the queen, surely he would have had him killed before now. And what of Wilfrid? How did the young novice fit in with everything? Could he have betrayed Beobrand to his future father-in-law? Perhaps Dalfinus had no knowledge until this very moment that Beobrand would recognise Agobard, thus reaching the inevitable conclusion of his plot against the queen.

All these thoughts flashed through his mind in a muddle, like snowflakes in a blizzard, too fast and fragile to be caught and examined. He shook his head in an effort to clear it. Halinard tugged at his sleeve.

"Lord," Halinard said in a voice barely above a whisper, "look."

His eyes were wide. The Frankish warrior was usually calm and controlled, but now his face was twisted with an emotion Beobrand could not place. Halinard pulled again at his kirtle and, with a start, Beobrand realised that the man's hand was trembling.

Following Halinard's stare, Beobrand looked past Agobard, Dalfinus and Wilfrid to where the crates were stacked. A fat man had lifted one of the sheets, revealing what was beneath. The sight twisted Beobrand's stomach. It was a stoutly made crate, bars of oak as thick as a forearm. But it was not the enclosure that shook Beobrand, but its contents. Within the cage, blinking against the sudden bright light, was Binyamin, the man who had buried his father not two weeks previously. His bearded face was mottled with bruises. He stared out and saw Beobrand. For the briefest time hope lit his face, only to be replaced a moment later by resignation. Binyamin bit his lower lip and looked down, shutting out the murmured sigh that had rippled across the gathered nobles.

Beobrand's guts churned. So this was what they hunted at Dalfinus' special events. Beobrand wondered what lay beneath the other sheets. How many men? Were there women there too? Children? He could feel the beast of his anger rousing deep within him. He had kept it in its own cage these last weeks, but he sensed the moment was not far away when he would need to call upon his unfettered fury.

"The whoresons," he snarled, barely aware that he had spoken. Without conscious thought, he groped for his sword, forgetting it was not at his side.

Then the man who had pulled aside the sheet covering Binyamin's cage turned towards Beobrand and in that instant he knew it was not the sight of the poor Iudeisc man inside the cage that had shocked Halinard so.

The fat man's jowls quivered. He wore the finest silks and yet he seemed dishevelled, as if he had slept in his clothes. Where most of the men present had well-groomed beards, some long, many cut short and trimmed, this man's beard was neither. He had what appeared to be a few days of stubble covering his face and bulbous neck. Beobrand had only seen the man once, several years before, but he would never forget those cold, emotionless eyes.

"Vulmar," he hissed.

Halinard tensed beside him, as if the name itself had power. The man had been Halinard's master for many years. He was a monster; a man of power who abused his position to take whatever he desired. He had violated Halinard's daughter, Joveta, and had planned to do the same to Beobrand's child, Ardith.

Beobrand had dreamt of one day facing Vulmar and ending his existence once and for all. The Frankish noble had sent men to kill him, all the way to Northumbria. He yet lived, and all they had succeeded in doing was to start the war between Deira and Bernicia. Now, after all those years, the man was standing before him. Beobrand drew his seax from the sheath that hung beneath his belt. He did not need his sword to slay the likes of Vulmar.

"Easy, Beobrand," said Gram, taking stock of the situation quickly. "There are too many of them."

It was true. He wanted to rush at Vulmar and strike him down, but Gram was right. The arena was filled with nobles, servants and a score of warriors loyal to Dalfinus. It would be all they could do to escape with their lives. If Woden smiled upon them, maybe they would survive long enough to be able to face Vulmar again. Dalfinus, who was clearly a player in this complex game of tafl in which Beobrand now found himself, would need to face justice too, but Beobrand had no idea how he could bring this to pass, surrounded by foes, as they were. No, the time to confront Dalfinus and Vulmar for their treachery would need to wait for another day. All Beobrand and his friends could do now was flee.

The moment he'd made the decision, Dalfinus must have seen it on his face, for as Beobrand turned towards the guarded doors, the *comes* of Liyon shouted, "Kill them!"

Halinard was still rooted to the sand, mouth agape as he stared at Vulmar. Beobrand pulled at his shoulder.

"Come on," he hissed, "we will kill him another day."

Gram was already moving. He shoved past a couple of servants, sending plates and cups flying, and hurried towards the double doors. The guards around the perimeter were confused as to what was happening. They had not yet begun to move. Once they had regained their wits, there would be no way for the three of them to escape. At the moment, there were only four guardsmen before the doors. If they were faced with twenty, they would be slain, or captured, and most likely placed inside those cages alongside Binyamin, for whatever perverse game Dalfinus had planned for his captives.

Marcoul stepped into Beobrand's path, reaching for him in an effort to hinder his movement. Perhaps the man thought he was showing bravery by standing before the tall, fair-haired warrior from the north. Maybe he thought the worst that could happen to him would be for Beobrand to shove him aside. Whatever thoughts went through Marcoul's mind as he blocked Beobrand's path were quickly silenced.

Without hesitation Beobrand slapped away the man's clutching hands and plunged his seax blade into Marcoul's right eye. The blade punched through the soft tissue and drove into the man's brain. Such was the speed and force of the blow that the metal tip of the blade scraped the rear of Marcoul's skull before he started to fall. He was dead in a heartbeat, and Beobrand wrenched his seax free from the socket, as the corpse tumbled to the sand.

Beobrand stepped over the crumpled form without a second glance. One less enemy to worry about. Halinard had drawn his own knife now and had regained his usual composure. He snarled at the men around them and they stepped back, wary of the naked blades and shocked by Marcoul's sudden slaying.

Ahead of them, Gram was almost at the doors. The guards had dropped into defensive stances, lowering their spears. Beobrand scanned the perimeter and saw that some of the other wardens were on the move, snapped out of their hesitation by the sight of bloodshed.

Vulmar shouted something over the sudden din, his voice whining and angry. Beobrand could not make out the words, but he understood Dalfinus' response well enough.

"Things change, my friend."

Beobrand ignored the two of them and rushed after Gram. There was no time to think now. Their only chance was to overpower the spear-men at the doors before the others closed in. The guards were well-trained and they held their ground with spears levelled and shields raised. Without looking, Beobrand could sense the movement of the other guards from around the amphitheatre. In moments, they would face overwhelming numbers and be surrounded.

"Death!" he shouted in his battle-voice. Halinard was by his side now, and together they joined Gram, pushing forward in a frenzied assault.

Beobrand ducked beneath a spear thrust, grabbing the haft in his left hand and forcing the iron blade away and up. Sliding his half-hand along the smooth haft, he pressed forward. A second spear-tip flashed towards his face and he caught it on his seax blade with a clang. Then he was too near for the guards to bring their spears to bear. They had positioned themselves with their backs to the oak doors, so when their attackers grew close, their long spears became unwieldy in the confined space, constrained by the timber behind them.

Beobrand stabbed savagely into the exposed throat of the owner of the spear he held in his left hand. The guard beside him, realising his spear was too long to use against Beobrand, dropped his weapon and swung a punch at the Bernician thegn. The calm of battle had descended upon Beobrand now and he saw the blow coming. With more space, he might have been able to avoid the punch altogether, but Halinard and Gram were close beside him, and he could not risk losing his grip on the blood-slick handle of his seax, so all Beobrand could do was sway his head to lessen the impact. The powerful blow glanced off his cheek and snapped his head back. Beobrand grunted, but barely felt the impact. The pain would come later.

If he lived.

Beobrand tugged his seax blade free from the first man's throat. Hot blood gushed and Beobrand slashed the knife's sharp edge across the second warrior's knuckles as he was pulling back for another punch. The man howled and tried to step back, but there was nowhere to flee. His back collided with the barred doors. Without pause, Beobrand hacked the seax down the length of the man's face, cutting across his forehead, and splitting his nose and lip. In an instant the warden's face was a crimson mask. He slid away and down, whimpering and mewling, all fight fled.

To either side of Beobrand, Halinard and Gram had got the better of their adversaries. Halinard had somehow managed to wrest his opponent's spear from him and, stepping away for space, had then pierced the guard's chest with his own weapon.

Gram had disarmed his enemy and was now repeatedly plunging his seax into the guard's belly. The man's face was white, his teeth bared as he clawed at Gram, desperate for any way of halting the savage attack that was tearing at his innards.

Beobrand heaved at the bar that locked the doors. He cursed as he pulled the gates open and realised they could only be barred from this side.

Beobrand's mouth was filled with blood where his teeth had cut the inside of his cheek. He spat onto the sand.

Their strength, speed and skill had carried them this far because the guards had been taken by surprise, but the other guardsmen were on the move now. They would have close to twenty armed warriors on their heels. And there were countless more outside, if they managed to get out of the building. But that was a problem for later, now they needed to get into the dark tunnel as quickly as possible.

Beobrand ushered Halinard in before him. Turning, he snatched up a fallen spear and, without hesitation, threw it with all his strength at the closest approaching guard. The man did not even have time to look surprised. Beobrand was no expert spear-man, not like his gesith, Garr back at Ubbanford, but he was strong and, at such close range, he could not miss. The spear flew higher than he had anticipated, hitting the man in the right shoulder. It struck him so hard that he staggered backwards, spinning around before collapsing to the sand.

The other red-cloaked wardens, wary now, slowed their advance.

"Come on," snarled Beobrand, pulling Gram away from the man he was still stabbing over and over. He had never seen Gram lose himself in combat this way before, but it was impossible to tell when the battle-frenzy would take hold of a warrior. Perhaps this was a gift from Woden, sent to aid them in their escape.

Gram spun around at Beobrand's touch. He stepped back, raising his seax, ready to defend himself. Beobrand had seen men strike their friends before when blinded by the battle-madness.

"I am not your foe-man, Gram," he said in a stern voice.

Gram blinked, then his eyes cleared. Nodding, he hurried into the gloom beyond the open doors. Halinard was already halfway down the tunnel.

"Hurry," snapped Beobrand, shoving Gram forward. "There is no way to block the doors. They'll be on us in a heartbeat. Our only chance is to get out into the city and hope we can lose ourselves." As he said the words, it sounded like a futile plan, but he pushed aside his doubts. They must keep moving forward. There was no time to question, no time to show fear or uncertainty. To halt now would spell disaster.

He ran after Halinard. Gram took a few steps, then stumbled, falling to one knee. Beobrand ran back, offering a hand. Gram clutched the outstretched hand, groaning as he rose. It was then that Beobrand saw the dark stain on his thigh. Gram's face was pale in the sunlight that filtered into the tunnel through the open doors. The droplets of blood from the man he had killed were dark against his pallid skin.

"Wish I'd had a shield," Gram said, smiling thinly against the pain that had him in its grip.

Beobrand glanced down and saw a long rent in Gram's breeches. The wool was sodden and black with blood. In the pool of light from the doors, Beobrand could make out splashes of blood where Gram had staggered down the tunnel. Outside, the guards were gathering, darkening the entrance. In moments, they would gain enough valour to rush into the tunnel.

Gram leaned on the spear he had taken from one of the fallen guards.

"Go," he said simply. "See that those whoresons pay. And tell Bassus I died well."

Beobrand's vision blurred as his eyes brimmed with tears. Surely there must be something he could do, some way that Gram could escape from this. But as he looked into the older man's eyes, they both knew the truth.

"This is where I die, Beobrand. Whether for nought, or for something depends on you. Go! I will hold them here. Flee and find Cynan and the others and make sure my life buys your freedom."

Turning away, Gram faced the light. He hefted the spear, and took a couple of stiff-legged steps towards the doors.

Blinking away his tears, Beobrand ran in the other direction. He could not believe that Gram would die. He had known him for so long. Gram had always seemed invincible to Beobrand. But he knew that no man could escape the cold hand of death. Whether it came in the flicker of steel of a spear's blade, or the slow, crushing breathlessness of old age and decrepitude, death would find them all in the end; both the weak and the strong.

That thought, and Gram's words, spurred him on. He must escape from this place and find Cynan and the rest of his gesithas. Could they already be dead? He had not seen Thagmar in the amphitheatre. Had he been sent into the city to dispatch Beobrand's men while he was lured to his doom here?

"Gram?" asked Halinard, as Beobrand approached.

Beobrand shook his head. There was no need for words.

The light in the tunnel dimmed and there was a sudden roar of men and the clash of weapons. Someone screamed out. Others shouted.

Beobrand did not turn to see Gram's last stand. He knew he

would acquit himself well, but in order for his death to have some meaning, they must escape.

"Ready?"

Halinard nodded, his face grim in the shadows.

"Come then," said Beobrand, "let us be free of this place while we still have the chance."

Side by side, they sprinted down the remainder of the tunnel, slamming their shoulders into the doors.

PART THREE

FLIGHT INTO DARKNESS

Chapter 21

Cynan's head throbbed. Opening his eyes, he winced as the bright light lanced into his brain. With a groan, he pushed himself up on his elbow and looked about him. Slowly, the night before came back to him. Beobrand had left early with Gram and Halinard, wishing to be fresh for the big hunt. Cynan and the others had remained at Genofeva's, where they had drunk too much of her good wine. Ingwald and Bleddyn were asleep on the floor nearby. There was no sign of any of the others. Cynan had a vague recollection of Eadgard mentioning a brothel. Grindan had been keen to go with his brother. They all knew he had been smitten by one of the girls there. A pretty young thing from a far-off land called Suriyah. Grindan spent much of his time, and all of his wealth, visiting the girl. Cynan had told him it was a bad idea to get so enthralled with a whore, but Grindan had merely shrugged and said with a twisted, sad smile, "I can no more choose what my heart will desire, than a man can choose his wyrd."

Cynan could not argue with that, but he knew it would be hard on the man when it came time to leave. The rest of the men had been in high spirits as the drink flowed, and though they might not have been so enraptured as Grindan, they each had favourite girls they wished to visit before they departed Liyon.

Cynan had long since decided he would not seek solace between a stranger's thighs. He wanted to continue drinking. Bleddyn, still moping over having had to leave Alpaida, was happy enough to join him. Ingwald had dutifully stayed too. Cynan knew the man had found a plump redhead he would have surely liked to see, so he urged him to go, but the older man declined.

"Emma will only cry when I tell her I must leave," Ingwald had said. "And what man likes to hear a woman's wailing?"

"Then don't tell her you're leaving," Cynan had replied. "I thought you said you could barely understand each other anyway."

"But if I said nothing, lord, that would be dishonest. Besides, a woman always knows such things, no matter if the man speaks the words or not. No, I will stay and drink with you until I can no longer understand anybody, or indeed speak."

Cynan had not pressed him further, but he had never seen Ingwald so keen to drink himself into oblivion. He thought of what Grindan had said and wondered if Ingwald too might not have found love where he had not sought it.

"Good morning." The cheery voice sliced through Cynan's thoughts. He grimaced at the loud sound.

"Genofeva," he said, looking up at the woman who had her back to him. She was kneading bread on a tabletop, every now and again picking up the dough and slapping it back on the board. Each thwack of the dough made Cynan flinch. Genofeva smiled at his discomfort. She muttered something that he did not fully understand, but from the tone seemed to be an admonition about drinking too much.

Nodding, he pushed himself to his feet. It was warm in the room with fires already blazing ready for cooking the copious amounts of food the widow served.

"Drink," Genofeva said.

The thought of drinking more made Cynan's stomach heave, but she smiled and pointed to a jug on a nearby table. "Water."

He stepped over Ingwald's snoring form and filled one of the wooden cups beside the earthenware pitcher. He sniffed the contents, then, satisfied that it was indeed water, he took a sip.

"Thank you," he said.

Genofeva grunted.

He thought back to the night before, trying to make sense of awakening here. He remembered saying they should return to the palace, and then nothing more after that but a blur of food, wine and riotous laughter. Genofeva must have allowed them to sleep on her floor.

He prodded Ingwald with his foot.

The bald man did not awaken, but his snoring stuttered to a halt. He rolled over, throwing his arm across his face to cover his eyes. In moments his breathing had slowed and he was once again fast asleep.

Beside him Bleddyn opened his eyes blearily.

"Lord?"

"Water," said Cynan, nodding to the jug and cups.

Bleddyn rose, rubbing a hand across his face. He poured himself a cup and drank.

"Wake up," Cynan said, and poked Ingwald again. He could tell from the angle of the sun through the windows that it was very early, but they had imposed on Genofeva enough already and now they were cluttering up her kitchen. Cynan kicked Ingwald again, harder this time, but still the older man made no sign of moving.

Refilling his cup, Cynan dashed the cold contents over Ingwald's partially covered face. The warrior sat up spluttering and cursing.

"Time to be up," Cynan said, handing him a cup of water.

Ingwald glared at him, but after a moment, he took the cup and drank.

Genofeva kindly gave them a loaf of yesterday's bread and, despite their tender heads and roiling stomachs, they thanked her and staggered out into the courtyard.

"Perhaps we could go back to the palace and get some sleep." Ingwald hawked and spat into the slow-moving waters of the Sona.

The three of them had finished the bread as they sat on the wharf, watching the boats sliding up and down the wide river. The sun gleamed on the water, making them squint against the brightness. The thought of sleeping was tempting, but Beobrand had told them they would be leaving on the morrow no matter what happened today.

"No," Cynan said, "we must purchase what we need for the next part of our journey. When we are done, we can rest. It is early, and if we make a start now, we might be done by midday."

"You think we will be heading north or south?" asked Bleddyn.

Cynan pondered for a moment. A gull swooped low, watching them as it flew past, no doubt investigating whether the men had any bread left or if they had discarded any crumbs.

"I know not," he said, truthfully. The decision hinged on Wilfrid and his relationship with the nobles of Liyon. The possibilities were too confusing to contemplate and Cynan shook his head. "But no matter. Whichever direction we travel, we will need the same supplies. Beobrand gave me coins enough and instructions to be ready to travel tomorrow morning. I have known Beobrand longer than you, but I think you would both agree that we do not wish to displease our lord by sleeping during the day."

As they had walked down to the wharf, he had weighed the small leather purse that hung from his belt. To his relief, it was still heavy with the gold coins that the people of Liyon used. Fleetingly he had worried that he might have spent too much of what Beobrand had given him, or perhaps lost it in the drunken haze of the previous night. He was certain that he had used at least a couple of the gold coins to purchase more wine and food. Closing his eyes, he had an image of handing several coins to Genofeva. It was little wonder she had allowed them to sleep on her floor without complaint. He had given her more gold in one night than most men would spend in her establishment in a month. Thank the gods Genofeva was an honest woman. They would have made easy targets for thieves while they snored drunkenly in her kitchen.

"There is one problem," said Bleddyn.

Without warning, Ingwald rose and stumbled away from them to lean on a mooring post that jutted up from the edge of the timber wharf. There he drew in deep breaths and looked up at the pale blue of the morning sky, as if praying that the bread and water would remain in his belly.

"Two, if you count Ingwald's puking," continued Bleddyn.

"I am not going to puke," Ingwald said, angrily waving a hand at them. His pallid, sweat-beaded skin told a different tale, but he valiantly fought against the evident revolt of his stomach, panting open-mouthed.

Cynan turned back to Bleddyn. "What problem?"

"We do not have Halinard or Wilfrid with us."

Cynan frowned for a moment before the reality dawned on him.

"Between the three of us we will make ourselves understood," he said, hoping he was right.

"I'm not sure how much use Ingwald will be," said Bleddyn with a grin.

Cynan turned in time to see Ingwald vomit noisily into the river.

"You drunken whoreson," yelled an enraged voice from out of sight beneath the raised wharf. Ingwald could not stop himself retching again, but he staggered back, away from the river's edge in an attempt to avoid whoever he had inadvertently splashed.

The cursing and shouting from beneath the wharf continued. There were dozens of wherries, skiffs and barges all along the wharf, some large vessels too. One of the smaller boats must have come close to the wharf without them noticing. The boat had been in the wrong place at the worst time. Cynan hurried forward to see who the unlucky sailor was. Even now the man was bellowing imprecations to the "goat-swiving whoreson" who had showered him in puke.

As he reached the edge of the timber quay, it struck Cynan that he understood the man's words. The sailor was cursing in the Anglisc tongue. Glancing at Bleddyn, who raised his eyebrows, Cynan peered down to the river. There, hitherto completely hidden from where they had been sitting, rested a six-oared boat. There were three men at the oars and a fourth manned the rudder. The boat was low in the water, heavily laden with sacks. One of the sacks and the steersman were splattered with Ingwald's undigested breakfast.

The oarsman closest to the rudder began to laugh. The helmsman snapped at him angrily in Frankish. The sailor fell silent, biting his lip. They were clearly a skilled crew, for in moments, they had shipped their oars and slid alongside the wharf. The sailor at the prow stood, a coiled rope in his hand. For a heartbeat, he seemed to toy with the idea of throwing it to Cynan or Bleddyn, but evidently deciding that neither of them would be capable of catching it or indeed securing the boat, instead he stepped up onto the boat's wale and leapt onto the timber structure of the wharf. Nimbly he scrambled up to where the two men looked on in stunned silence. Ignoring them and Ingwald, who was still bent over a few paces away, the sailor looped the hawser around the mooring post and pulled the boat close in to the wharf. Another rope snaked up to him. He snatched it expertly from the air and secured it to the bollard.

An instant later, the vomit-splattered helmsman, face twisted with rage, appeared over the lip of the wharf and rushed towards Ingwald. The man was stocky, with strong arms and short, thick legs. He was not old, but his skin was lined and weathered. The steersman was yelling abuse at Ingwald now in Frankish so rapid Cynan could make no sense of it. He wondered if he had imagined the man speaking in Anglisc. Perhaps it had been one of the other sailors.

And yet, as the man ranted at Ingwald, who was sheepishly apologising in his faltering Frankish, there was something familiar in the sailor's gait. Cynan recognised the pugnacious manner in which the man jutted his face at Ingwald, the way he stood, hands on his hips, as if daring him to vomit on him again. Cynan shook his head.

Surely it could not be.

The other sailors had climbed onto the quay and, in spite of their smiles, Cynan was aware that they were watching their skipper closely, ready to jump to his defence if needed. Bleddyn moved beside Cynan. He saw that Bleddyn's hand rested on the hilt of his sword. Cynan shook his head. Beobrand would not forgive them for fighting on their last day in the city.

Stepping closer, Cynan touched the squat sailor on the shoulder. The burly man spun about, fists raised. There could be no doubt now, though Cynan could make no sense of what his eyes beheld.

"Sigulf?" he said.

The stocky sailor fell silent, peering up at Cynan. Slowly, his eyes widened.

"Cynan?" The sun was full on the man's face and he shifted his head so that Cynan's shadow fell on him, making it possible for him to better see the Waelisc warrior. "Cynan!" he exclaimed. "It is you!"

They had not seen each other for years, but without hesitation, the two men embraced. After a moment, Cynan pushed him away. The smell of Ingwald's vomit made him gag and he fought not to disgrace himself by puking too.

"By Christ's bones, brother," said Sigulf, and the use of that title brought so many memories to Cynan, rushing back like the freezing waters of the Narrow Sea. He thought of the chaos of betrayal in Mantican's hall. Of the bitterly cold surf washing over them as they fought Draca and his pirates on a snow-riven beach. The image of blood soaking into the sand; Cargást's sad eyes and Bearn's broken, lifeless body. Sigulf was no warrior, but he was a brave man and had earned the right to call himself Cynan's brother.

"How long has it been?" Sigulf asked. "It must be getting on for ten years."

"Yes," replied Cynan, his mind still reeling from the unexpected meeting with a man he had never thought to see again, and certainly not here, in this Burgundian city.

"You look like you are in need of a drink," said Sigulf, smiling broadly. "Let me buy you a jug of wine. Then you can tell me what in Christ's name you are doing in Liyon."

The thought of more wine was almost enough to undo Cynan, but he took a long breath and held his stomach in check. His mind was racing. He had many questions for this man, but he could not risk frittering the day away on idle chat with old friends.

Ingwald, still pale, but upright now and with the worst of his sickness past, for the time being at least, wiped his sleeve across his mouth.

"I am sorry," he muttered to Sigulf.

Sigulf shook his head.

"It is already forgotten," he said. "I've had worse things dropped on me from the wharf of Liyon before, I can tell you." He clapped Ingwald on the shoulder as if they were old friends.

"I don't know about Cynan and Ingwald," said Bleddyn, stepping close and offering his hand to Sigulf, "but I for one would appreciate a drink and perhaps something to eat." He looked from Ingwald to Cynan, gauging their reaction. "To settle my stomach."

Sigulf grasped Bleddyn's forearm tightly in the warrior grip.

"Then it is agreed," he said, beaming a wide smile. "I know a place near here that serves wonderful food and wine."

Without waiting for a response, he turned to his sailors and barked a quick succession of orders to them in perfect Frankish. Bleddyn glanced at Cynan.

"And they say Beobrand is the lucky one," he whispered, then louder to Sigulf: "Tell me, Sigulf, how it is that you know Cynan. And are you busy for the rest of the day?"

"I am no scop, but there is a tale to tell there. And I can always find time to catch up with an old friend," he nodded at Bleddyn, "and new, over a cup or three of wine."

"That is like music to my ears," replied Bleddyn with a grin. "But after a drink, there is something else you could do for us."

"Oh, and what is that?"

"We are in need of an interpreter."

Chapter 22

The doors flew open and Halinard and Beobrand ran out into the sunlight. This side of the building was in shade, but it was still bright after the dark tunnel. The door wards must have heard the tumult from inside the amphitheatre for they were facing the doors. One had been standing close enough that the door Beobrand had barged through struck him. The guard flailed backwards, and toppled over onto the cobbles. Beobrand saw it was the red-faced, bearded leader, but there was no time to gloat.

The other men stepped back in surprise. By the horses, a dozen or more city guards turned to see what had caused the commotion. With a pang, Beobrand looked down at the wooden chest that held Nægling and Halinard's sword. It was shut and they could not spare a moment or risk turning their backs on the door wards to look for their weapons. Behind them, the sounds of fighting had been replaced by the echoing slaps of running feet on the flagstones. Cursing, Beobrand sprinted in the opposite direction to the horses. They could not hope to fight the guards and survive, so they would have to make do with no mounts and no weapons beyond their seaxes. Their situation was desperate, but while they lived, there was still hope.

"This way," he shouted, heading across the open ground and

making his way towards a narrow alley between two buildings. Shouts came from close behind them and Beobrand pushed himself to run faster. He was tall, and his strides were long. Fast and fleet of foot as he was when facing an opponent with sword and shield, he was no runner. His injuries over the years had slowed him down. Cynan could beat most men in foot races. Beobrand could not. Halinard was even slower. He was older than Beobrand and had a limp from where he had been injured last year in Rheged.

Glancing back, Beobrand saw that Halinard was falling behind. There were half a dozen guards in pursuit, with more following further away. Beobrand slowed his pace a little, until he was beside Halinard.

"Run," he panted. "Do you want us to get captured and killed? What of Joveta and Gisela? Would you leave them?"

With a growl, Halinard urged his body to greater speed.

"Good!" shouted Beobrand. "Run, you Frankish bastard, run!"

Halinard did not reply, but sprinted on faster than Beobrand had ever seen him move before.

Briefly, they ran through bright sunlight, the dark mouth of the alley yawning before them. They were almost at the entrance to the alleyway when a spear clattered nearby, skittering across the cobbles. Halinard tripped on the weapon and almost fell, but Beobrand pulled him upright and pushed him on. Stooping, he snatched up the spear, offering up a silent prayer to Woden to turn away any more projectiles that might be flung at their backs. His breath was rasping now, his lungs burning. He wished he had made more of an effort at training over the last weeks. But then, in the sun-filled lazy days of spring, he had not felt the need. This gods-forsaken city had made them all soft.

Another spear struck the timber wall of the building to the right as Halinard sped into the alley. Beobrand was a step behind him and in an instant, they were both once again in cool shade.

The ground squelched beneath their feet and the acrid odour of piss and shit enveloped them. They did not slow as the alleyway turned sharply to the left at the end of the first house.

The moment they rounded the bend, Beobrand halted. Halinard carried on running for several paces before realising his lord had stopped. He turned, bent double and dragging in great breaths of the foetid air. He was about to speak, when the first of their pursuers reached the corner. With a roar, Beobrand drove his stolen spear into the man's chest, shoving him backwards, where he tangled with the rest of the guards who had rushed into the narrow alleyway.

Leaping onto the man, using the spear that jutted from his body to steady himself, Beobrand drew his bloody seax again and hacked and hewed at the guards. His tiredness was forgotten now.

"Death! Death!" he bellowed at them.

The heavy seax blade struck flesh and cracked bones and the men's screams filled the shadowed passageway. The man he had speared held a sword in his weakening hand. Beobrand yanked the weapon free, then turned on his heel, leaving chaos behind him.

Pushing Halinard before him, the two of them ran on, slipping and sliding in the muck as they headed ever downhill. The guards shouted and cursed as they pulled their injured and dying out of the way so that they could resume their pursuit.

Beobrand slipped in the mire as they sped around a corner. He fell, his hands plunging into the cold mud. Halinard hauled him up. After several more turns, they entered a small yard, criss-crossed with wattle fences. There was a large hog in one of the small enclosures. The others were empty apart from several hens that were pecking in the mud. The birds squawked and clucked as Beobrand hurdled the fence, scattering them. Halinard's foot caught on the top of the fence as he followed his lord and he sprawled onto the earth. The pig squealed in dismay. Dogs barked in nearby houses, adding their yapping cries to the mayhem.

Beobrand dragged Halinard to his feet and the two of them stood for a while in breathless silence, swallowing great lungfuls of air. Beobrand straightened and listened. He could hear shouts far off, but the sounds of the guards were fainter than before.

"They must have taken the wrong turning back there," said Halinard.

"There are many of them," panted Beobrand. "They will find us soon enough. We cannot stop here."

They were still winded, but had both recovered enough to be able to carry on. They set off once again, more slowly now, but still with haste. Climbing over the far fence, they headed between what looked like two storage sheds.

"We are heading for the river?" asked Halinard.

Beobrand could think of nowhere better.

"If we can get across the bridge, perhaps we can find Cynan and the others."

"Genofeva's will be the first place Thagmar will look for them."

Beobrand said nothing. Halinard was right. It would be dangerous for them to head to the tavern, but it was the only place where he thought they might find their friends. A woman leant out of a small window and shouted something at them as they passed. Her voice was strident and brash, but Beobrand did not understand her words. She was just as likely to be encouraging them as giving away their position to the guards.

A strong smell suddenly assailed them as they turned another corner. It was similar to the stench of piss and shit in the first alley, but much more potent. It hit them like a physical thing, making them gag and spit. Before them three men, with cloths tied about their faces, stood over great ponds filled with a noxious mixture of water, urine and excrement. The nearest man set aside the great paddle he was using to stir the liquid and the sheets of tanning leather within. Without a word, he pointed along a lane that sloped down in the direction of the river. Before today, Beobrand had always travelled by the main road, never by these alleys and back ways, but by his reckoning, the lane the tanner was indicating would take them out on the road beside the river, close to the bridge.

For a heartbeat, Beobrand hesitated, wondering if the tanner might perhaps be sending them into a trap. But what alternative did he have than to accept the man's directions without questioning his motives? Offering him a nod of thanks, Beobrand ran into the steeply sloped lane.

They careened down the hill, sensing that speed was all that could save them now. If they could reach the bridge before Dalfinus' men, they could cross and might evade capture in the bustling west side of Liyon.

They passed several warehouses, barns and sheds, the morning sunlight flickering bright and warm as they sped between the puddles of shade. The main road was before them now. Beobrand recognised it. There was the small leatherworker's shop where he had often stopped to peruse the satchels, flasks and purses that hung from its beams. It was as he had thought, they were only a few dozen paces away from the bridge over the Sona.

Halting at the edge of the building, he leant out and peered up the road towards the palace, and beyond that, the amphitheatre. His heart sank as he saw more than a dozen red-cloaked guardsmen moving at speed towards his position. They were shouting and yelling as they came.

"Not far now," Beobrand hissed. "But we must hurry." He meant to turn towards the bridge and make a run for it. They were far enough from the guards that they would surely be able to outrun them, even as tired as they were.

Halinard grabbed hold of his kirtle and pulled him back.

"Too late, lord," he whispered.

Beobrand followed his pointing finger and saw a line of

perhaps ten guards at the entrance to the bridge. As he saw them, so some of the warriors noticed him and Halinard. They shouted, and more cries answered them as the guards coming down the road saw their quarry too.

Cursing, Beobrand and Halinard hurried back up the lane.

Not too distant, perhaps just beyond the tanners, they could make out the shouts of other pursuers.

They were surrounded. Trapped.

"To the river!" snapped Beobrand, turning left beside a dilapidated warehouse.

The sounds of pursuit from the main road grew louder as guards entered the lane. Too late Beobrand realised he had led them into a dead end where three warehouses met. The timbers of the buildings were weathered and cracked and for a moment Beobrand wondered whether they might be able to break through the walls. He had the sword he had taken, but a sword was not much use when it came to cutting through wood. He scanned the shingled roof of one building, and the dark, mossy thatch of the others. Could they climb up and escape that way?

Something crunched beneath Beobrand's foot. Looking down he saw it was the desiccated corpse of a gull; skeletal body blackened and twisted, once white feathers begrimed and straggled. He shuddered, remembering Nelda's curse and her bird that he had struck down. Surely such a thing could only be a bad omen here in this place. Was this then how his tale would end? After all the battles, the shieldwalls, the clashes of kings for whom he had been champion, was he to be hacked down like a common thief in a stinking alleyway in Frankia?

Well, if this was to be his end, he would make them pay dearly for taking his life. He was Beobrand of Ubbanford and he would not go quietly. He longed to seek vengeance on Vulmar, and Dalfinus for his betrayal, but he could hear the guards closing in. It seemed Woden had finally turned his back on him. The All-father loved blood and chaos. Beobrand spat a gobbet of blood into the mud. If the gods indeed watched the lives of men so far south, he would give them something to remember him by.

"Tonight we will feast in Woden's corpse hall, my friend," he said, patting Halinard on the shoulder. "I am sorry for leading you here."

Halinard smiled and there was true warmth there, in spite of their dire predicament.

"You gave me life when I thought it had ended, lord," he said. "You saved my kin and took my oath. Where else should I be, but at your side?"

Beobrand nodded, his throat thick with emotion.

"Let's make them remember this day," he snarled, turning to face the opening of the alley between the warehouses. They could hear many voices now, calling and shouting to each other. There was fear in those voices. The city guards were hesitant, nervous of what they might find. The men they chased had already killed or wounded several of their number, and now, despite their overwhelming odds, they came cautiously.

And yet, Beobrand knew it was only a matter of time before the warriors rushed them. Halinard and he would exact a high blood-price, but they would succumb in the end. There could be no other outcome. He looked up at the bright blue of the sky and wondered if Eanflæd saw the same sky. Did she ever think of him, as he thought so often of her? He thought then of Ardith and the grandchild he had never met. He thought of Octa, his angry son, with whom he would never find peace. The thoughts of what he was losing filled him with an all-consuming rage, and he growled deep in his throat. Holding his seax in his left half-hand, he raised the stolen sword in his right and took another step towards the sound of the oncoming enemies.

Let them come! They would pay with their blood for all they had stolen from him.

There was a moment of calm. The shouts and voices were quietened. And yet he could make out the shifting of positions, the jangle of byrnies, the scrape of metal as blades were readied. They were so close now that he would have been able to smell them if not for the pervasive stench of the tannery nearby.

He imagined the warriors, just out of sight, looking into each other's frightened eyes, pointing and signalling who would be the first to attack.

Beobrand crouched in the warrior stance. He cared not who would be first to die on his blade. But he was done with waiting. And fleeing. Now was the time of death.

He took a deep breath, grimacing at the tang of the tanners' pools in his throat. He turned to Halinard. The Frank was grim-faced and pale now, but he held his seax before him, resolute and ready. Beobrand nodded and Halinard returned the gesture. No words were needed now.

For several heartbeats they stood like that, looking towards the alleyway where their enemies were gathered.

All was silent for a time, and then the guards came in a rush.

Chapter 23

"Tell him we'll pick them up first thing in the morning," said Cynan. His head throbbed and sweat soaked his kirtle. They had been traipsing through the noisy alleyways and streets of the city for much of the morning and he'd had enough. He was glad this was the last trader he needed to deal with. The sun was high in the sky and the day hot, and Cynan longed for the cool shade of Dalfinus' stone palace. Tomorrow they would be on the road, but this afternoon, with any luck, they could doze a while in comfort while Beobrand and the others sweated with the Frankish nobles on their special hunt.

Sigulf uttered a few quick words to the rat-faced man. The glover had tried their patience, but it seemed a bargain had finally been struck. The man rubbed the back of his hand over his long nose and nodded before replying.

"He says you must pay now," interpreted Sigulf.

Cynan sighed. He held out one shiny gold coin. He had thought they were done with winter and could barely believe they needed to buy gloves. But Sigulf had warned them about riding over the mountains to the south. Despite the warmth here, there would be snow and ice up there, and they would freeze without warm clothes.

"Tell him half now, the rest when we collect. And tell him

to have them all ready by dawn." Cynan doubted they would be here so early, but he did not want to be kept waiting. He imagined with some pleasure the sharp-nosed man growing frustrated and impatient when they did not arrive with the first light of the morning.

The glover stared at the gleaming metal for a heartbeat, then, licking his lips, he nodded in agreement. Cynan handed him the gold and turned on his heel, glad to be rid of the troublesome man.

Walking down the slope away from the overcrowded streets and towards the quieter pastures where cattle and sheep grazed to the west of the Sona, Cynan turned to Sigulf.

"I owe you my thanks. Without your help that bastard would have charged me double."

"At least!" said Sigulf. "He is as cunning as a fox, that one, but we know each other well and he has some of the best cloth in all of Frankia. The haggling can be tedious, but you won't be sorry with the results. His gloves will keep your fingers from freezing off, which must be worth a couple of coins."

"Again, I thank you. It has been a wonder to see you again after all these years." They walked beneath the shade of a couple of elms that grew beside the road. Cynan welcomed the coolness and toyed with the notion of sitting down to rest beneath the trees. He dismissed it as soon as the thought had come to him. He could not face any longer with Sigulf than was necessary.

"It has indeed been a marvel," said the sailor. "I still can scarcely believe we are together again."

Cynan glanced over at Ingwald and thought he saw the man roll his eyes before he turned away. He could not blame him. It was true that he had been pleased to see Sigulf at first, and the man had undoubtedly helped them to negotiate fair prices with the local traders, but much of the conversation that morning had been like this. Expressions of disbelief at meeting in the south of Frankia after so long. There was little of interest or substance in the man's talk and Cynan, along with his men, quickly grew tired of Sigulf's company. Cynan had forgotten what a difficult man he was, but it soon came back to him. It was Sigulf who had attempted to turn *Brimblæd*'s crew against Beobrand. He had questioned every decision and demanded fair payment for the risks the men endured. He was a good man, but he was dogged and defiant, and he was as cantankerous and quarrelsome as he was steadfast in a fight. These were useful traits when dealing with hard-nosed merchants, but his constant criticisms and needling, coupled with their wine-sickness from the overindulgence the night before, made him a less than perfect companion.

After their meeting at the wharf, Sigulf had led them back to Genofeva's, where Cynan had allowed him to buy them ale, some fresh bread and cheese. The widow had shaken her head to see them back so soon, but she'd greeted Sigulf by name and served them quickly enough.

Sigulf had told them of how he had used the wealth Beobrand had given him following Ardith's rescue to purchase his own boat. After plying his trade as a merchant along the coast of the Narrow Sea, he had travelled further south. Sigulf was a canny man with a keen eye for trade and he now carried all manner of goods, from earthenware pots of olive oil to bolts of silk along the coasts of the Great Sea and inland along the largest rivers. He often came to Liyon, but it had been years since he had returned to Cantware or seen anyone from his old life.

"From time to time I hear stories of Beobrand," he'd said, "but I never thought I would see him, or you, again."

He had asked Cynan for tidings of Albion and to hear the truth behind some of the stories he had heard of Beobrand and his Black Shields. Sigulf had sat leaning against Genofeva's wall, chewing on his bread and washing it down with swigs from the jug of wine he'd ordered for himself. He was prepared for tales of daring and adventure, but Cynan had answered tersely, in no mood for chatter. The humour of the group had curdled as it became obvious that Cynan was not going to regale Sigulf with his and Beobrand's exploits.

Cynan looked sidelong at Sigulf as they trudged out of the shade of the elm trees and walked between a small orchard and a fenced-off plot of land that housed half a dozen scruffy goats. A young boy, with a scab on the bridge of his nose, sat atop the fence, throwing pebbles at the animals. Silently, the boy halted his sport and watched the men pass. Sigulf spoke in a gruff voice to the lad. The boy retorted, jutting his chin out defiantly. Sigulf halted, turning to glower at the boy. When he took a step towards him, the youth leapt from the fence into the enclosure and hurried through the goats to the other side. There he leant against a fencepost with feigned indifference and observed Sigulf darkly.

Sigulf said nothing further, but turned and continued on his way. Gone was his jovial spirit of earlier. Cynan suspected he regretted agreeing to help them. The truth was they had little in common save for those few shared days when years before they had sailed aboard *Brimblæd* in search of Ardith. But still, they had fought side by side and that was a bond that could not easily be forgotten. And Sigulf was a good man, and true to his word. And yet, now that they had purchased all the supplies they required, Cynan did not think the sailor would be overly upset to part company with the surly warriors.

At one point in the morning, Sigulf's face had lit up. He had witnessed Attor as he came ambling down one of the muddy streets towards them. Attor had been as surprised as Cynan to see the sailor, and he had awkwardly allowed Sigulf to embrace him. But Sigulf's joy at the reunion was short-lived. Despite having sailed on *Brimblæd*, Attor seemed barely to remember him. Besides, the thin warrior was in a dark mood, having bidden farewell to the widow he had been seeing these last weeks.

At mid-morning, they had passed the brothel that the rest

of the gesithas favoured. It was a rambling building built long ago of brick with a tiled roof. The plaster was cracked now and had fallen from the walls in many places, and several of the age-darkened clay tiles had been replaced recently with bright, new earthenware shingles, giving the roof a mottled look. Still, it was an impressive place and once must have been a palace. There was an inner courtyard that was always thronged with women and drunken men. Cynan had been tempted to seek out the shade of the yard, but feared he would not be strong enough to resist the delights on offer. So he had sent Bleddyn in to rouse the men while the rest of them waited outside. The warriors had emerged, one by one, heavy of head from too much drink, and heart-weary from the knowledge that they were to leave behind the warm beds, whores and luxuries to which they had grown accustomed.

None of them knew Sigulf, and so were not that interested in the man. They had heard from the mouths of warriors they respected the tales of Ardith's rescue and had no desire to hear the story again from a sailor who was a stranger to them. And so, after polite nods and exchanges of pleasantries with the man from Hithe, they fell into their own conversations about the revelry of the night before and the journey that awaited them on the days ahead. They had grumbled at having to follow Cynan around the town, but he had insisted and now they were laden with all but the most cumbersome supplies. As the strongest, Eadgard carried the heaviest load of two large cheeses in a sack. Grindan, while slimmer than his bear of a brother, still bore his own share of the provisions: a dry cured ham. Attor had scowled, but had not complained when it fell to him to carry a sack of hard-baked bread. Bleddyn and Ingwald both had sacks of salted, dried sausages over their shoulders. By the time they reached the river, they were all drenched in sweat and moaning of aching backs and arms.

"The labour will do you all good," said Cynan. "You have

spent too long with the perfumed womenfolk of this city. You are soft."

The mention of women brought the image of Eadgyth into his mind. She was so far away and the thought of her filled him with frustrated anger. Perhaps he should have visited the old palace the men frequented. Why should he forsake the pleasures on offer there? Eadgyth would understand. He was a man, with needs. By all the gods, he was not even wed to the woman. And yet he had told himself he would not lie with another until he had spoken with Eadgyth and told her how he felt about her. He had often regretted his stubbornness, but at least now he did not have the added pain of needing to abandon a new woman in Liyon.

They were at the bridge now, and Cynan halted in a small patch of shade. One of the pair of city guards posted on the western edge of the bridge glanced in their direction, but showed little interest in the small gathering of men. Cynan wiped the sweat from his forehead with his sleeve. He wanted nothing more than to get to the palace and stretch out in the quiet shadows of the walled gardens. But he could not merely walk away from Sigulf, not after all his help.

"It has been a hot morning," he said. "I don't know what we would have done, if we had not found you."

"You would be a lot poorer, that's for certain," replied Sigulf with a broad smile.

Cynan laughed dutifully.

"Let me buy you a drink with some of that gold you have saved us."

Sigulf looked at the sweat-streaked faces of the other men. None of them returned his smile.

"You are kind," he said, holding his hands palms upward, "but alas, I must attend to my own affairs. It has been wonderful to see you again, Cynan. Please, pass on my greetings to Beobrand."

"Of course," replied Cynan, relief washing over him. "Perhaps we will see you again in one of the ports between here and Roma."

"Perhaps," said Sigulf, though each man knew there was very little likelihood of that.

"Waes hael," said Cynan, taking Sigulf's arm in the warrior grip. "May the wind always fill your sails."

Sigulf beamed and his eyes glistened with emotion.

"Good fortune on your journey," he said. He was turning to head down towards the wharf when a sudden commotion stopped him.

A dozen red-cloaked warriors of the city watch were sprinting across the bridge towards them. One of the guards near where Cynan and the others were saying their farewells shouted out to the running men, asking for the cause of their haste. As they drew closer, the leader of the group gave a hurried, breathless reply. He spoke too fast for Cynan to understand, but the sharpness of his tone and his obvious anxiety sent a tingling of unease down Cynan's spine.

"What did he say?" he asked Sigulf.

The sailor seemed unable to talk, but his pale face said much without words.

"What is it?" hissed Cynan. "Speak, man! What has happened?"

"He says…" Sigulf stuttered. "He says the men from Albion…" He drifted into silence, as if to utter the words pained him.

Where the bridge met the western shore, the guards were still talking loudly, voices raised in consternation, disbelief and anger. Sigulf cocked his head, listening, eyes widening at what he was hearing.

"What?" snapped Cynan, his frustration and apprehension building. "Speak!"

Sigulf's eyes flicked back to stare at the Waelisc warrior.

"They say Beobrand was like a wild animal, that he attacked the *comes* and his guests."

Cynan winced. He knew not what had occurred, but Beobrand's anger was legendary.

"Where is he? Does he—" He hesitated. "Does he yet live?"

Sigulf was still listening to the guards on the bridge. He nodded slowly.

"I think so. It seems he fled the amphitheatre and has disappeared. They are searching for him and another warrior who is with him. It sounds like there was much killing in their escape."

Cynan's stomach lurched and his head pounded. Beobrand had gone to the hunt with Halinard and Gram.

"Only one other warrior?" he asked.

"That is what they are saying."

A bellowing cry came from the guards at the bridge. One of them, a heavy-set man, whose helm sported a white plume of feathers, was pointing at the gesithas gathered in the shade.

"They seem to have recognised him," said Sigulf, nodding towards Eadgard, who towered above them all.

Cynan cursed. Of course, half the city knew Eadgard after his fight with Gunthar.

"Hey, you!" shouted the guard, advancing towards them. "You are from Albion, aren't you?" Cynan knew enough Frankish to understand the man's words. Following the guard's lead, the other warriors fell in beside him. Hesitantly at first, they began to close on them.

"Surely there has been some misunderstanding," whispered Sigulf. "I am sure this will be cleared up by nightfall."

Cynan had no such hope. He cast about for a way out of this, but he saw no escape.

"No," he said. "We cannot allow them to capture us." He recalled the man Dalfinus had ordered put to death on the journey from Paris. "We are strangers here, and if what you have heard is true, any friend of Beobrand's will be as good as dead if taken by the guard."

"You want us to fight then?" rumbled Eadgard, dropping his heavy sack and rolling his neck to loosen his muscles.

Cynan scanned the approaching men. Their faces were flushed and wet with sweat. Their eyes shone as brightly as the blades of their spears. There was fear in those eyes, but death lurked there too.

"If it comes to it," said Cynan, placing his hand on his sword's pommel, "we will fight."

"You will be killed," said Sigulf.

"Perhaps," replied Cynan, drawing his sword. "But this is our fight, not yours."

Sigulf, pale-faced, pulled a seax from the sheath that hung below his belt.

"We are brothers, are we not?" he said, jutting out his chin in the defiant manner Cynan recalled from when they had sailed together.

Cynan's heart swelled with a mixture of pride and sorrow. He wished they had not met Sigulf that morning. But a man could no more change the past than he could stop the tides.

"Aye, Sigulf," he said, offering a grim smile to the man, "that we are." He glanced around him. The Black Shields had shed their burdens and were all now readying themselves for battle. The guards were close now. There were two of them for each man of Albion, and they came with spears and shields. "If we are to be slain here," said Cynan, overwhelmed by a sudden sense of doom, "I could not ask for braver companions."

He wanted to say more. He wished he had longer to prepare the men for combat. They were weary from the night of carousing and the heat of the morning, but he knew they would acquit themselves well, even outnumbered as they were. He had stood beside them all before and knew of their worth. He opened his mouth to say as much, but there was no more time.

Seeing the men of Albion discarding their loads, drawing their blades and dropping into the warrior stance, the white-plumed leader shouted an order and the scarlet-cloaked guards lowered their spears. The time for talking was over.

With a roar, the Franks ran towards them.

Chapter 24

"What have you got there?"

The harsh voice spoke in Frankish. Beobrand held his breath and stifled the need to gag. The stench of the freshly cured leather was noxious and all-pervasive. He had thought the smell would become more bearable as he grew accustomed to it. He was wrong.

Beside him, Halinard tensed, as he too listened to the guards addressing the tanner. It wasn't the first time that the waggon they rode in had come to a halt, pausing at some obstacle in the path. But this was different. The tanner had whispered to them a few moments ago that they were approaching the city gate. Halinard had barely had time enough to hiss a translation to Beobrand before the lumbering vehicle creaked to a standstill.

There had followed a long pause. Beobrand had strained to hear any sign of what was happening, but all he heard were the muffled sounds of the city and his own blood rushing in his ears. After a time they had moved on, the waggon shifting and groaning beneath the weight of the hides, many of which were piled on top of Beobrand and Halinard. After a dozen heartbeats, the waggon had halted again, then, after a short time, the tanner had clicked his tongue at his mules, and they had trundled onward once more.

Beobrand, lying in the noisome dark, tried to picture what he remembered of the gate where they had entered the city all those weeks before. They must be in the queue of people threading their way out of Liyon. Beobrand had said that it might have been better to have waited, to leave closer to nightfall, when there would be fewer travellers and merchants on the road. The tanner had shaken his head and spoken quickly to Halinard. The Frank warrior had nodded in agreement.

"He says that if we leave at dusk, the guards will be suspicious. Also, if we set off now, so close to the time of our escape, it gives the watch less time to summon more men. The longer we leave it, the more likely they will search the cart. Setting off now is wise. The guards will not believe we have arranged an escape from the city so quick."

Beobrand could barely believe it himself. One moment they had been standing in the alleyway, weapons in hand, ready for the guards to overcome their fear and rush them, the next they had been slithering through the dark, pulling themselves through the slimy mud beneath one of the warehouses.

It had been Halinard who had first felt the tanner's touch on his foot. Halinard had been as taut as a bowstring, ready for combat, and had almost sliced through the man's wrist without pausing for thought. He might have done so, if he'd had a sword in his hand. Luckily for the tanner, and them, the shorter seax blade provided Halinard with the extra instant in which to take stock.

An outstretched hand tugged at the leather of his shoe, and a mud-smeared face seemed to peer from the bottom of the warehouse wall. It took only a heartbeat for both Halinard and Beobrand to understand. The warehouse was built raised up from the ground, perhaps to keep the contents away from rats, or out of the river should it flood. This dead end was clearly used as a dumping ground. A shattered barrel, some mildewed sacks, what looked like the broken frame of a box bed, and all manner of other refuse was piled in the corners and against the walls, obscuring the shadowed recess beneath the warehouses.

The hand had beckoned and Beobrand had shoved Halinard down. There was no time for deliberation. The Frank had dropped to his chest and squeezed into the space beneath the building, following their rescuer into the gloom. Beobrand had followed as quickly as he could, throwing his sword and seax into the darkness before him. The moment he was completely under the building, he reached for a torn piece of sackcloth and a broken bucket, pulling them over the hole they had passed through. A heartbeat later, he saw the mud-caked shoes of the guards as they ran into the alley.

Beobrand listened to their confused shouts as he pulled himself into the darkness on his stomach like a serpent. He expected the rubbish to be snatched away, exposing them, but the guards seemed not to have noticed the space under the buildings. They argued, their raised voices obscuring the sounds of Halinard and Beobrand's passing under the warehouse behind their mysterious rescuer.

As they had emerged into the light, sweating and begrimed, they had seen the man was one of the tanners. The smell of the tanning pools scratched at their throats, as the other two tanners helped pull them from beneath the warehouse and, without hesitation, began wrapping cloth about their faces. They did not speak as they unceremoniously pushed hats onto Beobrand and Halinard's heads and tied leather aprons about their waists. Seeing the glint of gold on his arm, one of the men tugged at the arm ring. Beobrand tensed, then allowed the man to remove the gold and slip it into a pouch. Gold was of no value to a dead man. When they were dressed as tanners, the men thrust long wooden paddles into their hands.

None of them uttered a word, but Beobrand and Halinard understood what they must do without explanation. They stood close to the foul pools that filled the air with their putrid stink, where they had seen the tanners at their work. Beobrand headed for the further pool, Halinard for the closer one. Stepping onto the timber planks that had been placed over the ponds, both men dipped their paddles into the disgusting liquid. The smell had been bad from a distance, but here, standing over the pools, it made breathing difficult. The mask that had been tied over Beobrand's face seemed to do nothing to lessen the stench, but he wondered if it might be even worse without it. He retched. Surely it could be no worse than this.

The guards sped around the corner then, shouting and yelling.

Beobrand felt his stomach clench and he fought against the urge to vomit. He must not puke.

The guards halted on the edge of the tannery yard and were shouting. One of the tanners, perhaps even the man who had rescued them, replied and pointed up the alley that led back in the direction of the amphitheatre. The guard shook his head. He shouted something about it being impossible. His eyes roved over the other tanners until his gaze rested on the tall, broad-shouldered one stirring the repulsive brew that removed the fur from the animal pelts.

Beobrand willed himself to appear shorter, hunching his shoulders. He did not dare meet the guard's stare for fear that his piercing blue eyes would give him away. Could the man see his golden hair, despite the filth and the small hat jammed on his head. Just as Beobrand was certain that the guard had recognised him, Halinard drew the man's attention by raising his dripping paddle and signalling in the same direction as the first tanner had indicated.

"It is true, master," he said in a rough voice that Beobrand could barely recognise. Halinard said a few more words that Beobrand did not comprehend.

The guard pondered for a heartbeat, then, clearly deciding that he should waste no more time on these foul men who surrounded themselves all day with excrement, he barked an order and the guardsmen sprinted up the alley.

When they were certain the guards had gone, Beobrand followed the tanners into one of the ramshackle buildings. Treated and untreated hides were piled in the gloom. The air was thick with flies and the smell was terrible. But after the acrid burning stench of the pools, the air tasted almost fresh.

"What did you say to them?" Beobrand asked Halinard.

The Frankish warrior swatted a fly away from his face.

"I said those bastard northerners had run that way. And they looked terrified."

Beobrand grinned, sudden relief washing through him. But they were not safe yet. The tanner who had taken his arm ring stepped close and handed the golden band back to Beobrand. He accepted it with a nod, surprised to see it again. The man also offered him his seax and the sword he had taken from the guard. Beobrand sheathed the seax, but he had no scabbard for the sword, so held it loosely in his half-hand.

It was then that their rescuer, a man who introduced himself as Shimon, explained his plan to transport them out of the city hidden beneath a heap of hides.

The conversation had been fast and to the point. Beobrand had been unable to keep up and after a short time, Halinard stopped making any attempt to interpret.

"We must decide quickly," he said. "We cannot waste time."

Beobrand nodded in agreement. He felt powerless, but a moment before he had been sure he was going to die, so now he would put his life in the hands of these strangers who had saved him. A sudden thought gripped him then and he tugged at Halinard's dirt-encrusted sleeve.

"Thank him for me. Tell him if there is anything I can ever do for him, let him ask it, and I will do my best to repay him."

Remembering his golden arm ring, he tugged it free of his arm and held it out to Shimon.

Halinard said a few words to Shimon, who shook his head and waved the gold away.

"He says there is no need for payment. You have already done enough."

Beobrand did not understand the man's meaning, but decided not to push for an answer then.

After they had clambered into the rear of the tanners' waggon, and the heavy stinking hides had been placed over them, Beobrand had asked Halinard what Shimon had meant by his words.

"We spoke of it briefly," Halinard replied, but before he could elaborate, a bout of coughing seized him. "Gods, how this stinks."

The waggon had begun to rock and sway as they left the narrow lanes and entered the bustling city street. The muted sounds of Liyon came to them through the leather piled atop them. Beobrand heard hawkers shouting, dogs barking, shrill voices of women gossiping. All the usual sounds of the city at midday, which, when added to the hooves of the mules, the shouted commands that Shimon called to the beasts, and the rumble and creak of the waggon over the cobbles, would drown out all but the loudest of shouts coming from the men hidden beneath the stinking cargo. Even so, Beobrand and Halinard kept their voices to a whisper.

Beobrand wanted to spit to free his mouth of the stink and taste of the leather, but he swallowed and wished they'd had time to drink water before heading off on the waggon. The sun beat down on the loathsome load and it was stiflingly hot beneath the leather before they had travelled much of a distance.

"And what did Shimon say?" asked Beobrand, prompting Halinard to answer his previous query.

"He said they are Iudeisc, the other tanners and him. No good Christian wants to do that filthy work, so the Iudeisc do it."

Beobrand thought on this for a moment, wondering how this explained the man's actions.

"Was he kin of the people we met while outside of the city?"

"I don't think so," said Halinard. "But he said that word has travelled about what you did for those that Thagmar had abused."

Beobrand recalled Binyamin as he had stared out from the cage in the arena. Was the man dead now? Beobrand cursed. Would Binyamin's wife soon be cleaning another body for burial? Would she even be able to tend to her husband in the way of her people? By Friga, hadn't the woman suffered enough?

"I have done nothing but postpone the inevitable," he said.

"You did what you could, lord. The Iudeisc have few friends."

"I hope this does not bring the wrath of Dalfinus and Annemund upon them."

"That is a risk they are willing to take."

They had grown silent then for a time, each lost in his own hell of reeking heat and fetor. Beobrand played through the images he had witnessed in the arena, trying to make sense of it all. So much had happened so quickly. He thought of Agobard with his scarred hand and the horse-hoof crescent scar on his forehead. He was Dalfinus' man. So Brocard's hunch about the attack in the forest had been correct. And Marcoul had been involved, along with Dalfinus and Annemund.

And Vulmar. That verminous noble from Rodomo.

"I don't know how," Beobrand whispered into the foul-smelling darkness, "but we must kill Vulmar."

"Oh yes, lord," replied Halinard, "I feel God has allowed us to escape so that we might finally bring that fat bastard to justice."

"Justice?" Beobrand scoffed at the idea.

"A sword can deliver God's justice, can it not?" asked Halinard.

"I know nothing of God's justice," said Beobrand, his voice

hard, "but a blade is the best way to take vengeance. I swore a bloodfeud against Vulmar years ago. I never truly thought I would be able to act on it, as far away as we were. Even when we came to Frankia, I told myself that I must escort Wilfrid and Baducing, and could not seek out my enemy. But now…"

"You are not the only one with a need for revenge against that man," whispered Halinard.

"I know it."

"Now we are free of the duty of escorting Wilfrid, we can do what is needed."

"It will not be easy."

"Is anything of import ever easy?"

Beobrand thought of the weeks they had spent dining and drinking in Liyon. Growing fat and soft. His thoughts turned to Cynan and the others, but he could not bring himself to voice his concerns, not here, in the sweltering stinking black beneath the skins.

"Do you really believe God helped us to escape?" he asked instead. "I know Coenred would agree with you." The thought of one of his oldest friends far away on Lindisfarena saddened him.

"Perhaps," said Halinard. "Mayhap it was the Iudeisc god who aided us after you helped his people."

Beobrand sneered at that.

He thought of how he had prayed to Woden. The All-father would revel in this escape, changing themselves from warriors to filthy tanners and hiding under foul-smelling hides. It was like something from a scop's song, a cunning trick the gods might play on each other.

However it had happened, whether by chance, luck or divine intervention, it seemed to be his wyrd to escape. Whatever came now, Beobrand vowed silently, that if Woden kept him alive long enough to face Vulmar, he would give the Hanged One more mayhem and blood.

Along with Vulmar, Dalfinus and Annemund deserved to be punished for their part in the attack on Balthild, and for the hideous hunt in the arena.

"You think Wilfrid knew what Dalfinus had planned for us?" Beobrand asked. He saw Gram's face in the darkness. His jaw muscles bunched as he heard anew in his memory the sounds of Gram's death.

"I know not," replied Halinard, his voice quiet, doubtful. "But the boy is ambitious."

"Yes," said Beobrand, sensing the truth of Halinard's words. "He will do anything for advancement, it seems to me."

"Even betray us?"

"I think he might at that," said Beobrand, his words hard and sharp like splinters of iron. He had promised Eanflæd he would protect the novice, but if Wilfrid had truly betrayed them, did that oath still hold? Gods! If he harmed the youth, the queen would never forgive him. And yet, if Wilfrid's actions had led to Gram's death, Beobrand was not certain he would be able to stay his hand should they come face-to-face. "When next we meet Wilfrid," he said, wiping sweat from his eyes, "he had best watch himself."

"You think we will meet him again then?" asked Halinard.

"I think that Wilfrid will follow where Annemund and Dalfinus lead. And I mean to see them both again. And when I do, they will have to answer for their actions against me and their queen."

They had fallen silent again as they reached the queue of travellers passing through the city gate. A long time passed. Too long. Surely the city watch had seen through their feeble plan. Holding his breath, he listened for any sign that they had been detected. The sword's grip was slick with sweat in his hand. If they were to be captured, he would not make it easy for the guards. The instant the hides were pulled away, he would surge up, hacking and slashing with the stolen sword. Halinard and he would no doubt be overwhelmed, but their captors would pay a high price.

Shimon was saying something to the guard, but his voice was too soft to make out any words. The guard replied, his tone grating and angry. The waggon shifted and groaned as Shimon climbed down from the seat. For several heartbeats there was silence, then, without warning, the hides above Beobrand shifted, as they were pulled away. The oppressive weight that had pressed down upon him lessened. He tightened his grip on the sword, but held himself in check. It was still dark. Only some of the leather had been lifted. Halinard and he were yet hidden. He imagined the guard inspecting the goods. Any movement now would give them away. His lungs burnt and he realised he had not breathed for a long time. Still he dared not draw in breath, for fear the guard would discover them.

Shimon's voice grew louder. The guard replied, his gruff voice sounding more weary than angry now. Beobrand got the sense he was moving away, perhaps put off by the stench. The weight of the hides flopped back onto Beobrand and he struggled not to move.

The waggon rocked as Shimon pulled himself back up onto the seat. With a shouted order at the mules and a flick of the reins, the vehicle lumbered forward. Only when they had travelled some distance did Beobrand allow himself to breathe. He dragged in great lungfuls of the foetid air and for the first time he cared nothing for the smell.

Chapter 25

Wilfrid's stomach recoiled as he watched Vulmar sink his teeth into the slab of rare beef. One of the pale-faced thralls had carved the meat for him and now stood, eyes downcast, ready for the next order. Blood dribbled over the fat man's stubbled chin and trickled down his bulbous neck. The sight of the liquid brought back to Wilfrid the horrors he had witnessed that day. There had been so much blood.

Biting his lip, he cast about the palace hall in search of a friendly face. He would even have been happy to see Rotrudis, with her inane simpering. He had been surrounded by these men all day. Powerful men, with powerful appetites. He was exhausted. Is this what it meant to be a man of consequence? Did they all partake in such sickening acts of violence?

When it became clear that Beobrand and Halinard had escaped and were not going to be brought back into the arena immediately after their bid for freedom, Dalfinus had ordered his men to remove the corpses that littered the sand in Beobrand's wake, like a grisly high-tide mark of gory jetsam.

Wilfrid had seen Binyamin in the cage at the same time as Beobrand had noticed him. The realisation of the nature of this hunt and the character of the men with whom he had allied himself had made him tremble.

It was then that he had turned to Annemund, searching for an explanation, or at least reassurance. The bishop had been serious, his face set and sombre, but his words did little to comfort Wilfrid.

"They are criminals," he had said, in answer to the unspoken question on Wilfrid's face. "All have been sentenced to death. Their killing is just. What matter their executioners?"

Wilfrid had nodded, unable to speak. Of course, men and women who broke the laws of the land must be punished, but surely that chastisement should not bring pleasure. He said nothing of the words he had heard Vulmar shout as Beobrand fought his way free of the arena.

Wilfrid looked into his cup of wine. The dark crimson liquid reminded him of the blood that had gushed from Gram's wounds when his corpse was dragged out of the tunnel.

Some of the men had cheered at the sight. Others had clapped with glee. Wilfrid was sickened. By the bones of Christ, who were these people? Gram was no criminal. His only crime, it seemed, had been to follow Beobrand.

As the day had unfolded, Wilfrid had begun to fear for his own life. Vulmar had scowled when Wilfrid had been introduced and he heard the novice was from Albion. But even without his association to Beobrand, Wilfrid knew he had seen too much. He quickly understood that these men did not only share a passion for inflicting pain on condemned men and thralls. They had also conspired against the queen. To what end, he was not certain. But whatever Dalfinus' and Annemund's goal in seeking the queen's death, they would never allow him to leave now.

A dark voice whispered to him, deep within the most secret recesses of his soul. Would he have wanted to leave, even if he was able to do so? Beobrand must be dead by now, or would be very soon. It would be better to embrace his new family, the voice said to him, and to accept the influence the alliance would confer upon him. Perhaps he had no stomach for the nobles' violence, but he could not deny that the power to command the life and death of their subjects was intoxicating.

Having reached this conclusion, he decided that he should remain as inconspicuous as possible. He must learn all he could about these men and their plots. Speaking little, he had drawn to the edge of the arena, from where he listened and watched. Any knowledge he might glean could serve him well later. The first thing was to understand the relationships that governed all of the men in the arena. It was clear that Dalfinus was foremost in the group. Even his brother, the bishop, deferred to him in front of the others. Vulmar too, married to a cousin of the king himself, and lord of Rodomo, wielded great influence. The other nobles circled about those two, like ravens around a carcass, squabbling about who would get closest.

The death of Marcoul at Beobrand's hand had been as shocking to Wilfrid as it had been sudden. But after their initial consternation, neither Dalfinus nor Vulmar seemed overly concerned with the man's killing.

"He was ever a fool," spat Vulmar, looking down at Marcoul's body. He lay on his back, staring blindly up with one eye, the other socket brimming with blood. A fly landed on the man's cheek and edged ever closer to the darkening pool. "Believing he could stand before one such as Beobrand. Did you ever see such speed?"

Wilfrid had watched Vulmar as he talked. There was colour in the man's cheeks and as he took in the ruin of Marcoul's face, he licked his lips. He had enjoyed the spectacle of bloodletting. But he also appeared to admire Beobrand.

Wilfrid wondered at that. He knew of the past between the two men, and it was obvious that Vulmar had intended to slay Beobrand here this day. He had shouted as much to Dalfinus as the thegn of Ubbanford had escaped.

"You promised me I would be the one to slay him!" he had cried.

"Circumstances change, my friend," Dalfinus had replied.

In that exchange, Wilfrid had understood a great deal. He saw that this hunt was as much a trap as it was a diversion. Dalfinus had used him to lure Beobrand here to be killed. How much of what Dalfinus and Annemund had promised him over his time in Liyon had been to keep him, and therefore Beobrand, in the city, awaiting the arrival of Vulmar? The thought of it filled him with terror. Perhaps now that Beobrand had escaped they would have no role for him. He thought of the condemned men he had seen slain this day. Would he follow them soon, cut down with callous abandon by these murderous nobles?

But as the day wore on, so Wilfrid was treated as another valued member of the secret hunt. He yet lived, and now the sun had fallen and he had been seated at the high table in the palace alongside Dalfinus, Annemund and Vulmar.

"I have travelled all this way," said Vulmar suddenly, wiping meat juices from his chin, "and for what?" Flecks of his spittle flickered in the last rays of the sun lancing through the unshuttered windows.

"I did not see you complaining earlier," replied Dalfinus, his tone honeyed and smooth.

Vulmar grunted and shovelled into his mouth an egg that had been poached in wine.

"The hunt this year was certainly memorable," he said, dribbling yolk down his chin and onto the linen-covered board. He laughed at a memory. "Did you see my throw?"

"It was majestic," said Dalfinus. "Wasn't it, Wilfrid?" He turned to the young novice, asking with his eyes for help to mollify Vulmar. Wilfrid would have rather not been drawn into this conversation, but he sat at the high table, and there was nowhere for him to hide. He swallowed a mouthful of wine and forced a smile.

"The great Hector himself could not have made a better throw," he said.

Vulmar's eyes narrowed.

When the arena had been cleared of the bodies left behind by Beobrand and his gesithas, the inhabitants of the cages had been released one by one to be dispatched by the nobles in all manner of ways. Some had been slain by arrows, others in hand-to-hand combat, where only the noble possessed a weapon.

Binyamin had been given to Vulmar. The fat lord of Rodomo had killed him with a spear. The Iudeisc's hands had been tied behind his back. Guards had prodded him, encouraging him to flee. Bravely, he refused to run. He knew he would die, but he would not provide them with the sport they craved. Vulmar had raged at him, shouting abuse. And yet, even when the guards struck him hard, knocking him to the ground, the proud man would not give his tormentors the satisfaction of running. Furious, Vulmar had thrown his spear at him. It had missed, and he had been forced to take another weapon from one of the guards. He missed with that spear too, which sent him into a terrible rage. Taking a third spear, he had moved closer to the captive and then let fly again. That spear's tip had bitten into Binyamin's thigh. It had been a poor throw, and it had surely been chance that had guided the blade to sever the man's artery. Dark blood had pumped from the wound. In a matter of heartbeats, Binyamin had collapsed, unable to remain upright as his lifeblood soaked the sand all around him.

"A flatterer, I see," Vulmar said, his tone flat. "You will have to watch this one, Dalfinus." Wilfrid kept his expression blank, but his thoughts wheeled and spun. He would have to be careful. He had overstepped. Everyone there knew Vulmar had shown little skill. Clearly, Vulmar knew it too and was not impressed by Wilfrid's fawning. "Wilfrid, isn't it?" Vulmar went on. "You travelled with Beobrand all the way from Albion?"

"I did, Lord Vulmar," replied Wilfrid, keeping his tone respectful.

"Then why, pray," said Vulmar, turning to Dalfinus, "is he not in one of the cages? He is young and could provide us with sport."

Wilfrid's breath caught in his throat.

"My brother likes this one," replied Dalfinus.

Wilfrid noted Dalfinus did not say that he was fond of him.

"As does your daughter," said Annemund softly.

Dalfinus' face darkened.

"Yes," said Dalfinus, fixing Wilfrid with a hard stare, "Wilfrid's flattering tongue has opened Rotrudis' heart it seems."

"Only her heart?" Vulmar guffawed, almost choking on his food.

Dalfinus' jaw tensed and a small furrow appeared on his brow. Wilfrid wondered how much the *comes* of Liyon knew, or suspected. Had Annemund told him that Wilfrid had bedded Rotrudis? Did he know she was with child? Why allow him to wed her if he was unaware that she was no longer a maiden?

"We are speaking of my daughter, Vulmar," Dalfinus said, his tone sharp and low. "Do not forget yourself."

Vulmar swallowed.

"I merely jest, man."

Wilfrid could sense the mood of both men darkening. He felt as if he was walking across a narrow bridge over a treacherous gorge. A misstep, and he would fall to his doom. If he became the focus of their anger, there was no telling what they might do or what would become of him. Having studied the brothers' relationship, he was not sure that his friendship with Annemund would save him if Dalfinus turned against him. And whilst he was now betrothed to Rotrudis, he was in no doubt that Dalfinus' decision on that matter could shift as quickly as the wind.

He must distract them away from him.

"Any news of Beobrand?" Wilfrid asked, the words slicing through the tension that had engulfed them.

"The man is as slippery as an eel," said Dalfinus with what appeared to be grudging admiration. "The whoreson killed several more of my men in the city. Before he vanished."

"Vanished?"

"He somehow evaded the watch." Dalfinus shook his head. "I knew I should have kept Thagmar at the arena this morning. He's the only one I can trust to get things done. Beobrand was always going to be dangerous."

"You must catch the half-handed bastard," said Vulmar. "He should have been dead for years. Now I would see ended what he started when he crossed me."

"He will be captured soon enough," said Dalfinus. "I have doubled the watch, and as soon as Thagmar returns from his business, I will set my hound on Beobrand's scent."

Vulmar glowered, leaning forward so that his neck bulged beneath his chin. To Wilfrid he looked like a great toad.

"When your man finds him," Vulmar said, "I demand the pleasure of taking his life."

Dalfinus offered an easy smile that did not appear to reach his eyes.

"If he is brought in alive," he said, "the pleasure will be yours. I made a promise to you, my friend, and I will keep it, if I am able."

Vulmar nodded and took a deep draught of wine.

"What business does Thagmar have that is so pressing he would miss the hunt?" asked Annemund. "I do not believe I have known the man to ever miss a hunt before."

Dalfinus chuckled.

"Yes, he does relish the hunts. But today he went in search of something else that would bring him joy."

"Oh? I can think of nothing that he would enjoy so much as to miss the chance of showing off his skill with blade and bow."

Dalfinus shrugged.

"It all depends on who he is able to kill, I suppose. Today he set out on the trail of perhaps the one thing he hates more than Iudaea."

Annemund raised an eyebrow.

"And what is that, pray?"

"An enemy that has shamed him and evaded death."

"And who is this walking corpse?" asked Vulmar.

"That Waelisc warrior of Beobrand's, Cynan. And the rest of the men who travelled with them."

Wilfrid thought of those men. He had lived with them for months. They had often treated him with disrespect, ridiculing him and taunting him. But he knew this to be the warriors' way. They were not bad men. When Beobrand had believed him in danger, they had ridden after him. And when they had seen the violence perpetrated by Thagmar, they had rushed to halt it, confronting Thagmar's men with shields and swords. They had protected him, and now he was learning that they were most likely all dead, slain by the brute, Thagmar. Some of these thoughts must have been plain on his face, for Dalfinus was looking at him quizzically.

"I know you were friends with these men," he said. "But they cannot be allowed to live. They impeded Thagmar from carrying out my orders. They made a fool of him and me."

"I understand," replied Wilfrid. His mouth was dry, so he drained his glass. "They were foolish to defy you."

"Yes, they were." Dalfinus grinned, clicking his fingers for more wine. "I am glad you see things clearly."

"I told you, brother," said Annemund, accepting a refill of his glass from a young man, "Wilfrid is as cunning and as ruthless as they come."

"I see that."

Dalfinus drank, looking over the rim of his glass at Wilfrid. Vulmar was also staring at him with a strange expression that made Wilfrid's skin prickle and creep.

"But remember, Wilfrid, for your own good," Dalfinus said, setting down his glass and reaching for a poached egg. "It does not do to be too clever."

Wilfrid swallowed. The air was heavy with threats and again, he had the feeling he was treading on a precarious bridge, ready to slip to his death at any moment.

"I will endeavour to be just clever enough to please you," he said, with a wide smile.

Dalfinus scowled, perhaps looking for some insult in Wilfrid's words. But after a moment, he returned the grin and laughed.

"Yes, you do that." He continued laughing until Annemund and Vulmar joined in. Wilfrid let out a breath. He sipped his wine, vowing not to drink too much. He could not allow his tongue to undo him. He must remain sharp of mind. Despite the merriment in the hall, he could sense the danger lurking in every sidelong glance. These were men who killed without compunction, they would think nothing of killing him if they believed he had no value, or if they perceived him to be their enemy.

He would have to step with extreme caution. He ran a finger over the fine patterns in the glass of his goblet. Outside, the sun was setting and all around the hall, slaves were lighting candles against the darkness. The flames flickered and gleamed from silver platters. The stark shadows brought out the details of the carvings and masonry of the columns and walls. Yes, he would need to tread with care if he did not wish to lose his life to these powerful men, but the prize that awaited him was beyond anything he could have imagined. Wealth and influence to rival that of the kings of Albion.

"What tidings from Thagmar?" asked Annemund. "The sun sets. Shouldn't he have returned by now?"

A shadow passed over Dalfinus' face.

"He will return soon enough, brother. Have you ever known him not to fulfil his objective?"

"You have a short memory. As I recall, only days ago he did not return with all of your taxes, or the church's tithes."

"And that Waelisc whoreson will pay for that, if he hasn't already. I imagine Thagmar is taking his time in killing that one."

Wilfrid thought that slaying Cynan and the other Black Shields would not prove such an easy task as Dalfinus seemed to believe. But he said nothing, instead watching the men as they spoke, calculating, judging their motives. Annemund seemed intent on needling his older brother and Wilfrid wondered at that.

"Cynan is dangerous enough," Wilfrid said, making the decision to speak up. He knew the warriors from Bernicia better than anyone. This was how he must show his worth. "But it is Beobrand we need to worry about."

Annemund nodded, clearly pleased with Wilfrid's intervention.

"We," Dalfinus said, adding an emphasis to the word and raising an eyebrow to Wilfrid, "will have him soon enough. Thagmar will run him to ground. He has dozens of men at his disposal. Beobrand is alone, apart from the man he uses as his interpreter." He shook his head dismissively. "They will not get far."

"You are probably right," replied Wilfrid. "But what if he evades Thagmar and his men?"

"He will not," snapped Dalfinus. Was there a sliver of doubt in his eyes?

"He might not," Wilfrid said, "but make no mistake, Beobrand is no normal man. He is like a storm, or a raging tide. A force of nature. You saw how he fought his way out of the arena this morning."

"It is true," said Vulmar. "He killed some of my best men. I sent many strong warriors to kill him in the north. Only one returned. Beobrand has the luck of the Devil."

"Many have said as much. But luck or battle-skill, or both, Beobrand has survived all manner of obstacles in his life. He is no fat lord who sends others to do his bidding." He deliberately looked away from Vulmar as he spoke these words, but sensed the sudden fury coming off the man. Dalfinus and Annemund both grinned, seemingly pleased to see the lord of Rodomo insulted. "Beobrand is a warrior who stands in the shieldwall and leads his men from the front of any battle line." Wilfrid paused, taking a sip of wine. He had them now. His nerves had fled and they were listening intently to him. Even Vulmar sat in rapt silence. "If anyone can survive and escape Liyon," continued Wilfrid, "it would be Beobrand."

"Impossible," muttered Dalfinus without conviction.

"Would you have believed any man could fight his way out of the amphitheatre when it was swarming with your guards?"

"He did not lead from the front there," said Vulmar with a sneer. "He sacrificed one of his men while he fled."

"Is that what you saw?" Wilfrid shook his head. "I watched a brave warrior, a man beloved of Beobrand, who was willing to give up his life so that his lord could escape. Is this not what all lords wish from their sworn men? And can you imagine how much Gram's death will have angered Beobrand?"

"What do you think he will do?" asked Vulmar. He looked around the candlelit hall, as if he expected Beobrand to leap out of the shadows.

Wilfrid kept his expression blank, despite the disgust he felt at the fat man's obvious cowardice.

"He will want vengeance," he said. "But he is no fool. He knows he cannot attack you here, where you are surrounded by walls and armed men."

"So he will run," Vulmar said, "and we will seek him out."

"You think he will run?" Wilfrid allowed himself to sound incredulous.

"None of this matters," snapped Dalfinus. "Thagmar will bring him to us soon. Then it will be the lord Vulmar who will have his revenge."

Wilfrid nodded slowly, as if agreeing wholeheartedly with the *comes* of Liyon.

"But if Thagmar does not capture him," he said at last in a quiet voice that forced the listening men to lean in close to hear him, "Beobrand might know of a way to gain revenge on you all." He looked at each of them in turn. "He is a formidable warrior, but do not be fooled by his strength and his brutish face. The man is sharp of mind too."

"What revenge could he bring?" asked Dalfinus.

"Think about it." Wilfrid steeled himself. This was when he was at his most vulnerable. For he was not certain of the assumptions he had made about these men and their plots. "If Beobrand knows the truth…" He hesitated. With the next words he spoke, he would either cement himself amongst their number, or they would turn on him.

"What truth?" asked Annemund, narrowing his eyes.

"The truth about your plans for the queen." The men were staring at him, but they made no motion to move against him or to shout for the guards. "He may not know that your ultimate intention is to place Clovis' brother, the king of Austrasia, on the throne of Neustria, but Beobrand has a sharp mind."

Wilfrid was pleased to see that his words elicited a reaction, showing him that his deduction was correct. He held his face expressionless.

"Beobrand knows nothing," said Dalfinus.

Wilfrid sighed, shaking his head.

"Do you truly believe that? He recognised your man, Agobard. He remembered him from the forest. It was Beobrand's sword that pierced Agobard's hand and he picked up that scar on his head when he attacked Balthild's party." Wilfrid indicated his own forehead. "I was able to piece things together. I would wager in the moment when he saw Agobard, Beobrand knew enough."

Dalfinus lifted his goblet and drank. Was his hand trembling?

"Even if he knows everything," he said, "which I very much doubt, what could he do with such knowledge?" As he said the words, Wilfrid could see the reality of the situation dawning on Dalfinus' face. "You think he would go to the king?"

Wilfrid shrugged.

"As you say, Thagmar will surely bring him here soon enough. But, if he does not, there is a chance that Beobrand might expose you."

Annemund made the sign of the cross.

"We would all be hanged. Every last man in this hall, should the truth ever be known."

"We knew the risks," said Dalfinus. "That slave girl needs to be slain before she does more damage. That Jezebel has too long had the ear of the king and his *major domus*."

"If only Agobard had succeeded in his mission," said Annemund. "He could have rid us of the thrall-queen and Clovis' heir. With her gone, her fool of a husband could easily be swept aside, and Sigebert, the first-born prince, could assume his rightful place as king of all of the Franks.

"And yet Balthild still lives. She has given birth to a healthy son, and we have an enemy who might already be on his way to tell the king of our part in the plot against the queen."

Wilfrid released a long breath. They spoke freely before him of their conspiracy against the throne. Now he must not give them reason to doubt his loyalty to them. Or his value.

"We must hurry to court," he said. "If any should give an account of what has happened here, it should be us. We can discredit Beobrand before the king. With your status, that should not be difficult."

"Yes," Vulmar rubbed his jowls, smiling, "Beobrand is a foreigner and a lover of Iudaea. Clovis will listen to me, and Beobrand's name will soon be cursed within all the realms of Frankia."

Annemund frowned.

"But what if he later comes to court and tells them the truth?"

Wilfrid smiled, feeling at ease for the first time that long day. His path was clear to him now.

"The truth?" he said. "What is the truth? I suggest we make haste. For he who tells a tale first, controls the truth."

Chapter 26

When at last the waggon halted again and Shimon pulled back the skins, Halinard and Beobrand tumbled from their hiding place. They were drenched in sweat, smeared in muck and blood, and they smelled worse than a midden in high summer.

Blinking against the bright light of the afternoon, Beobrand looked about them. They were on the edge of the oak and beech woodland that grew to the west of Liyon. Shimon had spoken to them as they had climbed laboriously up the slope, telling them that they could not risk halting for fear of being seen by other travellers on the road or by the wardens on the wall. Such was the cloying heat beneath the hides that Beobrand had begun to believe he might pass out, or perhaps even die.

Now, stumbling into the cool fresh air of the forest, he fell to his knees gasping. Shimon pulled the stopper from a leather flask and handed it to him. Taking a great mouthful, Beobrand swallowed down the tepid water. It tasted faintly of leather and the instant the liquid hit his throat, he gagged. A moment later he was retching and puking into the leaf mould.

Halinard took the waterskin from him and stepped away, stiff-legged and scowling. Taking a sip, he swilled the water around his mouth and spat. When he was sure he could stomach it, he drank a little and returned to Beobrand's side. Pulling him to his feet, he handed him the flask again.

"Rinse your mouth, but do not drink yet."

Beobrand spat and eyed the waterskin dubiously.

"Go on," Halinard urged.

Beobrand sighed, then sipped from the skin. He spat out the water, ridding his mouth of some of the taste of bile. To his surprise, he did not vomit again. Taking a tentative swallow of the water, he nodded to Halinard. He made his way back to the waggon where Shimon was already pulling several items from where they had been secreted beneath the sheets of leather. He handed them a cloak each, a sack which contained a few provisions, no doubt the tanners' food for the day, and he gestured for them to keep the waterskin. It wasn't much, but with the sword and the two seaxes, it would be enough to get them to a settlement where they could purchase horses. The golden arm ring should be more than enough to buy mounts, but it was conspicuous, so they had decided to walk a ways from the city, travelling off the road until they were a safe distance. He slid the gold ring into the sack and slung it over his shoulder.

He had no scabbard for the sword, and carrying such a blade openly would mark him as no normal traveller. Only warriors and nobles bore swords. Or wolf-heads, who had stolen a weapon from one of their victims.

Without a word, Shimon took the blade from Beobrand and wrapped its length in some old sacking, tying the makeshift sheath with a long cord of leather. There was enough of the sack cloth left for it to be loosely draped over the sword's plain hilt and pommel. With a nod of thanks, Beobrand took the weapon from the tanner and examined it. With anything more than a cursory glance, it would be clear to any observer what was contained within the sacking. Thinking for a moment, he took the sack which held their provisions and tied it to the end of the wrapped sword. Then he rested the flat of the blade on his shoulder with the sack dangling behind.

Beobrand mourned the loss of Nægling, his byrnie, his fine helm and shield, but he told himself these were but objects. They could be replaced. Unlike the life that had been stolen from Gram. Darkness tugged at his mind, threatening to turn his thoughts towards Cynan and the rest of his gesithas. He was not yet ready to confront such thoughts, so he pushed them away.

Shimon said something. Halinard snorted.

"What does he say?" asked Beobrand.

"He said you look like a pilgrim."

Despite their situation, Beobrand smiled. Nobody had said this of them since they'd left Albion. And now, for the first time they were no longer making the pilgrimage to Roma.

"I don't believe pilgrims are meant to travel with thoughts of murder in their hearts," Beobrand said, spitting again and taking another swig of water. His stomach had calmed, but he still felt nervous. "Come, we must go. To tarry further here is to put Shimon at more risk."

The tanner seemed to understand the meaning of Beobrand's words and he climbed quickly up onto the waggon.

"Thank you," said Beobrand in Frankish. "For everything." Then, to Halinard: "Tell him I am in his debt."

Halinard relayed the message and Shimon nodded.

"Shalom," he said, and flicked the reins over the mules. The beasts lowered their heads and strained at the traces. The waggon began to move with a creaking of timber. They watched for a while as it pulled away from them, flickering as it passed through the dappled light beneath the trees.

"What did that word mean?" Beobrand asked.

"I believe it means peace, in the language of the Iudeisc."

Beobrand frowned and looked along the road. There was nobody in view apart from them and Shimon's waggon.

"Perhaps," Beobrand said with a sigh, "one day we will find

peace. But before then, let's get off the road before anyone sees us. We have justice to seek and people to kill."

They found a stream in the afternoon. Beneath the trees it was not as hot as it had been in the sun, and the stifling heat beneath the hides seemed like a distant memory. But the stink of the leather and their sweat clung to them like sodden linen. Beobrand would have welcomed water deep enough to submerge himself, but the stream was narrow with only a trickle running over its pebbled bed. Without a word, they both pulled off their clothes and proceeded to scrub their bodies in the cold water. When they were clean, they dipped their kirtles and breeches in the water too, clutching the wool in great handfuls and rubbing it against itself. Even after washing as best they could, they were not able to remove all of the muck and smell from the clothes, and after they had wrung them out, the garments were still heavy with water. They shivered as they redressed, but neither man complained.

"I fear I will have that smell in my nose till my death day," said Halinard, sniffing and grimacing.

"You will not die so soon, I think." Beobrand smiled, but the mention of death turned his mood bitter.

They walked on in silence for some time. The sun was low in the sky now, lancing through the trees as they trudged westward. The sound of galloping horses echoed to them from the road. They were too far away to see who might pass or to be seen by the riders, but they both felt exposed in the open, so, halting, they both crouched behind the bole of a great oak.

"Dalfinus' men?" Halinard asked when the thrum of hooves had all but vanished in the distance.

"Perhaps."

Beobrand shoved himself to his feet and they walked on once

more. His breeches were still damp and they chafed against his skin, but that was a small price to pay for not smelling as strongly of the tanners' uncured leather.

"We'll need to find somewhere to camp soon," he said. "Once it is dark, we will have to halt where we are, or risk walking into trees and falling down gullies."

"You think we can risk a fire?" Halinard sounded hopeful, but Beobrand shook his head.

"Even if Shimon had left us a flint and tinder," he said. "I think it would be best to find somewhere to shelter without a fire tonight."

Halinard nodded glumly. The forest was already noticeably cooler than it had been in the city and they wrapped their cloaks about them as a wind began to pick up, whispering and rustling in the leaves above them.

A short time later, they stumbled upon a clearing where a massive oak had fallen in some storm long ago. The great tree's roots had ripped from the earth and now provided a sheltered hollow. There were signs of a fire having been lit there, but the ashes were scattered, cold and old. Nobody had made camp in this place for a long time. They settled down in the wind-shadow of the tangle of roots and earth and examined the food Shimon had given them. There were two small, unleavened loaves, a slice of cheese and some kind of pastry. Beobrand sniffed it and tore it into two pieces. Inside was a mixture of white cheese and some green vegetable leaves. At the sight and smell of it, he realised how hungry he was.

They ate the small pastry in silence. It was good, spicy and satisfying and unlike anything either of them had tried before. They both took a drink from the skin and settled back as the gloaming closed in around them.

"This would be a cosy camp site with a fire," Halinard said.

Beobrand nodded. The place brought back memories of a similar fallen tree in a frozen winter forest long ago and far away.

He shivered at the ghosts of those memories. He too wished for a fire. Perhaps if he could stare into a fire, he would see something in the flickering flames to distract his mind. Instead, as night drew its dark shroud about them, all he saw in the gloom was the imploring face of Cathryn. He had barely known her, and yet she came to his nightmares so frequently that her features were as familiar to him as if she were kin. Whenever he thought of her a heavy sadness filled him. He had been unable to protect Cathryn, just as he had failed so many others over the years.

"You think Cynan and the others made it out of the city?"

Halinard's voice shattered Beobrand's sombre reverie. The land was black about them now and neither man had spoken for a long while. Beobrand had not wanted to think about his gesithas. But Halinard's question pulled his mind away from dwelling on a long-dead girl he had been unable to save, to men he considered his brothers.

"I should not have left them," he said, his tone bleak.

"Nothing you could do, lord," said Halinard softly.

"There never is, it seems to me."

"Speak not so." Halinard shifted his weight in the darkness, leaning closer to Beobrand. "Ardith does not live because of you? My family is not safe at Ubbanford? You cannot save everyone, Beobrand."

Beobrand sighed. He knew it was true, but the truth hurt all the same.

"They are my men," he said at last. "I should not have brought them here."

"You are not fair to them, lord. They are oath-sworn and stand beside you against any foe."

"But I was not at their side. To think of them being attacked by Thagmar, ambushed somewhere in the city..." His voice trailed off. He imagined Cynan and his gesithas fighting bravely, and yet if they were taken by surprise and outnumbered, no amount of valour would save them.

"We speak of Cynan here," said Halinard. Beobrand could hear the smile in his voice, even though he could make out nothing more than a dark shadow in the deep gloom. "And Attor, Eadgard, Grindan, Bleddyn, Ingwald. Brave men all. And cunning. I would not wager against them in a fight."

Beobrand nodded in the darkness.

"I hope you are right," he said. "I don't need any more reasons for vengeance. Besides," he sniffed, "I can only kill Vulmar and those accursed brothers once."

Halinard made a sound that could have been a chuckle. Beobrand wanted to say something to reassure the man, to tell him he would see Gisela and Joveta again, but tiredness smothered him like a thick blanket. Perhaps sensing Beobrand's weariness, though he too must have felt the same, Halinard placed a hand on his arm.

"Rest. I will take first watch."

Beobrand said nothing. He wrapped himself in his damp cloak and tried to make himself comfortable in the hollow beneath the roots of the oak. It was a cloudless night, and cold. He stared up at the patch of star-filled sky above the clearing and wondered whether the shades of those he had lost looked down. His mind was swarming with thoughts and he had believed slumber would elude him, but moments later, his eyes closed and he was quickly asleep.

Chapter 27

"Beobrand!"

The cry brought him awake with a start. Halinard had evidently succumbed to exhaustion and he snored quietly beside Beobrand. It was still night and the forest creaked and sighed in the breeze that had risen since nightfall.

Beobrand lay there in the dark, listening to the night and Halinard's even breathing. Had he imagined the scream? Surely if it had been real it would have woken Halinard too. It had been laced with such terror. But the night was quiet. He must have dreamt it. Beobrand closed his eyes again. For them both to sleep would mean there would be nobody on guard, but he was too tired to care.

The cry came again, loud and piercing in the gloom.

"Beobrand! Help me!"

It was a woman's voice. And not a dream. It reverberated around the forest, echoing in the hollow beneath the fallen oak's roots. It seemed to come from everywhere at once.

Beobrand pushed himself to his feet. Snatching up the sack-wrapped sword, he cast about him, listening for another call or any sound that would lead him to the woman calling his name.

Silence.

Nothing but the wind-whisper of the trees.

"Where are you?" he shouted, not caring if any other denizen of the forest should hear him. There was something about the woman's voice that spoke of unimaginable fear. The thought of leaving her alone out there in the forest filled him with dismay. He was about to call out again, when she screamed his name once more.

He stumbled off into the darkness in the direction of the voice. All else was quiet save for his rasping breath and the hushed voices of the beech and oak. Twigs and branches clawed at his face and clothing, as if the forest itself sought to hold him back.

Another scream. Closer now, wailing in abject horror before being abruptly cut off. The voice in that cry was familiar to him, but still he could not place it.

Stumbling over unseen roots, he flailed on through the woodland, desperate to reach the woman who was in such peril. Even though he still had no name to associate with the voice, Beobrand could not bear the thought of allowing harm to come to her. In some hidden, deep part of his soul he knew she was of the utmost importance to him. He would not be able to forgive himself if she should be killed like so many others had before her; men and women he had failed to save.

He ran on blindly, tripping and narrowly avoiding colliding with the gnarled trunk of an old beech tree in the darkness. He caught hold of a branch, righting himself, and scraping his left half-hand on its rough bark.

He paused, drawing in deep breaths. He could no longer hear the woman's screams and feared he was already too late. His panting breaths hung like ghosts for the briefest of moments in the chill air before him. Dawn must be close, for in the grey gloom he began to make out the shapes of the trees, looming and tall all about him; silent sentinels of the forest.

Movement ahead drew his eye. Dark shadows moved there. The silvered edge of a blade caught the wolf-light of the predawn. Beobrand pressed on. The forms before him were quickly becoming clearer and he marvelled at the speed with which the sun rose at this time of year this far south.

Several men were converging on the slight form of a woman. Her long golden hair glimmered in the sunrise. The sun also gleamed from the naked steel in the men's hands.

Bellowing, Beobrand launched himself at them. The men turned to face him, but they were no match for the thegn of Ubbanford. He swept them aside, parrying and counter-attacking in a welter of blows and blood. As the third of his enemies fell, Beobrand saw a fourth reaching for the fair-haired woman at the edge of the clearing.

The sun was bright now, and Beobrand saw her face as the warrior caught hold of her long tresses and pulled her head back. She screamed and turned towards Beobrand. With a pain as sharp as if he had been stabbed, he saw that it was Sunniva, her beauty undimmed by death. Letting out a scream of frustrated rage, he hurdled the dying body of the third foe-man. But even as he ran, he knew he was too far away to save her.

Sunniva's eyes opened wide as the warrior dragged his sword across her throat. Beobrand roared with such fury and anguish that the sound was barely human. Bounding forward, he hacked his bloody blade into the man's head, smashing it open and sending him tumbling to the earth.

Dropping his weapon, Beobrand caught Sunniva in his arms, lowering her to the ground. Blood sheeted from her throat, drenching her chest. It poured warm and wet over his hands.

"I'm sorry," he whimpered. "I'm sorry."

Tears streaked his face as he looked down and saw Sunniva's belly was swollen with their unborn son, Octa. How could this be? He did not understand, but his sorrow was as visceral and deep as the moment he had first lost his wife all those years before. Looking back up to her face, his sobbing breath caught in his throat. It was not Sunniva he held in his arms, but another golden-haired beauty.

Balthild, Queen of Frankia, stared up at him with her intelligent, sorrowful eyes.

"Beobrand!"

At this new shout Beobrand's head snapped up. His eyes were blurred from weeping, but he could see clearly enough to recognise who stood there on the edge of the glade.

Cynan's face glowed in the dawn light. He was smiling that infuriating smirk of his as he stepped out of the trees. Beobrand shook his head, unable to make sense of what was happening.

"How?" was all he uttered.

There were shadowy forms moving behind Cynan, and despite the horror and grief that yet gripped him, Beobrand felt a surge of relief to see his gesithas, his shield-brothers, had escaped from Liyon.

But as he watched, he saw that these were not his men. The low sun fell on the red-cloaked warriors as they stepped behind Cynan. The man closest to the Waelisc had hair even paler than Beobrand's and with a wrenching of his guts, Beobrand recognised Dalfinus' captain.

Thagmar grinned at Beobrand as he unsheathed a knife and moved in as close as a lover to Cynan. He was so near that Cynan must have heard him approach. He must have even smelled his sweat; felt his breath on his cheek. Why then did Cynan not realise the danger?

Beobrand opened his mouth to scream out a warning. But try as he might, no sound issued from his lips. He made to stand, to rush to Cynan's aid, but despite straining with all his strength, the corpse of the queen weighed him down, holding him pressed against the cold earth.

Thagmar leered and, unhindered, he placed the sharp edge of his knife against Cynan's throat.

Too late, Beobrand found his voice and screamed.

Chapter 28

Beobrand sat up, blinking in the bright morning sunshine. The ghost of his scream was in his ears and he stared about him for a moment in confusion, searching for the enemies that had surrounded him. He clutched the sword tightly, its wooden grip warm to the touch, as if he had slept with it in his hand all night. The air was cold and damp. A light mist hovered over the earth, drifting wraith-like between the boles of the trees.

It was shortly after dawn and there was no movement in the clearing. The wind that had blown in at dusk had died away, and the world of the forest was still and peaceful. Only the birds made a sound, their chorus welcoming the sun.

"Lord, you are well?" Halinard rose, rubbing at his eyes and glancing about the glade for signs of danger. That at least was true then. Halinard had fallen asleep and had not roused Beobrand. "I thought I heard someone cry out."

With each heartbeat, the jagged memory of the dream's horror ebbed away, leaving Beobrand feeling empty and spent.

"Lord?" prompted Halinard, looking at Beobrand sidelong.

"I am well enough," growled Beobrand. "A bad dream, nothing more." He scowled at Halinard, as if daring him to question him further. After a moment, the Frankish warrior looked away. Beobrand frowned. "I suppose we must thank the gods that no brigands passed this way," he said, "for your snoring would have attracted anyone within a thousand paces."

"Sorry," muttered Halinard, holding out his hand. Beobrand clasped it and allowed Halinard to heave him to his feet. In the man's apology he heard the faint echo of his own regrets as he'd sobbed to Sunniva's shade.

"We were both tired," he said, clearing his throat. He did not wish to think of the dream. "We needed the rest."

A bout of coughing seized Beobrand without warning and he bent double. Eventually the coughs abated.

"By Tiw's cock," he said, hawking and spitting phlegm into the leaf mould away from their camp. "I thought I was rid of that damned cough."

"It was cold in the night with no fire. And," Halinard gave a small shrug, "we did sleep in wet clothes."

Perhaps they should have tried to light a fire after all, but too late for that now. There was nothing to be gained from worrying about what they might have done, only in what they would do next.

Beobrand took the cool morning air deep into his lungs, paying close attention to the sensations of his body. His chest felt clear and did not hurt, apart from the dull ache where his ribs had been cracked in battle a lifetime ago. That reminder of his first battle had so long been a part of him, he barely noticed it. Beobrand stretched his arms and twisted a few times until his back popped, then he made his way over to the edge of the clearing where he had tied their sack to a branch high above the ground. Retrieving the bag, he rummaged within it and pulled forth one of the small loaves. This he broke in two and handed half to Halinard. He used his seax to divide the cheese between them too.

They ate in silence for a while, washing down the food with mouthfuls of the water from the skin. It was cool and refreshing and Beobrand could feel the strength returning to his limbs after the exertions of the previous day.

The sun was warm on his face and the mist already thinning.

"Come," he said, "we are wasting daylight. I would find a settlement where we can buy horses before day's end."

Without waiting for a response, Beobrand slung the wrapped sword, with the now lighter sack reattached, over his shoulder and strode off into the north-west. Halinard jogged to catch up, then fell into step beside him.

"It is far enough from Liyon?" he asked. "We have not covered much ground on foot."

"It will have to be," replied Beobrand. "There is no time to lose, if we are to take what we know to the king."

Beobrand walked on, the sun behind him as it rose ever higher in the sky. The visions of his dream assailed his thoughts. He tried to ignore them, instead focusing on the bright day and the life around them. He listened to the birdsong that filled the forest. He could make out the thin warbling of a group of dunnocks, the high-pitched chirrups of sparrows and the angry screech of a jay somewhere in the distance. As the day grew warmer, the mist burnt away and the air became alive with the hum and buzz of insects.

He did not wish to think of his dream, but he could not prevent himself from remembering Sunniva's eyes. Or had they been Balthild's? Had Dalfinus and his conspirators already murdered her, as they had tried to before? The most recent tidings he had heard, a couple of weeks before, were that the queen had given birth to a healthy son at Cala. But that had been gossip that had travelled to Liyon with traders and merchants over weeks. The gods alone knew what had happened in the intervening time since the birth of the royal heir. Balthild might have been assassinated, just as she had been in his nightmare. Mayhap her son had been slain too, or he might have died of some ailment. Babes were so fragile. Beobrand recalled his own fear that something would befall Octa when he was an infant. By Woden, he still worried about his son, and Octa was a man now; a warrior and a killer.

And what of Cynan? Had his dream been sent by the gods to tell him what had already happened, or what would come to pass? Was Cynan already dead? The thought pained Beobrand, but he would not dwell on such dark speculation. He walked on, pushing himself to ever greater speed until the sweat ran down his face and soaked his kirtle.

Halinard limped along, first at his side, then increasingly several paces behind him, without complaint. It was only when Beobrand paused for a brief rest around midday that he noticed the man's discomfort. Halinard trudged out of the shade beneath the trees to where Beobrand waited beside a small stream. The Frank groaned, gritting his teeth as he lowered himself down to lean his back against the mossy trunk of a willow that grew at the water's edge. He massaged his outstretched leg and grimaced.

Cursing silently to himself, Beobrand pulled out the last flat loaf. It was hard and stale, but would still be good with water to moisten it. Tearing it in two, he handed half to Halinard, then dropped to his knee beside the stream to fill the waterskin. When it was full, he sat down beside Halinard and offered him the skin. He took it and drank deeply. Beobrand bit off a piece of the bread and chewed it absently, while he looked out over the thinning woodland ahead of them. They had kept to the forest all day and had seen no other travellers. Once more, far off on the road, they had heard the passing of several horses hurrying by at a canter. They were far from the road and the sound echoed from the trunks of the trees, making it impossible to tell whether the horsemen were heading towards or away from Liyon.

Beyond the woodland, there were fields of green barley. Beobrand remembered a village in the next valley. He peered into the distance and thought he might be able to make out a slight haze in the air, perhaps from cooking fires, but his eyesight was not good enough to be certain.

"Can you walk as far as the next settlement?" he asked. "The other side of that hill."

"I can walk as far as I need to walk," Halinard replied. He bit off another piece of stale bread.

"We need horses," said Beobrand.

Halinard looked at him sharply and swallowed.

"I will not slow you down."

"I know, Halinard," he said. "But we will not reach Paris until harvest time if we walk all the way. Besides, I had forgotten your injury." He turned to face Halinard. "I am sorry." It seemed all he did was apologise, but he felt keenly that he did not deserve the loyalty of his men when he was such a poor leader. He should have known that some treachery was brewing in Liyon. He could have led his men to safety weeks ago, instead he had grown complacent and soft. Angry too, but what good was anger without action?

"It is nothing," said Halinard, rubbing a hand across his chin.

Beobrand set a slower pace as the sun dipped into the west. Halinard said nothing, but his jaw was set as he trudged beside Beobrand. A couple of times after they cleared the forest and began walking across the fields of barley, Beobrand halted to take a drink and to survey the land around them. Halinard was pleased for these respites, and while the interruptions to their progress frustrated Beobrand, he knew it could not be helped. There was no point in forcing a speed that Halinard could not match. Eventually, he would do more damage to his leg and if he could not walk at all, what would Beobrand do?

He could not countenance abandoning him. Besides, even if he convinced himself it was necessary to do so, how would he fare travelling across the breadth of Frankia alone without anyone to interpret for him? No, the best course of action was to buy mounts and then ride as quickly as they were able towards Paris.

With any luck, Dalfinus would still have his men scouring the city for them, while they would be well on their way to the royal palace and the king. Of course, Beobrand did not trust to luck, and so, as they walked he scanned the distant road for riders. They saw a couple of carts, a large flock of sheep, and a cattle drover with a dozen dun-coloured cows, but they did not spot anything that looked threatening. No armed men and no horsemen.

It was possible that the travellers on the road had seen them as they climbed the rise, but there was nothing to mark them out as anything more than peasants. There was no gleam of metal from weapons or armour, their once rich clothes were dirty and drab, and they each wore threadbare brown cloaks. And if they were to procure horses, they would need to risk approaching the road eventually.

The first sign they had of the man's approach was the barking of his dog. They were still some way off from the settlement, but they had crested the hill and they could make out the buildings scattered seemingly randomly where the road forded a river. The day was clear and the sun bright and warm, and Beobrand was pleased to see he had been right. The pale smudge in the sky was the pall of smoke that drifted up above the village. It would take them a while yet to reach the settlement, especially at Halinard's pace, but there was still plenty of light in the sky, and it was possible they would be able to find horses and provisions there.

The dog's barking startled them both. Beobrand turned to face the threat that came from behind them. Without thinking, he swung the sword from his shoulder, shaking the now almost empty sack off, then holding the weapon in front of him. It was still wrapped in cloth, but there could be little chance of anyone mistaking what was in the tall man's hand. Halinard rested his fingers on the hilt of the seax that hung from his belt.

A grey, white and black hound came bounding towards them. Its tail was flapping vigorously, but its barking mouth showed an array of large sharp teeth. When it was yet a few paces from them, a voice snapped an order and the animal dropped to the ground, where it eyed Beobrand and Halinard balefully.

Beobrand flicked his gaze to the man who strode towards them. He was not overly tall, but he walked with long, distance-devouring strides. The man was older than both Halinard and Beobrand. He had a full white beard and thick, silver hair, pulled back from his lined face and tied at the nape of his neck. He wore simple shoes and black breeches, and a fawn-coloured shirt that looked to be made of deerskin. Over his shoulder he carried a large axe.

The man and his dog had come from a copse of hazel and hawthorn off to the west, but due to their quicker speed, they had caught up with them easily. Beobrand cursed his lack of attention. How had he not seen the man sooner?

"I talk," hissed Halinard under his breath as the dog fell silent.

There was no time for Beobrand to answer, so he merely nodded and stood his ground, watching intently the interaction between the men and trying to understand as much as he could of the Frankish words they spoke.

The old man stopped next to his dog and, reaching down, stroked between its ears. Despite the axe he carried in his meaty hands, he gave no indication of being a threat. He smiled broadly, looking first at Beobrand and then Halinard.

"Good health to you," he said. Beobrand nodded, understanding the common greeting. Halinard replied and in moments they were speaking too quickly for Beobrand to follow. He watched Halinard's stance, and listened to his tone, ready to defend them if his gesith gave him a warning. But the conversation went on for some time, and as they spoke, both Halinard and the old man visibly relaxed.

They continued to speak at length until the silver-haired man pointed down to the road. His tone became harder. Beobrand heard Halinard mention Dalfinus then, and on hearing the name of the *comes* of Liyon, the old man spat. Beobrand tightened his grip on the sword, readying himself for combat. If the stranger should set his dog on them and come in swinging that axe of his, it would be messy. There would be no guarantee that they would escape unscathed. He left the sword's point resting on the tilled earth, but was ready to whip it up the instant he was given cause to doubt the man's good faith.

But the silver-haired man did not attack, or even raise his voice. Instead he shook his head and took a flask from a pack that was slung over his shoulder. He stepped close, offering it to Halinard.

"It is wine," he said, when Halinard hesitated, and Beobrand understood the Frankish words.

With a shrug, Halinard took the leather flask and drank.

"It is good," he said, and passed it to Beobrand.

Beobrand took a swig. Halinard was right. It was good. Sweet and fresh-tasting and not something he would have expected from the skin of a ceorl. He handed it back with a nod of thanks. The man swallowed a deep draught, then stoppered the flask and stowed it in his pack once more.

Halinard turned the conversation to horses, and despite not being able to comprehend all the words, Beobrand understood that the man had animals on his farm. When Halinard asked if they could buy some, he thought a while, then nodded. Without waiting for a reply, he strode off once more, his hound gambolling through the green shoots of barley.

"Come," he said, beckoning over his shoulder, before shouting something else Beobrand did not understand.

"His name is Dudon," said Halinard in a whisper, "and he will sell us horses and provender."

"What was that about Dalfinus?"

"He hates the man. Says he taxes him unfairly."

Beobrand nodded, wondering if any of Dalfinus' people loved their lord, or if he ruled them all through fear.

"What did you tell him about us?"

"Nothing really. Just that we need horses. He asked if we preferred not to meet any of Dalfinus' men. I couldn't ignore the question, so I said we want to travel quietly. He told me some guards rode through here, but none since yesterday. He knows we are on the run, I think, but he cares nought for our story. In his eyes someone fleeing from Dalfinus cannot be bad."

Dudon was some way down the slope now. Turning, he called to them.

"We can talk more later," said Halinard, limping after Dudon. "For now, just hope he has good horses."

Far off in the distance, they could hear the unmistakable metal-on-metal sounds of a smith at work.

They traipsed down the hill behind the old man. Soon he moved off the field and headed down a dirt path that led towards the settlement. Dudon set a gruelling pace and Halinard was struggling when they reached the river and the first of the buildings. They passed a barn, then the forge, where a smith hammered a glowing piece of iron. The leather-aproned man examined the hinge he was fashioning, then plunged it into a bucket of water in a hiss of steam. Dudon called out a greeting. The smith waved, staring with open interest at the men accompanying Dudon.

The path led along beside the river for a time. Willows and alders grew lush and thick there, obscuring the rest of the buildings from view. It was only when they reached the ford, where the wider road passed through a broad rocky shallow of the river, that the houses, other barns and storerooms, and the hall itself became visible to Beobrand and Halinard.

Beobrand recalled the place well now that he saw it again. It had the air of a well-managed steading. The buildings bore no sign of decay and any damage from the previous winter had already been mended. The roofs were all clean and moss-free, the thatch glowing golden in the light of the lowering sun. The whole place had an air of prosperity, and Beobrand wondered at the silver-bearded Dudon with his plain-spun breeches and deerskin shirt. He looked more like a woodsman than a farmer, but if this steading and the land about it were his, he was a rich man indeed.

The feeling was only reinforced when they rounded the house nearest the ford and were able to see beyond it a fenced-off corral that held perhaps a dozen horses. At a glance Beobrand could see it was good horseflesh. They were riding horses, not the stocky, heavily-muscled stock that farmers bred to pull carts and ploughs. His spirit soared to see such animals. On a couple of those beasts, they would make it to Paris more quickly than he would have thought possible.

But something scratched at his mind as he watched the horses cropping at the grass in the paddock. Like a pebble in a shoe, he could not rid himself of a nagging thought. What need would a farmer have for so many steeds?

Before he had time to seek an answer to this question, Dudon disappeared around the far side of the hall. Moments later, several men stepped from the shadows into the afternoon light.

Beside Beobrand, Halinard cursed.

Most of the men wore crimson cloaks. The low sun glinted from their burnished byrnies. The steel blades of their swords gleamed as they were drawn from tooled leather scabbards. In an instant, Beobrand knew the truth. The horses were not Dudon's, they belonged to Dalfinus' men.

Beobrand recognised some of the faces of the red-cloaked warriors, but the man at their centre was well-known to him. He stood a head taller than the next tallest of the guards. Bright teeth showed in his thick beard as he grinned.

Gunthar.

Beobrand cast about him for a means of escape, but it was

no use. Even if Halinard was able to run, there was nowhere for them to go. Dudon had cunningly brought them along the riverside path so that they would only spy the horses at the last moment and now, Dalfinus' men, who must have been resting in Dudon's hall, were close enough that if they tried to flee, they would be run down in a few heartbeats.

Halinard spat and pulled his seax from its sheath.

"No, friend," said Beobrand, placing a hand on his arm. "They are too many."

It was true. He counted eight of them, all armed and armoured. Gunthar alone, with his brute strength and savagery, would have been tough to beat. The two of them, no matter their battle-skill and bravery, could not hope to prevail against such odds.

Offering up a silent curse to Woden, Beobrand threw his sword to the earth and held his hands out, waiting for the guards to approach.

Chapter 29

The punch snapped Beobrand's head back and crunched his lips into his teeth. His vision blurred and he staggered backwards a couple of steps. Willing himself not to fall, he straightened and stared defiantly at Gunthar who loomed over him, massive fist raised, ready to inflict another punishing blow. Beobrand's mouth filled with the salt-metal taste of blood and he spat into the dust at Gunthar's feet.

Gunthar was as fast and unpredictable as he was strong, but Beobrand berated himself for not seeing the punch coming. He had been caught off guard by the smiling giant who delivered the crushing jab without warning.

Gunthar stooped and lifted the sword from where Beobrand had dropped it. Beobrand wished now that he had not relinquished the blade. His fists clenched at his sides, his muscles trembling with fury. He could have slain this brute before becoming overrun by the superior numbers of the guards. He ran his tongue along his teeth, but none felt loose. His mouth was full of blood. He spat again.

He should not have told Halinard to surrender. He had stupidly thought that by not resisting, Dalfinus' men might be lenient with Halinard, but now he saw that was madness. Surely Vulmar and Dalfinus would want them both dead. There would be no mercy for either of them. It was possible that they would be kept alive until they could be questioned about what they knew and who they might have spoken to, but even if they lived long enough to be tortured somewhere in the bowels of Liyon, they would be killed all too soon.

They should have fought. If they were to die, better a warrior's death, quickly cut down in battle.

Beobrand glanced at Dudon. The old man would not look him in the eye. No amount of shame would save him if Beobrand was able to swing a blade again. The man had betrayed him and would pay the price with his life, if Beobrand had his way. He looked longingly at the sword in Gunthar's hand, and the seax he had also thrown to the ground. Fleetingly, he wondered if he could snatch up the long knife and rush Dudon before Gunthar struck him down. Shaking his head and spitting blood once more, Beobrand smiled thinly. He would not be able to seek vengeance. Soon he would be trussed up and carried back to the city, if he was not slain outright here at Dudon's steading.

Gunthar examined the sword in his great hands, turning it this way and that so that the afternoon sunshine glimmered on its plain blade. He said something to Halinard, his voice a low grumble like distant thunder. When Halinard said nothing, Gunthar leapt forward. Halinard let out a cry and fell, sprawling in the dirt. For a dreadful moment Beobrand thought Gunthar had driven the sword's blade into his friend. Then he saw the blood on Halinard's face. It streamed from his nose, soaking his lips and beard. Gunthar had punched him too.

Shaking his head and spitting, Halinard pushed himself to his feet. He glowered at Gunthar, showing no fear, and Beobrand was filled with pride for his Frankish gesith. Gunthar spoke again, his voice low and menacing. This time, Halinard replied, addressing Beobrand.

"He says the sword belonged to his friend."

Beobrand sneered. He had been wrong to surrender, but perhaps he could yet force a fight.

"Tell him he can keep it," he said. "It is more use than his dead friend."

Halinard sighed and wiped blood from his nose on his sleeve. He spoke briefly, earning a backhanded slap from Gunthar that spun his head and sent him staggering. This time he did not fall.

A couple of the guards chuckled. They were crowded in close now, eager to see their leader's treatment of their captives. Gunthar stalked over to Beobrand and made to strike him again, but this time Beobrand was ready, and he stepped quickly back.

Gunthar snarled, lifting the sword high. Beobrand had seen Gunthar fight. He was hugely strong, fast and skilled. But his weakness was his temper. He could be goaded into rashness. Gunthar took a step closer. Beobrand did not move. He paused for a heartbeat, then spat a gobbet of bloody spittle into Gunthar's face.

For an eye-blink Gunthar did not react, then, bellowing like a bull, he surged forward swinging the sword in a great arc. Beobrand felt the cold thrill of battle wash through him. Better to fight and be killed quickly now, than tortured for the pleasure of that bastard Vulmar and Dalfinus' other conspirators.

As the sword flickered downward through the warm afternoon air, Beobrand sprang forward and gripped Gunthar's wrists. The warrior's strength was prodigious and whilst Beobrand was broad and strong, he was no match for Gunthar, especially as it was his weaker half-hand that grasped Gunthar's sword arm. The sword's movement was halted momentarily, but Gunthar growled, using his bulk to lever the blade down.

Beobrand grunted with the effort, but knew instantly that he could not hope to beat Gunthar in a show of strength. He was dimly aware of the rest of the guardsmen shouting and calling out. There was movement behind Gunthar and he imagined Halinard had also seized this opportunity to strike out, to find a better death than the one that awaited them in Liyon. But Beobrand could not divert his attention away from Gunthar. His world shrunk to encompass only his opponent as he heaved and struggled with the great brute.

Bracing himself against the man's terrible strength, Beobrand felt the leather of his shoes slip in the dry dust. Gunthar's leering face grew ever closer. Beobrand could not hold him for long. It was only a matter of time before Gunthar would overpower him.

The sounds of the other guards grew louder, but still Beobrand could not divert his attention from his foe. Without warning, Beobrand suddenly relaxed, allowing Gunthar to push him back a step. The massive man was momentarily off balance and in that instant, Beobrand snapped his head forward. All of his fury was in that blow. All his sorrow at what he had lost. All of his anger at his poor decisions that had brought them to this place. All his self-loathing at his weakness and poor leadership. He had led Halinard and his gesithas unto their deaths. He did not deserve such loyalty and he would seek to repay it by fighting as hard as he could.

Beobrand's forehead crunched into Gunthar's nose like a hammer blow. Pain bloomed in Beobrand's head and bright light flared, blinding him. Blood spurted as Gunthar's nose was broken. Most men would have been felled by such a blow, but Gunthar was no normal man. He was as strong as an ox. And perhaps as senseless. But he was yet a man, and despite his strength he was shaken by the head-butt. Sensing Gunthar's hold on the sword weaken, Beobrand tightened his grasp on Gunthar's wrist. He dug his fingers into the man's flesh, but his mutilated left hand was not strong enough to cause Gunthar to release the weapon. Beobrand's fingers began to slip on Gunthar's brawny forearm and he knew that he would lose that battle of force in scant moments. He could not allow Gunthar to bring the sword to bear, so, seeing no alternative, Beobrand grasped as tightly as he was able and flung himself backwards, pulling the giant with him. Gunthar blinked at the sudden shift in momentum, but he was still dazed from the previous blow and unable to hold Beobrand upright. Together they collapsed onto the hard earth.

The air was driven from Beobrand's lungs and he lost his grip on Gunthar. The sword skittered away in the dust. In a flash, the huge warrior straddled Beobrand and began raining down blows. Undaunted at losing hold of the blade, Gunthar seemed content to use his knuckles. Given his size and strength, Beobrand thought the outcome would be the same. Already his vision was darkening and blurring with each strike from Gunthar's stone-like fists. The sound of the blows echoed and grew, filling Beobrand's world. It was as if the whole of middle earth was filled with fighting, and Beobrand imagined he could hear many men struggling; the familiar clamour of weapons on shields, the shouts of the dying. It seemed fitting to him that after so many wars, so much blood and death, he should die with these sounds ringing in his ears. His face was slick with blood, both his own and that of his attacker that dripped from Gunthar's shattered nose.

Beobrand struggled beneath Gunthar, but to no avail. His arms were pinned by the man's knees and it was all he could do to twist his head in an effort to lessen the power of the man's punches. All he could see now was Gunthar's bloody face surrounded by a halo of encroaching darkness. He would lose consciousness soon, he thought. And after that, death would come swiftly, or he would be forced to endure endless torture. He shook and heaved against Gunthar's weight, but it was useless.

Abruptly, the blows stopped.

Was this death then, coming for him after he had eluded its clutches for so many years? Beobrand peered up into the sudden brightness where Gunthar's shadow had been a moment before. With a start, he realised the man's weight atop him had gone.

Another shadow replaced Gunthar's and Beobrand squinted, trying to make sense of what he saw through his rapidly swelling eyes. In Gunthar's place there loomed another giant and Beobrand braced himself for the assault on his body to be renewed.

But instead of further attacks, a huge hand was lowered towards him, fingers outstretched in an offer of assistance. Blinking and groaning with the pain of the beating he had suffered, Beobrand clutched the proffered hand and allowed himself to be heaved to his feet. He swayed there for a spell, looking down in disbelief at Gunthar. The man's eyes were open, staring sightlessly back at Beobrand. His face was awash with blood from his shattered nose and the blow that had slain him. His skull was sundered. Blood, brains and bone had tumbled from the gaping wound.

"What?" said Beobrand stupidly. His head rang like a smith's anvil. He shook it to clear the fog and instantly regretted the motion. Turning slowly, he looked up at the man who had raised him to his feet. "How?" he asked, finally recognising the warrior.

"I told him in the arena," said Eadgard, spitting onto Gunthar's body. "He should fight men his own size."

"Am I dead?" Beobrand asked.

Eadgard frowned.

"You are talking to me, lord," he said, "so I hope not. He is though." He nodded towards Gunthar's motionless form, in case Beobrand was in any doubt to whom he was referring.

Beobrand was still unsure about what was happening, but his mind began to clear somewhat. Quickly, he stooped to retrieve the sword. He was dizzy and his head swam as he stood upright once more. He did not know how much use he would be in a fight, and he had no idea how Eadgard had come to be there, but if his gesithas were here, he would stand with them.

He looked about for Halinard. He sighed with relief when he saw the Frank yet lived. Halinard had a gash across his forehead, but otherwise, he appeared hale and whole. Beobrand's vision was clearing now, and he saw there would be no need for further fighting. As he watched, Attor cut down the last of the guards. Another of the red-cloaked warriors cried out for mercy, but he received none. Ingwald, face splattered with blood, stalked towards him, and drove a spear into the man's chest, silencing his pleas.

Beyond the bodies strewn across the road, several horses milled about on the path. They were lathered in sweat, and he wondered how he had not heard their arrival.

Near the hall, Dudon stood with the villagers, open-mouthed and wide-eyed at the sudden slaughter and the drastic reversal of his fortunes.

Cynan was striding towards Beobrand, his face split in a grin. Beobrand was overjoyed to see him, but the sight of the silver-haired farmer had rekindled the fires of his ire.

"Gunthar's fists have not improved your looks," said Cynan with a smile. "It seems we arrived just in time."

Beobrand nodded in welcome, but did not reply. Instead he brushed past Cynan and walked determinedly towards the hall.

"Lord?" called out Cynan.

"It gives me joy to see you," Beobrand said over his shoulder, glaring all the while at Dudon. "I would hear your tale over food and ale. But before I can rest, there is one more man who must die this day."

Chapter 30

Cynan walked into the hall, accepting a cup of ale from Bleddyn. The men were gathered around a table that had been set up against the far wall. They conversed in whispers, the mood in the room subdued and sombre.

"What have you done with them?" asked Beobrand, looking through the smoke-hazed air. Cynan winced at the sight of him. Beobrand had cleaned his face of blood, but it was swollen and bruised. In the coming days those bruises would mottle like storm clouds at sunset. Still, it could have been much worse.

"They are in the barn," said Cynan. "Grindan and Eadgard are watching them."

"They are not to be harmed," said Beobrand.

Cynan nodded. Short of killing them all, there was nothing for it but to leave the villagers behind when the men of Albion rode on in the morning.

"As soon as we are gone, they will carry word to the city of what occurred here," he said. "Dalfinus will know where we are heading."

"Then it is lucky you brought extra horses," said Beobrand. "With the guards' mounts and those you rode on, we have spares and should make good time. We will leave at dawn and trust to Woden that we will reach Paris before those vipers."

Beobrand was slumped in a large chair that must have belonged to the master of the farm. The farmer would not be needing it any longer. The old man had made a good show of standing up to Beobrand. He did not flee as most men would have done. Seeing his advanced years, every warrior there had known how a fight between the two men would end, but to his credit, Dudon had hefted his great axe and stepped out to meet the tall thegn of Ubbanford without hesitation or sign of fear. He was a brave man, of that there could be no doubt. The womenfolk had wept, and his dog had barked, as one of the children held it back by its collar, but Dudon had not flinched and had not wasted his breath on worthless words. He knew he had betrayed Beobrand, and looking into the battered and bruised face of the fair-haired warrior, he saw the approach of death.

It was over in a heartbeat. Dudon swept his axe towards Beobrand, who knocked it aside and hacked his sword into the old man's neck. Beobrand did not show any sign of pleasure in what he had done. He had turned away as the womenfolk began to wail.

Dudon had not made a sound, even as the blade struck him and his spirit departed. He slumped onto the dry earth, surrounded by his kin. He died silently.

They had allowed the womenfolk to care for Dudon's body, and Cynan, seeing that Beobrand was still stunned from the beating he had received, had ordered the men to round up the rest of the villagers and secure them in the largest barn. Two of the women from the settlement were now at the hearth in the hall preparing food. The scent of lamb and onions hung in the air and Cynan's stomach grumbled. It had been a long time since he'd had a proper meal. He sighed, taking a swig of the ale. It was slightly sour, perhaps a few days old, but it was good enough, and he relished the sweet hint of yarrow from the gruit as the liquid washed the dust of travel from his mouth.

"Ask them how long for the food," he said to Halinard. The Frank had been dozing, head sagging, chin on his chest. Seeing him thus made Cynan wonder how bad the wound on his head was. But Halinard opened his eyes and muttered a few words to the women by the fire. The older of the two hissed a reply and fixed first Halinard and then Beobrand with a stare of such malevolence that Cynan thought she would slit their throats the moment their backs were turned. He had thought to leave the women in the hall during the night to tend to the men, serving them ale and food, but now he vowed he would have them moved to the barn as soon as the stew was served. He sniffed, wondering what the women might have added to the pottage. It smelled rich and wholesome, but he supposed it was possible that they could have poisoned the food.

"She says if you want to eat hard carrots and raw lamb, then you can help yourself. But it takes as long as it takes." Halinard shrugged. "She will tell us when it is ready."

"Tell her she must feed some of it to her children before we eat."

Halinard raised an eyebrow, but translated the words. The woman hissed again, glowering at him for a moment before returning to her work.

Cynan wondered if there was something he was missing. He sipped the ale again, as he settled himself down on the nearest bench. He was exhausted. The responsibility for the men's lives had weighed heavily on him. He had thought Beobrand would step into the role of leader as soon as they were reunited, but he could see that the older warrior needed time to rest.

"How is your leg?" Cynan asked Attor.

"I'll live," said the slim warrior. That was more than could be said for the guard who had wounded him. He had taken a spear thrust in his thigh from the white-plumed leader of the guard at the western side of the bridge. Attor had spun inside the reach of the sharp blade, somehow avoiding the deadly cut to the artery that ran inside the thigh, then, in one fluid motion, he had hacked his long seax into the guard's throat.

"Tell me," said Beobrand, rousing himself from his reverie, "how it is that you came to be here, mounted and armed, but, as far as I can see, without your byrnies, shields, helms or any of the provisions I had commanded you to acquire."

"Well, lord," said Cynan, in an effort to make light of their situation, "it seems that someone upset the nobles' hunt, which made men of Albion less than welcome in the fine city of Liyon."

Beobrand did not smile.

"They killed Gram," he said, his tone flat. "It was a trap. Vulmar was there."

"Vulmar?"

"Aye. Dalfinus invited him. All this while he has been feeding us and filling our cups with fine wine, he was waiting for Vulmar to come."

Cynan tried to understand, but there were too many players in this deadly game.

"They set a trap for you? At the hunt?" he asked.

"It was no hunt. Not for animals." Beobrand sipped his ale. He stared at the fire on the hearth stone for a time, as if he could see images in the flames. "They use the amphitheatre as the men of old Roma did. They had men there. Caged. This hunt is nothing more than a slaughter for the nobles' amusement." Beobrand emptied his cup. Grindan reached for a jug and refilled it. "They would have killed me for Vulmar's pleasure too," Beobrand went on, "if I had not recognised the man from the forest."

"What man?"

"You remember after the attack on Balthild, one of the brigands got a hoof to the head?"

Cynan nodded uncertainly, not liking to be reminded of his own clumsy fall when the injured horse had unseated him.

"I'd already skewered his hand and, after that horse's hoof struck him, I believed him dead," said Beobrand. "I could scarcely believe that a man could survive such a blow, but there he was. His name is Agobard. He is one of Dalfinus' men."

"So Brocard was right!" exclaimed Cynan.

"So it seems," Beobrand's bruised face was dour. "The attack was organised by men wishing to put an end to the queen."

"And her heir too." Cynan thought of the manner of men who would seek to kill a woman heavy with child for their own gain. He clutched his cup firmly.

"There are many of them," said Beobrand. "They must hate that she is freeing thralls. Vulmar is one of the bastards who plotted against her. The moment I saw him and this Agobard it all fell into place. We fought our way free..." His voice faltered and Cynan was certain that he was thinking of Gram. "Then, with the help of some tanners, we made it out of the city."

"Ah, yes. We met Shimon on the road."

Beobrand sat up straight.

"You met the tanner?"

"We did, and if it had not been for him, we would not have found you so quickly. He recognised us as your companions and called out to us. We were not certain at first."

"*You* were not certain," said Attor.

Cynan chose to ignore Attor. They had quarrelled over approaching the Iudeisc tanner. In the end Attor had ignored Cynan and ridden up to the man in his waggon.

"It took us a while to make out what he was saying," Cynan continued. "But in the end we understood—"

"I understood," interjected Attor.

Cynan raised an eyebrow, but did not rise to the bait.

"Shimon said you had escaped the city and told us the direction you were heading. We thought you would not risk the road for a time, so we followed through the forest. Attor," Cynan bowed dramatically to the older warrior, "cut your sign in the woods this morning and tracked you here."

"I can barely credit it," said Beobrand. "You met Shimon? And our tracks led you here?"

"Yes," replied Cynan, nodding. "And he is not the only friend who has crossed our path these last days."

"No?"

Cynan told Beobrand then of how they had met Sigulf and how he had helped them. Beobrand shook his head in disbelief.

"If I did not know you, I would say you were lying."

"It is no lie, Beobrand."

"But here, in Frankia." Beobrand whistled. "Wyrd is truly a strange thing that none can comprehend."

"This is not wyrd, lord," said Attor, his eyes bright in the shadows of the hall. "The Lord Almighty's hand is in this."

Beobrand scowled.

"Do not speak to me of your Christ god, Attor. Is he not the same god whose followers torment the Iudeisc?" Beobrand's voice rose in pitch, his anger simmering close to the surface. "Is Annemund not one of your god's most sacred servants? And yet the man joins his brother in their infernal hunt of men, and together they conspire against their queen."

"But, lord—"

"No!" Beobrand cut Attor off. "Is not Wilfrid one of your Christ's chosen ones? And yet he has betrayed us."

"God is good," said Attor, his voice quiet, but firm. Everyone knew Attor to be a brave man, but Cynan respected him more than ever in that moment as he stood by his beliefs. He knew it was no easy thing to defy Beobrand.

"Good?" barked Beobrand. "I see much evil carried out in the Christ's name."

Attor was pale.

"I do not understand all the ways of God," he said. "No man does. But Coenred has told me that every man is free to choose his own path. God is not evil, He is good. Some men choose not to follow the truth of His teachings." He paused, staring into

Beobrand's ice-cold glare. "Just as there are some pagans who choose to do good, lord. Coenred told me once that you can turn your back on the Almighty, but He will never turn his back on you. I believe God Himself sent Sigulf to aid us, and Shimon and the tanners to help you."

Beobrand glowered, but said no more on the matter. Perhaps it was the mention of his friend, Coenred, or maybe it was because there was no way to win such a debate. Whatever the reason, Beobrand shook his head and drank more ale.

"Tell me," Beobrand said after a time, ignoring Attor and turning back to Cynan, "how Sigulf helped you to leave Liyon."

"I will tell that tale as we eat," Cynan said.

The women had finished the stew and began to silently dish it out into wooden bowls. True to his word, Cynan ordered Bleddyn to fetch one of the children from the barn. He returned with a girl of perhaps ten summers. Her freckled cheeks were tear-streaked. She shook her head at first, refusing to do what the woman asked of her. The grey-haired woman snapped at the girl and raised her hand to strike her. The child bit back her retort and ate, staring with wide, red-rimmed eyes at the warriors in the hall as she spooned some of the pottage into her mouth. Content that the food was not poisoned, Cynan allowed the women to dish out a bowlful for each of the men and then had Halinard tell them to take the rest of the stew to their kin.

Eadgard helped Bleddyn carry the cauldron to the barn and the rest of them were soon seated at the table with bread, ale and the rich-smelling stew before them. The food did not last long. They had all been hungry and within moments they were mopping the bowls with the crusts of the bread.

"I could have eaten another bowl of that," grumbled Ingwald.

"I feel like I haven't eaten in days. You are too kind to give them so much."

Cynan shrugged.

"These people have done nothing wrong. This is their food. Would you see them go hungry? The children? The women?"

"Not the children," said Ingwald, chastened by Cynan's words.

"These people are innocent," said Cynan. "They could not defy Gunthar and his guards even if they had wanted to." He flicked a glance at Beobrand. His bruised face was set in a scowl. Cynan knew him well enough to imagine what he was thinking. "There was only one of their number who deserved to be punished, and he has paid the blood-price for his actions."

Beobrand said nothing. He stared morosely into his cup. Cynan wondered whether he regretted slaying the old farmer. Beobrand would never admit such a thing, but Cynan had often heard his lord roused from a restless sleep by nightmares that had him whimpering the names of men he had killed. Beobrand killed with ease, but the ghosts of the dead never left him.

While the men chewed on the last of the bread and refilled their cups with the sour ale, Cynan told Beobrand how they had bought all of the provisions he had requested and were on their way back to the palace when they were spotted by the guards at the bridge. He recalled how they had fought their way free, despite being outnumbered.

"The men fought like lions," he said, proudly. "And Sigulf stood with us."

"He fought?" Beobrand sounded surprised.

Cynan smiled as he remembered the sailor screaming at the guards, hacking and stabbing with his seax.

"He was ever a brave one," he said. "I told him it was not his fight, but he reminded me what you had said to the men on *Brimblæd*."

"What I said?" Beobrand narrowed his eyes, as if peering back through the years to recollect his words.

"Well," said Cynan with a smile, "Sigulf remembered, even if you do not."

"What did I say?"

"That after we had stood together in battle, we were brothers." Beobrand smiled sadly at the memory, then grimaced as his bruises stretched.

"Just like a brother," continued Cynan, "Sigulf can be vexing. But he stood with us and without him, I fear we would have been lost. The alarm had been raised and more guards were coming, but Sigulf led us through back alleys down to his boat." Cynan remembered the headlong rush through the midday heat. All about them the shouts of pursuit, and the echoes of rushing feet. Attor had been bleeding badly and his feet had dragged along the ground where he dangled between Eadgard and Grindan. Somehow they had made it to the wharf without further impediment, and in moments, Sigulf had them all aboard his boat and pushing out into the crowded waters of the Sona. "We rowed out of Liyon as members of Sigulf's crew."

"Where did you get the horses?" asked Beobrand.

"Sigulf knew a man just south of the city. He sold us the animals. For much more than they are worth, but there was no time to strike a good bargain. I'm sorry, but the pouch of gold you gave me is empty."

"It is not so bad," said Beobrand, lifting his shoulders as if willing himself to a better humour. "There is food here that we can take with us. And we have spare horses now, and those cost us nothing save some sweat and a few bruises." He smiled lopsidedly, his swollen face dark and misshapen in the flickering light of the fire and the rush lights.

Halinard reached for the ale jug, shaking his head.

"Nothing, he says," his voice dripping with exaggerated

outrage. Reaching up, he dabbed his fingers at the scab that had formed on the long cut to his forehead.

Beobrand snorted.

"I fared worse than you," he said, pointing at his own face. "That is just a scratch. And what oath-sworn gesith would not take a hundred such cuts for his lord?"

The moment of levity was instantly shattered as Beobrand realised what he had said. None of them spoke for a time as their thoughts turned to the man who was missing from their ranks.

Eventually, Beobrand pushed himself to his feet.

"To Gram," he said, raising his cup. "A braver man, I have not known."

They all drank, but the sour mood had returned to the hall once more, and soon the exertions of the day caught up with them. Conversation waned. Attor yawned and rose from the bench. Following him, one by one, they stretched out, wrapped in cloaks and blankets, and tried to find sleep.

Cynan opened his eyes in the darkness and listened to the night. It was not the first time he had awoken. Bleddyn and Ingwald had exchanged places with Eadgard and Grindan some time before. They probably believed they were being quiet but they had scraped against the benches and Eadgard had cursed loudly when he'd stumbled over Attor's sleeping form.

Eadgard's snoring now echoed in the gloom, drowning out any other night-time sounds. Cynan sensed movement and peered into the darkness. Dim moonlight spilt into the hall as the door was pulled open and a tall shadow slipped into the night. It appeared that Cynan was not the only one unable to sleep. He lay still, listening to Eadgard's rumbling snores for a few moments more, then, acknowledging that sleep would elude him, he pushed himself to his feet. Carefully, he threaded his way past the slumbering men. The door, like all of Dudon's settlement, was well made and maintained. Its hinges were oiled with pig fat and made barely a sound as he opened it and stepped into the cool darkness outside.

Beobrand was standing with his back to the hall, staring out over the open land that was limned in the silver glow of the moon. Pulling his cloak about his shoulders, Cynan moved towards his lord. He cleared his throat as he approached so as not to startle him. Beobrand stiffened, but did not turn. Nor did he speak for a long time after Cynan stood beside him. Cynan had long ago stopped trying to converse with Beobrand when a dark mood seized him. It was enough that he was there, close by.

He flicked a glance at Beobrand. It was too dark to make out his features, but Cynan could picture the bruises, the swollen eyes and the split lip. When they had galloped to Beobrand and Halinard's aid that afternoon, there had been a moment when he had believed they were too late. Beobrand had fallen and that brute, Gunthar, had dropped onto him. Cynan had felt an almost physical pain at the sight. He had failed to protect his lord. The men had felt it too and had struck Gunthar's guards with savage ferocity, fighting their way to Beobrand with abandon. The shared sensation of relief when Eadgard had pulled the thegn of Ubbanford to his feet had lifted their spirits for the first time since fleeing Liyon.

A light breeze rustled through the leaves of the trees down by the river. Somewhere close by an owl hooted. The eastern sky was tinged with the first steel-grey light of the predawn. It was peaceful here, but Cynan could not shake the thought that this was the calm before they entered another storm.

"I wonder if this thing I seek to do is madness," said Beobrand, his voice not much more than a whisper, but loud all the same in the still of the night.

Cynan sighed, thinking of all the times he had followed Beobrand. The clash of shieldwalls. The towering waves crashing over the deck of *Brimblæd*, the sea biting with ice and snow as they had tumbled into the surf. The thrumming hooves as they galloped through the night to Hunwald's hall.

"It will not be the first time that what you do seems like folly. But many times, lord, what has looked like foolishness has led to great things. To victories that appeared impossible."

"Do you seek to flatter me, Cynan?"

"I know better than that," said Cynan. "I merely speak the truth. You have won great victories when oftentimes all has seemed lost. Many deem you to be lucky, though I know you hate it."

"Almost as much as I resent being called an instrument of the Christ God," said Beobrand. "It was bad enough when Oswald said as much, but to hear Attor utter those words makes me sick to the stomach. I am neither lucky, nor holy."

"I could not speak to the truth of that," said Cynan. "But the men do not follow you because they believe you to be lucky or touched by God. They love you for your fire, and because you seek to do what is right, not that which is safe."

A gust of wind shook the trees on the riverbank, as if the night whispered a reply to Cynan's words.

"Of course," he said, smiling in the gloom in an effort to lighten the mood, "that you are a wealthy, gift-giving lord helps too."

Beobrand seemed not to have heard him.

"It is true that we have faced terrible odds before," said Beobrand, gazing off towards the lightening eastern sky. A bright star glimmered there still, high above the horizon. Cynan wondered if the gods were watching them. "But this is different," Beobrand went on. "We are far from home. We are but few, and we are surrounded by a forest of foes. To ride to Paris is surely folly."

Cynan had been thinking how best they could safely escape Frankia and he seized upon Beobrand's doubts.

"Then do not go," he said. "Let us ride from here, past Paris and head straight to the coast." As the words came, so the attraction of the thought grew within him. He spoke quickly, excited at having found the answer. "These are not our people here," he said. "We can find a ship to take us back to Albion, away from this accursed land, with its intrigues and treacherous nobles."

And back to Eadgyth, he thought.

Beobrand chuckled.

"Back to Northumbria?" he asked.

"Yes," Cynan responded eagerly.

"Where the nobles do not plot and there is no strife?" Beobrand's voice oozed with sarcasm.

"At least there we know who our enemies are."

Beobrand sighed, perhaps thinking of how they had been taken in by Annemund and Dalfinus.

"There is some truth to that," he said. "But I cannot turn my back on Balthild. I have thought much on this and I must do this thing. I must warn the queen of the plot against her, even if it means I ride to my death."

Cynan sighed. He had known as much and had not truly thought Beobrand would head back to Albion, avoiding further conflict. It was not in his nature. Cynan remembered how he had defied Beobrand and ridden into Rheged to aid Sulis. The danger had not mattered. He understood Beobrand all too well in this.

"Wherever you ride, lord," he said, "we will be at your side."

"I have thought on that also," said Beobrand, his tone strangely flat and hollow. "You are right. These are not our people, and I cannot ask you to give up your life for them. I free you from your bond to me. The rest of the men too. Ride for the coast and return to Albion."

Cynan was aghast.

"We are your oath-sworn men, lord," he said, his voice as brittle and sharp as slate. "We could no more ride away and leave you to your wyrd than you could turn your back on the queen. Do not dishonour us by imagining we would leave your side."

Beobrand did not speak for some time. At last he said, "I hear you, Cynan. I meant no harm by it. But sometimes the weight of your lives is too much to bear."

"We each gave our oath to you freely, Beobrand," said Cynan, his tone softer now. He understood Beobrand's burden. "You accepted our oaths and they cannot so easily be broken."

At the mention of broken oaths, Beobrand turned his back on Cynan and walked over to the paddock where the horses stood dozing in the dawn. Beobrand leant on the fence and spat. Cynan hesitated, sensing Beobrand's dark mood returning. After a few heartbeats, he followed him, standing beside the tall thegn and watching the shadowy shapes of the horses. One of them, a tall, strong animal with plaited mane, shook its head and snorted at the men's proximity.

"We will ride with you Beobrand," Cynan said into the quiet, "wherever you lead. Never doubt that. And do not again seek to spare me or the men from danger. We have each chosen to give you our lives, and we know you would not throw them away needlessly." He paused, turning his next words over in his mind like a man searching for just the right stone to place in a wall. "But if riding to Paris directly is madness, as you say, then perhaps we should seek another way of warning the queen."

"What do you have in mind?"

Cynan opened his mouth to reply, but before he could speak, the crunch of steps on the path alerted him to someone's approach. Turning, he could just make out Bleddyn's features in the dawning light.

"It seems that nobody is sleeping this night," Cynan said.

Bleddyn joined them at the fence, leaning his forearms on the wood and staring at the horses.

"Well, with Eadgard's snoring," he said, "and all the comings and goings, and the worries about what we are heading into, it is not surprising to me that we're finding it hard to sleep." Bleddyn hawked and spat into the be-dewed grass. "Still," he said, "it could be worse."

Beobrand turned to look incredulously at the Waelisc man.

"And just how could it be worse?" he asked, his tone hard and as bleak as winter. "Gram is dead. Wilfrid, the man I swore to protect, has betrayed us. Vulmar means to slay me. Queen Balthild, our only ally in these lands, is beset by plotting nobles who mean to kill her and her newborn babe. We aim to ride into the vipers' nest of King Clovis' court to bring tidings of the conspiracy, despite not knowing what we might face there. And yet you say things are not so bad."

Beobrand had kept his voice quiet, but Cynan could sense his anger in the stiffness of his shoulders. His hands were clenched into fists, gripping the fence railing as if to prevent him from striking Bleddyn.

Bleddyn turned to face Beobrand, and Cynan marvelled to see that he was smiling, his teeth glinting in the dawn light. To think Bleddyn had been a thrall until the year before. He had been quiet and subservient. Now he felt able to jest with the lord of Ubbanford. Cynan was proud of him, but he shook his head at the man's audacity.

"Well," Bleddyn said, "if we are to ride to Paris, then at the very least I might get to see Alpaida again."

Chapter 31

"I still think the danger is too great," said Grindan.

Beobrand sighed. He was tired of the arguing and wished to snap at Grindan for silence. But the man was ever loyal and had earned the right to question him. Besides, he merely sought to improve what was admittedly a weak plan. Grindan had been opposed to it from the beginning, constantly seeking ways to make it safer, probing for weaknesses and looking for unforeseen dangers they might face.

"We have had this conversation more times than I wish to remember," said Beobrand, leaning forward to prod the embers of the fire with a stick he had been whittling. "No matter how often we go over it, there will always be risk. The best we can do is for you to remain outside the city. Then, if things do not go well, you can take the truth with you and ride for the coast."

"It is not right that we should leave you to go to the palace alone," said Eadgard, adding his voice to his brother's protestations.

"I will not be alone," replied Beobrand, his tone betraying his frustration. Gods, they had been over this countless times in the days since they had left Liyon. He wished they were riding to war. He knew where he was in a shieldwall. The terror of it would gnaw at his innards, but the joy of it would grip him too, as it always did, and he would prevail. These intrigues in which he found himself now entangled were another kind of warfare to which he was not so adept. By Woden, what he would not give for the simplicity of a sword in his hand and an armed enemy to confront.

He tossed a small log onto the fire, watching the sparks as they rose up into the cloudless sky above the clearing. They mingled for a moment with the stars there before winking out. The sudden flaring of flame illuminated the men's faces. Grindan, his features etched in worry, shook his head. Eadgard frowned. Halinard, Bleddyn and Ingwald sat expressionless, staring into the fire. They had long since resigned themselves to the dangers to him and themselves, and were as tired as Beobrand of going over the different possibilities.

"I have made up my mind," said Beobrand. "There is no more to discuss. We ride at first light."

Not waiting for a response, he rose and walked into the darkness. Outside the pool of flickering firelight he could see the shadowed forms of Attor and Cynan where they stood on guard, backs to the flames so as not to spoil their night vision. Not wishing to speak to anyone, Beobrand walked down the slope towards the stream where they had filled their water skins at sunset. It was very dark under the elm trees. Unseen twigs and thorns snagged at his cloak, tugging him back. Angrily, he pulled his shabby, woollen cloak free and moved on, further from their camp. A leafy bough fluttered against his face and he flinched, expecting the pain that had until recently come whenever anything had touched his face. Brushing the leaves aside, he was glad to note that his skin was no longer so sensitive. He thought of the image he would present before the king. He would have to hope that the truth of his words would be heard, for he knew he did not look like a noble, not even one from the savage northern kingdom across the Narrow Sea. His eyes were less swollen now, but his face was many coloured and mottled with ageing bruises. And gone were his sumptuous jewels, his tooled leather belt with its garnet-encrusted buckle, his war helm and his splendid sword Nægling. Now his clothes were dirty, shabby and torn and the simple sword at his side rested in a plain scabbard he had taken from one of Gunthar's men.

Glancing back over his shoulder, Beobrand could just make out the fire's glow reflected against the boles and branches of the trees. He didn't think the light would be visible from the road. For the first few days after they left Dudon's settlement, they had not risked a fire, but as they rode further north and saw no sign of pursuit from Liyon, they grew bolder. They were still cautious, avoiding the road when possible and not riding into any of the settlements they passed, but with each day that went by, the closer they got to Paris, and the more they began to believe they might see this thing through.

All except Grindan, it seemed, who had taken it upon himself to challenge the sense of their course of action. Beobrand knew him for a clever man, a deep thinker, and so he had listened to him attentively. At first, at least, before his concerns became repetitive and tiresome. But there was no denying that Grindan's inquiring mind had proven useful. Beobrand's first instinct had been to ride directly to the palace in Paris, announcing himself to Erchinoald in the hope that the steward would prove faithful to his word and bear the news to the king and queen. Grindan had not been alone in his scepticism of this plan, but it had been his idea to have the group separate. He had pointed out that so many mounted men would surely be accosted by the city guards, preventing them from even reaching the palace gates. They had debated the possibility of wearing the scarlet cloaks they had taken from the guards at Dudon's hall, and posing as men sent from Liyon. This would explain their weapons and mounts and would deter too much questioning at the gates of Paris. But in the end they had rejected the idea, as only Halinard could converse in the tongue of the Franks without being unmasked as a stranger.

After the seemingly incessant discussions while they rode and as they sat around their fires at night, they had finally decided what the best course was. Beobrand and Halinard, who would act as interpreter as usual, would head to the palace alone, leaving the rest of the men outside the city with the horses. It was, of course, not without risk, but they believed that two men on foot would attract little attention on the busy thoroughfares into the city. When at the palace, Beobrand hoped that showing the ring he had been given would gain him an audience with Erchinoald. The *major domus* had seemed genuine in his affection for the queen, so hopefully he would convey Beobrand and Halinard before the king himself. Cynan had protested, saying that he would not leave Beobrand's side; that it was his duty to protect him.

"I know we spoke of this before," Beobrand had said to him a couple of nights previously, "and I know you wish to protect me from harm. But, Cynan, truly you must know that once we enter the palace there will be nothing we can do should things turn against us. I am Beobrand of Ubbanford, Thegn of Oswiu of Northumbria. This should give me some protection. But if things go badly for me, they would not hesitate to kill you. It is your duty to lead the men to safety."

"And if I refuse?" Cynan had said stubbornly.

"As you reminded me, you are yet my oath-sworn man, is that not so?"

Cynan nodded, but did not speak. Beobrand could see from the set of Cynan's jaw that he knew what was coming, and he did not like it.

"And I have your oath?" Beobrand asked.

"You know it to be so," Cynan growled, angry at being trapped by his own words.

"Then I command you not to follow me into Paris. You will

wait with the horses for one day and night and, if I have not sent word, you are to lead the men to safety."

Cynan had been sullen and quiet ever since the exchange, but Beobrand was adamant. There was no good reason to place his gesithas in undue danger.

Ever since he had seen Vulmar standing beside the cages in Liyon and understood who was behind the conspiracy against the queen, he had been filled with a burning need to inform Balthild and her husband, the king. Balthild reminded him so much of Sunniva that the thought of her being harmed filled him with a seething fury. But more than wishing to keep the queen safe from future attacks, he wanted to see Vulmar, Dalfinus and the other conspirators face justice. They had killed Gram and no doubt they had slaughtered the men inside those cages. How many of these so-called hunts had Dalfinus held? And for what? The gratification of taking another man's life? Binyamin had been no criminal to face death at their hands. His only crimes were to be poor and to be born Iudeisc.

Whenever he thought of that day in the amphitheatre, Beobrand could feel the beast of his anger deep inside him, straining against its chains. To think that Wilfrid, the very reason for them being here in Frankia, had betrayed them enraged him. Why had the young man done it? Why side with Annemund and Dalfinus over his travel companions? Beobrand shook his head in the darkness, smiling thinly at his own stupidity. What was it that drove all ambitious men? Fortune and power. There was nothing else such men cared for. The Christ followers spoke of goodness and truth, but they were no different from other men, consumed with lusts of the flesh and the desire for wealth.

Somewhere off in the cool night a bird called, its shrill whistling song rising and falling. One of the horses stamped and snorted. Another whinnied quietly. Perhaps there was a wolf or a fox nearby. Turning, Beobrand began to trudge back up the hill. He would check on the animals before returning to the fire.

Tomorrow would be a long day and the gods alone knew what it would bring. He should get some rest.

The horses were tied at the edge of the copse, where the men had camped. It was a clear night and Beobrand could soon make out the shadowed shapes of the animals. One turned its long head towards Beobrand, letting out a low nicker of welcome. Beobrand reached out his hand and stroked the horse's soft snout.

The gods had smiled on them since they had been reunited at Dudon's settlement. Apart from two days when low cloud had wreathed the land and a light drizzle had fallen, the days and nights had been dry. And they made good time, the number of horses allowing them to change mounts regularly.

Even the misfortune of one of the horses breaking its leg in a rabbit warren had proven in the end to be more a blessing than a curse. The sun had been low in the sky on the fourth day and the provisions they had taken from Dudon's hall were dwindling. When at first the chestnut stallion had tumbled over, throwing Ingwald to the earth, Beobrand had feared the worst. Ingwald was not a gifted rider and he fell awkwardly, lying still, unmoving. The horse had thrashed and screamed as it struggled upright, but its right foreleg was shattered at the fetlock and the hoof dangled uselessly. Cynan and Attor dismounted quickly, grabbing hold of the beast's reins, preventing it from further harming itself or kicking Ingwald's prostrate form.

Moments later, Ingwald had pushed himself to his knees with a groan. He'd suffered nothing more than a knock to the head. Beobrand had sighed with relief that the man was not badly injured. The loss of one of the horses they had taken from the guards was regrettable, but they still had plenty of mounts for the journey.

The horse's screams had reminded Beobrand of a time long ago when he had forced a horse into a small shieldwall. That steed had been injured beyond saving, as was the stallion that stood trembling and rolling its eyes at the men who stood around it nervously gazing at the flopping hoof. Beobrand had caught Attor's eye and a silent understanding passed between them. Attor pulled out one of his seaxes and, whispering comforting words into the animal's ear, plunged the knife deep into its throat. The horse pulled away, kicking and bucking. Attor backed away, favouring his bandaged leg, but in moments the animal had collapsed, shivering and panting as its lifeblood gushed from its neck.

Seeing that Ingwald had recovered his senses, Beobrand had ordered him to butcher the beast.

"It is the way of things," he'd said. "You caused the animal to be killed, now you must cut up its flesh to feed us."

Ingwald had opened his mouth as if to contest Beobrand's command, then thought better of it. Dropping to his knees beside the animal, he'd begun the gory work. Bleddyn had helped him and that night they ate fresh horsemeat. They carried what they could from the carcass, but neither Ingwald nor Bleddyn were skilled butchers, so much was left to the crows and beasts of the wild.

As well as the horses and provisions they had taken from the settlement, Gunthar's men had also supplied them with weapons, some byrnies, shields and several gold coins. These they'd used to buy more supplies when they had grown tired of horsemeat. Halinard had ridden down to a small farm, leading a horse behind him. He had returned with fresh eggs, flour, a round of cheese, and a string of cured sausages.

Beobrand recalled the meal they had eaten that night. They had a couple of pots and a griddle pan they had taken from Dudon's hall, and Halinard had prepared a sumptuous feast of fresh bread, poached eggs and fried slices of the spicy sausages. Afterwards, all of them had sat back replete and contented. It had then been a sennight since the fight and they felt far from danger. It was easy to forget they rode through a foreign land.

The weather was mild, and their journey took them over gentle terrain. They were never hungry, and the days were warm. At night they slept well under the stars, wrapped in their blankets, dreaming of the women they had left behind and the kin that awaited them back in Bernicia. Yes, thought Beobrand, the gods had smiled upon them.

The night bird he had heard before called again. Beobrand cocked his head, trying to place the sound. A heartbeat later, and much closer, came the ululating hoot of an owl. One of the horses snorted, scraping a hoof against the turf. Beobrand scanned the animals' shadowy shapes. Their heads were up, ears pricked. They stood rigid and nervous, peering into the darkness. There was something out there, whether a wolf, a fox, or something else, Beobrand did not know. Surely no wild beast would come so close to the fire, not with the smell of men so near. Even so, perhaps it would be a good idea to tell one of the sentries to come down to stand guard over the horses.

Beobrand turned in the direction that the horses were looking and squinted into the gloom. He could see nothing out there. The world was shrouded in the black cloak of night.

He was just about to head back to the camp when the bird call came again, high-pitched and warbling. It seemed very close. The horses were more agitated now, several of them pawing at the earth, blowing and whinnying. Whatever animal was out there, it was getting closer. The hair on Beobrand's neck prickled and he dropped his hand to the seax that hung from his belt. He wondered whether he should call out for Cynan.

Before he could make a sound, the quiet of the night was rent by a bellowing roar, followed by the shouting of many men and the unmistakable clang of metal on metal.

Chapter 32

Cursing, Beobrand tugged the seax from its scabbard. The horses had done their best to warn him that something was out there. His mistake had been to assume it had been an animal, intent on feasting on the mounts' flesh. What actually lurked in the darkness was far deadlier. And its prey was not the horses.

Sprinting up the rise, Beobrand searched the night for signs of the attackers' location, but the darkness was a chaos of echoed grunts, shouts and the clatter of steel. The sounds seemed to come from all around him and he struggled to make sense of it in the darkness. Closing in on the camp, he saw that someone had kicked the fire, scattering the embers. The dimly lit shapes of fighting men flitted across the clearing. From his vantage point, Beobrand could not make out who was friend and who was enemy. Iron gleamed red in the ember-glow. Sparks flew as a warrior stamped on a burning brand. Sword blades collided with a terrible, piercing din.

Where had these men come from? Such was the confusion in the clearing Beobrand could not easily count the attackers, but it was clear they outnumbered his gesithas. He noted in the dim illumination that none of them appeared to wear armour or any ornament that might catch the light and give them away. They were as dark as shadows and must have been as silent as wraiths as they had closed in on the camp site. Beobrand cursed himself for allowing the fires that must have guided their foes to them as clearly as a hunting horn blown in the forest.

Taking another step closer, Beobrand scanned the fighting, trying to see how he could best attack and where he could make the most impact. With the surprise of the assault and the numbers of attackers, victory for the men of Albion seemed unlikely, but if he could find the right place to strike, perhaps Beobrand could sway the outcome of the clash.

He saw that his men had not had time to form a shieldwall. Cynan fought alone, his back against the trunk of a great tree. Attor too was on his own, spinning and leaping, the injury to his leg seemingly forgotten, as he sliced and stabbed with a seax in each hand at the several men who surrounded him. Beobrand watched Eadgard, standing back-to-back with his brother, Grindan, swinging the huge axe that had belonged to Dudon. Their adversaries were wary of the weapon and seemed reluctant to approach. Beobrand saw no sign of Halinard, Bleddyn or Ingwald. He hoped they were at the far side of the clearing, rather than lying bleeding or dead in the leaves beneath the trees.

Transferring the seax to his left half-hand, Beobrand drew the sword from its scabbard, glad that he had been cautious enough not to leave the weapon in the camp when he ventured out into the night. There were four warriors around Attor, and Beobrand determined that this would be where he would strike. The older warrior was formidable, but he was not fully recovered from his wound and even he could not stand against so many and hope to remain unscathed.

Beobrand moved to his right, using the boles of the trees as cover to reach the place he had selected from which to rush to Attor's aid.

"Come and die on my blades, you shit-eating whoresons,"

screamed Attor, his seaxes parrying and slashing out to cut the forearm of one man. Another assailant darted in, thrusting his own seax at Attor's unprotected right flank. It was only Attor's experience and skill that saved him. With seemingly impossible speed, he twisted to deflect the blade away with his own. He was standing firm against terrible odds, but it was only a matter of time until one of them would get through his defence.

Beobrand lifted his sword and ran forward. He had taken no more than three steps, when he sensed movement to his right. In battle, Beobrand was even faster than Attor, and with the speed that made him legendary in Albion, he spun to face this new threat. A black-garbed figure loomed out of the darkness, and with instincts alone Beobrand parried a downward slicing sword blade.

There were more warriors than those fighting in the clearing! Beobrand grew cold at the thought of how close he had come to being slain. Had he lost his wits? But there was no time now for such concerns. Pushing aside his self-doubt, Beobrand feinted with his sword at his attacker's face. The man raised his own blade to block the strike. Beobrand sprang forward, plunging his seax into the man's stomach. He grunted, letting out a cloud of warm breath that reeked of garlic and ripe cheese. Beobrand could not see the man's face, even though they stood as close as lovers. It was a killing blow, but his opponent was not dead yet and he was lithe and strong. He attempted to pull away, to make room to swing his own sword. Beobrand could not allow that. A dying man's blade was just as deadly as that of a living warrior. Twisting the seax in his hand, Beobrand shoved forward and threw his bulk into the dying man. His foe-man's feet tangled with a root and together they fell to the earth. The fall drove the air from the man's lungs and Beobrand's seax blade sank deeper into his body. Viciously, Beobrand pulled the weapon from the sucking flesh. Dark blood bubbled and the man trembled beneath him. Without hesitation, Beobrand drove the seax back into the man's body again and again. With a shuddering sighing cough of his foetid breath, the man died.

Pushing himself to his feet, Beobrand searched the gloom for another assailant. But now all of the fighting seemed to be contained within the small glade where they had camped. Beobrand was shaken. He had assumed that all of the attackers were engaged in the fight. Such an assumption had almost cost him his life. He could not make such an error again, but with the night filled with the shouts and clash of battle, he wondered whether he would have the chance to make more mistakes.

There was barely enough light to see by now that the fire had been kicked out, but the ruddy glow of the coals strewn in the clearing enabled Beobrand to see that the fight was not going well for his men. Snatching up his weapons once more, he hurried forwards.

"Halt!" boomed a voice, sudden, loud and shocking in the gloom. The voice was unknown to Beobrand, but it held the tone of command and the men in the clearing all paused in their struggles, uncertain for a heartbeat. Beobrand too hesitated on the edge of the open space, scouring the dark shapes for an indication of what had happened and what he should do. He felt helpless at his lack of understanding of the events, and he berated himself again for allowing such a thing to happen. They had become complacent. They had thought any attack that might come would arrive in the darkest part of the night, when men were at their lowest ebb. They had never expected an attack to arrive when they had still been awake. They had chatted and told tales around the fire, foolishly believing themselves safe. These men, all dressed in dark-coloured clothes, with faces stained with soot or mud, had crept close under cover of the night. If they had approached after the men had been sleeping, the sentries might well have heard them, but as it was, any sound they had made was covered by the noise of the men they came to attack and so they had been able to ambush them unimpeded.

"Drop your weapons," said the voice into the sudden stillness, "or I will slice this one's throat like a pig at slaughter." The man spoke in Anglisc, but he was not a native of the island. His accent was thick and reminded Beobrand of Halinard. Taking a step closer, Beobrand peered into the darkness. His eyes had adjusted to the gloom now. Stepping from the absolute dark beneath the trees into the glade where the faint pool of light from the stars and moon added to the scant glow from the scattered embers, Beobrand was able to discern that the speaker held a knife at Cynan's throat. They were a few steps from the tree that Cynan had been using to shield his back while he fought. A corpse lay sprawled before the Waelisc warrior. Beobrand imagined that Cynan, having dispatched his enemy, had been moving to aid Attor when the man who now held him had slipped out from his hiding place in the trees to take him unawares.

How many more men lurked in the darkness?

"Don't listen to him, lord," Cynan said, showing no fear. "Kill them all!"

For the briefest of moments Beobrand contemplated doing what Cynan said, ignoring the man who held the knife and commanding his gesithas to continue fighting. The thought had barely formed in his mind before he dismissed it. He still could not see Halinard, Bleddyn or Ingwald. For all he knew they were already slain. And yet, even if they were still alive and able to fight, the number of enemies was still too great. They could not hope to triumph. And Cynan would surely be killed the instant Beobrand called out to his warriors. Beobrand would not sacrifice Cynan's life for nothing.

"Who are you?" he asked, stepping into the clearing.

"Ah, the great Beobrand," said the man, his face in shadow. "You have proven to be as lucky as they say. You have avoided my blade many times, but I think this time fortune has finally abandoned you."

Beobrand's mouth was filled with the bitter taste of defeat.

This was not bad luck, it was his own foolishness. And still he had no idea who this enemy was.

"We have fought before?" Beobrand asked, praying silently to Woden that he might see some way to extricate them from this predicament.

"More than once, I should have seen you die," said the mysterious man, "but perhaps you do not remember. You should have died in Eoferwic many years ago, and yet you escaped, with the help of another."

Beobrand reeled as the man's meaning became clear.

"You are Vulmar's man? You tried to murder me by the church."

"I am no-one's man," the shadowy stranger replied, his sneer twisting his voice. "But it is true that Vulmar often pays the most gold. And yet that is not the only time our paths have crossed."

Beobrand remembered the fight by the church in Eoferwic. He had been lured to a meeting after dark, then attacked by five men. Only one had escaped. Beobrand would have been killed, if not for Wulfstan's intervention.

"When else have we fought?" Beobrand asked, barely able to believe this was the same man who had run from that night-time ambush with a cut to his arm.

"I watched you fight with your back to your king's in the forest of Deira."

Beobrand recalled the assassination attempt that had resulted in Fordraed's death. Oswiu had been convinced that it was Oswine who had sent the men to kill him, but Beobrand had known otherwise. There were many similarities in that attack with this one. Those men too had blackened their faces with soot and had approached in the dark.

"We killed all of the men who attacked the king," Beobrand said, shaking his head. "There were no survivors."

The man shrugged. As he did so, Cynan tensed. Perhaps he thought to pull away from the man, or to push back and upset his footing. Whatever he had imagined would happen, the man was prepared, and tightening his grip on Cynan he pressed the knife more firmly into his neck, splitting the skin there. Blood welled and began to trickle from the cut. It looked black in the gloom. Cynan's breath hissed.

"Do that again," said the man, "and I will slay you. I would prefer to take you alive. There are others who wish to see you again. But I will not hesitate to cut your throat if you push me." Cynan grew still. The man's dark eyes focused once more on Beobrand. "That attack in Deira was a mistake on my part. I believed five would suffice in the circumstances. I underestimated you and your king. Oswiu fought well. This time, I come with enough men."

The man certainly liked to hear himself speak, thought Beobrand. He looked around the clearing, vainly searching for anything he could use to his advantage.

"But it was after you crossed me in the forests south of Quentovic," said the man, "that I swore I would slay you."

Suddenly Beobrand knew who this man must be.

"Agobard," he hissed, remembering the name of the man he had seen in the amphitheatre in Liyon.

"Ah," said Agobard, "it is strange to hear my name on your lips. I have for so long known yours, and wanted nothing more than to kill you. But now, sadly, I have been paid to bring you alive, so that others might have that pleasure. Now, drop your weapons and command your men to do the same."

"Kill him, lord," Cynan said, his words clipped and sharp. "Kill them all. The moment you drop your sword he will slay me anyway."

Agobard stared at Beobrand unmoving. His face was in complete shadow, only his unblinking eyes were visible from the red gleam of the embers reflected there. What Cynan said was almost certainly true and Beobrand's stomach churned to think of losing the man who had been at his side for so long. But he could see no way out of this. If he could buy them more time, perhaps a way of escape might present itself. If they fought on now, they would all be killed.

"Know this," said Beobrand, his voice brittle and hard as flint, "if you harm any of my men, I will kill you."

Agobard laughed.

"Given a chance, you would kill me whether I hurt your men or not. But whether you believe me or not, I give you my word that none of your men will face further harm from me or my men tonight, if you surrender now."

Beobrand did not trust him, but he could see no alternative to surrender, or seeing his men cut down. By the gods, how he wished he had never left Albion.

"Put down your weapons, my brave gesithas," he said, his mouth sour and dry.

With a sigh, Beobrand dropped the blood-smeared seax and his sword to the earth.

Chapter 33

The dog was small, not much larger than the rats it was bred to hunt. But despite its size, the wire-haired terrier was noisy as it barked and snapped at Cynan's horse's hocks. The stallion shied away from the snarling hound, sidestepping and attempting to wheel about so that it could kick out at the annoying canine. Cynan cursed, clamping his thighs tightly to the horse's flanks to avoid being thrown. His hands, like those of all the other Black Shields, were tied behind his back. Being a skilled horseman, despite not being able to grasp the reins, Cynan was able to keep his seat and, after a few tense moments, bring the stallion under control. But not before it had careened into Ingwald's mare.

They were riding past a large crumbling house that was being repaired. The owner of the dog, a grizzled-looking man who had been busy planing a beam for the construction, ran after his animal, adding his own shouts to those of Agobard's men.

Ingwald cried out as his mare reared up. The animal was usually docile and calm, which was the main reason Cynan had chosen it for the older gesith after his fall from the stallion a few days earlier, but now it snapped its teeth at Cynan's horse and kicked out at the yapping dog.

The dog continued barking. Its owner, whose beard and hair

was the same shade as the animal's, making them look strangely like kin, stood back and yelled ineffectually, clearly scared of the horse's flailing hooves.

Ingwald remained in the saddle for longer than Cynan had expected, but he soon tumbled from the animal's back. He landed heavily and lay unmoving. Cynan gritted his teeth, grimacing at the sight and the sound of the impact that had been loud enough to hear over the tumult of angry shouts, barks and stamping horses. By the gods, Ingwald was no rider! The road, while covered in mud and ordure, was made up of slabs of stone and smaller cobbles. A bad fall could see a man break bones, or crack his skull.

A couple of Agobard's men, faces still streaked with soot from their night-time assault, slipped from their saddles. The carpenter had managed to loop a string over the dog's neck, but the animal still strained and barked. The man was swearing now, shouting and spitting at the riders, somehow enraged by what had happened, or seeking to justify his dog's actions with his own barking bluster. Agobard's men stepped close, showing the man the swords they wore. The fight instantly left him and he pulled his dog away, tethering it beside the house he was working on.

Ingwald's mare was terrified. It had tried to run from the column of riders, but, like all the other horses, her harness was tied with a lead rope to the saddle of one of Agobard's men.

Agobard shouted something Cynan could not understand, but the tone was clear enough. Ingwald groaned and pushed himself up from the manure-strewn cobbles. Agobard's men hurried to get him back onto his horse. Relief washed through Cynan. There was a welt on Ingwald's forehead and his eyes had a dazed appearance, but he seemed hale enough as the two warriors hoisted him into his saddle. Without delay, they were riding on, leaving the carpenter and his barking dog behind.

"Glad you did not break your head," Cynan said. "When we get out of this, I must teach you how to ride. A man of your age should at least know the first rule of riding. If you do not master it soon, I fear the worst for you."

"What is the first rule?"

"To stay in the saddle," Cynan offered him a sidelong smile. "If you keep falling like you do, the earth might win the fight one of these days."

"It will take more than a barking dog and a cobblestone to send me to the afterlife," Ingwald said. He grinned, but Cynan could see he was in pain.

"Perhaps a couple of dozen warriors, who attack you in the night, you mean?"

Ingwald winced at the reminder of their grim situation.

"I'm not dead yet," he said, grunting as he shifted his position in the saddle. "Never mind my head. How's yours?"

"Well enough," lied Cynan.

The moment Beobrand had dropped his weapons and given the command for the others to do likewise, Agobard had removed the blade from Cynan's throat. Cynan had fully expected Vulmar's man to cut into the thick artery in his neck. He was determined not to give in, no matter what Beobrand had said, and yet, before he could move to defend himself, Agobard had struck him hard with the hilt of his seax across the back of the head. Such was the force of the blow that Cynan had collapsed, blacking out.

When he came to his senses, Beobrand and the others had already been bound. His own hands had been tied while he was insensate, so he could not reach up to touch his head and feel the extent of the damage. He did not need to. He knew it was bad enough. The hair at the nape of his neck was wet and sticky with his blood and his head throbbed without cease. If he moved suddenly, his vision blurred and he grew dizzy. Shortly after he had first mounted and they'd ridden down the hill to the road to Paris, waves of nausea had washed over him and he had vomited, barely avoiding falling from the saddle. He had felt somewhat better since then, but the bright sunlight lanced into his eyes, and with each jolt of the stallion's gait, Cynan's head felt as though it might shatter.

Ahead of them, across the Secoana, the sky was hazed with the fug of hundreds of cooking fires. The wind was in their face and the stink of the city filled his nostrils. It did nothing to help him prevent his stomach from roiling. Ingwald gave him a sidelong glance as they rode on through the streets of Paris.

"You are sure you are well?"

In spite of the ache in his head, Cynan smiled.

"I'm not sure I'd say I am well, but it will take more than a bastard's seax pommel to kill me."

Ingwald returned his smile, but Cynan could tell that the bald man was unconvinced. Both of them knew his head hurt more than he was letting on. They also knew that they were heading to almost certain death. There was nothing any of them could do about his head or anything else, so Cynan saw no reason to further burden Ingwald with worries.

"As long as there are no more barking dogs or seax pommels, we should be fine."

Looking to the head of the column of riders, Cynan watched Beobrand. He sat rigid and straight-backed in the saddle. Even though he could only see the back of Beobrand's head, Cynan could well imagine his lord's furious expression. Agobard was speaking to him incessantly, seemingly pleased to converse with the man he had sought to kill on so many occasions. Cynan wondered what drove the man. Whatever it was, he was clearly overjoyed at having finally captured the famed lord of Ubbanford, and he revelled in having a captive audience for his gleeful boasting.

Beobrand had not spoken to Cynan since their capture. When they had been led to the horses at dawn, and each of the men had been lifted onto his beast's back, Beobrand had shaken his head at Cynan. The thegn's face was haggard, the paling bruises not hiding his dismay.

"I am sorry, lord," Cynan had said.

The first rays of the morning sun lit the land in a fogged, golden haze. It was going to be a beautiful day, but Cynan felt nothing but abject sorrow and the stabbing pain in his skull.

"It is not your fault, Cynan," Beobrand had replied.

Despite Beobrand's words, Cynan felt the full responsibility for what had happened. He had counselled Beobrand against riding to Paris, saying it was too dangerous, but once he had agreed to follow his hlaford there, it was his oath-sworn duty to protect him.

And he had failed.

Cynan had been on guard duty when the attack came. The fact that none of them had expected it, or detected the attackers' approach, was no consolation to him.

They were now being led to the king's palace, where surely they would be killed. He could see no other reason that Agobard would take them there. And it had been Cynan who had permitted Agobard and his men to close on the camp unhindered. Then, after he had allowed himself to be captured by Agobard, Beobrand had felt forced to surrender.

No matter what Beobrand said, they both knew the truth. If they were to die in Paris, Cynan would be to blame.

They reached the river without incident. Children, barefoot and grubby, ran behind the large group of riders. Men and women paused in their daily labours and stared as they passed. As they rode across the bridge, Cynan looked down at the dark waters of the Secoana. A barge laden with bulging sacks was being rowed beneath the bridge and for a fleeting moment, he imagined leaping from the horse into the vessel and escaping aboard the boat, as they had in Liyon. But the barge was far below where the road was carried over the water. If the fall did not kill or cripple him, the slow-moving vessel would be easily detained. He toyed with the idea of flinging himself into the river's waters, but with his hands tied, he would surely drown. He would rather find what fate awaited him in the palace than to take his own life in the cold darkness beneath the surface of the Secoana.

They halted at the gates of the palace. Agobard called out to the guards, who peered from the walls. Cynan, head pounding, stared up with more defiance than he felt into the faces of the Franks who stared down at them. The door wards did not keep them waiting long, and in moments the gates were heaved open. Agobard trotted his horse beneath the arch and into the courtyard. The rest of the riders followed. At the tug on his lead rope, Cynan's stallion fell into step.

Cynan craned his neck painfully to look behind him to where Bleddyn rode. He nodded at Cynan, but his humour was gone now. Cynan felt another pang of guilt at having brought the man with him to Frankia. He was loyal and steadfast yet, whilst brave enough, he could barely be called a warrior. Cynan nodded to Bleddyn reassuringly, feeling regret at his own thoughts. It was not the man's fault that he'd not had more time to train with shield and blade. What did any of that matter now? Whatever each man's skill in battle, they were unlikely to receive an honourable death.

The gate closed behind them and a great oaken bar was dropped into place, securing the palace from intruders. The sound was as heavy and final as death. Cynan wondered if they would ever leave this place again.

All around the courtyard were blue-cloaked royal guards. They observed the new arrivals with interest, their faces grim and unwelcoming, as if bad tidings had preceded them. Cynan searched their ranks for a familiar face, but he recognised none of the men. Evidently, Brocard and his warband were not in the palace, or at least not part of the welcome guard.

Agobard swung down from his mount with ease. At a curt command, his men dismounted and began to help the men from Albion to do likewise. A flash of scarlet caught Cynan's attention and he turned to see several men hurrying down the steps from the royal hall. His stomach tightened and a sudden sharp pain pierced his head. These were men he knew all too well, but the sight of them brought him no joy.

They each wore the red cloaks of the guards of Liyon. They were led by the fair-haired Thagmar.

"Agobard!" the captain of the guard shouted, grinning. He said more, but Cynan could not follow the words. Agobard indicated his captives with a sweeping gesture and both men laughed. Beobrand had already been dragged from his horse and he stood now before Thagmar, his shoulders set, his chin jutting forward. He towered over Thagmar and Agobard. His hands were still tied behind his back, but the men approached him warily, such was the aura of danger about him. Beobrand's hands were bunched into fists. The muscles of his arms bulged and the cords of his neck stood out as if he were straining to snap his bonds. Beobrand's whole body was tensed and ready for action, but he did not move, instead motionlessly menacing the men with his formidable presence. Cynan could not see Beobrand's eyes from where he sat astride his stallion, but he could imagine the cold fire in his lord's blue glare.

Without warning, hands grabbed Cynan roughly, pulling him from the saddle and dumping him unceremoniously on the hard ground. Gasping at the stabbing pain in his head, Cynan's vision darkened and clouded. For a moment, the noises of men and horses were as if heard from afar, distant and echoing. He staggered and almost fell. Halinard, already dismounted, moved quickly to his side, preventing him from toppling over. A heartbeat later, Ingwald was at his other side, his features a mask of anxiety.

"I am well," said Cynan, knowing he neither looked nor

sounded well. After a time his sight cleared and sounds returned to normal. He could hear Thagmar's strident tone as he addressed Beobrand.

Cynan did not comprehend the words, and was about to ask Halinard to interpret when Agobard spoke in Anglisc, his voice carrying easily to all of the gathered men.

"Thagmar says it looks as though you have allowed your men to practice for the arena using your face as a target."

Beobrand chuckled, the sound of his mirth out of place surrounded as he was by enemies.

"Tell him this was the best that Gunthar could do," he said. "But the brute looks a lot worse than I do, of that he can be certain."

Agobard translated Beobrand's words with some relish it seemed to Cynan. Thagmar's face grew pale.

"Tell him," Beobrand went on, "that what Eadgard had started with his fists in the arena, he finished with a blade. It is an easy mistake to choose the wrong weapon in a fight, but not a mistake Gunthar will make again."

Cynan grinned at Beobrand's bravado. Eadgard and Attor laughed out loud. Cynan marvelled at how, even though defeated and possibly close to death, Beobrand was able to lift his gesithas' spirits.

Thagmar stepped in close to Beobrand, whispering something much too quietly for any save Agobard and Beobrand to hear.

Cynan wondered what would happen to them all now they had reached the palace. He surveyed the faces of the crimson-cloaked warriors flanking Thagmar. They must have ridden directly from Liyon to Paris without delay to have arrived before them, he thought. What fate awaited them now might depend on who had ridden with them. Had Thagmar travelled with his men alone, or was Dalfinus here in the court of the king of Frankia? Cynan recognised most of the men who stood with Thagmar. A couple of them looked his way, scowling at him.

They had not offered him any kind of friendship while in Liyon, so he was not surprised.

Then he recognised Hincmar's weathered face. After the fight at the Iudeisc farm, Hincmar had avoided him, which had saddened Cynan. For a heartbeat, their eyes met, before Hincmar looked away, unable to hold the Waelisc man's gaze.

In that look Cynan saw many things. Perhaps a flash of the man's guilt at what he had done in the name of his lord. Maybe a sadness at the loss of a friendship that might have been. But above all, the sombre knowledge that he was staring at a man who would soon be dead.

As this dark realisation came to Cynan, so the tall figure of Erchinoald strode out of the hall. He descended the steps with rapid grace, hurrying to where Beobrand stood with Agobard and Thagmar. The *major domus* took in the scene quickly. There was a sombreness about him as he looked at Beobrand. He said something in a low voice, shaking his head. Beobrand replied, but his voice was too quiet to be heard now.

Erchinoald inclined his head, then, with a click of his fingers, he turned and made his way back up the steps into the palace. Thagmar pushed Beobrand to follow him. Agobard and the red-cloaked guards from Liyon fell into step behind them.

In moments they had disappeared into the hall, leaving Cynan and the rest of the Black Shields of Bernicia, standing, bound and defenceless, to await their wyrd.

Chapter 34

Beobrand strode into the hall, his head held high. His shoulders were straight and he defiantly met the eyes of each of the people who stared at him as he followed Erchinoald into the cavernous room.

Despite the bright sunshine outside, it was gloomy in the palace. Shafts of light from narrow windows speared the haze. Dozens of beeswax candles flickered, making the sumptuous decorations glitter and gleam. The silks worn by the nobles who appeared to be awaiting Beobrand's arrival shimmered, and the gold and jewels that adorned their bodies glimmered. There had been a buzz of conversation behind the doors, but everyone fell silent as the two immaculately dressed wardens pulled them open. The people in the hall had surely received warning that the northern thegn had been captured and would be brought before the king, for the hall was crowded and men and women peered with interest to see the huge warrior from Albion. Beobrand's eyes narrowed as he wondered what lies they might have been told about him.

Erchinoald paused in the doorway.

Agobard began to speak, but the *major domus* hissed something, making a cutting gesture with his slender, clean hand.

Agobard, face still besmirched with soot and clothes dusty from travel, swallowed and fell silent. He glared at Erchinoald, but the noble did not avert his gaze and a heartbeat later, Agobard looked away. He had talked and boasted of his victory without pause all that long morning, but this battle of wills was one he could not hope to win. The meaning was clear. Erchinoald did not appear happy with this turn of events and was no doubt unable to ignore orders that must have come from the king himself. And yet here, inside the walls of the palace, Erchinoald was Agobard's superior and would be obeyed.

Erchinoald turned to Beobrand.

"Ready?" he asked, with what seemed an almost apologetic tone.

Beobrand knew not what he was supposed to be prepared for, but he was sure it would be nothing good. The thin *major domus* of the palace had the air about him of one who had been forced to do something he did not agree with. Beobrand wondered at the powers at play here, and what the *major domus* would do if he said he was not ready. Beobrand smiled without humour, but nodded.

Erchinoald turned and began to walk solemnly towards the dais at the far end of the hall. Beobrand forced his face to remain emotionless and followed. Agobard and Thagmar were close behind him, but he purposely ignored them. The leather thong that bound his wrists chafed. In the darkness that morning, before they had mounted and ridden to Paris, Beobrand had strained at the cords, hoping to snap them, but all he had managed to do was to dig them painfully into his skin. He had ridden with as much dignity as he could summon, listening to Agobard's bragging and wishing for nothing more than to be able to reach out and strangle the man. But the men were watching, and to see their lord scream abuse and insults would have done little to bolster their morale. Instead he had spoken sparingly, vowing not to give Agobard the pleasure of seeing him react to his taunting. He had remained silent as the man had told of carrying the tidings of Beobrand's whereabouts to Rodomo. Agobard had sniggered as he recounted how Vulmar had sent word to Dalfinus to keep Beobrand in Liyon, so that the fat lord might have the pleasure of killing the Bernician thegn. All the while, Beobrand had held his tongue, but when he had seen Thagmar, he had not been able to resist the comments about Gunthar. To hear some of his gesithas laugh in the face of such adversity had lightened his own dark humour, but the truth was, no matter the face he put on, he could see no way out of this for any of them.

All that morning he had tried to devise a way they might escape, but nothing had presented itself. They were outnumbered, and their bonds were tight and strong. Without being able to free themselves, there was nothing they could do.

He had ridden on through the morning, silently berating himself and riddled with guilt, but not allowing any of those feelings to show. He should not have led them to Paris. It had been folly all along. Cynan had told him to head straight for the coast and now he knew his Waelisc friend had been right. Was it pride that had made him head for Paris? He had told himself it was his sense of duty to Balthild, but perhaps it had more to do with his own desire to see Vulmar and Dalfinus fall. Had he truly believed he would be able to best such powerful men in their own land? Not only had he grown soft in Liyon, he had become complacent and arrogant. His arrogance, he feared, would destroy them all, and the weight of his shame sat heavily on him as he walked the length of the hall under the inquisitive eyes of the gathered Frankish nobility.

Still, he would show no weakness to any of them. If he were to die, he would do so with defiance, as his gesithas expected of him. He glowered at the faces he passed. Most of the men sneered with disapproval. Some of the women, too, looked on with disdain. Others held different emotions behind their lashes.

Their eyes glistened and there was a hunger there as they took in his tall, muscled frame, bruised face and tousled blond hair.

Looking beyond the dozens of faces that stared at him with ire, lust or disgust at his travel-worn appearance and battered face, Beobrand's jaw tightened. It would be a struggle to remain calm, for there, on the dais, stood Vulmar and Dalfinus. A woman was seated near them, and for a moment Beobrand thought it might be Balthild and his mood lifted. His hopes for an ally were shattered when he saw it was not the queen, but Erchinoald's diminutive wife, Leutsinde. She glowered at Beobrand with undisguised loathing and he wondered again at what she might have been told about him. What would prompt such hatred?

On the raised platform was an ornately carved throne. It was surrounded by a multitude of candles that made the young man seated there glow like a god. The gleaming figure was very young, probably a few years younger even than Octa, but, like Beobrand's son, he was handsome, with clear skin. His gleaming hair was swept back from his face, and held in place by a golden circlet that crowned his head. His hair was extraordinarily long and cascaded over his shoulders like a maiden's locks. Despite being seated, Beobrand could see that the young man was slim, yet strong. His shoulders were wide, his well-muscled legs stretched out languidly. He had intelligent eyes, but there was a certain softness about his mouth that gave him a hint of childish petulance. Again, something he had in common with Octa, who frequently acted without sufficient forethought. This must be Clovis, king of the Franks. Beobrand met the king's cold stare and understood something else. Like his son, this young man was full of self-belief and was frightened of nothing. They were both dangerous men. But Clovis held the power over life and death in his kingdom.

Beobrand felt the bony finger of fear scratch down his spine. A single word from this man would see them all killed. And

Beobrand's enemies, the lords of Rodomo and Liyon, stood beside his throne.

Vulmar, jowls quivering, turned and whispered something to Clovis. The young king's eyes narrowed, but he held Beobrand's gaze, never once wavering.

Beobrand lowered his eyes. It would do neither him nor his gesithas any good for him to antagonise the king. It had taken him many long years to learn as much.

He frowned.

Queen Balthild was nowhere to be seen. Nor could he spy Wilfrid anywhere. Could the novice have remained in Liyon? Annemund did not appear to be in the hall, so it was possible. If he managed to escape this situation with his life, Beobrand vowed he would seek out the young novice and make him pay for his part in this betrayal.

Erchinoald gestured for Beobrand, Agobard and Thagmar to halt, while he stepped up onto the dais. The air was redolent of burning beeswax and freshly cut rushes. He was determined to show them no weakness, but the attention of so many made him uncomfortable. He heard whispers that he could not understand. He had stood before kings many times in his life, confronted men who had sought his death and destruction. But he had never felt as vulnerable as he did in that moment with his hands tied, and even his ability to defend himself with words curtailed by his poor grasp of the Frankish tongue.

Erchinoald introduced Beobrand, his voice strong in declamation. First he addressed the king. Beobrand watched the young man's face closely. Clovis stared at him all the while without changing expression. Here was a man who had learnt to veil his feelings. The king appeared calm, but there was a hard cruelty about his eyes that unnerved Beobrand.

Erchinoald spoke at length, but Beobrand was unable to keep up with his words and understood but little more than his name when it was mentioned. When the *major domus* had finished,

Clovis spoke. His voice was deep and sonorous, almost musical. Beobrand could imagine him being trained to speak before his subjects, coached in how to hold their attention and command an audience in the way that warriors were trained in the use of spear and shield. As he spoke, the king looked away from Beobrand for the first time. He directed his speech at the men and women who thronged the hall and their silence was absolute as they listened.

When Clovis finished speaking, for a time nobody uttered a sound. Erchinoald was the first to break the spell. He snapped a command at Agobard.

The assassin glowered at him, then, clearing his throat, he said in Anglisc: "King Clovis, second of his name, Lord of Neustria and Burgundia, king of all the Franks, wishes to know why you, Beobrand of Bernicia, journeyed all the way from Albion to murder his subjects, his queen and the fruit of his loins, prince Clothar, the heir to the throne."

Beobrand shook his head in disbelief. He had known there would have been lies about him whispered into the king's ear, but he had not expected to be accused of the attack against the queen. That was so far from the truth as to be laughable. Of course, the men who plotted against Clovis and Balthild needed to discredit Beobrand completely, if they were to avoid him casting doubt on their allegiances and loyalty. He wondered why they had not had Agobard kill him when he'd had the chance. Perhaps they were so vain that they believed they could control events completely. Staring at the king's handsome, yet inscrutable features, he thought it more likely that Clovis had ordered to see this man from Albion whom they accused of such heinous crimes.

Beobrand swallowed. His throat was dry. He cast a glance over the dais, but there were no allies there. Erchinoald seemed sympathetic to his plight, but did not seem inclined to speak up in his favour. Vulmar's lip curled in a sneer. The fat lord was barely able to disguise his glee at the trap that had been laid for Beobrand. Dalfinus' expression was harder to read. The grey-haired *comes* of Liyon watched Beobrand from beneath shadowed brows.

"Answer the king," whispered Erchinoald.

Beobrand frowned. He knew enough Frankish to understand the order, but he still held back, weighing up the different options open to him. This was the first time King Clovis had laid eyes on him, and here were powerful men, oath-sworn vassals and nobility condemning him, a stranger to these lands. What could he say that would sway the king's opinion of him? The silence had drawn on too long for comfort now. Someone in the audience coughed. Erchinoald was anxiously gesturing for Beobrand to speak. There was nothing for it but to tell the truth and trust in his wyrd. Or at least that the king would hear the sincerity in his words.

"Lord king," he said, bowing and forcing his tone to remain calm, "I stand before you accused of crimes I did not commit. I am a thegn of Bernicia, sworn man of Oswiu, King of all of Northumbria. I have been tasked by my queen, Eanflæd, to escort Christ's servants, Wilfrid and Baducing, on a holy pilgrimage to the sacred city of Roma. We were merely travelling through your lands when we witnessed the attack on your queen. We were not part of that attack. We came to her defence."

The king held up his hand for Beobrand to stop talking. He nodded to Agobard, who said a few words in Frankish. He spoke very quickly, but it was plain that he had not relayed all of what Beobrand had said.

Anger began to writhe within him at the injustice of this. The very man he must rely on to translate his words was a killer who had attempted to take his life and was in the employ of the very conspirators who wished to see the queen killed. His muscles bunched as, unthinking, he pulled at his constraints. The leather cords cut deeper into his wrists, the pain bringing him to his senses. He must not lose his temper. When a man screams in anger, it becomes nigh impossible to listen to the meaning behind his words.

"Those men," said Beobrand, his voice taking on a hard edge as he nodded at Vulmar and Dalfinus, "are responsible for the attack on the queen."

Agobard said nothing.

"This man, Agobard, led the attackers," said Beobrand, his voice raising as his hold on his anger began to slip. He tried to calm himself, but despite having learnt many hard lessons since his youth, his ire was still not easily tamed. With each furious word he growled, he sensed his chances of convincing the king of his innocence draining away like wine from a cracked pot.

Agobard remained silent. The king's face was passive, almost disinterested in its lack of expression. Despite knowing the foolishness of it, Beobrand allowed his rage to burst free.

"Ask Agobard how he got that scar on his forehead," he shouted. He wanted to indicate what he was referring to, but of course, his hands were held tightly behind his back.

Still Agobard was silent, so Beobrand tried to convey his message in broken Frankish.

"These men, Vulmar, Dalfinus and Agobard, want kill queen."

A crashing blow to the side of his head sent him reeling. Staggering, he lost his balance, then tumbled over. His fast reflexes allowed him to twist his body so that his shoulder collided painfully with the flagstone floor, rather than his face. Cursing, he looked up to see Thagmar standing over him. Beobrand had been staring at the king, so had been taken completely unawares by Thagmar's vicious punch.

The gathered nobles gasped. Vulmar was speaking quickly to Clovis, no doubt refuting Beobrand's words. Beobrand noticed that Leutsinde had risen and was adding her own voice to that of the conspirator who petitioned the king. Dalfinus watched on in stony silence.

With his hands bound behind his back, Beobrand struggled to rise. Thagmar, face dark, stepped close. Beobrand tensed, readying himself for the inevitable kick in the face. Agobard seemed frozen by what had happened. This was a very different battlefield than he was used to. He was a man who thrived in the shadows, not lit by the flames of hundreds of candles for royalty and nobles to scrutinise.

Before Thagmar could strike Beobrand again, Erchinoald stepped from the dais, halting him with a curt word of command. Reaching down, the *major domus* helped Beobrand to his feet. The hall was still in chaos as so many voices vied to be heard. Beobrand's ears were ringing. Turning slowly, he faced Thagmar.

"You snivelling whoreson," he whispered, his voice barely audible.

"What is that?" asked the captain of the guard of Liyon.

"You pig-swiving nithing," Beobrand muttered.

Thagmar's eyes narrowed. He sensed he was being insulted, but could not hear Beobrand's words. He took a step closer. Anticipating the move, Beobrand sprang forward at the same moment, snapping his forehead into Thagmar's face. His height and speed ensured he made contact, but Thagmar was also fast and he was no fool. He swayed back, so that what might have been a devastating blow, lost much of its force. Still, Beobrand's forehead crashed into his nose with a satisfying crunch and as Thagmar staggered back, blood began to flow from his nostrils. He was about to surge forward when Dalfinus bellowed in a voice that cut through the din.

"Silence!"

The voices stilled and quiet descended on the hall, rippling out from the dais until everyone was again hushed and watching the king and the man from Albion. People were shocked by the sudden violence. Thagmar glowered at Beobrand. Touching a hand to his face, he looked at his blood-slick fingers.

He growled a command and two warriors hurried forward, grabbing Beobrand roughly by the arms.

"I will kill you," Thagmar hissed. His words were clear in the new stillness and Beobrand understood their meaning well enough. Fury raged within him and he wanted to shout his defiance at Thagmar, to tell him he would fight him to the death right there. And yet much of his rage was directed at himself. By releasing his hold on his anger, he might have doomed them all. His men were relying on him and he was a fool to react so. Clenching his fists firmly behind him, Beobrand turned back to the king. Clovis still watched the proceedings from his throne. His expression had not changed, though Beobrand thought perhaps he detected a flush of colour in his cheeks that had not been there earlier.

"King Clovis," Beobrand said in Frankish, "I can speak your tongue bad. Please, call my man, Halinard. He speak for me." He searched for the words he needed to convey his message. "Agobard not speak my words. You hear my words." If he could talk to the king, he could explain everything.

For a long while, Clovis held Beobrand's glowering stare, unspeaking. Beside Beobrand, Thagmar sniffed and wiped at his face, smearing blood on his hand and cheek. Vulmar sidled close to the throne and whispered.

At last, Clovis stood, taking a step towards Beobrand.

"Repeat my words exactly so that Beobrand of Bernicia can understand them," he said to Agobard. Agobard nodded and proceeded to interpret for the king. As far as Beobrand could comprehend, he did so faithfully, and the more he spoke, the more lost Beobrand felt.

"It is clear to any who looks upon you that you are a dangerous man," said the king through Agobard. "Lords Dalfinus and Vulmar have told me of your violence, and now I have seen it here, in my hall. And you wish to bring one of your men here so that you might speak more freely?"

Beobrand nodded.

"Your request is denied." Agobard translated the words impassively, but Beobrand thought he detected a hint of his earlier bragging in his tone.

"But, lord king," said Beobrand, "I do not trust this man to speak my words. He is my enemy. He was one of the men who sought to kill your queen and unborn child, ordered by Vulmar, Dalfinus and others who plot against you." Again Beobrand sensed his temper unravelling, his voice rising in pitch. With difficulty, he restrained himself.

Agobard hesitated, but after a nod from Dalfinus, he spoke. To Beobrand's surprise, from what he understood, the man recounted his words accurately.

Clovis listened patiently. When he spoke, Beobrand understood why Dalfinus seemed unafraid.

"Vulmar and Dalfinus told me you would say these things. That you would sully their names with your evil."

"They lie," shouted Beobrand, unable to control his ire. But even as his words echoed from the high ceiling of the hall, he knew that his protests would avail him nothing.

"You accuse nobles of my realm of lying," Clovis said, "but why should I trust you?" Beobrand wanted to reply, but Agobard continued to speak the king's words. "I know these men. They have been faithful and they pay tribute to me. All I know of you is that you are a heathen who attacks my people."

"No, it is not so."

Dalfinus whispered something into the king's ear. Clovis nodded.

"Is it not true that you attacked and killed several of Lord Dalfinus' men in Liyon?"

"They were going to kill me!" Beobrand yelled. He thought of Gram standing in the tunnel as he fled with Halinard. "One of my men was slain."

When Clovis heard Agobard's translation, he showed emotion for the first time.

"You cannot deny it, can you?" he cried. He slammed his right fist into his left palm. The sound was as loud as a slap. "Can you?"

Beobrand sighed. With sword and shield, his fury served him well, but if there had ever been a chance of winning here, it was his anger that had defeated him.

"I fought to save my men," he said, his tone desolate with the realisation he had failed.

Clovis shook his head. Vulmar smiled. Dalfinus glowered.

"The men of Burgundia are Franks," said the king. "I am their ruler. You killed my subjects."

Beobrand had lost this battle of words, so he decided to steer the fight back to the safer ground and the more important matter of the attack on the queen. His motives there could not be questioned.

"But I did not harm Queen Balthild," he said. "I protected her." He fixed Clovis with his ice blue stare, forcing himself to speak evenly. "I protected her and your child."

Clovis seemed to ignore his words and Beobrand wondered if Agobard had interpreted his meaning. Instead, the king turned the conversation to earlier events.

"Vulmar tells me you attacked and killed some of his men in Rodomo. Is this true?"

Beobrand would not deny this.

"That whoreson had my daughter."

Agobard translated and Clovis turned to Vulmar with a raised eyebrow. Vulmar spoke softly, holding out his hands and shrugging.

"The girl was his thrall. Bought with good Frankish gold."

"Like Balthild?" replied Beobrand in Frankish.

There was a sharp intake of breath from someone in the throng. Erchinoald stiffened.

Clovis' smooth brow wrinkled in a frown.

"It is true that Balthild was a thrall," he said, "but now she is my queen and you are keeping me from her when we have been apart all these months."

Understanding suddenly dawned on Beobrand.

"You have not seen her? Have you spoken with your wife since she was attacked?"

Erchinoald hissed something and Agobard translated.

"It is not your place to question the king." He paused, but after a command from Erchinoald, he went on. "King Clovis has just returned from meeting allies and inspecting estates in the south, following his glorious victory over the rebels on the marches of Septimania."

"Lord king," said Beobrand, raising his voice to be heard over the mutterings in the hall, "you must speak to Balthild. Ask her what happened in the forest south of Quentovic. She will tell you my part in all this, and she will recognise this man too as one of those who sought her death." He pointed with his chin at Agobard.

"Silence," snapped Clovis, his patience evidently exhausted. "I would be done with this. I do not trust you, Beobrand of Bernicia. By your own admission you have killed Vulmar's and Dalfinus' men, and I hear that while I was fighting rebels in Septimania you have been consorting with Iudaea in Liyon. Can you deny any of this?"

Beobrand closed his eyes for a heartbeat. He could see no way out of this now. If only he had followed Cynan's advice and led the men directly to the coast. And yet here he was, standing, beaten and alone, before the king of the Franks.

"Can you deny these things?" Agobard repeated Clovis' question.

"I cannot," replied Beobrand. "But I did not harm Balthild. I came here to warn her that these men—"

Clovis cut him off and Agobard eagerly translated his words, raising his voice to drown out Beobrand's explanation.

"You admit the crimes my trusted men accuse you of. They

also say that you plotted against my queen and I am inclined to believe them over you. I am decided. Danger has followed you ever since you arrived in my kingdom and I would see this threat removed once and for all. I decree that your men be slain, and that before sunset, your own life be taken, that we can be free of your treachery."

The words reverberated in Beobrand's mind. He strained again at his bonds, but they held fast. The two guards restrained him firmly, allowing him no freedom to move. Erchinoald was speaking to the king now, and it seemed to Beobrand that the man was defending him. He knew the truth of it, and fleetingly Beobrand wondered why the *major domus* had not spoken out before. And yet, even as Erchinoald raised his voice above the sudden clamour in the hall, Clovis waved his protestations away.

Beobrand could barely believe what he had heard. He did not truly care that his own life was forfeit. He should have died many times before that day and it was his foolish pride that had brought him here. But to think that he had led his men to this place where they would be executed for crimes they had not committed filled him with a despairing rage. Dimly, he was aware of his own voice soaring in fury. He bellowed and roared, struggling to free himself from the strong hands that grasped him. Shame washed through him like a dark flood. This was not the way for a warrior to face his death. But he did not fight for himself. He fought for his gesithas. They did not deserve this, it was not their wyrd, but his.

Thagmar stepped close and punched Beobrand hard in the face, snapping his head back and leaving him dazed. He tasted the salty metal tang of blood and spat. He still tried to fight. If he could escape his captors and his bonds, perhaps he could see a way to free his men from this doom that he had brought on them. He had always found a way before.

Another hammer blow from Thagmar made Beobrand's legs buckle and his head droop. Erchinoald's face was suddenly close. The *major domus* said something, but Beobrand could not be sure if he spoke to him or to Thagmar. Whoever he addressed, Beobrand did not understand the man's words. But Thagmar did not strike him again and his head began to clear as he was half-dragged by the guards towards the open doors of the hall.

The men and women were filing outside, keen to watch the executions. For what better entertainment could there be for these nobles than the killing of strangers to their lands?

Beobrand could not bear for his men to see him thus, carried by the burly warriors either side of him. So, after a few steps, he got his feet under him and, despite being a captive still, he walked out of the palace and into the courtyard where his gesithas and he would be put to death.

Chapter 35

The instant the doors of the palace opened, Cynan knew Beobrand's luck had finally run out. Several red-cloaked warriors hurried down the steps and made their way to the men guarding the Black Shields. The Franks spoke in muttered whispers, but Cynan ignored them, instead scouring the crowd of people flooding out of the hall for a sign of his hlaford. Perhaps two dozen men and women, all finely dressed in silks and adorned with gold and jewels, poured out of the double doors and gathered on the steps, chattering excitedly in the bright midday sunshine as if they were attending a festival. Many of them stared at the men from Albion with open interest. Cynan looked beyond them.

Where was Beobrand? He had not been inside for a long time. Long enough to have been killed, whispered a small, malicious voice in his mind. At the thought, Cynan's heart seemed to constrict in his chest. Beobrand was never an easy man. To follow him had often led to heartache and pain, but he had freed Cynan from thralldom and given him more than his liberty. Cynan was a warrior, with a hall and gesithas of his own because of Beobrand. To imagine him slain filled Cynan with a terrible, aching despair.

The warriors who guarded Cynan and the others must have

received orders from the men who had left the hall, for they began pulling the Northumbrians to their feet and pushing them towards the steps that led up to the palace.

"Take care what you do," growled Eadgard as one of the guards twisted his arm painfully. By way of answer, the man punched Eadgard in the back to start him walking, much as he might goad an ox. Eadgard turned and faced his tormentor. Eadgard was a huge man and if he had not been bound, the guard would not have been so bold. But, like the rest of them, Eadgard was tied with knots he could not break and he could do nothing more than glare. The guard hesitated for a heartbeat, then he drew his sword and prodded the giant with it.

"Do as they wish," said Cynan. There was nothing for it but to obey. Looking at the numbers of warriors there, even if the Bernicians had been freed and given byrnies and arms, they would not have lasted long.

Eadgard fixed the man with a cold stare, then looked down slowly at the sword blade pressing against his kirtle as if to say, "your puny sword does not frighten me."

"Where do you think they are taking us?" asked Eadgard to Cynan, not deigning to give the guard more of his attention.

"I don't know," replied Cynan, "but there is no need to give them a reason to kill you."

"You think if we do not provoke them there is a way we live to see the sunset?" asked Grindan in a quiet, calm voice, as he was hauled to his feet and shoved after his brother.

Cynan did not answer. What could he say? The men were not fools. They all saw how this day would end. Gods, if only Beobrand had listened to him. At the thought, he could almost hear old Bassus' voice rumbling in Sunniva's hall at Ubbanford. "There is nothing to be gained in looking to the past and what might have been, young Cynan. It cannot be changed. You can only act on what is happening now and prepare for the future."

Bassus was right. Cynan knew that. But knowing the right of

it made it no easier to ignore what had transpired to lead them to this place.

Strong hands grabbed him and a voice whispered close to his ear.

"Sorry," the voice said in Frankish.

Cynan recognised the voice. Turning, he saw it was Hincmar.

"What will happen to us?" Cynan asked in his faltering Frankish.

Hincmar did not speak. He just shook his head, then lowered his gaze. Nothing more was needed. He had confirmed Cynan's fears. With a gentle push, Hincmar sent him walking along with the other prisoners.

It was at that moment that Cynan saw Beobrand. For the briefest time the sight of the lord of Ubbanford filled him with joy. His elation was as short-lived as spit in a fire. Beobrand's face bore a dazed look, and two stern-faced guards supported him on either side. With them strode the odious Thagmar and that bastard, Agobard. Thagmar was dabbing at his face with a cloth, wiping away blood that oozed from his nose. A trickle of blood also ran from Beobrand's mouth. Cynan did not know what had happened inside the hall, but somehow Beobrand had succeeded in bloodying his foe, even bound as he was.

"Stand straight, lads," said Attor, who had also spotted Beobrand. "There is our lord and it seems he has been having words with that godforsaken nithing, Thagmar."

"But how?" asked Bleddyn, peering at the men at the top of the steps. "His hands are tied." There was an edge of fear in his voice. Cynan could not blame him for it. They could all see where this was leading. His heart swelled with pride that none of them openly showed their concern.

"His hands are tied all right," said Attor with a chuckle. "But Beobrand has ever had a hard head. I would wager Thagmar found that out the painful way."

The crowd of nobles had congregated at the bottom of the

steps. They parted now to let the men from Albion pass, guided by their stern-faced guards.

Ingwald and Eadgard joined in with Attor's laughter and soon, as they ascended the steps walking upright and proud, the Black Shields of Ubbanford were all laughing, the sound incongruous yet somehow comforting to Cynan. The laughter reminded him of good times. Happier times. He yearned to hear Eadgyth's light laughter. To see her one last time. To sit in companionable silence in the hall at Stagga while the fire burnt low. But if he was to die here, he could think of no better men to die with than these. Unbidden, Cynan found himself laughing with them.

If he needed any further proof of what awaited them when they reached the top of the steps, Cynan saw Dalfinus step into the daylight, flanked by a young, radiant man who must surely be the king himself. On the other side of the king waddled a fat man with quivering jowls. Cynan recognised Vulmar from years before in Rodomo.

So, Beobrand's foe-men had reached the king before them. Cynan could feel the threads of wyrd fraying in the hands of the sisters who weaved their destinies.

"Where is the queen?" he called out to Beobrand. Surely only her word could save them now, and he scanned the crowd in vain for her.

Beobrand shook his head as if to clear it.

"She is not here, Cynan." He held Cynan's eyes for a moment, then looked away.

Cynan's laughter had ceased, replaced by a grimace.

"You were unable to use your charm to convince the king of our innocence?"

Beobrand hawked and spat. He shook his head.

"Do not feel bad, lord," call Attor, "at least you were able to break that whoreson Thagmar's nose." The warriors laughed again. Thagmar snarled something to his men and the guard leading Attor struck him a blow on the back of his head. Attor stumbled, but did not fall. "These Franks don't know how to hit," he said. "This one is trying to tickle me."

Cynan could see that Attor's courage was buoying the men's spirits and when he looked at Beobrand, he noted that he also took heart from his gesithas' bravery.

They reached the top of the steps. Behind them the great doors of the hall had been shut. At the bottom of the stairs, all of the nobles and the guards on duty stared upwards at the spectacle to come.

"What now?" asked Attor.

Cynan could see Beobrand struggling to find an answer, but at last he looked directly at Attor.

"It seems I have led you down a dark path, my brave gesithas. We will not be seeing the holy city of Roma after all, I fear."

Attor nodded in grim understanding.

"Probably better in my dreams anyway," he said. "Still, I will be at the side of Jesu Christ the Almighty soon enough, which must be better than any earthly city."

The young man Cynan assumed was the king said something to Erchinoald, who turned to address the crowd. He spoke at length in a strong voice that carried easily over the gathered throng. Beyond the walls Cynan saw a great flock of starlings wheel up into the bright sky as if startled by something in the bustle of the city. To think that out there life went on as normal for the men, women and children of Paris, while here, in this sheltered courtyard men's lives were soon to be cut short.

As the *major domus* of the palace called out the crimes for which they were to be executed, the guards positioned Cynan and the others to face the steps, and the nobles below. Then, with quick kicks to the backs of their legs, the guards knocked them down onto their knees.

Cynan heard swords being drawn from scabbards, but he did not turn. He did not wish to see Hincmar's tanned face again. Fear struck Cynan then, as sudden and hard as a blow.

Without warning, he began to shiver despite the warmth of the day. He knew this feeling. It always gripped him as he waited in a shieldwall for the slaughter that would come in a storm of steel. But this was different. His battle-skill could not help him now. His death was certain, and Cynan fought hard to lessen his trembling. He closed his eyes and tried to picture Eadgyth's face.

Erchinoald finished speaking. A hush fell upon the gathering.

"Halinard," shouted Beobrand, "tell them—"

Cynan's eyes snapped open in time to see Thagmar silence Beobrand with a savage punch to the gut that doubled him over.

"That one first," Thagmar said, pointing at Attor.

"Place a blade in his hand, you bastards," said Eadgard. The guards ignored him and Eadgard bellowed again, furious that his friend would face death without a weapon in his hand to mark him as a warrior.

"I need no sword in my hand to tell God where to find me," said Attor.

He smiled at Eadgard, who ceased his shouting. A single tear trickled down his dirt-smeared face. Attor looked over at Cynan from where he knelt. The older warrior was pale, but smiling. He was muttering something, and it took Cynan a few heartbeats to understand that it was the prayer all Christ followers knew and recited at each mass.

The guard behind Attor stepped forward, raising his sword so that the sun caught its polished steel blade. There was a dreadful beauty in the scene. Nobody spoke now, and all those gathered seemed to be holding their breath. Some of the starlings Cynan had seen before passed overhead, dark against the pallid blue sky. Far off, came the sound of horses' hooves clattering over the bridge. The flag lofted above the roof of the palace caught the wind, fluttering and flapping like a luffing sail.

Cynan wanted to say something that might halt this nightmare. He longed to leap to his feet, snatch up a sword and fight his way to freedom. But these thoughts were merely fancies. His bonds bit into his wrists as he shook with impotent anger. Powerless, his breath caught in his throat as he watched on in horrified silence.

"Do it," hissed Thagmar.

As if his voice had cut a cord that had held the guard motionless, the warrior who stood above Attor moved with sudden, deadly intent. Inverting his sword, so that the blade's point rested between Attor's neck and his left shoulder, the guard rammed the weapon downward without hesitation. Attor's eyes widened as the last words of the Lord's prayer died on his lips.

Cynan watched aghast as the sword blade sunk deeply into Attor's flesh. He had slain many men and could imagine all too well how it felt to drive the metal into the man's body. Cynan shuddered at the moment Attor jerked as the sword pierced his heart. Tears welled in Cynan's eyes. His breath returned to him in a great sobbing cry.

Beobrand let out a scream of anguish. He panted, perhaps as much from the punch to his stomach as from witnessing Attor's death. But Beobrand was raving now, bucking and struggling against the men who held him. Thagmar, a smirk on his blood-stained lips, turned to face him.

"I'll kill you!" screamed Beobrand, striving to reach the captain. "I'll kill you!"

Thagmar might not have understood the Anglisc words, but the sentiment behind them was clear, and he laughed at Beobrand's impotence. He raised his fist, ready to strike Beobrand again.

His blow never fell.

A thundering of hooves outside the palace walls was followed by a loud hammering of a fist on solid timber.

"Open the gates," came a loud voice in Frankish. The banging on the huge doors was insistent. "Open the gates in the name of Queen Balthild."

Chapter 36

Beobrand fought against the men holding him. Heaving and straining, he screamed at Thagmar.

Attor's body slumped forward. Light gleamed on the guard's sword blade as it slid out of Attor's dying body. The warrior, always so full of vitality, toppled forward, his mouth still working to utter the words of the Christ follower's prayer. Beobrand noticed there was almost no blood on the sword, as if Attor's body did not wish to relinquish it and did not know it had been slain. That soon changed. As Attor fell forward, bright blood began to pump out of him and soak the stone steps.

Dead!

Attor was dead.

All Beobrand could think of was claiming the blood-price for his gesith's murder. Thagmar was closest, so he would die first. Raging, Beobrand pulled against his guards, but even his prodigious strength was not enough to allow him to break free. Thagmar stepped back to avoid Beobrand's frenzied fury, then, when he saw he was in no danger from the Bernician, he stepped close once more, raising his fist and sneering.

Beobrand braced himself for the blow he knew would come. He would welcome the pain, accept it. He deserved to be hurt for his part in Attor's death. Gods, all of his gesithas here would die and their blood, like that of so many others, would be on his hands. He spat at Thagmar, taunting him, willing him to strike.

Thagmar hesitated.

At first Beobrand believed the man to be toying with him in some way. Mayhap he didn't wish to beat him more for fear he would pass out and thus be spared the torture of watching his men executed.

Thagmar, distracted now, looked away, down into the courtyard. He frowned.

Beobrand followed his gaze. The sound of someone shouting and hammering on the gates finally reached him, piercing his senses where sorrow and anger had rendered him deaf.

There was something familiar in the shouted voice that came from without the palace. Beobrand did not understand the words, but as he watched, guards hurried to withdraw the locking bar and pull open the great doors.

There followed a commotion in the courtyard as more than a score of riders trotted through the gates, scattering the men and women. The horsemen wore the blue cloaks of the royal guard and at their head rode Brocard. The tall captain leapt from his horse and rushed to another rider, offering his hand. To his amazement, Beobrand saw the second rider was not a guard, but none other than the queen herself.

Balthild wore the garb of a guardsman, but it was impossible to conceal her feminine curves. Her head had been covered with a simple helm of iron. She removed this and her lustrous golden hair tumbled free. The nobles and guards alike gasped, as much at her beauty as for her audacity to have ridden here thus, astride a horse like a common warrior.

Handing her helmet to another of the riders, Balthild strode up the steps, Brocard at her side. The horsemen were dismounting and Beobrand noted how they pulled their shields from their saddles, shoving men and women aside as they formed up together into a defensive wedge.

One of the dismounted horsemen who did not wear the distinctive cloak of Brocard's men, hurried after the pair as they ascended the steps. With a shock that rocked him almost as much as Thagmar's gut punch had, Beobrand recognised the man. This was no warrior. The face was fine-boned and handsome, with clever eyes and delicate lips.

"Wilfrid!" Beobrand bellowed, finding his voice again. "You are a dead man."

Wilfrid flinched. His face was pale as he took in the scene. His mouth fell open in shock when he saw Attor's crumpled form, lying in an ever-expanding pool of blood.

"It is not what you think, Lord Beobrand," said Wilfrid. His voice trembled, but was loud enough to carry over the noise of the warriors and the angry shouts of noblemen and women being shoved aside to make space for the queen's guardsmen. There was chaos in the courtyard, but Beobrand ignored what was occurring there.

He could barely breathe, such was the rush of anger that swept through him.

"I think you are a treacherous whoreson," he hissed, "who has betrayed us for power."

"No," replied Wilfrid. "I have done what I was able to see you safe."

By Woden, how easily the youth lied.

"You were there in the amphitheatre, Wilfrid," said Beobrand, his words as jagged as broken ice. "You saw what they planned for us. You led us there. Gram is dead because of you. Attor…" His voice cracked. "Attor too."

"Lord Beobrand." Queen Balthild's soft, melodious tone quietened Beobrand, who still shook with anger.

She had been whispering to Clovis and Erchinoald, but now Balthild approached Beobrand. He saw that, where before all eyes had been on the king, the *major domus* and the condemned men, now nobody could look elsewhere but at the queen. Even dressed in the travel garb of a man, her presence was captivating.

"Wilfrid speaks the truth," she said. "I trust him."

"You do not know what he has done," spat Beobrand, unable to contain his anger, even in the face of Balthild's calm. "The men whom Wilfrid names as his friends. Annemund. Dalfinus. Vulmar. They are all snakes." He stared into her eyes. She must understand the truth of it. "It was by their will that you were attacked," he went on. "They sought to see you and your child slain. I rode here to warn you."

"Wilfrid has told me all about the plots against me," Balthild said. She sighed, seeming more disappointed and sad than angry. "He told me also of how they planned to slay you."

"Then you know he cannot be trusted. No friend of such men is worthy enough to have your ear."

Balthild smiled. Beobrand blinked. The sun seemed brighter and warmer.

"And yet," the queen said, "were you not taken in by Dalfinus and Annemund? Did you not consider them your friends? Could it not be that one younger and less experienced than you also fell foul of their charm?"

Beobrand glowered at Wilfrid, but said nothing. What Balthild said was true. He had allowed himself to be seduced by the brothers' wealth and power, accepting their friendship and the pleasures of life surrounded by the riches to be found in Liyon.

A movement in the courtyard tugged at Beobrand's attention. He glanced down at the open gates, realising with a start that he was no longer being held. The guards on the steps had gone.

And so had Thagmar.

Spinning about, Beobrand searched the top of the steps for the blond captain. Dalfinus stood close to Erchinoald and the king, but there was no sign of Thagmar, Vulmar or Agobard.

Beobrand did not wish to douse the flames of his fury at Wilfrid, but the young novice could wait.

"They have escaped," he hissed, his voice tight with emotion. The queen frowned.

"Your enemies have escaped," Beobrand said, certain that he spoke the truth. "You must free me so that I can hunt them." The thought of Vulmar and the others slipping away without punishment filled him with dismay and a new seething rage that could not be quelled.

Balthild understood the situation at once. She spoke quickly to Brocard, who in turn shouted down to the courtyard. In response to the captain's command, Beobrand saw Fulbert, the scar on his face bright in the sunshine, leap into his saddle once more. Several other blue-cloaked warriors mounted up and in moments they had galloped through the palace gates.

"I should ride with them," Beobrand said. "Those men have done me much wrong."

"There is no time for that," replied Balthild. "Fulbert will run them to ground and bring them back here to face justice soon enough."

"There can be only one form of justice for the likes of Vulmar," growled Beobrand. "I would be there to witness it."

"We can speak of all of these things in time," Balthild went on, brushing aside an unruly lock of hair and tucking it behind her ear. "But for now do you give me your word that neither you nor any of your men will seek to cause Wilfrid harm when you are freed?"

Beobrand glared at the young novice, then down at Attor's still, huddled form. Eadgard, face crimson with his own emotions, looked as though he would rip Wilfrid apart with his bare hands if he was given the chance. Beobrand sucked in a long, calming breath. The sounds of the palace and the city beyond became clearer as he gained control of his ire. Balthild was right. Wilfrid could wait. There were others who must die first.

"Vulmar has fled," Beobrand murmured quietly so that only the queen might hear him. "But one of the serpents stands near the king. Tell Brocard to protect your husband."

Calmly, Balthild turned to Brocard. With a flick of her hand and some unspoken command, he pulled a seax from his belt and held it at Dalfinus' throat. The *comes* of Liyon seemed unsurprised and made no effort to escape.

Balthild placed a hand on Beobrand's shoulder.

"Even bound, you seek to protect my family," she said, looking back to Beobrand. "I have already told my husband of your innocence. He is most contrite for what happened here, but he is easily led and prone to excesses of passion." She offered Beobrand a thin smile, as if she spoke of a wayward child. Clovis seemed to understand that she was speaking of him, for when Beobrand looked at him, the young king averted his gaze, apparently abashed and ashamed.

"Now," Balthild said, moving quickly on from the king's actions, "order your men not to harm Wilfrid, and we can be about the business of meting out justice to Dalfinus here, and that fat rat, Vulmar, and their servants."

Beobrand looked down at the open gates, imagining Fulbert and his guardsmen even now dragging Vulmar, Thagmar and Agobard back to the palace.

"Do not fear, Lord Beobrand," Balthild said. "Vulmar and the others will pay the blood-price for their crimes. They will be brought before the king and tried for treason. Justice will be meted out, by the king. And you can be sure it will be swift."

Beobrand glanced at where Attor's corpse lay, still warm in the afternoon sunshine. He had seen Clovis' justice at work.

"Not too swift, I hope," he said.

Balthild ignored the comment.

"Do I have your word, Beobrand?"

Biting his lip, Beobrand nodded. With a gesture from Balthild, one of her guards stepped forward and cut Beobrand's bonds.

Rubbing his wrists, he turned to face his kneeling men.

"You are not to harm Wilfrid. You hear me?" he said. "I have given my word."

"We hear you, lord," said Grindan.

Cynan nodded. The Waelisc man was pale. Attor's death had shaken him too.

"Eadgard?" said Beobrand.

"I hear you," said the huge warrior. "You have my word. Which is worth more than that of the nithing, Wilfrid." He spat. Wilfrid took a step backward, away from Eadgard's unbridled anger. The novice's foot slipped on the top step and he almost fell.

Beobrand did not like to be reminded of what little value could be placed in a man's word. Once his word had been iron, now it felt weak and riddled with rot.

"And the rest of you?" he asked.

Bleddyn, Grindan, Halinard and Ingwald all nodded. Their faces were sombre and grim. He thought that none of them had put aside their anger at Wilfrid, but there would be time to confront the youth later.

"You have our word," said Beobrand to Balthild.

Before Balthild could give the order for them to be freed, several horses clattered into the courtyard.

The riders wore blue cloaks and Beobrand marvelled at how quickly Fulbert had been able to capture the men who had fled. Then he saw that several of the horses were riderless. One of the guardsmen rode a pale horse. Blood trickled down its flank from a deep cut in its rider's arm.

Beobrand recognised Fulbert as he dismounted and ran up the steps. The man's face was flushed almost as red as the scar that marred his once-handsome features. Fulbert dropped to his knees before the queen, speaking quickly, his voice strained.

Beobrand could not understand all of the words, but Fulbert's expression, the empty saddles and the blood told Beobrand all he needed to know: Vulmar and the others had turned on their pursuers and fought their way free.

PART FOUR

THE WILD HUNT

Chapter 37

Beobrand scanned the faces of the people who hurried out of the way of the column of horsemen. He saw nobody he recognised from the palace courtyard. None of Agobard's mercenaries. No guardsmen from Liyon. Those who had fled the palace were surely far away by now, or hidden within the jumble of buildings on the southern bank of the Secoana. Certainly none of them would be foolish enough to show their face. Beobrand cursed. They would have no chance of finding Vulmar and his lackeys if they had gone to ground in Paris. There were too many places for them to hide and countless ways out of the city.

They had pinned all their hopes of finding Vulmar on Halinard. Beobrand trusted the Frank with his life. He just hoped the man's instinct in this was good. And that his memory served him well.

Halinard rode with Fulbert at the front of the group of riders. Fulbert bellowed for the people of Paris to make way. He was furious that he had lost Vulmar and the others. Halinard pointed out the route the horsemen should follow. Beobrand hoped Halinard was right. As they had galloped through the streets, they had seen no sign of Vulmar or the other men who had fled the palace, but that had not surprised Beobrand. It had been some time since Fulbert's small band had been ambushed, and after his return with the sorry tidings, they had been forced to linger in the palace before setting off in pursuit. Beobrand just hoped the delay wouldn't prove to have been too long.

After they had been freed of their bonds, Clovis had ordered the men from Albion to be equipped from his guards' stores. Beobrand had wanted nothing more than to chase after his enemy, but the king would not hear of them riding into peril without weapons and armour. With every moment that passed, their quarry slipped further away, but no matter what Beobrand said, there was nothing he could do until the king allowed them to leave.

At least the setback had allowed them to tend to Attor. Cynan had been sitting beside the dead gesith, cradling Attor's head in his lap. Cynan looked up as Beobrand approached. His eyes shone and his skin was sallow. He looked older than his years, ashen and tired. Beobrand understood how he felt.

"We all loved Attor," he said in a quiet voice. "Let us take him inside."

He stooped to help Cynan carry their friend's body, but a powerful hand on his shoulder stopped him. Beobrand's nerves were frayed and he spun about quickly, ready to face a new threat. His head ached from the sudden movement.

He let out a sigh. It was Eadgard. The big man's face was pale, his eyes red and puffy.

"Let me carry him, lord," he said.

Beobrand hesitated, then stepped aside. He could see that Eadgard needed this.

Together, Cynan and Eadgard lifted Attor's limp form and carried it into a small guardroom. The rest of the Black Shields followed mutely, heads lowered. None of them spoke as Cynan and Eadgard placed Attor's pallid, cooling corpse atop a bench. They stepped back and the men from Bernicia stared down at their dead comrade.

"He died bravely," muttered Grindan.

The men murmured and nodded. Beobrand could still hear Attor's quips as he faced his end. It takes courage to stand in battle, but it is braver still to accept death with dignity. Beobrand's eyes prickled with tears.

"He will be missed," he said. His voice caught in his throat. It felt swollen, and he swallowed to clear the lump there. "Look at us. Attor would tell us not to mourn him like women. He would want us to drink to his memory, to tell tales of his exploits long into the night."

"And he would want us to seek revenge," Cynan said, his voice thin and sharp as a blade's edge.

"He would want his soul commending to the Lord Almighty," Wilfrid said from the doorway. "I will pray over him."

The grieving men moved away from the young Christ follower, as if to touch him might infect them with some malady. Eadgard stepped into the gap they left. He loomed over Wilfrid. To the novice's credit, he did not back away.

"Have you not done enough already, monk?" said Eadgard, his voice a menacing growl. Beobrand noticed that the man's hands were balled into fists at his side. Muscles in his neck bunched and bulged.

"I understand your anger, Eadgard," replied Wilfrid, staring up into the giant warrior's furious eyes. "I too grieve for Attor." He glanced over at Beobrand. "And Gram. But please believe me when I tell you I never wanted any of this."

Eadgard gnarred in the back of his throat. Beobrand thought he was going to leap on the youth. He decided he would do nothing to prevent Eadgard. His task of protecting Wilfrid seemed unimportant now. The novice monk's actions had surely removed that obligation from him.

But before Eadgard could move, Wilfrid spoke again, his voice steady.

"You think me guilty of betraying you." The men grumbled. Again Wilfrid glanced at Beobrand and it seemed to him that

Wilfrid spoke as much for his benefit as for Eadgard's. "But this is not the truth. What would you have had me do? When I discovered what these men were about, I was in their midst. But I am no warrior. I could not fight my way free from the nest of vipers I found myself in. So I bided my time. I used what skills God has given me." He tapped his temple with a long finger. The ring he wore flashed in the gloom of the guardroom. "I listened. I planned. And when an opportunity presented itself, I encouraged them to come hither, to Paris. I knew Lord Beobrand would come here. We all know he made a promise to protect the queen and he would not forsake her."

Beobrand wondered if Wilfrid said these words for his ears, to remind him that he had promised the queen of Northumbria to protect him also. He scowled, not liking to be made aware of his own shortcomings. Too often of late he had been forced to break his oaths. He did not need Wilfrid to tell him so.

"But," continued Wilfrid, holding up his be-ringed finger, "I never foresaw this outcome. I did not wish to see any of you killed." He looked each of them in the face for a moment, willing them to believe him. "You came to my aid when I was in need. Do not think I would forget such a thing. I sought to do the same for you. The instant that we reached Paris, I slipped away and rode with all haste to Cala. I had learnt that Queen Balthild was still there and I knew that only her word could save you from Dalfinus' and Vulmar's poisonous lies. I did what I could." He looked down at the corpse on the bench and sighed. "I only wish I could have reached here in time to save Attor. But the least I can do now is to pray for his everlasting soul. He was a follower of the one true God and I believe he would have welcomed my prayers."

Wilfrid held Eadgard's glowering stare. Eventually, the huge warrior let out a ragged breath. He turned to look once more at Attor's lifeless form. Beobrand saw that a change had come over the corpse. The face was still recognisable as the man he had lived and fought beside all these years, but it was clear now that Attor was gone. What lay on the bench was meat and bones now. All life had vanished like smoke on a breeze. A wave of sorrow washed over him.

Eadgard turned back to Wilfrid.

"Do what you wish," he said, pushing the novice aside, and stepping into the light.

Silently, Beobrand and the others followed Eadgard, leaving Wilfrid alone with Attor's corpse inside the darkened room.

Outside, weapons and armour were being set out for Beobrand's men. It was while Clovis' guards brought out shields, helms, swords and the short axes so beloved of the Franks, spreading them out for the men of Albion to choose, that Halinard had approached Beobrand.

"I know where the monster has gone," he'd said, swinging one of the Frankish axes to test its weight and balance.

Beobrand did not need to ask him to whom he was referring.

"Tell me," he said. He had no time for conversation. They should already have been hurrying after Vulmar and yet they milled about the palace courtyard, his men perusing the arms on offer like womenfolk looking over the wares of a pedlar.

"I told you I came to Paris with Vulmar before."

Beobrand nodded. He remembered.

"There was a place he would go when not at the palace. A friendly hall. The home of Lord Nithard. Just to the south of the city."

"You think he has gone there?" Beobrand frowned. The lord of Rodomo could be anywhere. He could feel his chances of capturing him slipping away with each passing moment.

"Where else can he go?" Halinard scratched at his beard. "He has allies there. Men who..." he hesitated. "Men who share his tastes. His secrets. Men who will protect him."

Beobrand gripped his shoulder.

"You are sure?"

Halinard shrugged. He looked old, haggard.

"Who is sure of anything?" he asked forlornly.

Beobrand sighed. After the events of that day, he understood Halinard's sentiment.

Of course, Vulmar might not be where Halinard supposed, but when they questioned Fulbert and the other survivors of the ambush, they told of Vulmar, Thagmar, Agobard and several of the assassin's warriors escaping. When asked in which direction they had headed, they all agreed that it was to the south, backing up Halinard's idea. With no better plan than that, they had set off southward in the hope they would find them at the hall Halinard spoke of.

When servants had brought out refreshments and placed jugs of wine and platters of pastries upon trestles in the sunshine, Beobrand had lost his temper.

"Enough of this," he had bellowed. "We leave now." Draining a cup of wine, he had thrown the empty vessel to a bewildered servant. The boy, shocked and frightened of the tall brute of a warrior, with his mutilated hand, bruised face and piercing blue eyes, juggled the cup for a moment before it clattered to the ground.

Balthild watched him with a knowing expression on her flawless features. Ignoring her, and the stares from the courtiers, Beobrand strode towards the horses.

"To me, my gesithas," he shouted. His men hurried to follow him, snatching up their weapons, finishing their drinks and cramming the last morsels of food into their mouths.

The queen signalled to Brocard, and the captain of her guard barked orders at his men. They rushed to their horses, as anxious to ride as Beobrand. He cursed himself for not having pushed them to leave sooner.

"Halinard," he snapped, swinging himself up onto the mount

he had ridden since Dudon's farm, "tell Brocard where we are going."

And so they galloped through the streets of Paris, wary of another ambush, peering down shaded alleys for any sign of their quarry. They saw none. Fulbert had said that Vulmar and Thagmar had been mounted, but that most of Agobard's men had fled on foot.

Beobrand had thought of Vulmar's bulk and cursed the man's luck.

"That fat bastard would not have got far on foot."

"A horse can only carry such a load for a short distance," Halinard had replied. "And Vulmar is no rider."

After crossing the bridge, but still within sight of the palace, Fulbert had halted the column, calling down to a group of rivermen who sat in the afternoon sun, playing dice. They spoke briefly. The boatmen pointed south.

"They saw Vulmar and Thagmar ride this way," Halinard said, excitement tingeing his voice.

There was no sign of the others though. Agobard was a wily one. Beobrand imagined him telling his men after the ambush on Fulbert to split up and disappear into the labyrinth of alleyways, roads, yards, meadows, orchards and fields, perhaps with instructions to reunite at a designated meeting place.

They had reached the outskirts of the city now. The houses thinned out and there were fewer people on the road, meaning they could push the horses faster. A sudden snarling and barking made Beobrand turn in his saddle. They were passing the same building that was being repaired from that morning. The carpenter was splitting timber with wooden wedges and a mallet. He watched the men as they rode past. Ingwald flinched at the sound of the barking dog, clinging to his reins as if fearing he would be thrown yet again. But the dog was tethered now, and though it snapped and barked at the horses, it could do them no harm. The carpenter, recognising them, raised a callused hand and called something Beobrand could not make out over the thrum of the horses' hooves. The man's face was cracked in a grin and he waved happily.

"I hope you and your dog get the bloody flux," shouted Ingwald, smiling back at the carpenter and his angry hound.

Some of the men chuckled, but their mood was sober and grim. They thundered on, towards the wooded hills that rose to the south of Paris. Beobrand and his men had been captured nearby and he wondered where this hall that Halinard spoke of could be. They had seen no such place that morning.

Halinard rode close to Beobrand and pointed to the south and west.

"Lord Nithard's hall is that way," he said. "There is a path off the road after that hill."

The road crested a slope and their horses, tired now from being pushed hard, lumbered up the incline, blowing and panting. Fulbert reined in, allowing the rest of the horsemen to catch up. The great gash to his face was now fully healed, but the scar was red, puckered and angry-looking in the bright light of the lowering sun.

Fulbert spoke quickly to Brocard. The captain of the guard nodded to Halinard to interpret.

"Nearly there now," he said. "We leave the road and the path leads between two hills with forest on both sides. We must go careful from here."

"You think Agobard and his men might have made it here before us?" Beobrand asked.

"Perhaps," ventured Halinard. "And I was thinking. Vulmar is no fool. He knows I am with you and he must suspect I will bring you here."

"You think he has set us another trap?"

"I think yes, if he can. Nithard has men. And if Agobard is somehow here ahead of us..." His words petered out, but he did not need to say more. None of them could be certain what awaited them, but if there was one thing they knew about Agobard, it was that he liked to set traps and ambushes for his enemies.

Beobrand glanced up at the sky, which was the hue of molten iron as the sun set.

"It will be dark soon, we cannot tarry. If night falls before we have run him to ground, I fear Vulmar will slip away and we might never find him."

Halinard nodded.

"He is a slippery one, it's true. I think he will take a new mount and strike out for the coast. But his wealth is without end and he has allies everywhere."

"So there is no knowing where he will go, if we lose him. He understands the king will know the truth by now, so he will flee these lands and we might lose him for good."

"I was thinking much on this," said Halinard. "If you want to listen, lord. I have a plan."

Chapter 38

Cynan halted, leaning against the rough bark of an oak. Drawing in a deep breath, he held it and listened to the men making their way through the foliage. They were noisy to his ears. Close by, Eadgard's cloak snagged on a twig. As the massive man moved forward, the branch flicked back into his brother's face. Grindan muttered a curse. By the gods, it would be a miracle if they were not heard long before they reached their destination.

It was dusk now and already dark under the trees. Cynan watched the shadows of the men move with as much stealth as they were able to muster. They flitted from tree to tree, but each of their footfalls was clear to him and he wondered how distant they were from their foes. It couldn't be too far now. Letting out his breath slowly, he set off once more.

He missed Attor's calming presence. The scout had been able to move as silently as a ghost through dense undergrowth. He had been helped by his slender form and his reluctance to wear an iron-knit shirt, but there was a natural grace about him too. It always felt as though he could step on twigs without snapping them, and wade through brambles without their thorns catching on his garments. Cynan had never learnt how Attor was able to move with such stealth. Now he never would. He sensed his grief welling up within him like milk boiling in a pot. His head ached terribly, but he pushed away the pain, focusing on the men around him and on the obstacles before them. Now was not the time to succumb to his hurts or the heartache of loss. Healing and mourning would have to wait for later.

If they survived the night.

They pressed on, as quietly as possible. They could not slow too much, for when they heard the signal, Fulbert would be relying on them to do their part.

Brocard had been unsure of the plan at first, but Beobrand's support for Halinard had finally swayed the captain enough for him to order his men to dismount and approach the hall on foot. With each moment that passed, Cynan had sensed Beobrand's tension building. He imagined Vulmar escaping into the gathering night, disappearing and evading justice. Cynan understood Beobrand's frustration. Of late it had seemed as if the gods had forsaken them. If Beobrand had once been considered lucky, that good fortune had vanished.

They had left their horses guarded by a couple of Brocard's men and started along the path that wound its way westward through dense woodland. Halinard knew the land and after a short way he had told them to halt where the track rose up a steep slope. Leading Cynan, Brocard, the scar-faced Fulbert and Beobrand up to the brow of the hill, Halinard had whispered, "Down there is where I would place an ambush."

They moved off the path and crouched in the shade of a great ash. From the cover of the tree, they stared down at the path as it looped southward before vanishing again into the forest. To either side of the trail, the woods sloped up, creating in the narrow valley a perfect place for an ambush. The sun had touched the treetops to the west and would soon drop behind the horizon. The shadows were long and dark. Brocard, still unconvinced, wanted to return for the horses. But the gods who had seemed to have turned their backs on Beobrand and his men recently,

had perhaps decided to smile upon them once more. Just before
they turned away, the setting sun had glinted from an uncovered
blade in the forest. It was only for an eye-blink, but there was
no mistaking what they had seen. There were men in those trees.
Men with cold iron. Agobard might well be leading those men.
The area was uncannily similar to the site of the ambush on the
queen. But Agobard, who seemed to be so careful and cunning,
had been left little time to prepare. Perhaps that haste had led
to his men not concealing their weapons. Whatever the reason
for the mistake, they now knew there were men lying in wait
amongst the trees. It was all that was needed for Brocard to
agree to put Halinard's plan into action.

They had slipped back down to the men who waited on the
path. There had been very little time for discussion. The sun
would be gone soon. Beobrand had taken charge, relaying orders
which Halinard interpreted.

"Brocard, you take your men to the south, I will go to the
north with my men. Cynan will lead the Black Shields and I will
carry on to Nithard's hall with Halinard. When it is full dark,
and we have had time to reach the building, Fulbert will blow
his horn and you will attack from north and south at the same
time. Thus, the hunters become the prey."

"I do not like this," Cynan had said. "You cannot go with
Halinard alone. You do not know how many men will be at the
hall. I will come with you. My place is at your side."

"No, Cynan. I need you to lead the men. There is none better
for this task." Attor could have led them well through the dark
forest, Cynan had thought, but he'd said nothing. "There is no
time for argument," Beobrand went on. "We must hurry."

"Then take some of the men with you," Cynan urged, but
Beobrand shook his head.

Brocard had remained silent as the men argued, but now
he stepped between them and spoke quickly, in hushed tones.
Halinard relayed his meaning.

"The plan is a good one, but Cynan is right. Two of you alone might not be enough. Brocard goes with us to the hall with half a dozen men. The others follow Fulbert. Now, there is no time for more talk. Wait for full dark. If the horn sounds before we reach the hall, Vulmar hears and we may lose him."

There had been no further argument. Cynan had grudgingly accepted the role that Beobrand had given him but he could not shake the feeling that he was neglecting his duty as he watched the lord of Ubbanford, Halinard, Brocard and six of his blue-cloaked warriors disappear into the encroaching darkness beneath the trees. Noise of their passage through the bracken, nettles and briars reached them for a short time, and then there was nothing more than the hushed sounds of the forest. Wood pigeons hooted. A woodpecker drummed somewhere far off.

Cynan nodded to Fulbert, indicating the long hunting horn that hung at his belt and miming blowing it.

"Full dark," he said in Frankish.

Fulbert nodded, his scarred face serious. With a whispered command to the remaining dozen guardsmen, Fulbert turned and made his way into the woodland. His men followed him and they were soon swallowed up by the forest.

Cynan had hurried at first. They had further to travel, needing to head west and then turn south, before circling back eastward to where the ambushers were lurking. Fulbert's men only had to go a short way to the south and then head through the woods westward before they would meet Agobard's warriors, if that was indeed who waited for them. Cynan hoped Fulbert would give them long enough to get into position. He worried too about Beobrand, Halinard, Brocard and his men. They had even further to travel and the footing was treacherous in the gloom. Halinard had said they would head over the wooded hillside, dropping down the far side where they would then follow a stream that ran past the hall.

Cynan peered up through the foliage. There was still the

afterglow of the sun in the sky, but it would not last long. Here, beneath the tree canopy, it was dark and the cool of the night began to seep out of the loamy soil. The gloaming was heavy with the scent of decaying vegetation. It was hard to be certain, but Cynan guessed they had travelled as far as they needed in a generally westerly direction. He tapped Grindan on the shoulder and pointed south. Grindan's face was a pale smudge in the gloom. He nodded and passed on the message. As quietly as possible, the men of Albion began to make their way towards where they thought their adversaries were hiding.

It was difficult to make out anything but the large trunks of the trees, but in spite of the darkness, rather than slowing their pace, an urgency came over them. They could sense their time running out, and so they pressed on. Someone slipped and fell with a grunt. They all halted, holding their breath and listening to the night. The forest was silent. Cynan made his way stealthily back to the man who had fallen. He found Ingwald climbing to his feet with a groan. Cynan thought of the bad fall he had taken when thrown by the horse. Ingwald's body must be bruised and battered.

"Sorry, lord," Ingwald hissed.

Cynan squeezed his arm, but said nothing. They stood in silence for a moment, but everything remained still. They moved on. Cynan breathed through his mouth, straining to hear any indication of the ambushers ahead. The sounds of the men around him were too loud. He was sure that they would be overheard. For the first time he drew the sword he had taken from the palace from its plain scabbard. The grip was cool, the heft of the weapon reassuring in his hand. He stepped forward again, wincing at the shuffling and cracking of the Black Shields as they seemed to make as much noise as pigs snuffling for mast under the trees.

It was almost fully dark now, but he judged there was still a way to go. He wondered whether Beobrand had reached the hall and hoped Fulbert would hold his nerve a while longer.

As if in answer to his last thought, the hush of the night was ripped by the howling blast of a hunting horn. The sound seemed to come from some way off to Cynan's left, but there was little time to pinpoint its location before the sound was cut off.

Cynan cursed.

An instant later, the roar of a dozen men rushing into battle filled the darkness. More voices joined the clamouring, followed by the crash of steel.

Cynan cursed again. They were not in position, but the need for silence was over. Still, perhaps the presence of the Black Shields was yet unknown, so he called his men to him, keeping his voice low. They crowded close, pressing their heads together.

"It seems Fulbert has blown his horn too soon."

"It can happen to any man," said Ingwald.

The men chuckled in the darkness. Cynan ignored Ingwald's jest, but he was gladdened that the men were able to find humour still.

"Ready yourselves for a fight, brothers," Cynan said. He listened as blades were drawn, shields readied, helms straightened. "Don't let them know we're here until we hit them," he hissed. "Now, follow me. Let's make this the last time that Agobard lays an ambush. We are the Black Shields and what do we bring?"

"Death!" they replied as one.

Saying no more, Cynan turned and ran through the gloom towards the sounds of intense fighting. The ground sloped downward and he slipped and slid, catching himself on branches to slow his careening motion. Twigs and boughs whipped and clawed at his face. He ducked and sprinted onward. Behind him he could hear the Bernicians crashing through the brush. But loud as they were, the noise they made was nothing when compared to the clash of battle before them.

There was a faint light ahead where the tree cover lessened and the glow from the sky filtered down onto the path. Men fought there, blades gleaming dully. Cynan was the first to reach the path where Fulbert's men struggled with the ambushers. He raised his sword and lifted his borrowed shield.

The moment before he crashed into the backs of the men who had planned to kill them, he screamed out a battle cry. The cry was taken up by the other warriors who were only a few paces behind him. His heart soared as they burst forth from the forest gloom and smashed into their foe-men.

"Death!" they cried. And that is what they brought with them from the darkness.

Chapter 39

Sweat drenched Beobrand despite the cooling of the air as night fell. He had found a byrnie that fitted him well enough amongst the pile of things laid out for them by the apparently repentant Clovis, but as they hurried through the brooding gloom, Beobrand had begun to wish he had not donned the thing. His shoulders ached, his head throbbed and his lungs burnt. Again he thought of how weak he had become from their stay in Liyon. Or perhaps he had still not recovered his full strength after the fever that had laid him low in the winter. An insidious voice whispered to him that his fatigue was a sign he was growing old, but he thrust that worry deep down within himself to the secret place where he buried all his fears and doubts. With a grunt of effort, he pushed himself to greater speed.

The thought of the weight of his years pressing on him and recalling the hacking, debilitating cough brought into his mind the image of Attor. He could scarcely believe the man was gone. He would yet live if it had not been for that viper, Vulmar, and his lies. Beobrand prayed to Woden and any other god who might listen that the lord of Rodomo was indeed where Halinard thought he would be. The thought of him having slipped away into the night and escaping the punishment that awaited him, turned Beobrand's stomach. He should have come in search of the man years ago, instead he had chosen to ignore the threat. There had always been some other enemy to confront that was closer, more pressing. He had allowed Vulmar to live for too long. That would end tonight. And if the bastard had fled, Beobrand vowed he would not rest until he found him. The journey to Roma be damned. If he had to chase after Vulmar across the whole of Frankia and beyond, he would. Wilfrid could make his own way to the holy city.

While they had ridden from the palace, Beobrand had thought much on what Wilfrid had said. He shared Eadgard's anger at the boy. It was no easy thing to brush aside Wilfrid's betrayal. He had been certain he knew the novice's heart ever since that moment in the amphitheatre when Wilfrid had remained with Dalfinus, merely watching as Beobrand, Halinard and Gram fought their way free. But now, as so often in life, things were not so simple. Balthild had made Beobrand question himself. Had he too not been taken in by Dalfinus? And it seemed that as soon as he was able, the novice had turned away from his erstwhile friends and done all he could to save Beobrand and his warriors from Vulmar and Dalfinus' machinations. The thoughts swirled about his mind like a swarm of bees, buzzing and droning, but seldom settling.

He needed a clear head this night. If he still lived tomorrow, he would turn once more to Wilfrid and what should be done with him, but for now, these preoccupations were unimportant. Wiping the sweat from his brow, Beobrand pushed on through the dusk-enshrouded forest.

They had decided soon after leaving Cynan, Fulbert and the others that their greatest challenge would be reaching the hall in time, so they had ignored any efforts to traverse the woodland stealthily. They still moved without speaking, knowing that voices travelled far in the wilderness, but they cared not for snapping twigs, breaking saplings or trampling through bracken and gorse.

Halinard, panting from the exertion, halted. For a moment he bent double, catching his breath, as the others caught up. They had reached the summit of the hill. From this vantage point, they could glimpse the land that lay before them to the west. There was still a ruddy glow in the western sky, but the sun was already partly behind the horizon. The day's last rays picked out the dense forest that swept down into a cleft in the hills. Some way off to the south-west was a bright, golden slab of light. Beobrand squinted. It was too far away for him to be certain, but he thought it was the roof of a hall, agleam in the falling sun's light.

Brocard and his men crowded around them. All of them were breathing heavily, but none of them seemed as tired as Beobrand and Halinard. Beobrand clenched his jaw tight. He would show no weakness before these Franks. They were all younger than him by at least ten years and they had not received the same beatings or endured the same gruelling travel as he, but he would not use such things to excuse his shortcomings. No, he was the lord of Ubbanford, commander of the fabled Black Shields, and before the night was through, these younger men would see why songs were sung of him in halls across Albion.

Pushing himself upright, Beobrand cuffed the sweat from his face and forced his breathing to slow. He touched Halinard on the back and the Frank straightened too.

"Come," Beobrand said, "we cannot waste time. It will be dark soon."

Brocard said something in a hushed tone. Halinard replied, but Beobrand could not make out the meaning of his words.

"Not much further," Halinard said. "There is a stream at the bottom of this hill. When we reach it, turn left and soon we be upon the buildings." Halinard's breathing had returned to normal now, and while he repeated his words to the Franks, Beobrand set out down the steep slope.

The ground was soft underfoot, thick with leaf matter and loam. After the moment of sunlight, it was soon very dark beneath the trees. Beobrand, rushing down the hill, did not see the stream before he had slipped down its sheer bank and plunged up to his knees in cold water. The stream bed was deep mud that pulled at his shoes. Grimacing, but pleased he had not fallen, Beobrand turned and waded southward. Behind him he heard the others sliding and splashing into the water. The air was chill here in the cleft cut by the beck. The squelching, churned mud released an unpleasant stench of decay that caught in Beobrand's throat. Insects whirred near his ears, and he batted them away with his right hand. In his left, weaker hand, he held a shield he had taken from the palace. It was painted blue like the cloaks of the royal guards of Neustria. But here, in the darkness of the forest stream, it looked black.

They made good time along the stream bed despite the clinging mud that seemed intent on sucking the shoes from their feet. The sun had set and the world was rapidly being swallowed by night when they came out of the forest and into a large clearing. There was still enough light in the sky to clearly see the looming shape of a hall. A couple of smaller buildings were off to Beobrand's left, where the tunnel-like darkness between the trees showed the place the path exited the woods.

Begrimed, wet and cold, Beobrand climbed out of the brook. He scanned the buildings while the others clambered up from the muddy ditch. They all breathed easily now. They had slowed their pace as they approached the buildings. The men around him drew swords from scabbards and pulled axes from where they had carried them wedged into their belts. Beobrand tugged his stolen sword from the scabbard he had taken from one of Gunthar's men. The weapon's smooth grip and the weight of the blade felt good in his hand. But it was still unfamiliar to him. He missed Nægling and fleetingly wondered whether he would ever see that great sword again.

Brocard whispered something and his men fell into line beside him. Despite the gathering darkness, Beobrand felt exposed standing there in the open, a few dozen paces away from the door of the hall. Beobrand signalled to Halinard and the two of them joined the small rank of warriors on the right flank, the end nearest the stream that continued past the hall and was lost to sight in the gloaming.

They stood in silence, listening to the night. There was no sound of fighting. The hall itself was quiet, but a faint light oozed out from beneath the doors.

"No door wards?" Beobrand hissed to Halinard.

The Frank peered at the hall, then shook his head.

"I see nobody," he whispered. He repeated the conversation, whispering in Frankish.

Brocard nodded, and signalled for them to make their way forward.

As one, they stepped towards the hall. A crow flapped across the sky. Beobrand shivered, wondering if this was an omen from Woden. Good or ill, he could not say.

Stealthily, they moved closer. The stillness of the hall unnerved Beobrand. Surely Vulmar would have placed a sentry at the door if he was there. The man was many things, but he was no fool. Perhaps they had been wrong all along and Vulmar was far from this place. Maybe the blade they had seen picked out by the sun's dying light in the forest was nothing more than a woodsman's axe.

Without warning, a horn blared in the distance. The blast was short, but loud enough to carry far, the sound piercing and out of place in the hush of the darkening forest. Within the hall, a dog began to bark.

Brocard hissed a curse.

There was no wind, but the sounds of men fighting drifted to them, echoing through the trees and over the hill that separated the buildings from the path where Fulbert and Cynan must have sprung their trap on the ambushers.

Beobrand tensed, ready for what his wyrd would bring. The warriors around him loosened their wrists, rolled their heads to free up tight neck muscles, preparing for battle. Brocard hesitated. Beobrand had thought the Frank captain would take the lead, but in the hurried preparations, they had not thought to agree what would happen when the time came to close for battle. Indecision now could prove disastrous. Beobrand made up his mind. He would lead the men forward as best he could. His command of Frankish was not good, but he knew how to command men. He was about to utter an order, when the door of the hall swung open.

The noise of the barking dog grew louder and someone shouted at the animal for quiet. The red glow of firelight pooled out of the hall. If it had been full dark as they had agreed with Fulbert, the man in the hall's doorway might not have seen Beobrand and the warriors lurking at the edge of the clearing near the stream. As it was, there was yet enough of the sunset's afterglow in the sky for him to see them almost immediately. He shouted urgently over his shoulder, stared at the small group of warriors briefly, as if making sure his eyes had not deceived him, then slammed the door.

Whatever hope of surprise they had was lost. The only thing left in their favour was that they were armed and ready to fight. Speed was imperative now. If they could cross the ground to the hall and force their way inside before the inhabitants had time to arm themselves, they might yet retain some advantage. They had no way of knowing how many men were inside, but there was no time to think of such things.

"Come," shouted Beobrand in Frankish, not knowing what else to say.

He ran forward, Halinard limping at his side. For a heartbeat

Beobrand thought he might have misjudged Brocard, but then the captain snapped a command and he and his men sprinted to catch up with Beobrand and Halinard.

They had taken perhaps a dozen paces when the hall door flew open once more.

Chapter 40

Eight men ran out into the dusk, blocking the path to the hall. Light from the doorway glinted from their helms and byrnies. In their hands they bore shields. Some carried spears, others swords. A couple of them wielded short-hafted axes. They must have already been prepared for battle. Perhaps they had been waiting for just such an attack, or they had been on the verge of sending reinforcements to the men who watched the path. Whatever the reason for their preparedness, Beobrand, Halinard, Brocard and the six guardsmen found themselves facing a rapidly formed shieldwall before the open door of the hall.

Cursing, Beobrand did not slow down. He was ahead of the others, but trusted they would take their positions in the line, so, choosing the man second from the end of the shieldwall as his target, he sped forward, letting out a bellow of rage in his booming battle-voice.

His adversary was a burly, thickset man with receding hair and a dense hedge of beard. He was armed with one of the Frankish hand axes. Beobrand's height, speed and the length of his sword would make it difficult for the man to strike him. Beobrand grinned as the man stepped forward to meet him shield to shield.

A flicker of firelight from the axe's blade gave Beobrand an instant's warning that the man had thrown the weapon. The axe flew true and it was only his cat-like reflexes that saved Beobrand. Without thinking, he ducked and raised his shield. He felt the impact of the axe's blade as it bit briefly into the hide and willow boards before tumbling to the earth.

The axe had not found its mark, but perhaps it had served its purpose. Beobrand had lost his momentum. Looking over his shield rim, he saw his opponent had drawn a vicious-looking long seax.

The smile died on Beobrand's lips. He had underestimated his adversary. A mistake that proved to be many warriors' last. Along the line the other warriors clashed. The night was loud with the clatter of blades against shields. Grunts and shouts. Swearing and insults in the tongue of the Franks.

To his right Halinard lunged at his opponent and the man deflected the blow on his shield's rim. But Beobrand was only dimly aware of this. He watched the eyes of his foe-man, focusing on nothing more than anticipating which way he would strike. The short warrior was patient. He stood his ground, jabbing and feinting, but not opening himself up for an attack. Beobrand soaked up the man's blows, looking for a gap in his defences. But this was clearly a warrior who had stood against many enemies and had lived. He would not fall easily.

Beobrand swung a blow over his shield. The man parried it with ease. A feint to his head was ignored; the subsequent low blow blocked with his shield. Beobrand traded a few more attacks with the man, blocking with his shield and allowing his own strikes to be caught on the man's linden board. All the while Beobrand was watching for weaknesses, but he could see none.

Beobrand ignored a scream of agony that came from his left. He didn't know if it was one of the queen's guards who had fallen, or a warrior from the hall. He could not take his eyes from the man before him. To his right, he sensed that Halinard was on the offensive. Somewhere in the distance he thought he heard the sound of a horse whinnying. He had seen no horses outside the hall. But there was no time to dwell on that now. His opponent sent a flurry of blows at him, Beobrand parried or blocked them all, but he allowed the man to push him backward slowly.

Beobrand staggered back a pace, as if shaken by the ferocity of the man's attacks. He had fought enough men to know that sometimes a warrior only revealed his weakness when he believed he was winning. As Beobrand retreated, he kept his shield in a protective high position, leaving his left leg temptingly uncovered and open for a strike. He was not sure his enemy would take the bait, but an eye-blink after Beobrand had raised his shield so that the lower rim was above his knee, the man leapt forward, darting his blade towards his exposed shin.

The bearded warrior snarled, grinning savagely. He believed he was about to wound the tall, fair-haired warrior from Albion. But his blade never connected with Beobrand's flesh. His seax found only air where Beobrand's leg had been. As the shorter man lunged forward, so Beobrand pulled back his left leg and thrust his sword over his shield's rim. The move caught his foe springing forward and off balance. The steel of Beobrand's sword disappeared into the Frank's bushy beard and plunged deep into his throat. At almost the same moment, Beobrand smashed his shield down into the man's extended sword arm.

The warrior dropped his weapon. His eyes were wide with the shock of his sudden defeat. Beobrand twisted the blade that was lodged in the Frank's neck. Blood bubbled black in the darkness, running from the man's mouth and down the sword blade. Shuddering, the stocky warrior fell to his knees. Beobrand stepped back, pulling his sword free and allowing the man to collapse onto the earth, where he floundered like a beached fish, gasping and drowning on his lifeblood.

Beobrand looked along the line. Brocard and his men were

still locked in a savage struggle. One of the defenders had fallen, but Beobrand saw at least two of the queen's guards had been wounded. To his right, Halinard used his shield to lever his assailant's away from his body. Then, skipping to his right, he hammered his axe into the man's face. With a shriek, the man fell back.

Seeing his gesith was victorious, Beobrand turned to aid Brocard and his men.

"To me, Halinard!" he shouted over the tumult. Within the hall the dog was barking again and Beobrand worried they might release the hound to attack them. In the distance, he again heard the frightened whinnying of a horse.

"No, lord," said Halinard. He reached out and pulled Beobrand back. Beobrand glanced at him. Was he wounded? Halinard was breathless from the fight, but seemed uninjured. He could see no blood on him.

"No?" Beobrand asked, frowning. Halinard was either brave or foolish to refuse his lord's command. There was no time for dissent here. The battle raged and every heartbeat could spell triumph or defeat.

"The stable is at the rear of the hall, lord," said Halinard. "I think these men are sent to delay us."

Beobrand understood instantly. Nodding, he turned his back on Brocard and the guardsmen. They could fend for themselves against these warriors. Beobrand would not tarry here and allow Vulmar to escape.

"Lead the way," he said.

Without hesitation, Halinard ran into the darkness. Beobrand, his earlier tiredness forgotten, sprinted after him, bloody sword in hand.

Chapter 41

Beobrand hurried after Halinard. As he ran around the corner, the sounds of fighting were instantly muffled. It was darker here too. Lost was the light that came from the open door, but after only a few paces Beobrand noticed a new source of illumination ahead, glowing from behind the building. The sounds of horses was louder now, and Beobrand could make out voices talking urgently. Halinard was several steps ahead, and Beobrand wanted to call after him to wait. But not wishing to alert whoever was behind the hall of their presence, he watched in silence as the Frankish warrior rushed around the shadowed corner and out of sight. Beobrand charged after him, skidding out of the dark and into the dim light of a burning torch.

An elderly man, seemingly unarmed, held the brand aloft. The flickering light from its flame picked out the stable and two riders fighting for control of their mounts. The stable was a large building, perhaps a spear's throw behind the hall. The man with the torch had not yet seen Halinard and Beobrand, but watched on as the horses, evidently scared by the sounds of fighting, bucked and pranced.

Despite the distance and the gloom, Beobrand recognised both riders instantly. Vulmar clung to the reins of the larger horse, a white mare. His face was a pale mask of fear and he looked as though he might be thrown from the animal's back at any moment.

The other horse carried a slimmer man, fair hair bright in the darkness, reflecting the torchlight like gold.

Thagmar.

Beobrand knew him to be a skilled warrior, and now, seeing how he wheeled his mount around on the spot, remaining in the saddle with apparent ease despite the creature's efforts to unseat him, he saw that Thagmar was also a far superior rider to the lord of Rodomo.

Halinard did not slow down his limping run. He lurched towards the riders. Beobrand, now able to see the land before him, increased his own speed. His longer legs ate up the distance and he began to close the gap with Halinard.

They had almost reached the riders and the man with the torch when they were spotted. Thagmar must have seen their movement for he glanced in their direction and shouted something.

Vulmar, fear etched on his features, kicked his heels into his horse's flanks, desperate for escape from the approaching warriors. The beast valiantly carried its rider's bulk off at a canter. The lord of Rodomo would soon be enveloped in the darkness.

Beobrand cursed. Gods, they had come so close. He could see they would never reach him in time. Vulmar would even now manage to evade them. At best they would have to find mounts and ride after him in the dark.

It seemed Halinard refused to let that happen.

With a scream of anger, he snapped his right hand forward, letting fly the axe he had taken from the palace. Beobrand lost track of its flight in the darkness, then saw it strike Vulmar in the back. With a shout of triumph, Halinard rushed onward.

Thagmar spun his horse around, kicking it forward to

intercept him. Halinard, intent on his quarry, did not notice the threat until it was too late. Thagmar's horse's chest crashed into him, throwing him from his feet. With a grunt of pain, Halinard tumbled away and was lost to sight in the darkness of the stream bed.

Without halting his steed, Thagmar swung his right leg over the horse's neck and leapt from the saddle. He hit the earth at a run, pulling his sword from its scabbard. He glanced after Halinard, but knew Beobrand posed the greater hazard, so turned to meet him.

There was still light coming from the torch and Beobrand hoped the torch bearer would not enter the fray, striking him from behind while he tackled Thagmar. The man might be old, but a sharp blade was still deadly in a weak hand. He pushed the thought aside, he could not be distracted from his adversary. Thagmar stood before him, his nose swollen and eyes darkened from where Beobrand had smashed his head into his face. There were few men he wished to slay more than the captain of the guard of Liyon. From what he had seen of Thagmar in the arena and in combat, there were also few men more skilled with a blade in all of Frankia. He could not underestimate this opponent. To do so would surely lead to his death.

"Now I will kill you, Beobrand," sneered Thagmar.

Beobrand did not answer. He would not waste his strength on empty words and threats. His body was tired; bruised and battered. He could still taste blood in his mouth from the split lip Thagmar had given him in the palace. Beobrand had been bound then and had still managed to strike a blow on Thagmar. His head still ached from it. But he was not tied now, and there was nobody to hold him back. This time, he would slay Thagmar, or die in the attempt.

Seeing that Thagmar had not had time to retrieve his shield from his horse, Beobrand threw himself forward without slowing his pace. Thagmar was quick and skilled, but so was

Beobrand, and the Frank had not anticipated that Beobrand would continue his charge without halting.

Thagmar sidestepped, flicking his blade at Beobrand's exposed legs. But Beobrand was ready. Twisting his body to the right, he parried the low cut with his sword's blade, the metal clanging like a bell. Then, using his momentum to carry him forward, he swung his shield into Thagmar's face. He did not connect with the iron boss, but the splintered board smacked into Thagmar's broken nose. He let out a howl of pain, and both men collapsed in a tangle of limbs.

They rolled on the earth, each fighting for supremacy. Beobrand lost his grip on the shield. Finding himself atop Thagmar, he hacked down with his sword at the Burgundian's face. But Thagmar was quick. He pulled his head to the side and the blade bit into the earth. Before Beobrand could lift the sword again, Thagmar flicked his head back and bit into Beobrand's right hand. His teeth ripped skin, grinding against the bones. Beobrand screamed, recoiling from the pain and losing his grip on his weapon.

Thagmar rolled to the side, trapping the relinquished sword beneath his body. Where Thagmar's weapon was, Beobrand had no idea. He thought of pulling his seax from its sheath, but before he could move, Thagmar's hands wrapped around his throat.

The blond captain of the guard snarled and spat up at Beobrand. He had Beobrand's life in his grasp now and was going to squeeze it from him. Thagmar held him up at arm's length, his strong fingers digging into Beobrand's windpipe. Beobrand could not breathe. Panicking, he clutched and scratched at Thagmar's wrists, but his left hand's grip was not strong enough, and his right hand was slick with blood and slipped away. His vision began to blur. He could feel his strength ebbing.

The darkness drew in around him until all he could see were Thagmar's furious, bruised eyes. In moments, he knew, he would pass out. Then all would be lost. He would die here, strangled in the dirt after so many battles with sword and shield. With that thought, a realisation came to Beobrand, as if he had heard a whispered voice in the night. Thagmar was fast, strong and deadly. Like Beobrand himself. But with a blade, Beobrand would have had an advantage over him. He was taller than Thagmar.

His reach was longer.

Beobrand ceased trying to pull his opponent's powerful hands from his throat and with the last of his strength, he punched down, ramming a thumb into each of Thagmar's glaring eyes. Pressing down as hard as he could, he felt the eyeballs bulge, then burst beneath the pressure. Thagmar howled like an animal. He released his grip on Beobrand and thrashed in agony.

Gasping for breath, Beobrand rolled away. His thumbs dripped with gore. His throat burnt and it hurt when he swallowed, but the cool evening air felt good as it filled his lungs.

Thagmar was raving now, writhing and kicking like a madman. He pressed his hands to his face, whimpering and screaming. Beobrand snatched up the sword that had been uncovered by Thagmar's movements. Climbing to his feet, he looked down at his enemy, thinking of the suffering the captain had inflicted on the poor Iudeisc people in Burgundia. For a moment he considered leaving him thus, blinded and in agony. To live in constant anguish, each day remembering who had done this to him. Condemned to think of the man he had been and what he had become. Beobrand drew in another scratching breath, the night air burning his damaged throat. Even an animal such as Thagmar deserved a merciful death.

Beobrand waited until Thagmar rolled close to him. Slicing down with his sword, he cleaved deeply into Thagmar's skull. Instantly, the weeping and screaming halted. Thagmar's whole body tensed, his back arching. Beobrand yanked the sword blade free. Blood, bone and brains spilled onto the earth. Thagmar's body flopped down and lay still.

Beobrand coughed. His throat was raw and his mouth had filled with blood again where his scabbed lip had split open in the fight. He spat onto Thagmar's corpse, then looked up to see what had befallen Halinard and Vulmar.

Thagmar's horse had galloped into the night, but Vulmar's white mare stood some way off in the shadows, cropping at the grass. The old man with the torch was still there, standing mouth agape and staring at Beobrand.

Taking a step towards the man, Beobrand growled and gestured with his sword. Thagmar's blood flicked from the blade. He wasn't sure his swollen throat would allow him to speak, but the grunting snarl and the weapon in his hand conveyed his message well enough. The man dropped the torch at his feet, turned and fled.

Beobrand scooped up the brand and scanned the darkness. There was no sign of Vulmar or Halinard. Had the lord of Rodomo escaped on foot? Was Halinard lying in the stream bed? Perhaps the collision with the horse had broken his bones and he was unable to climb out. Mayhap he was insensible. The thought he might be dead gripped Beobrand's heart, and he hurried toward the stream.

It was then that he heard the pleading. A moment later, the light from the torch fell on the men who had been hidden from Beobrand's view behind the white mare. Vulmar was on his knees. The flame light glimmered in the tears and snot that streaked his face as he begged for mercy to the figure from nightmare who stood over him. It was Halinard, covered in mud, glistening and slick with the stuff like a nihtgenga, a monster from legend. In his hand he held a sword. The blade was clean and glimmering, aflame with torchlight.

Beobrand walked slowly towards the pair. He made no effort to speak. There was nothing for him to say.

Vulmar spoke quickly, his tone first wheedling, and then plaintive. When Halinard ignored him, Vulmar raised his voice in anger. All the while, Halinard stared at him in silence. Beobrand could see the tension in the man, the set of his shoulders, the trembling of the hand that held the sword.

Without warning, a shout came from behind Beobrand, from the direction of the hall. Spinning around, he raised his sword, ready to fight again. The torchlight fell on Brocard's face. Four of his men came with him, and Beobrand realised the sounds of fighting from the other side of the building had ceased. He nodded in greeting at Brocard, turning back to Vulmar and Halinard.

"Don't kill him," Brocard shouted at Halinard. "He must be taken before the king."

Vulmar looked up at Halinard, new hope in his eyes.

Halinard did not acknowledge Brocard, but whispered something to Vulmar. His voice was too quiet to hear, but Vulmar flinched as if struck, his eyes widening in fear.

"No!" shouted Brocard, but he was too far away to intervene.

Halinard drove his sword into Vulmar's belly. The fat lord fell back, shaking and mewling in terror and pain.

Brocard was incensed. He continued to shout as he hurried forward. He spoke too quickly now for Beobrand to make out his words, but it was clear that he was furious with Halinard and was threatening him with all manner of punishments. Beobrand recalled how Balthild had made him promise that they would capture Vulmar alive. And yet, he could not begrudge Halinard the satisfaction of slaying the man who had forced himself on his daughter, and countless other girls. The man was a monster, who revelled in causing pain, sating his abhorrent lusts with innocent flesh. But Halinard was a lowly warrior. And he was also a Frank who had once, long ago, sworn an oath to Vulmar. Could it be that he would be made to face justice for taking his lord's life? Beobrand could not be certain, but he could well imagine that Clovis might insist he be made to pay the blood-price for Vulmar's death.

Beobrand could not permit that to happen. Halinard was his man now and there was no more loyal gesith in his warband. Hurrying to where the warrior stood gazing down at the dying Vulmar, Beobrand shoved Halinard aside. Then, with a single stroke of his sword, he took Vulmar's head from his shoulders.

Brocard shouted out in anger.

Blood spurted and gushed from Vulmar's neck. His plump body toppled to the side. His head thudded onto the earth, where it rolled until it stared up at Halinard and Beobrand. The man's bestubbled face seemed to be pouting in surprise.

Halinard and Beobrand, both breathing heavily, looked down at the headless corpse, each lost in his own thoughts.

Brocard walked up to them.

"You should not have done that," he said, shaking his head.

Beobrand turned to Halinard. For a long while they stared into each other's eyes. No words were spoken, but much was said in that lingering look. They had shared a vengeance they had long dreamt of. They were fathers who had avenged the wrongs Vulmar had perpetrated on Joveta, and the suffering he had caused Ardith. Who could say what crimes the lord of Rodomo had committed on countless others? Halinard nodded, in thanks and understanding to his hlaford.

"You should not have killed Vulmar," Brocard said.

Beobrand turned away from the corpse. The monster was dead and it felt good to have been there at his end.

"I disagree," he said, and walked back towards the hall.

Chapter 42

The sun shone brightly from a clear sky. Cynan was glad he had found another straw hat to protect him from the worst of the late spring sun's glare, but he could not deny he enjoyed the warmth. Stretching out his legs, he winced at the pain in his ankle. He had forgotten about it as he'd sat drinking, but the movement jarred it once more, reminding him it had not yet fully healed. He had sprained it on the mad dash through the darkness. It had been swollen and bruised for days, and he could barely place his weight on it. It was still stiff, but at least now he could limp along on it well enough. Thankfully, his head no longer ached from the blow he had taken. Though given how much they were drinking, he feared it would pain him tomorrow as much as when Agobard had struck him.

Leaning back and sipping his ale, he watched the carpenters at work at the centre of the busy square. The open area before the church of Saint Germanus was teeming with people who had come to celebrate the first day of summer, what the men of Northumbria would call Thrimilci, and Cynan's people from the west of Albion, Bealltainn. But it was the timber frame at the heart of the field that commanded the view. Of course, the church loomed higher and was solidly constructed of stone, but everyone's eyes were drawn to the temporary wooden edifice.

They knew its dark purpose, and that was of much more interest than a cold church building. It had taken two days to erect the structure, but the scaffold was almost complete. There was still much of the afternoon left for the men to complete building it. That would be plenty of time.

The hangings were not due until the morrow.

One of the carpenters climbed down from the platform and walked into the shade where his dog was asleep. He reached down and patted the animal, then looked over to where Cynan and the others sat. He raised his hand in greeting. Cynan waved back with a grin.

"I still can't believe that man is in charge of the craftsmen building the gallows," said Grindan.

"He should hang that damned dog of his to test it," said Ingwald, still bitter at the tumble he had taken when the hound had rushed at his horse.

The men laughed. It was a good sound, and one Cynan had not heard much of late. Reaching for the jug of ale, he filled his own cup, then passed it over to Bleddyn. The ale was not as good as Genofeva's, but it was decent enough. Cool and heady. They had been drinking since early in the morning, which perhaps explained the ease with which they now laughed.

There had been little to amuse them since the night they had chased Vulmar to the hall. That had been a week ago, and despite them being victorious, and Halinard and Beobrand finding vengeance at last, a pall of sorrow and worry had descended over them. They had stayed in the hall that night. There had been no happiness at their victory. Brocard had been furious that his queen's orders had been disobeyed, but more than that, he had lost three men in the attack on the hall. Another had been slain in the fight in the forest, and several of the queen's guards were wounded. Of the men Cynan had led through the woods, only Eadgard had been badly injured. He had taken a long cut to his right shin and they had needed to half-carry him up to the hall after the last of Agobard's men had been dispatched.

Cynan took a deep draught of the ale and rotated his left foot, grimacing. Looking down towards the river, he saw Eadgard, head and shoulders taller than the men and women of Paris who thronged the fair. The huge warrior hobbled over to where Cynan and the others sat in the sun. He had gone to relieve himself into the river. Grindan smiled to see his brother returning. Cynan had sensed the nervous tension in the smaller of the brothers when Eadgard had pushed himself up, leaning on his makeshift crutch and limping away towards the Secoana. Grindan had wanted to go with him, that much was clear, but he knew better than to offer his brother assistance. Eadgard was proud, and to have been unable to move without aid these last few days had gnawed at him.

Cynan could understand Grindan's nervousness. He had almost lost Eadgard. The wound to his leg had festered and it had seemed that he might lose the limb, or even die. Until the previous day, Eadgard had been confined to a house of healing where he had been cared for. He had lost some of his bulk, and the ravages of his injury were plain to see on his sallow face and dark circled eyes. But the fever had broken at last, the monks' treatments and prayers finally healing him. When Eadgard had heard of the festivities and the hangings, he had refused to remain resting at Saint Christophoros' any longer. The healers had complained that it was unwise for him to move so soon, that he should stay abed another week. But none of them, not Grindan, nor even Beobrand, had spoken against him leaving. Now, seeing him tottering towards them, grinning as he took in the chaos of the open area that was filled with stalls and entertainers of all kinds, Cynan was just pleased to see him up and about. He had scarcely dared to believe it, but he had seen men with less grave wounds succumb and die.

Smoke from a nearby fire wafted on the light breeze to where the warriors sat. A sweat-soaked, soot-stained man was turning a long spit over the coals of a fire that had burnt brightly in the early morning, but now smouldered with intense heat. Several birds were skewered on the spit. A trio of plump chickens, a partridge, two ducks and a goose all roasting over the embers, fat oozing from their flesh and dropping into the fire, sizzling and spitting. The smell was wonderful.

"I'm hungry," said Eadgard, sitting down carefully to avoid jarring his leg.

"You're always hungry," said Cynan, thinking it was a good sign that Eadgard's recovery was progressing well.

Taking a coin from his pouch, Cynan handed it to Bleddyn.

"Get us some meat, and a couple of loaves from that baker we saw," Cynan said, gesturing airily to where earlier they had seen a man setting out his stall of bread, pies and pastries. There were too many people now to see the man's stall and Cynan hoped they had not left it too late to go in search of bread. He was still shocked at how quickly a city could consume food. The baker had a hand cart heaped high with his wares, but with this many hungry people milling about, it was very possible there would be nothing left now.

Bleddyn emptied his cup and rose without a word. He was a good man, and again Cynan was pleased with his decision to accept Bleddyn's oath. In the forest battle, he had once more proven to be brave and resourceful.

And he had saved Cynan's life.

When he had turned his ankle, falling at the feet of one of Agobard's woodsmen, Bleddyn had rushed to his aid, blocking a scything sword strike on his shield and giving Cynan enough time to clamber back to his feet. Cynan had gutted their attacker, but it had been Bleddyn's shield that had kept him alive.

And it had been Bleddyn who had slain Agobard.

Cynan had spied the man who had bested him the previous night and had hobbled towards him, screaming his name. Despite the chaos and numbers of warriors attacking the ambushers, Agobard had shown no fear, stepping in to meet Cynan, his teeth visible in a savage grin.

Cynan had known he was in trouble as soon as their sword blades met. His ankle was agony and the agility he relied on in combat was lost to him. He soaked up a flurry of Agobard's blows on his shield, but could find no opening in his enemy's defence. He was beginning to despair when a spear lanced in from the darkness, piercing Agobard's right side. Twisting the blade, as Cynan had taught him, Bleddyn tugged it free. Agobard fell dying into the darkness. Cynan had momentarily regretted it had not been his blade to take Agobard's life, but then he saw Bleddyn's pale face in the gloom and could feel no anger. The man had fulfilled his duty as gesith, and Cynan had clapped Bleddyn on the back, laughing as the ambushers died around them and it became clear the battle was won.

Apart from Eadgard's injury and Cynan's misstep, caused by the headlong dash through the dark, the men of Albion had come out of the fight well. Later, they had argued with Fulbert that he had sounded the horn before the agreed time. He swore it was already fully dark when he put the horn to his lips, and he would listen to none of the gainsayers. Even when his own commander, Brocard, had said he had blown early, Fulbert had refused to admit he was wrong. The other warriors had taunted him mercilessly.

One of Brocard's men, a thin whip of a man who never seemed to tire of jesting, had said something that made the others howl with laughter. When pressed on what he had said, Halinard, who had seemed weary and desolate since slaying Vulmar, translated for them in a sombre tone that only served to make it even funnier.

"He says that with his scarred face and," he waved his hand, searching for the words, "the sounding of his horn too soon, he pities any woman Fulbert might lie with."

"I did not sound my horn too soon," Fulbert had shouted.

The guard had smiled and fluttered his eyelashes.

"Do not worry, Fulbert," he'd said in a high-pitched voice, "it happens to many men."

"Not to me!" Fulbert had bellowed and the men had roared with laughter. That had been the one brief moment of humour during that long evening in the hall, but there had been no merriment on the ride back to Paris the next day.

Whether he had blown his horn early or not, did not matter. As it turned out, the fact that Cynan and the Black Shields had not been in position proved to work in their favour. Agobard's men had been crouched in the bushes on either side of the path, but when Fulbert's men attacked the ambushers from the east, those on the west side of the path had rushed across to their aid. When Cynan's men hit them from the west they were taken completely by surprise. Fulbert's men had been struggling against so many, and one of their number had already fallen with a spear in his guts. But the instant the men of Albion joined the fray, it was over in moments. The slaughter was savage and quick. It was only when a handful of the ambushers turned to flee into the forest that Eadgard was injured. With his usual abandon in battle, he chased after them, bellowing and swinging his great axe. Grindan had rushed after him, and they had become separated from the rest of the Bernicians in the gloom. It was while they fought that one of the ambushers, who had hidden behind a large oak, darted out and plunged his spear into Eadgard's leg. Eadgard split his skull a heartbeat later and soon all the ambushers were dead, but Cynan had berated the huge axeman for his foolhardiness.

"One day, your rashness will get you killed," he'd shouted. He knew Eadgard would not listen, he never did. But that had been before the wound-rot set in and the gash almost cost him his life. Perhaps now he would be more cautious in battle. Though Cynan doubted it.

Bleddyn returned, threading his way through the crowd of people that had congregated around the man roasting the birds. Cynan hoped he'd sell all his meat soon, or perhaps that the people of Paris would become less hungry. The throng blocked his view of the open area. There were so many sights to see that it had been an entertaining morning. There were dozens of tents and stalls, and animal pens. Hawkers, fighters, tradesmen, scops with their lyres and drums, dancers, all peddled their wares. Cynan enjoyed watching them all. One act in particular had caught his eye: a lithe girl who juggled knives as she climbed on the shoulders of a man Cynan assumed was her father. The mass of people waiting for roasted meat now obscured the juggling act from his view.

Bleddyn placed a single loaf on the table before them and beckoned for the wizened ale woman to bring them another jug.

"That was the last one," he said. "The meat man says the goose is not done yet. But I've paid him and he'll have his boy bring it over to us when it is well-cooked."

"But I am hungry now," moaned Eadgard. "Why didn't you just get a chicken?"

"I prefer goose," Bleddyn said with a grin. "And unless you plan on hopping over there, you will have goose too."

Eadgard frowned. The others laughed.

The old woman, whose ale they were drinking, brought over another earthenware jug and slammed it down on the table. She made to take the other pitcher away and Ingwald held up a hand, indicating she should wait. Taking the jug, he poured the last dregs from it into his cup, then handed the empty vessel to the crone. She said something unintelligible and winked at him before returning to where she sat beside her barrels.

"Looks like you will have someone to warm your bed tonight," laughed Grindan.

For a moment Ingwald looked horrified at the thought, but then shrugged.

"Perhaps if she allows me to drink for free."

"I would need to drink more ale than there is water in the Secoana to bed that hag," said Grindan.

"Funny, that is just what she said about you."

They all laughed again, but when their cups were filled once more, Cynan grew serious. He missed Gram's mirth. The tall warrior was always quick with a joke and he had been a good drinking companion. Cynan could barely believe he would never see the man again. Gram had been at Ubbanford when Cynan had arrived. He was like kin to him. But even worse than the ache of losing Gram was the stabbing anguish he felt whenever he thought of Attor.

They had buried him in the holy ground of Saint Germanus. King Clovis and Queen Balthild had been in attendance and the ceremony was conducted by Bishop Landericus with much pomp, chanting acolytes and wafting incense. Wilfrid had insisted that he be allowed to pray at the funeral. He spoke well, conducting himself as one born to stand before a congregation, but Cynan had been glad that Eadgard was too ill to attend, for the giant would never have permitted Wilfrid to speak without a confrontation. He was still furious with the novice. His anger had not abated even when they had informed him that it was Wilfrid who had petitioned Bishop Landericus to admit Eadgard into his house of healing. Landericus was famed all over Neustria for his knowledge of healing, and the newly founded hostel dedicated to Saint Christophoros was renowned for its success in curing the seriously ill.

When he had heard about Wilfrid's eulogy at Attor's funeral, and that Wilfrid had gifted some of his gold to the church in order that prayers would be recited for Attor's soul, Eadgard had lashed out, flinging a cup of water across the infirmary.

"Well he can try to make amends now," he'd growled. "Attor would yet live if it had not been for Wilfrid's treachery."

Cynan thought it was more likely that they would all have

followed Attor to the afterlife without Wilfrid's gallop to the queen and Balthild's intervention, but it had become clear that Eadgard would not listen to reason. Perhaps one day he would cease to be angry with Wilfrid, but that day had not yet come.

Truth be told, none of them much liked Wilfrid. The young man was arrogant and too clever by far. And yet, he had risked his privileged position and perhaps even his life, to save them, and actions spoke with a resoundingly loud voice.

If it had not been for the men they had lost, Wilfrid would probably have considered this whole affair a success. He might even believe that the loss of Gram and Attor was a price worth paying. Things had certainly worked out for Wilfrid. Clovis had rewarded him for his part in unmasking the conspirators. The king had gifted him with a hundred gold coins and a letter of commendation for him to carry to the *Pontifex* along with the letter from the queen of Northumbria. The young man's ambition and quick wits had certainly seen him climb high in his short life, and Cynan wondered what future awaited Wilfrid.

He recalled a conversation Beobrand had told him of just the day before. The two of them had been sitting quietly in a dark corner of the palace. It was difficult to find peace in such a crowded place, especially with the recent events and upcoming festivities, and for a time, Beobrand and Cynan had sat in silence, enjoying the stillness after so many days of tortured screams echoing about the halls as the captured plotters had been questioned.

Cynan knew that, like Eadgard, Beobrand was still not sure about Wilfrid. He disliked the youth instinctively, but he could not deny the part the novice had played in saving them all from execution.

After a time of sitting in companionable silence, Beobrand had told him there was something that still did not sit right with him.

"I asked Wilfrid," said Beobrand, as if shaken from a dream

by the memory, "to explain why he hadn't chosen to side with Annemund and Dalfinus. He seemed content with them and he could have taken the mantle of the bishop's heir. If he had done so, he would now be basking in the riches of the bishop's palace in Liyon."

Cynan said nothing.

"You know what he told me?" Beobrand said.

Cynan shook his head.

"He said he did not wish to spend the rest of his days with Rotrudis."

"That I can understand," said Cynan. "The girl is no beauty."

"True," Beobrand smiled, "but there is more. He had drunk much of the king's wine and his tongue was loose. And I sensed he soon regretted speaking so openly."

"What did he say?"

"He said that if truth be told, he did not wish to be in the thrall of the bishop of Liyon. Or to anyone." Beobrand snorted, as if what he was about to say amused him. "He said that he should only have to answer to God."

Cynan whistled. Wilfrid's arrogance was astounding.

"What about the *Pontifex maximus*?" he asked. "I thought even a bishop answers to the bishop of Roma."

"I said as much and he conceded, grudgingly, it seemed to me, that he would have to answer to the *Pontifex*." Beobrand held up his hands in seeming disbelief at the reply he'd received. "But none of this truly surprised me. It was what he said next that gave me a glimpse of his true self."

Cynan waited for his hlaford to continue, wondering what Wilfrid could have said to unsettle Beobrand so.

"He said: 'it would have been foolish to side with Annemund and those depraved idiots'. It was clear to him they would be discovered and in the end they would all be slain. He said he wanted no part of that." Beobrand took a deep breath. "I remember the next words he said. 'Riches and power for a few months is nothing,' he said. 'I want a long life of luxury, not a season.'" Beobrand shook his head at the memory. "He said that by giving up the conspirators, he had rid himself of the dreadful situation he was in and..." Beobrand's voice trailed off, as if he regretted beginning to tell this tale.

Cynan knew him well enough to remain silent.

"And then he said he now had a thegn of Bernicia in his debt."

"He said that? To you?" Cynan was incredulous that Wilfrid would be so bold.

"I asked him if he truly believed I was in his debt. He asked for my pardon, said he had spoken rashly. He even looked a little frightened." Beobrand shook his head at the memory and chuckled without humour. "But no sooner had he begged my pardon, than he was reminding me that if it had not been for him, we would all have died on the steps of this very hall."

Cynan recalled the feeling of the hard, cold stone beneath his knees. The sound of the city, muted and muffled beyond the palace walls. The sun glinting from the drawn swords. Hincmar's whispered apology. Then Attor's brave smile, before the blade pierced his heart.

How Cynan wished they had never come to Frankia. The place had brought them nothing but pain and loss.

The noise of laughter brought him back to the present. The gesithas were chattering around him, their voices raised from the ale they had consumed and against the growing noise of the festival crowds. The men's camaraderie made him feel their shield-brothers' absence more acutely.

Cynan held his cup aloft.

"To Gram and Attor," he said.

The men hesitated. Eadgard broke the silence.

"May they find mead, riddles and women," he said, his voice lusty and loud.

"I hope the afterlife has plenty of mead and riddles," said Ingwald, "but I could do without the nagging of women."

"It is not their nagging I hope for," replied Eadgard with a grin.

The men laughed and drank, but a sour mood fell over them, as if a dark cloud had covered the sun. They grew morose as they thought of their dead friends and the women they had each left behind. Even Bleddyn, who had been overjoyed to be reunited with Alpaida, now frowned into his cup as he was reminded that they would be leaving soon.

Their sombre humour was interrupted by a scrawny boy carrying a wooden platter, atop which rested the roasted goose. Its skin was crisped and charred, and the plate was swimming in fat and meat juices that ran from the bird.

Cynan gave the boy a sliver of hacksilver from his pouch. The lad beamed, secreting the precious metal inside his kirtle, before running back to his master.

"Is there enough for me?"

A shadow fell over the table. Cynan looked up to see Beobrand. The swelling on his face had vanished, the paling bruises ghosts of the fights he had recently lost.

"There is barely enough for me, lord," said Eadgard with a groan.

Halinard rose and offered Beobrand his stool. Looking around for another seat, he saw none.

"I can stand, lord," he said. The Frankish warrior had been quick to show his respect to Beobrand at every opportunity since they had slain Vulmar. Cynan had heard what had transpired behind the hall. Beobrand had spoken little of his part in Vulmar's killing, but it seemed clear to Cynan that his intervention had saved Halinard from punishment. Brocard had been furious at first, but he must have decided there was nothing to be gained from blaming the thegn of Bernicia, who was being feted by the king and queen for foiling the plot against them, which, if successful, would have seen them both killed and Clovis' brother, Sigebert, King of Austrasia, seize the throne of Neustria.

By the time they had returned to Paris, Brocard was declaring that it was he who had killed Vulmar in the fight. Beobrand seemed pleased with the captain's assertion, and Cynan wondered whether he might have suggested that path to Brocard. Nobody contradicted Brocard's description of the events, and both Clovis and Balthild seemed content with the outcome. Cynan was not so certain Halinard would have been forgiven as readily.

With a nod of thanks to Halinard, Beobrand sat, and accepted from Bleddyn a slice of goose on a hunk of bread.

"No Wilfrid?" Cynan asked. Beobrand had been with the novice when they had left the palace.

"You know him," Beobrand said. "He prefers the company of the king and his nobles to the likes of us."

"Better for him that way," muttered Eadgard, around a mouthful of meat and bread.

"How are things at the palace?" Cynan asked, keen to move the conversation away from Wilfrid.

"Everything is set for tomorrow," said Beobrand, glancing over at the gibbet. "Dalfinus has given up close to a dozen of his allies. Wilfrid has helped identify several more that he saw in Liyon."

The men ate quietly for a moment, perhaps all thinking of the screams that had reverberated around the palace since their return. Dalfinus may have been a strong warrior and even a brave man in combat, but he was no match for Clovis' torturer. Rumour was that Dalfinus had held out for a whole two days before confessing, but confess he did. And before he talked, Nithard, the old lord from the hall outside of Paris, had already admitted his part in everything. As first Wilfrid, then Nithard and finally Dalfinus gave the names of the plotters, so contingents of the king's guard were sent to drag his enemies back to the palace for justice. Tomorrow that justice would be delivered for all to see.

"What about Annemund?" asked Grindan.

"Clovis has sent riders to Burgundia, but I doubt Annemund will be foolish enough to have remained in the city. And he is not the only conspirator to have escaped. There will be more executions after tomorrow. This will not be the end of it."

"It will for us," said Cynan.

Beobrand swallowed the food he was chewing.

"Aye, for us it will." He had already told them they would be riding on the day after the summer day festivities were over. Cynan just wished it was going to be northward, instead of south, towards the land of the Langobards and then on to Roma. But even though perhaps Beobrand did not feel as indebted to Wilfrid as the novice would have liked, he had given his word to Eanflæd to deliver him safely to the holy city. And now that Wilfrid had shown he had never sought to betray them, Beobrand planned to escort him as promised.

But before then, they would enjoy the food and drink of Paris. King Clovis had been generous to Beobrand, and the lord of Ubbanford had ever been a gift-giving hlaford to his gesithas. When the goose was nothing but bones, Beobrand sent Bleddyn off in search of more food, and the old woman continued to bring jugs of ale to their small table. Their cups were never empty, and as the day wore on, the sounds of the crowds became muffled and distant to Cynan's ears. It became increasingly difficult to focus on the faces of the people passing by. He tried for a time to watch the juggling acrobatic girl, but as she danced and clambered onto her father's shoulders, the image of her blurred.

The sun had begun to slide down towards the western horizon now and Cynan was contemplating whether he should cease drinking for the day. He knew the wise answer to that, but his wisdom appeared to have vanished sometime earlier that long, warm afternoon.

He needed a piss. With a grunt, he pushed himself to his feet, swaying slightly. He'd forgotten about his ankle again, but as he placed his weight on it, the pain was as blurred as his vision. In the morning, he might regret drinking so much, but in the warm sunshine, he could think of nothing better than more ale. Except perhaps...

"Fetch us wine," he slurred to the old woman who served them.

Eadgard cheered. Cynan was unsure the woman had understood him, or indeed if she had any wine, but he did not wait for a response. Turning quickly, he staggered, wincing at the dull pain of his swollen ankle. Concentrating, so as not to lose his balance again, he made his way towards the river where men had been relieving themselves all day.

He had not gone far when a figure blocked his path. Cynan stepped to the side, but the man moved in front of him once more. Cynan blinked, trying to focus. The man was slender and of medium build. He wore a simple robe of undyed wool, tied at the waist with a hemp rope. Around his neck hung a plain wooden rood symbol, identifying him as a Christ follower. He appeared to be a monk, but his hair marked him out as a stranger to these lands. For where the monks of Frankia bore the tonsure that left the top of their heads bald, encircled by a fringe of hair like the crown of thorns used to torment Jesu, this monk's hair hung long behind his ears, covering the nape of his neck. Rather than the top of his head, it was his forehead that had been shaved.

"Cynan," said the monk, with an open smile, "praise the Lord. I thought I would never find you in such a throng."

Cynan blinked.

"Coenred? Is that you?"

"Your eyes do not deceive," replied the monk. "Though judging from your speech, perhaps your eyes are not working quite as well as they might. Have you been drinking all day?" Coenred did his best to sound disapproving, but he could not hide the glimmer of humour in his eyes.

The monk was one of Beobrand's oldest friends. What he was doing here, in Paris, Cynan had no idea.

"I have, Coenred," said Cynan, aware of how he was drawing out his words. "You see with the eyes of a hawk and are wise beyond your years. But I thought you were at Lindisfarena."

"And I believed you to be in Roma."

Cynan sighed.

"There is a tale there," he said, swaying slightly as if in a strong wind despite the afternoon being still and warm, "and I would hear your story too. But I fear that if I do not piss soon, I will wet my breeches."

"Look who I found," Cynan called out as they made their way through the crowd to where Beobrand and his gesithas sat.

The amazement on the faces of the men made both Cynan and Coenred laugh.

"I believe the truth is that I found you, Cynan," said the monk.

"Coenred!" shouted Beobrand, surging to his feet. "What are you doing here?"

"I could well ask the same of you, Beo," replied Coenred.

Beobrand embraced the monk like a brother, slapping him hard on the back.

"Our tale is a long one," he said. "And it is far from happy."

Coenred scanned the faces of the seated warriors and frowned, no doubt recognising that some of their number were missing.

"Baducing and Wilfrid are in Roma?" he asked.

Beobrand let out a long sigh.

"Baducing may well be for all I know. But Wilfrid is here."

"In Paris?"

"That is where we are," Beobrand replied with a lopsided smile. The change in Beobrand was astounding, thought Cynan. Coenred's presence had immediately lifted his spirits.

Coenred glanced over at the now completed gallows. Four of the king's guards protected the structure, their spear points gleaming in the bright afternoon sun.

"You have something to do with that?" the monk asked.

"You know me well," Beobrand said. "But come, sit with us and we will tell you our tale and you must tell us yours."

"It is Sunnandæg," said Coenred, looking over at the church of Saint Germanus. "I really should not be drinking. And Vespers will begin soon."

Beobrand waved a hand, brushing away Coenred's protests.

"It is a hot day, Coenred. Surely God would not begrudge you a drink with old friends."

Coenred hesitated, but only for a heartbeat.

"God is good," he said, smiling, "and the Lord shows mercy to sinners like me. And the sun is warm. And I am thirsty." Bleddyn arrived carrying a tray of pies he had procured from somewhere. The men moved their cups to make room for the tray. The savoury aroma from the pies filled the air. "And," continued Coenred, grinning now, "I have not yet eaten today."

Halinard found an empty barrel for Coenred to sit on, and soon they each had a full cup of ale in one hand and a slice of pie in the other. The old woman seemed to have ignored Cynan's call for wine, for which he was thankful. He knew he should really stop drinking, but still he took a bite of the meat pie, followed by a deep draught of the ale. Both tasted good and he knew he would not cease drinking that day until he was unable to drink more.

Having arrived later than the rest of them from the palace, Beobrand's head was clearer and his questioning of Coenred more coherent than Cynan's slurred queries had been.

They all listened intently as Coenred told them tidings of events in Albion. He spoke of a new church being built on Lindisfarena, which none of the warriors was interested in. Then he told of unrest in the lands north of Bernicia, where it seemed Talorcan, son of Eanfrith and Finola, was raising an army and looked set to be crowned king of the Picts. This was of much more interest and for some time Beobrand peppered Coenred with questions. When it became clear how little the monk actually knew of the Picts and the threat they might pose to Northumbria, Coenred finally moved on to his reason for being in Frankia. He explained that he had travelled to Cala, bearing missives from the abbess Hild to her sister, Hereswitha.

"I also carried letters of greeting for Clovis and Balthild from Oswiu and Eanflæd. It was at the palace that I heard you were in Paris. The *major domus* told me where I might find you. Erchinoald is a pleasant enough man, but my Frankish is not the best, so I understood little else other than that you were here." Coenred took a bite of his pie and washed it down with ale. Seeing his cup was empty, Bleddyn refilled it. "I had assumed you were on your way back from Roma." He grew serious. "War is approaching once more in the north, I fear. There will be need of your swords before long. No matter what the queen said when she sent you away, Beo, you will need to return soon."

"Alas, I have yet to fulfil my promise to the queen to deliver Wilfrid to Roma. It will be months yet before I am able to return."

"Well, you had best hurry," said Coenred, taking another swallow of ale and smacking his lips appreciatively. "I do not think Oswiu would be pleased to learn that Beobrand of Ubbanford, Thegn of Bernicia and leader of the famed Black Shields is sitting drinking ale in the sun in Paris when he has already had enough time to reach Roma and return."

"Oswiu need never find out, my friend. Just as your abbot need never hear of how you enjoyed ale with us rather than singing songs for Vespers."

Coenred smirked and raised his cup in acknowledgement.

"That is indeed true," he said.

"Besides," said Beobrand, "we will be on our way soon

enough, old friend. And when you hear our tale you will know we have not been dawdling."

"I am sure of that," said Coenred. "But you know Oswiu is a less forgiving man than most. When will you be heading out for Roma?"

"The day after tomorrow."

"Why not tomorrow itself? Why wait another day?"

Beobrand shook his head.

"An extra day will make no difference. The men need to rest after our ordeal. And in any event, there is something we must see on the morrow."

Coenred looked at him over his cup as he drank.

"And what is that?"

"We must watch Lord Dalfinus, brother of the bishop of Liyon, swing from those gallows."

Coenred's eyes widened.

"God have mercy on the man's soul."

"The man is scum," said Beobrand savagely. "He was part of a plot to kill the queen and to remove the king from his throne."

Coenred blanched and made the sign of the cross over his chest.

"How I pity the poor bishop, who must live knowing that his brother raised his hand against his earthly rulers."

"Indeed," continued Beobrand, enjoying the reaction his words were having on Coenred, "it is just a pity we cannot stay longer."

"Why is that?" asked Coenred hesitantly.

"We will miss seeing Dalfinus' brother, Annemund, the most eminent bishop of Liyon, slain for his crimes too."

Historical Note

Writing *Forest of Foes* brought a whole new set of challenges. At the end of *For Lord and Land*, Beobrand and company are on the cusp of escorting young Wilfrid to Rome, and like most readers, I imagine, I had naively expected the following book to detail their adventures in that holy city.

So imagine my surprise when I started researching Wilfrid's life in more detail and discovered how his tale entwines with the story of the bishop of Lyon and the Frankish queen, Balthild (also known as Bealdhild, Bathilda, Bauthieult). Before writing this book, I knew practically nothing about the Merovingian monarchs, and whilst I vaguely recalled reading about Wilfrid's adventures in Frankia, I wasn't really prepared for the details.

According to *Vita Sancti Wilfrithi* (*Life of Saint Wilfrid*), a hagiography written shortly after Wilfrid's life, there was just so much that happened to him in Frankia. The more I read, it soon became obvious there was ample material around which to base a whole novel.

The bishop of Lyon is named as Dalfinus in the *Vita*, but in reality, the bishop at the time was called Annemund (also Annemundus, or Ennemond). According to some sources, Dalfinus could be Annemund's brother, and so I chose to include them both and have them rule the secular and ecclesiastical sides of Lyon respectively.

In the *Life of Saint Wilfrid*, soon after meeting the young man from Britain, the bishop of Lyon (whatever his name was) offers Wilfrid lands to govern in perpetuity, and his niece's hand in marriage. The young Anglo-Saxon turns down the offer, but stays in Lyon for months before travelling on to Rome, where he remains for several more months, before returning to Lyon for a few years before the bishop is finally dragged before the queen, accused of treason. I have chosen to compress this timeline, which might make the generous offers from Annemund feel even more precipitated and unusual than they would have otherwise been, but in all honesty I find the idea of a bishop offering Wilfrid his niece and riches a little far-fetched, and makes me wonder what else was going on, especially given the later treason charges and execution.

Wilfrid did travel with a nobleman of "outstanding intelligence" who was also "hastening to Rome". This was Benedict Biscop (also known as Biscop Baducing). I decided to drop the "Biscop" (that is pronounced "bishop") to avoid confusion. After breaking their journey at Lyon, Baducing, Wilfrid's "austere guide", separated from him. As usual, there is little to go on, so I decided that Baducing was fed up with Wilfrid and what he perceived to be time-wasting in the city.

Beobrand visited Frankia earlier in the Bernicia Chronicles in *Storm of Steel*, but in that novel I barely scratched the surface of the complexity of Frankish history and the geopolitical situation of the seventh century. For this novel, I have had to delve deeper, but I still feel very much a novice when it comes to the Merovingian kingdoms and Frankia.

What we today know as France was split into smaller kingdoms: Austrasia, Neustria, Burgundia, Aquitaine and Septimania. Aquitaine was ruled independently, and was often quite detached from its Frankish overlords. Septimania was allied to the Visigothic kingdom that stretched across the Iberian Peninsula. The Frankish kingdoms of Austrasia and Neustria were ruled by the descendants of Merovech (hence Merovingian). Burgundia had no king at this time, but was subservient to Neustria.

At the time of this book, Austrasia and Neustria were ruled by two brothers, Sigebert III and Clovis II, whose father, Dagobert I, had ruled all of Frankia. Following Salic Law, Frankish kings divided their land between all surviving male heirs, which led to much strife and conflict. The Merovingian kings are sometimes known as the long-haired kings, as they believed that some of their royal authority came from their uncut locks.

Clovis and Sigebert are frequently referred to as the first so-called "do-nothing kings" (or *Rois fainéants*). Several later Merovingian kings were also given this less than flattering title as they seemed to have lost their forebears' power of dominion and increasingly relied on the "mayors of the palace" (*major domus*) to run the kingdom. This inevitably led to some of those influential administrators seizing power from the very kings they purported to serve.

Like many of the characters in the Bernicia Chronicles, Erchinoald was a real person. As the *major domus* he was one of the most powerful people in the kingdom. The story of Queen Balthild being a freed slave is perhaps apocryphal, but is mentioned in many sources, including the hagiography *Vita Domnae Balthildis* (*The Life of Lady Balthild*). It also describes how she was first owned by Erchinoald, who wanted to marry her, but who, after she hid from him, eventually gave her to his king to wed instead.

How much of this is true we can never know, and it is quite difficult to reconcile the story into a believable narrative. It is certainly true that Balthild went on to influence the laws of the land, outlawing the practice of enslaving Christians, and establishing several new religious sites, such as Corbie Abbey.

There are also stories of her buying slaves and freeing them. Whatever the truth behind the queen's background, she must have been a formidable character to have influenced society so and to have elicited such strong commentary from the author of the *Life of Wilfrid*, who describes her as a Jezebel who had nine bishops put to death.

There is one thing for certain: she must have been a forceful, intelligent woman, to be able to survive, and even dominate, in the male-oriented Merovingian court. If she had truly started out as a thrall, such accomplishments are even more remarkable. There are sources that say Clovis II had some form of mental or physical ailment, and perhaps it was this perceived weakness that allowed her, a clever, energetic woman with experience of the *major domus*' household and an eye for statecraft, to step up and help the king rule his kingdom. It is not inconceivable that Erchinoald placed her in that position, so that he could rule by proxy. Whatever the reasons behind her rise to prominence, it is easy to imagine why powerful men would wish to see her gone. It is not much of a stretch to think they might prefer to do away with her husband and the *major domus* too and place the perhaps more easily controlled Sigebert on the throne.

With all these titbits of information about Balthild, how could I not make the thrall-queen one of the central characters of *Forest of Foes*? There is so much intrigue and conflict surrounding her and on top of everything else, she is a beautiful, young, Anglo-Saxon woman, who might even be from royal stock. Beobrand would be powerless to resist her!

A quick note about language. Just as I have simplified the languages in the British Isles and have all the Anglo-Saxons effectively speaking one tongue, I have done the same for Frankia. The reality is that several languages and dialects would have been spoken in the different kingdoms, but it was already a challenge to have interpreters available for every scene without adding this complexity. I chose to have all the Franks understand the single language spoken by Halinard to simplify things.

Antisemitism has been a scourge on society for thousands of years. It was rife in early medieval Europe, and Frankia was no exception. Dagobert I had expelled all Jews who would not accept Christianity from his kingdom and it seems that many fled to the southern state of Septimania, where they were allowed to prosper under the rule of the Visigoths. Whilst it is possible that all Jews in Frankia either converted to Christianity or left the realm, it seems possible, even probable, that many Jews would have remained, perhaps openly conforming to the religion dictated by the ruling powers, but still secretly conducting their own rites behind closed doors.

In medieval society, Jews were often forced into marginal roles; tasks deemed un-Christian, or otherwise unsuitable and undesirable to most. Such a job would be tanning, which would be especially offensive to Jews, as Jewish law deemed tanners unclean. Luckily for Beobrand, the tanners he encounters are not only brave and resourceful, but honourable and willing to help one who has aided their people against their oppressor.

I have the men from Albion use the Old English word, Iudeisc, while the people of Frankia refer to Jews using the Latin term, Iudaea.

Lyon was, as Dalfinus says, the capital of Romano-Gaul and a much larger city than Paris. The history of the Roman remains and when they fell into disrepair is lost to time, but I liked the idea that Dalfinus would seek to rebuild some of the grandeur of Rome in his city. This, and his visits to Rome itself, will have a great impact on young Wilfrid, who later seeks to create his own legacy in stone monuments in Britain.

The image of a rich bishop being carried on a litter on the shoulders of perspiring slaves is striking. Such overt shows of power and pomp might also have influenced Wilfrid's ideas of what a bishop should be and how he should be treated later in life. There is no evidence that the bishop of Lyon was carried about like this, but it must have been a reasonably common occurrence, for in 675, the Third Council of Braga saw the need to order that bishops, when carrying relics of martyrs, must walk, and not be carried in a chair.

The saintly hermit used to lure Wilfrid out of Lyon, Saint Lienard, is loosely based on Saint Leonard of Noblac.

The waterfall he visits on the journey is just as loosely based on Cascade de la Fouge.

Much of the action takes place in Paris, which we all know to be the capital of France. In the mid-seventh century however, it was not the principal city in Frankia and was the location of only one of the many palaces owned by Clovis II. However, whilst other cities, such as Rheims, Metz and Aachen, would be prominent in the rules of other Frankish kings, Clovis II's grandfather, Chlothar II, had chosen Paris to be the city from which he would rule. Dagobert I had ruled from nearby Paris too, so it seemed likely that Clovis would carry on the family tradition. It also makes it easy for modern readers to associate the city with the ruling dynasty.

The Abbey of Chelles (Cala) was built at the behest of Queen Balthild and it attracted many other royal and aristocratic women to join the nuns there over the years. One such royal resident was Hereswitha of Northumbria, which gave me enough of a pretext for Coenred to visit, bearing letters from her sister, Hild of Whitby.

At the end of *Forest of Foes*, Beobrand and Halinard have finally taken their revenge on Vulmar and, once again, Beobrand has been instrumental in keeping a royal family in power, though this time in the foreign and strange land of the Franks. Being so far from home, with fewer of his gesithas around him than he is used to, and threatened by enemies on all sides, Beobrand has suffered terrible loss and heartache. His duty tells him he must press on for Rome to complete his mission, but his heart screams that there is war brewing in the north and he should return as quickly as possible to protect the land and his people.

Whatever course he chooses, you can be certain that Beobrand, Cynan and the Black Shields will find more action, adventure and intrigue, and maybe, just maybe, even love and peace.

But that is for another day, and other books.

Acknowledgements

As ever, my first thanks go to you, dear reader, for taking the time out of your busy life to read this tale. I hope you have enjoyed it. If you have, please spread the word to your family and friends.

Extra special thanks to Mary Faulkner, Jon McAfee and Emma Stone for their very generous patronage. To find out more about becoming a patron, and what rewards you can receive for doing so, please go to www.matthewharffy.com.

Thanks to my test readers, Gareth Jones, Simon Blunsdon, Shane Smart and Alex Forbes. Early feedback on the manuscript always helps improve the final version.

Thank you to my editors, Nicolas Cheetham and Greg Rees, and everyone else in the great team at Aries and Head of Zeus. They are all wonderful to work with and dedicated to creating beautiful books.

Thank you to the online community of historical fiction authors and readers who connect with me regularly on Facebook, Twitter and Instagram. I love to hear from readers, so please connect, and say hello.

And finally, as always, my undying love and thanks go to my beautiful daughters, Elora and Iona, and my incredible wife, Maite.

Matthew Harffy
Wiltshire, March 2022

About the Author

MATTHEW HARFFY grew up in Northumberland where the rugged terrain, ruined castles and rocky coastline had a huge impact on him. He now lives in Wiltshire, England, with his wife and their two daughters.

Follow Matthew at @MatthewHarffy and
www.matthewharffy.com